Review

When you open one of the books from Stefan Vučak's 'Shadow Gods' series, you know you are going on an exciting journey through an alternate star system. He successfully combines science fiction, terrorism and romance. The romance between Terr and Teena is allowed to slowly simmer as Terr goes from infatuation to deep love. I found it fascinating to watch their relationship develop even if it seems ill fated. Vucak is a master of dialogue; he never allows it to sound stiff or false. His plots are sharp and intricate. He is meticulous in paying attention to detail, and while the words flow smoothly, they also have a quality of passion.

Readers' Favorite

I0592614

Books by Stefan Vučak

General Fiction:
Cry of Eagles
All the Evils
Towers of Darkness
Strike for Honor
Proportional Response
Legitimate Power
Autumn Leaves
All My Sunsets
F/X-26
28th Amendment
Night Sirens
Broken Rose

Shadow Gods Saga:
In the Shadow of Death
Against the Gods of Shadow
A Whisper from Shadow
Shadow Masters
Immortal in Shadow
With Shadow and Thunder
Through the Valley of Shadow
Guardians of Shadow

Science Fiction:
Fulfillment
Lifeliners

Non-Fiction:
Writing Tips for Authors

Contact at:
www.stefanvucak.com

IMMORTAL IN SHADOW

By

Stefan Vučak

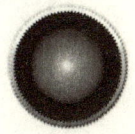

Stefan Vučak ©2005
ISBN-10: 0648473163
ISBN-13: 9780648473169

Dedication

To Mal ... a long path together

Acknowledgments

Crab Nebula – Credit: NASA, HST, and J. Hester (ASU).

Cover art by Laura Shinn.
http://laurashinn.yolasite.com

Map of the Serrll Combine

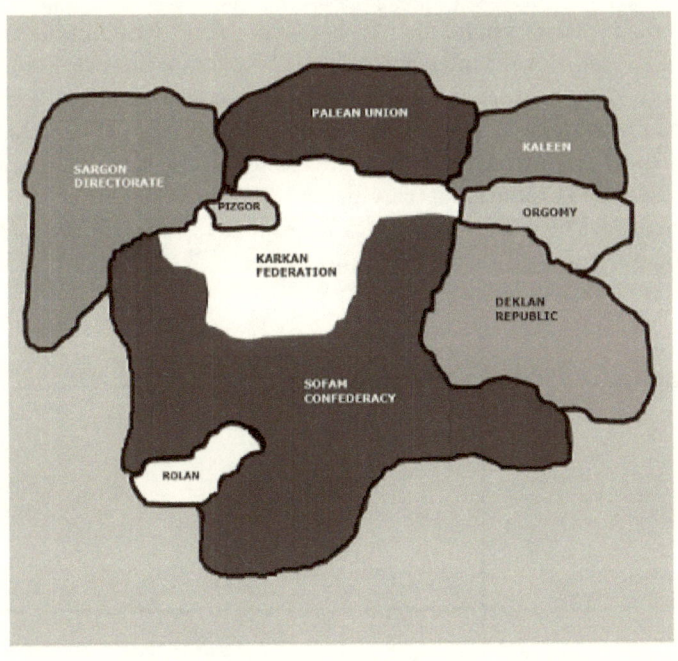

Composition of the Serrll Combine

The 247 star systems that make up the Serrll Combine is an association of six interstellar power blocks, split between two rival camps—the Servatory Party and the Revisionists. Each star system has a single representative in Captal's General Assembly from which members are elected to the ruling ten-seat Executive Council. Seats are based on a percentage of systems occupied by each power block in relation to the total number of systems in the Serrll Combine.

Name	No of Star Systems	Percentage of Total	Executive Council Seats
Sofam Confederacy	83	34	4
Deklan Republic	19	8	1
Palean Union	28	11	1
Karkan Federation	46	19	2
Sargon Directorate	32	12	1
Independents:		15	1
- Kaleen	8		
- Rolan	5		
- Orgomy	6		
- Pizgor	3		
- Other systems	17		
General Assembly	**247**	**100**	**10**
Outposts	40		
Protectorates	34		

Principal political blocks:

Revisionist Party:	Palean Union
	Deklan Republic
	Sofam Confederacy
Servatory Party:	Karkan Federation
	Sargon Directorate
	Nonaligned Independents

Composition of the Executive Council:

Security Council	Bureau of Colonial and Protectorate Affairs
	Bureau of Defense
	Bureau of Cultural Affairs
Administrative Council	Bureau of Administrative Affairs
	Bureau of Justice
Economics Council	Bureau of Economic Affairs
	Bureau of Technology and Development
Central Planning Council	Bureau of Central Planning and Development

Chapter One

Lying on the hard bunk, eyes closed, Tanard allowed the background hum to carry him into blackness and oblivion. It was but a small step to make, for the ship *was* carrying him into oblivion. It wasn't exactly death, but it might as well have been. Death was preferable to the nightmare of eternal imprisonment waiting for him when the prison transport made its last planetfall. Grounded, he would never again feel a deck beneath his feet or the tug of far stars. No, the tug would always be there, but he would not be able to answer it. It was perhaps greater cruelty. They should have shot him, it would have been a kinder fate, but they let him live and he planned to exact full toll for that oversight.

The ship whispered to him in the darkness of his mind.

Gravity changed and the deck shifted slightly, almost a tremble, as the transport dropped into normal space. His skin prickled and a hot flush raced through his body. Oblivion would have to wait, for a little while anyway. He lifted his head to meet Winn's steady gaze.

"Not long now," Tanard rasped and swallowed, absently touching the scar running across his neck and mangled throat. He ignored the dull burning left in the wake of his touch. The pain was familiar now, almost a friend; another companion in the dark, and one that was slowly killing him.

Winn grinned and slid his long legs off the bunk. His large black eyes, framed by a narrow triangular face, shone with anticipation. Freedom! Or at least a chance. He turned and shook the prone figure on the next bunk. The figure groaned, looked up and blinked vacantly.

1

"We there?" Railee mumbled indifferently.

"Depends on how far off we transited," Winn said.

Their eyes connected, the same thought clear on both their faces. After two years of hell it would all end soon, one way or another. That it could also end in their deaths didn't even occur to Winn. He was past caring. It was a luxury that got in the way of simply surviving, which he'd gotten tired of too. A real death now or death on Cantor later, there didn't seem to be much of a difference. Still, he wasn't about to give up on life just yet.

Railee did not particularly care whether he lived or died either. Captivity had toughened him, and the interrogations, first on Anar'on, then on Kalakan, made him hard beyond his years. His jailers were not cruel or in any way mistreated him physically. That would have been a sign of consideration, an acknowledgment he existed, that he mattered. No, what they did was far worse. They had taken away all hope, but he didn't hate, not exactly. His captors did what they needed to do. It was inevitable really. His fate was decided when he made his choice to join Tanard and become a raider. He could pretty it up with words of patriotism, a fight for Palean imperialism, because that's what it was. When the façade was stripped away, he had forsaken his commission in the Fleet and sold his soul to prey on helpless merchants. What price idealism?

It was a cosmic jest, but he was still to get the joke.

He planted both feet on the hard deck, stole a quick glance at his commander's scarred face, the disfigurement a comforting sight now rather than a shock it once was, nodded and strode into the bathroom.

Tanard watched his weapons officer and the corner of his mouth twitched. He caught Winn's amused expression and jerked his head at the bathroom door.

"He has come a long way."

"We've all come a long way," Winn said fatalistically, crossed his legs and stifled a yawn. Tanard grinned.

Was that his first officer talking? Railee may have lost his youth and innocence, lamentable perhaps, or perhaps not, but Winn had probably changed most of all. No longer timid and hesitant, he was now confident to the point of indifference. With nothing to live for, Winn now dared to even challenge him. Tanard approved of the transformation and wondered mildly if his first officer would revert to type if they ever managed to get off this rust bubble. He hoped not. For what he intended, he needed Winn cold and hard. They would all need to be cold and hard.

Railee emerged tugging down the tunic of his prison blues. He plopped on the bunk and propped himself against the bulkhead, hands locked behind his head.

"What's the name of this dump again?"

"Feron," Winn said and bobbed his head, his thin hands twining in a characteristic nervous gesture.

"Feron," Railee repeated in a high voice like it was something dirty and made a face. "Picking up more unfortunates for Cantor's fodder mill, I'll bet."

"Like you cared."

"You're right, I don't care. Why should I? Do any of them care what happens to *me*?"

"Probably not, and I don't care either."

"My friend." Railee looked disgusted.

Tanard frowned and the two of them fell silent. He wasn't conscious he showed any displeasure. He only knew their inane chatter distracted him. Over the last two years the other two came to know his moods intimately and acted without him having to say anything. They were better than a wife, he mused sardonically and his irritation evaporated.

He forced himself to sit still when every fiber in his body ached from the strain of waiting. Would the plan work? Would they be able to get off the ship? Once on the surface, how will they evade the inevitable hunt that would ensue? It could all be an elaborate trap, a plot to kill them. He was being a paranoid fool and knew it. Le Maran would not go to all this trouble merely to have him killed. If the Alikan Union Party Provisional Committee wanted him out of the way, he would already be dead. There would be no need for such elaborate sidestepping. His frown deepened.

The worst part being on board, none of them dared talk openly to vent their feelings and frustrations for fear the cabin might be monitored. It probably wasn't, but they couldn't take that chance. It was maddening. What he craved was a release, to pace around, to rage and storm, to let his bottled emotions free before they consumed him. Of course, that would never do. Even on a prison hulk, a commander's dignity must be preserved, which amused him intensely. Any dignity he might have had was stripped away on Anar'on by the unsmiling, shadowy Wanderer interrogators. At least the three of them had a cabin to themselves, for which he was thankful. Arranged that way?

He sensed the ship slow and stop. It was a subtle change in the background throb of small ship noises a lifetime of Fleet service he recognized instantly. The alarm siren wailed then, which made everyone jump, and the milky ceiling changed to pulsing amber. The hatch snapped open into the bulkhead with a sharp clang.

"Abandon ship! This is not a drill," the computer blared. "Everyone to their assigned survival blister."

Le Maran had done it!

Instead of excitement, Tanard felt a surprising calmness. Then again, it wasn't so surprising. Training had prepared him to face action with composed resolution, and he was certainly facing action now. He grunted, stood up in a single flowing motion and gathered the other two with a glance.

Now that the moment had come, Winn hesitated; mortified he could still feel indecision. Was he a coward after all? Then his mouth firmed and his eyes darkened as he turned to Tanard.

"Just don't let them take me…"

There was a wealth of emotion behind those simple words and Tanard was touched. Winn *had* changed, enough to realize

4

there were many kinds of death, not merely losing one's life.

"Then let's make this work, okay?"

Satisfied, Winn nodded, glanced at Railee and jabbed a long finger at the open hatch.

"Right! Let's get it on!"

Tanard lunged and grabbed his arm. "Wait!"

The young fool would get himself killed! He stepped to the hatchway and carefully peered into the corridor. Dazed prisoners peeked cautiously out of their cabins and looked uncertainly at each other. The computer repeated its warning and the passage began to fill. If the ship was indeed in danger, there was no time to waste. At the end of the corridor a hatch cycled open and two burly marines stepped through. Several prisoners made a dash past Tanard toward a row of four survival blisters at the far end of the passageway, their access hatches already gaping open.

"Stand to!" one of the marines bellowed and leveled his phase rifle. A pale violet beam struck one of the fleeing prisoners in the back. The man yelped, flung up his arms and crumpled to the deck in an untidy heap, unconscious.

With the siren still wailing, the prisoners now turned their attention on the marines. They had perhaps moments to escape from what may be a doomed ship and the guards were gunning them down. A heavyset individual, teeth bared, eyes glowing with blood lust and hate, launched himself in a flying leap at the two guards. The violet beam sizzled along the ceiling as others rushed into the melee; the ungainly, heavy rifles useless for any close-in work and the guards were dumb to bring them.

Tanard nodded. It was time to go.

"The far blister," he said and slapped Winn on the back. The three of them ran toward the open pods. Several inmates were already scrambling through the hatches.

The siren stopped its wail.

"Disregard! Disregard!" an angry voice boomed over the intercom. "Computer error. Everyone into their cabins now.

Repeat. Disregard abandon ship! All security sections, round up the prisoners!"

Hearing the command, some of the prisoners stopped and stood still, not quite sure what to believe. The downed guards lay still on the deck. The heavyset man picked up one of the rifles and marched deliberately toward the blister pods.

"Disregard be damned," he growled, trailing cronies in his wake.

Winn did not relish arguing it out with the guy. He reached the blister and dived through the hatch. Railee gave a triumphant yell and plunged in after him. A body sailed out of the hatch a moment later. Tanard elbowed aside the luckless individual trying to scramble back in and jumped into the gloomy interior.

"Go!"

Winn stabbed the pulsing yellow purge pad with a stiff finger and the hatch clanged shut, cutting off the panicked screams outside, leaving only the faint sound of futile pounding. Tanard piled onto a couch as the blister surged down the launch tube. The restraining field caught them, then released when the blister reached stable boost.

Winn quickly checked the main full-dimensional display plate. Three other blisters were clearing the stationary transport. Feron hung above them, a blue-green world covered in fluffy white gauze. After eleven days of staring at nothing but gray bulkheads, it was a gorgeous sight.

"Any threats?" Tanard demanded and leaned over Winn's shoulder.

"Showing three survival blisters in terminal descent," Winn said, scanning the display plates. "Make that four. Two VLBCs in a holding pattern nine hundred talans to port. No Fleet units within detection range, but this thing doesn't have much of a sensor suite," he added with an apologetic scowl.

The parked merchants, Very Large Bulk Carriers, were no threat. Tanard pursed his thin lips and allowed himself to relax.

The first and most difficult part of their escape had worked out well enough. He did not know who on the transport sabotaged the computer or how it was done, and he didn't particularly give a damn either. Le Maran had kept his promise and that was enough. Too bad it took him two years to get around to it, but Tanard could hardly blame his former controller. Busting them off Kalakan, the Fleet's premier Palean base, would probably have taken far more than Le Maran or the Committee was prepared to give. To the Committee's faceless men, the effort wasn't worth the return. Tanard's capture had caused them enough damage as it is. Even after two years the memories were poignantly sharp and he squirmed in his seat at some of the more unpleasant ones.

The aborted attack on *Zavian*, supposedly carrying the Unified Independent Front delegates, the subsequent running battle with young Terr and the loss of his arm, were all things that haunted his nights and stalked his days. On Anar'on, his Wanderer interrogators had peeled open his mind with detached indifference, laying bare the Committee's secrets, what he knew of them, which was enough, seeing how he was instrumental in the planning and setting up of the raider base on Lemos. Le Maran compromised—hard to see how that could have been avoided—and much of the Committee's operational arm with it. It must have been a grave setback for them, one that would probably take years to overcome, if at all. The Committee was exposed now and the hunters would be prowling. He could still see the probing orange eyes of his Wanderer captors and the image made his skin crawl. When they were done with him, they discarded him, an empty drained shell. The subsequent BueCult and Palean inquisitions on Kalakan were almost mild in comparison.

To have foregone those mind-wrenching sessions!

"You're on manual?" he snapped.

"On manual," Winn confirmed, "and I've shut off the transponder." It wouldn't do to let SC&C, Surface Command and

Control, take over the blister. Not after they came this far. That gag would land them at the nearest Field where grim marines, brandishing phase rifles, would be waiting for them to disembark, ready to haul them back into captivity. Winn wondered briefly if the other blister pilots remembered to be as careful, and then gave a mental shrug. It wasn't his problem.

Tanard reached over Winn's shoulder and punched in the nav coordinates he'd been given on Kalakan by an AUP agent.

"It appears we have a reprieve from purgatory," Railee piped, a huge smile wrapped across his face.

"That still remains to be seen," Tanard said gravely and looked at Winn. "How long to touchdown?"

"Three minutes. We'll be crossing the night terminator any moment now."

"Excellent." Darkness would not stop SC&C from tracking them, but it would hinder, if for a while, the local authorities in their efforts to find them once they were down. By the time the blister was located, he would be part of the background scenery. If everything worked out, he reminded himself. There were plenty of things that could still go wrong.

SC&C started squawking almost immediately, demanding they go automatic, they were tracked and would be fired upon if they did not comply. Tanard gave an irritated growl and Winn cut off the verbal tirade. It was an idle threat anyway. Feron was an insignificant world on the Palean/Karkan border and had the most rudimentary Fleet facilities. A transit station at best. Its sparse and scattered agricultural population shunned the metropolitan centers, and the city dwellers were happy to have it like that. It made for vigorous competition during the seasonal tourist trade. Not an advanced world, but its position in a minor shipping corridor ensured it would never be simply another backwater frontier world. That's why it was picked as a staging post for their escape. There were enough offworlders on the planet at any one time, and three more should not raise any excitement. By the time the authorities got themselves organized, he hoped to be off the planet. How were they supposed to *get* off the planet? One thing at a time, he told himself.

"Mr. Winn? Send a single comms ping on the thirty-one point-two C band," Tanard ordered.

Winn glanced at his commander, then punched in the frequency, his flash of resentment that Tanard kept aspects of their escape from him evaporated. It was only reasonable. If their flight from the transport had failed, he could not divulge information he did not have.

"Ping sent."

Almost immediately, a single sharp response shattered the blister's muted computer whispers.

Railee raised an appreciative eyebrow. "A welcoming committee?"

Tanard gave him a stern glance. "Our escape was meant to succeed."

"I am comforted," Railee said unabashed. "It would have been mildly disconcerting if this was simply someone's idea of a macabre prank."

Tanard suppressed a smile, but he was serious when he said their escape was meant to succeed. The Palean arm of the Alikan Union Party had gone to a lot of trouble to make sure the resistance network was ready to take them back in. At least he hoped that was the case. Le Maran never actually said they'd be assuming their old roles, or what roles they would really have at all. Tough to be an effective operator with the Serrll's entire security apparatus after you.

Winn rotated the blister as they crossed the terminator. Thick cloudbanks obscured the ground far below. Lightning flashes rippled silently through them, accompanied by brilliant red and blue sprites high in the stratosphere at the edge of space itself.

The blister angled to port and plunged into black clouds. Turbulence shook the little craft and Tanard's stomach squirmed as the deck suddenly fell away and the restraining field snapped on. A high-pitched shriek of tortured air set his teeth on edge. Then they were through and the ride became smooth. On their starboard side a checkered pattern of lights indicated a large settlement or small city. The blister slowed and steadied in its descent. In the blackness below an occasional solitary light identified a lone residence. The main display plate showed open countryside and planted fields crowding a ragged forest.

The blister descended quickly, paused, then settled with a gentle bump. It was kind of eerie to be on solid ground again.

"Adjust for local gravity," Tanard rasped.

"We have company." Winn touched glowing pads and nodded at the display plate. A combie was making a direct line for them, its nav lights blinking. It braked hard and dropped beside the blister.

"At least it's not an APC," Railee muttered darkly. An Armored Personnel Carrier would definitely have spoiled what had so far been a great day.

"Crack the hatch, Mr. Winn," Tanard ordered and stood up. The countryside appeared deserted, but someone was bound to come looking sooner or later and he did not wish to be around when that happened.

The hatch sighed open and warm, sweet air rushed in. It smelled of grass, freshly turned earth, and cut timber. It tasted good after days of canned ship's goo.

"Let's not admire the scenery!" an impatient voice shouted from the combie.

Tanard jumped out, ran to the combie and scrambled through the open doorway. Winn glanced at Railee and followed. The door snapped shut as Railee squeezed in and the combie immediately surged up. A green safety strip along the bottom of the curved shell offered feeble light in the darkened interior. The combie cleared the timberline and Winn muttered a silent thanks to the survival blister, then turned to study the approaching town with interest. There was little to see in the dark.

Tanard looked curiously at the driver. The Karkan glanced at him and smiled, his pointed tongue flicking briefly.

"Welcome to Feron," the driver hissed. "Before you start, I cannot tell you anything because I don't know anything. My job is only to get you out of here. When I set down, I will disappear and you'll be on your own." The Karkan gave a guttural hiss, his idea of a chuckle.

"My thanks for picking us up."

"Save it, Mister. I got paid plenty for picking you up."

Tanard nodded. To the local AUP chapter it may have been cold and calculating, but it also made very good tactical sense. Things can always go wrong in any operation. Why expose the local setup when you can hire someone else to run all the risks.

The township loomed before them. Surrounded by lesser buildings, three low towers climbed into a black sky, their color-reactive panels glowing pearly yellow. Traffic was thin this time of night. An occasional combie, communal, and private sled-pad crossed the flight lanes. The combie tilted and skirted the local spaceport. Tanard scanned the Field complex with detached regard. Access tubes tethered two cargo carriers and a bulky liner to the L-shaped terminus building. Maintenance hangars and repair facilities, lit by bright floodlights, crowded the terminal. He thought he saw an M-1 scout parked at the edge of the apron. That was not good.

For such a small town this was a pretty large facility. A major agricultural port?

The combie swept past the Field and descend in a leisurely sweep. It sagged and came down vertically behind what looked like a shopping complex. The door opened and the Karkan grinned.

"End of the line."

They piled out and watched the combie take off, its navigation lights bright. When it vanished, Tanard looked around. Surrounded by buildings the small quadrangle was deep in shadow. A thin breeze stirred invisible rubbish. Two combies lay parked side by side against a towering black wall.

"Mr. Tanard?" a disembodied voice came from the left machine. "No, don't come any closer. I cannot afford to be seen. When I leave, take the other combie. It's preset to take you to a local hotel. Suite 16-12. When you get there, do not attempt to use the combie again." There was a brief hiss as a door slid shut and the combie immediately lifted.

"Oh, that's terrific!" Railee retorted caustically, his fingers working in agitation. "What happens after we get to suite 16-12? And how are we supposed to get into the damned thing?"

"The lock is probably keyed to one of us," Winn ventured.

"Hopefully not under our real names," Railee added dryly.

"There is only one way to find out," Tanard said and headed for the lone combie.

It was a short flight. He wondered why their Karkan pickup had not taken them directly to the hotel, and then answered his own question. The Karkan was not meant to know, and what he didn't know, he could not divulge. They came down on one of the landing ramps protruding like a rude tongue from the building's side. They climbed out and the parking system whisked the combie away. Railee watched it disappear and shrugged.

Past the deserted foyer the corridor walls glowed soft beige, offsetting the pale blue of the ceiling. Tanard had no desire to be seen dressed in a prison coverall. Their footfalls made hollow echoes in the thick silence. They easily found the large double-door entrance to their apartment. Without hesitating, Tanard pressed his palm against the sensitized plate set waist-high beside the door. The lock cycled and the two panels slid into the opposite walls. They entered as the comfortable lounge flooded with light.

An opaque floor-to-ceiling window screen occupied the far wall. The wooden floor was polished to a dull sheen and the narrow boards made a pleasing linear pattern of brown and amber. Two formchairs flanked a low glass-topped table on which lay three pouches and what looked like ID tags. The entire right wall held a full-dimensional communications station. On the left the living area opened into an adequate kitchen.

"I could get used to this." Railee nodded in appreciation and sprawled into the nearest chair.

The Wall screen brightened.

"Welcome to the Circle Hotel, Mr. Vendam. You have a message. Do you wish to view message?" the housekeeping computer asked pleasantly.

"Display message," Tanard said.

The Wall cleared. Tanard was not surprised to see Le Maran's corpulent sleek face. It appeared that life was very comfortable for his old controller. He felt a pang of resentment and jealousy.

"Friend Tanard, I want to welcome you to Feron and congratulate you on your, ah, obviously successful extraction." Le Maran gave a tight smile, his fingers working themselves into knots. "Although eminently preferable, I regret that circumstances made it impossible for me to see you in person. On the table before you are new identity tags and travel documents. The IDs are genuine with verifiable local legends. Please study them. It was convenient to bring you all here this one time, but for obvious reasons you cannot remain together. As you may have surmised by now, your survival blister's landing point was not a random event.

"Mr. Railee and Mr. Winn, you have reservations at the local Field's transit lounge. Change your clothes, then go there immediately and check in for your flight. The liner leaves in the morning. Friend Tanard, your departure is somewhat more involved, for which I apologize in advance. You need to take a morning shuttle to Kumran, the planet's capital. A booking has already been made and you'll have enough time to make an off-planet connection that leaves in the afternoon. There will be security checks, but your IDs will hold, provided you don't miss your flights. Each of you will receive further instructions when you reach your respective destination. Until then…" The image faded and the Wall pooled into merging, confused patterns of color.

"A flight in the morning?" Winn demanded in outrage. "He's got to be kidding! Who is he, anyway?"

"He was the Committee's mission operations controller," Tanard said, mulling over the message.

There was a lot left unsaid there and a lot to be taken on faith. The elaborate planning and organization behind their escape completely dispelled any thought of betrayal.

"You mean, he's the schmuck who cooked up the Italan deal that got us caught by the Fleet?"

Tanard's grinned briefly. "I received my instructions from him, friend Winn, but I doubt he planned the operation."

"That's just great! And we're supposed to take his word and stroll to the Field with security crawling all over the place?"

"It's not a bad plan when you think about it," Tanard mused. "Your flight is obviously pre-booked and you'll be expected. Hardly something a freshly landed prisoner would be able to arrange."

"And if you're wrong?"

"I will apologize."

"Oh, that really helps." Winn snorted and shook his head. "Why should we listen to this guy at all? With new IDs and money we could make our own way—"

"To what?" Railee said and stood up. Tanard lifted his hand to silence him.

"Friend Winn, we discussed this already."

Winn took a deep breath and clasped his hands behind his back to mask his agitation. He hated this confrontation with his commander, but there was too much at stake to take things on the word of a mealy-mouthed bureaucrat. He had sampled one result of bureaucratic incompetence and did not relish being the

14

object of another such event.

"We discussed it, yes, but as I recall, nothing was decided. I am grateful to the Committee for getting our butts off that Cantor transport, but after what I've been through, I think this only makes us even. They used us on Lemos, and when Italan failed, they abandoned us. I'm not so anxious to trust them again."

Tanard appreciated the courage and strength it took Winn to say that. His first officer had changed, all right.

"I don't have an easy answer for you, friend Winn, and frankly, I'm too tired to give you the longwinded one. Yes, we were used, betrayed and discarded, and we may be discarded again. What we did on Lemos, did it make a difference in the larger scheme of things? Perhaps, but probably not, and I am fatalistic enough to realize it. Italan has always been a mad scheme doomed to failure and we were lucky to walk away from it alive."

"Rotting on Kalakan for two years, some luck."

"You could have been dead."

"I wouldn't have minded," Winn snapped. "If you knew Italan was doomed, why did we go there?"

"Because it's what we do!" Tanard thundered. "Because those were our orders, and like it or not, we're mercenaries, little better than the raider scum we used on Lemos. Paint it with patriotism, but that's what we were. Every cause demands payment in blood and we certainly paid for ours in full." Tanard glared at them and raised his cyberplast arm.

After failing to take *Zaviar*, his ship crippled, he knew death would be a preferable release to what the Fleet had in store for him. When Second Scout Terr boarded to take his surrender, he was about to kill the young officer, but fates conspired against him yet again. Instead of killing Terr, he lost his own arm in the ensuing firefight.

"There is very little patriotism in attacking an unarmed merchant," Tanard rasped wearily. "But patriotism or not, if they give me a ship, I'm going out there again."

"And walk into another half-baked scheme?" Winn hissed, greatly daring.

"No more wild schemes, friend Winn. This time it will be on my terms."

"Like we have a lot of options," Railee added flatly. "We're marked men and the Fleet won't rest until it has us recaptured. You've got to know that. How far do you think your new ID will take you on your own?"

"Far enough! I didn't mind throwing away my career. That was gone when I stepped on Lemos, but it was *my* choice! What I mind is being tossed aside on a crummy deal like Italan for the sake of expediency."

Tanard sighed and shook his head. Young and idealistic, and now disillusioned, his first officer was finding life's hard knocks tough to take. It was time for a reality check. He thrust out his jaw and leaned forward.

"What did you think we were doing on Lemos, eh? The AUP Provisional Committee needed killers and we were available. We know how to drive ships and how to kill them. We're good at it and why we got picked. If we manage to get out of here, you'll be killing more ships."

"Or get smeared by one more likely."

"If you want out, you're free to take your ID and go. I won't stop you."

"Not much of a choice, is it?" Winn muttered in resignation.

"You always have a choice," Tanard said harshly. "The problem is in picking which one to take."

The room was deathly silent as they stared at each other, knowing by committing themselves, even Cantor would not be an option anymore.

"Well, I only have my life to lose. How bad can it get?" Winn said with a small grin. He never really had any choice and Tanard probably knew it.

Railee laughed and slapped him on the back.

"That remains to be seen," Tanard murmured and absently massaged his cyberplast arm.

Next time, friend Terr, I won't miss.

* * *

Terr pursued the last bit of runny egg with a piece of toast and popped it into his mouth. Chewing, he leaned back and grinned broadly at Dhar, who was frowning suspiciously at a glass of purple juice.

"What's the matter? Something crawling in there?"

Dhar looked up and his scowl deepened. The vertical red slits of his large orange eyes squinted in concentration.

"I am not sure I like the taste," he said seriously.

Dhar's deep, soft voice reminded Terr of still nights, open sands and dark skies. Momentarily distracted, he took a long pull from his glass. The heavy juice had a zesty tartness that assaulted the mouth and left a lingering citrus aftertaste. It would never become his favorite, but it was the only palatable stuff the cargo tramp carried. The alternative, which the mostly Palean crew favored, wasn't worth drinking.

"It hasn't killed you yet," he said comfortably.

"It's a long haul, my brother. Give it time," Dhar remarked darkly.

"Every morning, you bitch about the damned juice—"

"And you keep riding me about it."

Terr grinned again and shook his head in resignation. "You're a sourpuss, you know that? But I'm not going to let your juice problems ruin my day."

A crewman left the serving counter and made for the exit, his thin hand wrapped around a large sandwich. He nodded to Terr as he strode past. Chairs scraped on the deck and there was a clatter of dishes and utensils as latecomers hurried off for the change of watch. The sounds echoed in the emptying mess.

The warmth and intimacy filling the room earlier, the carefree chatter of the crew, it was all gone. Stale smells of cold food and burnt toast lingered in the air; silent ghosts among silent voices.

Behind the counter, the serving order cook stared pointedly at the two lone figures deep in conversation. "You guys about finished?"

Terr looked up and scowled. "Excuse me? We on a timer or something?"

The order cook glanced at the ceiling and sighed. "I keep an open mess and what do I get? Lack of appreciation, that's what I get. I've been in a few clapped-out tramps in my day where they dish you a cold meal pack if you're lucky. Here, I try to do the right thing by everybody, and what do I get? Lack of appreciation."

Terr chuckled. "Doesn't seem right, does it?"

"A wise bird, eh? Well, let me tell you something, sonny. I got work to do. Not like some. You and your pal clear your asses out of here before I take a cleaver to you. Civilians, phaf!" Muttering at the injustice of it all, the cook dumped a load of dishes into the washer.

Dhar gulped down the last of the foul cloying liquid, placed the empty glass on the table with a loud click, and sat back. He folded his arms across his chest and studied his brother's look of sardonic amusement. His mouth lifted when Terr absently touched the scar above his left temple, a characteristic gesture of inner turmoil, he had learned. He knew every crease, every dimple and every mark on Sankri's finely molded, yet firm features. A strong face that reflected a resolute character and a sometimes stormy personality.

After their last brutal exchange with Kai Tanard two years ago, which cost the renegade Fleet officer his right arm, then on Anar'on where the Diplomatic Branch Resident made his clumsy attempt to recruit Terr into the Unified Independent

Front, Sankri had rebelled. He rebelled against what he had become and what others now expected of him as a result of his transfiguration as a Saddish-aa Wanderer. No, that was not quite true, Dhar reflected with brutal honesty and felt a momentary flush of guilt. The fact that his unselfish act saved Sankri's life was small compensation for the emotional struggle his brother now endured, or had endured. After the battle with Tanard, their ships battered and souls scarred, they were allowed a few days of precious leave on Anar'on. In the village of Dhar's fathers, among the rolling sands of the Saffal, Sankri had made a bargain with the god of Death that appeared to have given him a measure of inner peace. Over the last two years, Dhar had not seen his brother war with the demands of the Discipline or his newly found heritage—until this mission.

Tah, the gods will tell.

"I think we better do a fade," Terr said and pushed back his chair. "Unless, of course, you want another glass of juice," he added with malicious glee.

Dhar glared at him. "You have a cruel streak in you, Sankri, did you know that?"

"Yeah, so I've been told."

They took the cable-tube to the command deck. Its size matched everything else aboard the huge ship. The arrays of forward-sloping consoles were more suited to an M-4 than a bulk carrier. During one long uneventful watch, Terr questioned the watchstander about it. The arrangement was unusual and somewhat dated, he was told, but the ship was old and some of the perishable cargo they normally hauled required special attention. Besides, the watchstander admitted somewhat sheepishly, it gave the crew something to fiddle with. Listening to sterilized computer reports wasn't the same thing. Terr sympathized. Completely automated ships could be built, but they would lack that necessary human quality, the feel of being in control. Hence, manual over-instrumentation.

Beneath a brooding gray three-katalan-wide display plate,

the consoles were lined with rows of amber and green touch-sensitive pads. One of the largest navigation bubbles Terr had seen took up most of the curved ceiling. It was transparent. Stars peeked in, white and brittle. Brown gravity waves twisted and coiled about the ship as the bulk carrier tore through sub-space.

Three contoured formchairs faced the display plate and the console repeaters. Two were occupied. As the cable-tube hatch hissed shut, the center chair swiveled. The elderly Karkan Master Pilot frowned and his slightly flattened head tilted. His neck was long and slender, making the movement very graceful. Broad scales covered the pale green head. They glistened and changed color as he moved. Beneath a thin ridge of darker scales, fishy black eyes stared from horizontal slits. A thin pointed tongue flicked briefly from a flat mouth.

Thoran had spaced since he was fourteen years old and seen many things in that time, not all of them pleasant. He saw service in the Fleet Marines before the glamour wore off and life became merely dull shipboard drudgery and mindless drill. He left the Fleet and joined the merchant service—and found his place in life. Herding cargo ships lacked some of the excitement and intensity being a marine sometimes had, but what it did provide was security and predictability. Studying his two visitors, he had his doubts they were merely civilian engineers. They carried themselves with a distinctive and all too evident military bearing, no matter how much they tried to disguise it by what they thought was ordinary dirt hugger behavior. Even now, standing there relaxed, the young Kaplan wore his command presence like a cloak, one the pilot recognized immediately. He doubted that any of the crew noticed, and accepted the fact phlegmatically. He didn't know what the two of them were doing aboard his ship and moreover, he didn't particularly care. As long as they stayed out of his way, he was happy to keep his nose out of their business.

Thoran gave a low hiss and cleared his throat. "Gentle-men...The mess hall a bit dull, is it?"

Terr's mouth lifted and he nodded to the other watchstander. "Just stretching our legs, sir," he said.

"Cookie wasn't about to let you have it, was he?" Thoran mused, his eyes sparkling.

"He was a contributing reason," Terr said with a straight face and Thoran chuckled.

"If you're after some exercise, you should try a hike along the central spine. That'll give your legs a good stretching."

Terr winced and the memory made his legs ache. The VLBC was over thirteen hundred katalans long and he counted the walk as a unique experience, but it had not been *that* en-thralling to make him want to repeat it.

"I shall keep it in mind, thanks," he said dryly.

The proximity warning beeped and Thoran glanced at the nav plate. When he looked up, his eyes were dark with concern, the smile gone.

"We were tracking an anomalous contact for the past two hours or so and I suspect a raider. The damned thing is now on a direct intercept course. At our present closure rate, he'll be on us in fifty minutes. The scum are everywhere. Can't make a lift these days and they're on you. What good is having the Fleet if they can't protect us, eh?"

Terr sympathized. "IFF?" he asked and the watchstander shook his head. That ruled out a Fleet vessel.

"Nine months ago, I was jumped by one of those heathen," Thoran complained bitterly. "I was lucky and managed to get away. This son of a canal worm is making the same type of approach and I'm not hanging around to find out if he *is* a raider. I'd be obliged if you two would clear my command deck. I've got a ship to con," he snapped and glared at the watchstander. "Send the bastard a nav interrogative ping."

A few seconds later the watchstander looked up from his board.

"Bulk carrier *Virana* on a high-speed run to Rumini 3C, and he apologizes if he made us nervous."

Thoran's tongue flicked in a blur. "Apologizes for making us nervous? Son of a cow! Tell him to keep his distance," he snarled and swiveled in his seat. "You two still here?"

For a moment, Terr thought they were actually under attack, which would have made him very happy. An actual attack might cost the lives of the carrier's crew, but he could not afford to think about that. There was too much at stake. What was the worth of a life? His conscience gave a protesting stir, which he quickly killed. He had no time for that either.

Six days out of Naurun, he was impatient for something to happen, yet hoping it wouldn't, for there would surely be death in it for someone. The irony wasn't lost on him. He had a mission to capture one of a swarm of raiders who took to plundering Kaleen shipping of late. Raiders were one of society's less savory byproducts, but with fewer practical uses. If he believed the indignation of local politicians, the situation around Kaleen had become so desperate and the loss of cargo so severe, planetary economies were affected. If the nonsense was allowed to continue, it could potentially threaten the trading infrastructure and stability of Kaleen's eight systems.

Histrionics aside, everyone conceded that things were really not so bad, but it could become so if nothing was done to curb the raider threat. The similarity with raids on Pizgor's commerce two years ago was too striking to be merely coincidence. Discovery and subsequent destruction of the raider base on Lemos had solved Pizgor's immediate problem, but had it really resolved anything in the long run? Unable to eliminate Pizgor's carriers, it appeared that Sargon, and probably the Paleans as well, were out to strangle Pizgor's commerce by routing their ships away from its main shipping corridors. Had Sargon learned subtlety and were raids against Kaleen patterned along the same mold? First the club, then the gloved hand, was that it? Anabb seemed to think so and was the reason for Terr being out here, to get proof.

He and Dhar were posing as engineers shepherding two step-down fusion reactors to be installed on a Palean frontier world that skirted the Kaleen border. As far as the Very Large Bulk Carrier crew knew, they carried two civilian deadheads. The merchant service was understandably stuffy about getting itself involved in any Fleet skullduggery. The Master Pilot had nothing to grumble about, though. Passage was paid for the two of them, and no amount of checking by anyone could prove he and Dhar were anything else but Simplon engineers. The Diplomatic Branch was thorough about such small things. It was also a very good cover, which they had now used three times already, always on a carrier sub-contracted to Naurun or Omiron; both Kaleen frontier worlds whose shipping was at the moment enjoying concentrated raider attention, if that was the right word.

"Just leaving," Terr said and turned to the cable-tube hatch.

"Aw, stay if you like," Thoran growled, "but keep out of my way."

"Sir!" The watchstander gulped and went pale. "We have another contact and he is closing."

"Range?" Thoran barked, his eyes scanning the nav repeater plot.

"He's right on us, less than a light-minute below our port side…and *Virana* is also closing."

"Raiders!" Thoran snarled. "I knew it!"

Terr had to admire the raider tactics. The second ship must have been powered down, lying in wait in the shipping corridor for its prey to stumble on it. *Virana* was clearly a distraction, one now coming in for its share of the kill.

Just then, the comms console flickered and a sharp, guttural voice blared from the speakers.

"Bulk carrier, bulk carrier. You are about to be boarded. Drop normal and take to your survival blisters immediately. If you attempt to launch an emergency beacon or activate your transponders, I will destroy you in place. You have fifteen seconds before I fire on you."

"Be damned!" Thoran jumped out of his seat and thrust his jaw at the watchstander. "Set the transponder and dump the beacons."

"I wouldn't do that, Pilot," Terr said with quiet force and Thoran glared at him. The watchstander's finger was poised above the beacon ejection pad.

"And why the hell not? Once we're in our survival blisters, they'll cream us. Raiders don't like leaving any witnesses, Mister!"

"And if you piss them off, they will cream you for sure," Terr said and waited as Thoran struggled between his desire to defy the raider and duty to his nineteen-man crew. It wasn't much of a decision. The pilot's chest deflated with a long hiss and his shoulders sagged as he looked at the watchstander.

"Drop normal and order Engineering to secure the primary drive reactor," Thoran said and slumped onto the command couch. "Enable blister ejection sequence and alert everyone to stand by abandon ship routine." He shook his head and chuckled. "Twice in nine months. Would you believe it? I've had this ship for two years and now I'm going to lose her. Pits!"

The VLBC's nav shield changed polarity and the distortion field precursor discharged. The carrier dropped into normal space in a cascade of yellow and orange light from the collapsing drive field. Dead in space the carrier waited as the raider dropped normal less than eighty thousand talans ahead of them. It immediately boosted to close the gap.

Thoran slapped the armrests and stood up. "I'll let the owners worry about the hull and cargo. Right now, we better be leaving." He gave Terr a sidewise glance. "I'll be very disappointed in you, Mister, if that raider decides to come after my crew."

"I'll apologize," Terr said with a grin.

Thoran snorted and jerked his head at the watchstander.

"Give the abandon ship order, son, and your job is done. You two…" He pointed at Terr and Dhar. "You take a blister from the main loading dock with the others. I'll take one from here."

"Good luck, sir," Terr said and automatically stood to, realizing immediately he'd given himself away, but Thoran merely nodded, ignoring or choosing not to notice the gesture.

The cable hatch hissed open and Dhar stepped in. Without a backward glance, Terr turned and joined him.

"Main deck, Bay Three," Dhar growled as the hatch closed. A faint whine accompanied the falling car. There was a barely discernable ripple of shifting gravity as polarity changed and the hatch slid open.

Kalnar's cavernous loading bay was empty, the crew not anxious to chat with the coming visitors. This was only one of six bays on this level, designed to move cargo containers through the holds using enormous overhead cranes suspended from massive H rails running along the ship's spine. The carrier had four such levels. Two M-1s could have easily slipped side by side through the equally immense hatchway. It took a lot of power to move the fifteen million mikans fully loaded hull, and even more to keep it moving through subspace.

The VLBCs were valuable beyond price. If a raider was lucky enough to capture one that carried the right cargo and managed to sell it, its crew could live like potentates for ten lifetimes. Of course, a carrier's cargo was rarely that attractive, usually a mixed bag of commodities. Even when it was loaded with lucrative cargo the raider was by necessity forced to offload it at far below its actual commercial value, legitimate brokers shying away from such deals. That was what kept a raider running, unless he raided for reasons other than economic. There were plenty of religious and political zealots who saw destruction of an enemy's ability to trade, and thereby sustain its economy, a perfectly legitimate tactic if it brought an enemy to his knees.

It was a nasty way to do business.

It was also the kind of war that seemed to be waged right now against Naurun and Omiron. A large part of Terr's current job was to find out who was orchestrating it, which was the reason why he wanted to capture a raider intact. Getting hold of intact computer records would be a prize worth the lives of a carrier's crew. Wouldn't it? The Fleet had captured raiders before, but invariably the effort yielded them very little or nothing. The raider would trash the ship's computer before the marines could board and stop them. Modern methods of interrogation were only partially successful at best. What worked for the interrogators also worked for the raiders.

Sophisticated conditioning made it possible for a raider pilot or nav officer to forget everything of consequence by merely using a set of code words. It was frustrating. Of course, that same sophistication allowed an interrogator to break through the conditioning, but the process tended to be somewhat harsh and the subject was not much good for anything else afterward. It was a practice frowned upon by the authorities and forbidden by Fleet regulations. Despite the fact raiders were merely pirates, the law entitled them to due process, otherwise the Captal government would be no better than the raiders themselves. Once correct and moral behavior was sidestepped for the sake of expediency or some seemingly higher lofty goal, anarchy and dictatorship were not far behind.

It was sometimes inconvenient being the good guy.

But Terr was not a Fleet officer anymore, not technically, and he was undercover. It made the game a bit more even as far as he was concerned, although he knew Dhar held severe misgivings about the method he intended using to achieve his end.

Well, rit! A good guy was allowed to have a bit of fun now and then, no?

He gathered Dhar with his eyes and nodded at the docking console.

"Let's see what our raider friend is up to."

Immortal in Shadow

On the command deck the pilot watched as the cable-tube hatch closed behind the two odd individuals. He gave a low hiss, his tongue flicking rapidly from his mouth, and turned. With a last glance at the consoles, he jerked his head toward the two blister hatches pulsing soft amber. A solid yellow ring circled each hatch.

"Time we were going, son," he said and the grateful watchstander got up and hurried toward the nearest hatch. He pressed a yellow pad set waist-high and the hatch slid into the bulkhead with a raspy whisper. Without looking back, he scrambled inside. Thoran followed in a more dignified fashion. When he reached the blister, he paused and his eyes swept around the command deck one last time at a ship he had grown to love. He set his jaw and climbed into the blister.

He blinked in the gloomy interior and took the right seat. Without a word, he stabbed the yellow purge pad. The hatch clanged shut and the survival blister surged down the launch tube. He grunted as the restraining field held him in place. Then they were clear, the solid bulk of the carrier rotated above them from the blister's spin.

"Open a local comms link," Thoran said and the watchstander tapped pads on the simple console. The blister arrested its spin and boosted away from the carrier. Thoran thought he saw a long boxy shape close with his ship before darkness swallowed everything.

"Comms open," the watchstander said, somewhat intimidated by the pilot's close presence. Standing watch with his commanding officer was one thing, but having the pilot in his lap, so to speak, was unnerving.

"Everybody check in," Thoran ordered.

Three blisters reported in, accounting for his remaining eighteen crewmen. His two passengers were not on board any of the blisters. He was about to broadcast again, asking them to report in, then stopped himself. The raider could be monitoring this channel. If they realized two of the carrier's crew might still

27

be on board, they could possibly take action—against him. It could also conceivably compromise whatever those two individuals were up to. It wasn't his problem, he decided, and he never did figure the two for civilians. He ordered the blisters to form up on him and the little craft sped toward the stars.

The raider ship retracted its weapons projector dome and closed with the carrier. It slowed and crept toward the central port loading hatch, the vast hull of the VLBC dwarfing it even though the raider itself was not a small ship. The raider could not hope to take on board more than a fraction of the carrier's cargo, but with *Virana*, they could at least offload the more marketable items. If a patrolling Fleet picket happened to show up, the raid would still clear an operating profit. If there was time the hull would be taken to a remote system where it would be stripped and gutted.

The raider edged gingerly to fifteen katalans off the VLBC's sheer side, stopped and extended a forty-katalan-wide loading tube. The armored tube mated against the hatch bearing with a silent clang of locking clamps. Once the carrier was secured and its cargo analyzed, they would then extend additional loading tubes.

Standing before the docking console, Terr watched with keen interest as the raider first matched speed with the carrier, then slowly, but purposefully, drew closer. The image in the display plate grew until it swamped the stars. A moment later the loading tube connected and the snap of clamps echoed hollow through the hold.

"Time we made ourselves scarce," Dhar said gravely and turned. Terr grabbed his arm. Dhar stopped, but did not look back.

"Nightwings, I intend to disable, not kill."

Dhar slowly turned his head and looked down at his brother. His eyes burned with the fires of accusation and disapproval.

"It is not *right*, Sankri," he protested in righteous indignation.

For long seconds, Terr stared at his brother and felt keen disappointment. This was the first time Dhar had so openly disagreed with his decision on a course of action and he felt uneasy at the chasm of ideology that had opened between them. Out of necessity they came on board unarmed. If they were to face off with the raiders, there was only one way to do it—with Death in their hands.

"I don't have time to debate this," he said stiffly. "Will you support me or not?" He regretted the words even as he said them.

Dhar's features twisted with genuine pain. "Sankri, my brother, if you need to ask—"

"Nightwings..." Terr sighed and shook his head. Of all the times for this to come up! "Let's get into our hiding hole before we have every raider in that ship arguing with us."

Even as they hurried toward what looked like haphazardly stacked containers, Terr was desperately unhappy at what he was about to do. The words from the *Saftara* and the teachings of the Discipline didn't help him here, for the men he was about to face didn't live by a code of honor, or any code, for that matter. Did that justify *his* action, or merely excused it? Wryly, he reflected not for the first time the dichotomy of the Wanderer Discipline, born among the sands of the Saffal, nurtured by the collective wisdom of the Rahtir to meet the needs of the Wanderers and the brutal demands of chaos permeating the Serrll. It was a seemingly irreconcilable clash between order and upheaval. Though he walked in the shadow of the god of Death, he stood helpless in that chaos, unless he turned it against itself.

Two years ago, he stood on the warm sands of the Saffal with brittle stars hung in a sweeping tapestry above him and the lightnings of anguish coiled in his hands. When he loosed the lightnings, even the desert cried out at his pain. He did not want to be a child of Death, or carry the burden exercising such power exacted. He didn't want to be a god, but that power also made his blood sing and he walked immortal beneath its cloak. In a flash of brutal honesty, he knew himself unworthy of such a gift. The temptations for abuse were many. That night, among the shifting sands, he made a bargain with his god.

He would use the power the god had chosen to bestow on him and test the limits of the *Saftara* and its writings. To do otherwise would surely drive him to madness.

Why couldn't Nightwings understand? Couldn't his brother see if he could not play the immortal, the lightnings would consume him? He was not abandoning the Discipline or its teachings, but he had to live them on his terms in an environment alien as he was.

Dhar reached the containers, slipped into a gap and was gone. Terr paused. Behind him the ponderous bay hatch groaned and slid into the hull frame. He crouched into the opening between two containers and waited. Dhar's warm breath was comforting on the back of his neck and he made a decision. Torn with inner turmoil, he stilled his breathing and turned to face the tall, shadowy figure hunched before him. He reached with his right hand and placed his palm against Dhar's chest.

"Nightwings, we are brothers and I only wish to be at peace in your shadow," he whispered with fierce intensity, willing his eyes to reach across the gloom that separated them, to bridge the gap of understanding that had opened between them.

Dhar drew in his breath with a sharp hiss. This was not the time for Sankri to doubt himself because he disapproved of his ethics. Later, he would need to heal the wound in both of them, but not now. Sankri was right. They were one and that was all that mattered, what always would matter. Everything else was pettiness. He placed his own hand against Terr's chest.

"Then be at peace, my brother, for I shall always be with you," he said, his voice hoarse as it trembled deep within his chest.

Something flowed between them and Terr felt a stirring of power as Death touched him. The strength of Dhar's presence soothed and comforted him. Everything was all right and he was a fool to have doubted his brother.

With the shadow of Death on him, he silently mouthed the words from the *Saftara*.

"I shall walk in the shadow of Death. And it shall be with me all the days of my life. With shadow shall I smite my enemies and with thunder shall I purge their land." His hackles rose and he had an urge to raise his arms. Small blue lightnings slithered across his hands. "And all those who stand with me in the shadow of Death shall know my power and be comforted. With shadow and thunder shall I walk their land."

Death held ready in his hands and Dhar's comforting presence beside him, Terr was reassured. His brother had misgivings; unfounded, that was all. Who was to say Dhar wasn't right? Besides, a good stiff quarrel was a healthy thing and blew away the cobwebs of complacency. Didn't it? Unfortunately, he knew this particular squabble was not over yet. No matter. Differences aside, Dhar was with him now and the differences would be sorted out later.

He heard loud, high-pitched voices as the raiders boarded, Paleans, by the sound of them. A moment later one of the overhead cranes gave a low groan and there was a long hiss as it began to move. He heard cargo hatches open and the voices faded. He edged toward the opening and cautiously peered out. There was no one in sight, the raiders presumably busy checking out the cargo. The brightly lit loading tube beckoned and Terr sprinted across the ninety-odd katalans of open deck, his ship's boots soundless. He did not pause when he reached the tube, but quickly closed the short distance to the raider's cavernous hold. His nose wrinkled at the sharp acid smell of the air as he searched for the cable-tube hatch. Every ship carried its own peculiar ambient odor, one oblivious to its crew, of course. The bulk carrier's atmosphere had a soft, sweetish smell, reminding him of finely ground sugar and freshly baked buns.

"Here," Dhar whispered beside him and pointed at a hatch on the other side of the opening. Another short sprint, chests heaving from the exertion, they waited for the tube to open. Each second dragged on interminably and seemed to last an hour, increasing their chance of discovery and inevitable death.

"Come on!" Terr hissed with frustrated intensity and Dhar grinned, his eyes bright with excitement, the right or the wrong of it the least of his worries right now.

The tube hatch suddenly opened and Terr stood face to face with a tall, scruffy Palean. The Palean's enormous black eyes grew even larger and his small mouth opened in astonishment, but he was quick. Even as he reached for the powerful-looking needler stuck in his waistband, Terr shot out his arm.

"Naughty, naughty."

Small blue sparks jumped from his hand and struck the Palean's chest, defusing as they spread. The raider gasped in shocked agony and collapsed to the floor like a soggy rag.

Terr grimaced as he stared at the body. "Scum! Should have burned him."

"Sankri!"

"Never mind. Wishful thinking. Good thing he was alone."

"No matter," Dhar said beside him and Terr looked up. Dhar's wiry two point-three katalan frame was relaxed, but he looked ready for anything. Little blue sparks slithered along his arms. The vertical red slits of his orange eyes betrayed nothing. The thin membranes, designed to protect the eyes from fine sand, were retracted. His yellow skin looked dry, drawn tight over the bony ridges of his long face. His nose, broad and flat with flared nostrils, added to his skeletal appearance. No one could mistake him for anything but a creature of the desert. Terr had no trouble imagining him standing tall and aloof on a wind-swept dune, cape flying behind him, his eyes lost in the shimmering heat haze where an amber sky met the flowing sands.

He nodded once and they stepped into the tube. "Command deck," he snapped and the hatch slid shut. "If we're lucky the place will be deserted," he added musingly, not really believing it. They could expect at least two watchstanders on station, ready to maneuver the ship in case of an emergency.

"Mmm," was Dhar's skeptical comment.

"You take the left one and I'll take the right one," Terr said. "If there are more of them, just let them have it. They won't be armed and won't expect anything."

Dhar nodded meaningfully at the needler stuck in Terr's waist.

Terr sighed in exasperation, shook his head and crouched, his arm held level and ready. Nightwings was being a pain again. The hatch opened and he instantly loosed the lightnings. Bright arcs of blue lanced at the right command couch. The luckless watchstander hardly had time to swivel around as he was enveloped in a soft radiance that slithered and danced over his body. The Palean gave a choked gurgle, jerked uncontrollably and fell to the deck. His arms trembled as blue coils drained from his body. Terr glanced at the left couch, but it was all over. The second watchstander was slumped back, his eyes staring vacantly at the transparent nav bubble, mouth slack in contorted anguish.

Terr craned his neck and peered quickly around the deck. There was no one else about. He grabbed the Palean in the cable-tube by his left arm and dragged him partway out. The head gave a hollow thump as it bumped against the hatch slides. He stepped across the opening, leaned toward the small control panel set waist-high and tapped an orange contact pad. The pad turned green and locked the hatch open, preventing anyone else from getting to the command deck. The body blocking the hatch slides would also stop the tube from being reactivated in Engineering.

He glanced at Dhar and noticed the tension in his face. Dhar slowly turned his head and their eyes locked.

"It is better to give than to receive, eh?" Terr said with an amused smile.

"A dangerous thing we are playing with here, Sankri," Dhar said, looking grave. He pursed his lips and strode toward the three couches. His brother was right. The tingle of power still coursing through his body, the flash of joy and terrible certainty when he poured forth the wrath of Death, made him feel invulnerable before the puny creatures who dared stand before him. Sankri's irreverent remark rang too true for comfort.

An untidy heap on the left couch, the Palean's body looked crumpled and used. Small black burns charred the tunic around his chest. Dhar easily lifted the slight form with one arm and dropped it against the console. The Palean wasn't a consideration anymore. He would remain unconscious for several hours yet, although when he wakes, he would probably wish he were really dead. Dhar had experienced Death's touch and knew. The agony of returning life was seemingly an eternity of electric pins and needles eating at the whole body as feeling returned. He wiped his hand against his trousers in an absent gesture and leaned over the nav plot display plate.

Virana was still heading for them, but it would take her a bit longer now that the bulk carrier was dead in space and no longer under boost.

"The other raider is now one hour forty-nine minutes from intercept," he said.

Terr gave a small shrug. "You cannot have everything." *Virana* was an unpleasant complication, but not a fatal one. Unless, of course, his planned help took its time getting here. He pulled the heaped body away from the right couch, stepped to the comms panel and tapped in a preset frequency.

"Computer, issue an all-ships signify on the set channel," he ordered and reached for the ID tag in his trouser pocket. Satisfied, he settled himself onto the couch.

"All-ships signify transmitted," the computer answered in a strong, but soft voice. It did not take long. "Incoming transmission. Do you wish to respond?"

"Open channel," Terr said and looked at the main display plate as it cleared. A Palean First Scout stared at him with undisguised curiosity.

"Bulk carrier, you're transmitting on a restricted channel—"

"First Scout," Terr cut him off. "Designate your ship and distance."

The Palean arched his eyebrows. "SSF M-2 *Tahal*, four point—"

"Please close on my position at maximum boost and stand by for further instructions." It would take the M-2 over three hours to reach the bulk carrier, but the patrol ship could ferry prisoners, which would be useful. The First Scout would not be too happy, but Terr had no time right now for bruised egos. He inserted his ID card into a slot above the comms pads array. "My authentication and clearance codes are coming through now."

The Palean looked understandably annoyed until he saw the Diplomatic Branch authorization codes in his display plate. His eyes widened and he stood straighter.

"Codes received and verified, sir. Closing at maximum boost," he piped and the display plate cleared.

"You have another message," the computer announced. "Do you wish—"

"Open channel," Terr ordered.

A crusty old Karkan Master Scout stared coldly from the plate, his pointed tongue flicking from his mouth. Terr almost grinned at what he imagined would be the senior officer's reaction to his request.

"What in the pits is this, Mister?" the Master Scout demanded. "Do you realize—"

"Master Scout, please designate your ship and distance and

stand by for my authentication codes," Terr said calmly and pressed a touch-sensitive pad. The Karkan's fishy eyes bulged when he received the transmission.

"Of all the asinine…" The Karkan spluttered and hissed, but he had very little choice and Terr knew it. "SSF M-4 *Turin*, two point- three—"

Terr was very relieved. At one point-six lights an hour, it would take the M-4 one hour and thirty minutes to get to him, and an M-4 was a very handy force multiplier to have around.

"Please close on my position at maximum boost."

"Close on your position? What's going on, Mister?"

"A moment, sir," Terr said and tapped a pad, leaving the Karkan glaring at him. "Computer, cancel the all-ships signify." He tapped the pad again. "My associate and I have boarded a raider and we're in control of the command deck."

"Hah!"

"The raider crew are busy checking over the VLBC in which we were recently passengers. They don't know I have their command deck—yet."

"Hah!"

"There is an additional complication. Another raider vessel is closing on my position."

"I have him on my nav plot," the Karkan hissed. "You've got yourself a predicament, haven't you, Mister?"

"Master Scout! You will not intercept the target. You're authorized to call on any support to pursue it, but I need you here. You also have *Tahal*, an M-2, closing on me. I want him to carry any prisoners to Kalakan."

The Karkan was clearly not used to being ordered around like this, but then there was Terr's authority.

"Very well. There is more to this than meets the eye, I am sure, but we'll cover that later. Your authentication codes check out and I have no option but to comply. Closing on you at max boost," the Karkan said and the display plate turned pale gray.

Terr leaned back onto the couch and allowed himself a

small smile of satisfaction. He stretched his arms and grunted as the joints creaked.

"This time, my brother, we may have actually gotten away with it."

Dhar frowned and pointed at one of the display plates. "Perhaps not. According to these, there are two maintenance crawlways that lead to this deck and both are manually operated."

"You were studying the ship's schematics?"

"It seemed the thing to do."

"Okay, show me."

Dhar walked across the deck toward the cable-tube. Outlined on the right side of the hatch was a green door. He tugged it back and it slid into the bulkhead. On the floor was a thick panel covering a square manhole.

Terr pulled the needler from his waist, made an adjustment and fired at the clamp securing the panel. White smoke spurted from the panel and the clamp glowed dull red, then turned white. Molten metal flowed to the floor as acrid smoke filled the cubicle. He stopped firing, waved his hand through the smoke and looked brightly at Dhar.

Dhar studied the ruined panel. The lump of metal that was the clamp had already cooled. A thin wisp of white smoke struggled to rise. This would not hold back a determined assault from the crew armed with cutting equipment, but it was a satisfactory, if unorthodox solution to the immediate problem. Once the raider crew realized they were boarded and could not reach the command deck, it would take them some time to get around to try the crawlway. Hopefully, by that time the M-4 would have reached them.

Dhar pointed at a square panel directly under the nav bubble, set flush with the deck. Terr ran the needler beam around the edge of the panel, fusing it to the rest of the deck.

"Any other problems?"

"Command deck!" the inter-deck comms suddenly blared.

"You clowns asleep up there? Where in the bloody hell are my position checks?" demanded a harsh, guttural voice, which gave the impression of a large, angry predator.

Terr and Dhar exchanged glances.

"I would say this could be a problem," Dhar said dryly.

"Rit!" Terr swore, disgusted with himself. *Of course*, the raider commander would be on alert for prowling Fleet ships, ready to disengage from the bulk carrier and dash for a quick getaway. It was always the little things…

"Ren Lee?" the voice was softer now, clearly suspicious.

"When you were snooping around those schematics, did you happen to see if this tub has an auxiliary control room?" Terr asked, his forehead creased in concentration.

"There isn't one, but the ship can be maneuvered from Engineering," Dhar said.

"Maybe they can get this thing moving, but they cannot navigate." Terr nodded with satisfaction.

"Do you want to contact *Turin*?"

"And tell them what? This won't make her come faster. No, we'll sit tight and see what happens."

"Lee? If this is—" The harsh voice suddenly cut off.

"I think their curiosity is aroused, my brother," Dhar drawled and Terr smiled.

A moment later the green cable-tube control pad flickered and turned brown. The hatch jolted, but remained open, the body across the slides prevented it from closing. Terr was glad to see his first line of defense holding.

"I think we can expect visitors any time now," he said and waited.

After three minutes, dull clangs came from under the deck hatch and the maintenance alcove. The raiders were probably using personal communicators to have timed it so close. It was then that Terr sensed rather than saw a panel slide open on the left side of the cable-tube hatch. He automatically turned and raised his needler.

"Drop it!" the familiar guttural voice snarled from the gloomy alcove. Terr didn't hesitate and opened his hand. The weapon made a loud thud as it struck the deck. Death stirred within him and his shoulders twitched.

A tall imposing figure stepped out of the alcove, dressed in a black zip-jacket and gray pants. His round head was perfectly bald and he had thick, purple lips, now pressed tight beneath a broad nose and small pinpoint red eyes. His skin was midnight black with a faint oily sheen. The ugly snub-nosed needler was almost swallowed in his bulky hand.

The raider gave a mirthless smile and jerked back his head.

"I found this little access hideaway useful more than once."

"Yeah. I can see how it can be handy," Terr said, watching the other's eyes. A very tough customer, he decided. An immediate chemical hate passed between them and the raider pursed his lips.

"I don't know who you two birds are," the raider hissed, full of menace, "but I promise you'll sing to me before I kill you."

"Kadatar…" a muffled voice came from within the alcove's crawlway. The raider's eyes barely flickered, but that moment of distraction was enough.

Dhar did not move his arm to warn the raider. He merely lifted his left palm and there was a sharp crack as a bolt of blue light struck the raider on the chest. The raider screwed his eyes at the pain shooting through him and doubled up. He gave a strangled gasp, tried to bring up the needler and slowly toppled to the deck. His shoulders convulsed and he was still.

Dhar glanced at Terr and strode to the body. He went down on one knee, touched the raider's neck and looked up.

"He'll live," he said indifferently and looked into the alcove. It was the same setup as with the maintenance one. He picked up the raider's ugly needler and walked into the alcove. He touched a pad on the bulkhead beside the opening and watched as the inspection panel silently closed and sealed. He aimed the needler and traced the fine white beam around the seal. The acrid smoke irritated his throat and he coughed to clear it. When the job was done, he stared at the cooling metal for one long second, contemplating what he had done, and stepped out.

"You up there!" a high-pitched Palean voice came from the inter-deck comms. "What do you want? A cut of the action? We can talk."

"We'll talk when *Turin* gets here, you son of a canal worm," Terr muttered as he bent over Kadatar.

"I don't know what you clowns have in mind," the comms voice piped, "but this is what's going down. If you don't release the cable-tube, we're gonna turn off your air. You won't last an hour. Hear me?"

Terr swept his eyes around the deck, judging its size and snorted. They could easily last twice as long. Besides, if things got really desperate, there was always the command deck survival blister. He glanced at Dhar.

"Check the nav plot," he said and started searching through the raider's pockets. Nothing, not even a tissue. How then did the Palean know there were two of them? A personal communicator? He turned the body over and there it was, on the deck next to the outstretched left hand. Terr grinned, but it wasn't with humor as he reached for the little pebble device. He checked the setting, switched it off and waved the thing before his face.

Dhar nodded. "One hour, sixteen minutes before the M-4 closes," he said.

Around them the touch-sensitive pads blinked occasionally as the machines whispered among themselves. For the moment they were safe and he felt Death drain from him, leaving him with a disturbing emptiness. What concerned him more was the keen sense of regret that he no longer felt immortal, above the mere doings of foolish creatures. Was that the trap; the craving to loose the lightnings, followed by intoxication of wielding absolute power, and finally the addiction? If he, a native Saddish-aa Wanderer, was tempted, what must Sankri feel? The insight sobered him and he looked at his brother with new understanding.

"You okay?" Terr asked, noting Dhar's preoccupation.

The corner of Dhar's mouth turned up in a stillborn smile.

"I was reminded that standing beneath the hand of Death, its shadow can also a prison make."

"But who walks free, my brother? The person standing in shadow or the one who casts it?"

This time Dhar's smile was broad and genuine. "Ah, something for the Rahtir to contemplate," he said and sprawled his length onto the leftmost couch. Without hesitating, he lifted his long legs and planted them with a thump on the console frame. Terr raised an eyebrow. Normally, Dhar shunned all forms of flippancy and this display was most irregular and out of character.

"Why don't you relax," he offered quizzically.

Dhar sighed, leaned back and locked his hands behind his head. "I believe I will."

Terr shook his head and took the right seat.

Aware of his brother beside him, reassured by his presence, Terr closed his eyes. There was little they could do except wait. For him, waiting sometimes came hard, but he was learning patience. The influence of the Discipline was difficult to shake. He didn't really want to, but following it meant walking a rigid straight line, and he itched at such confinement. He preferred a degree of looseness. Having to be morally correct all the time had always been a tight fit for him.

There were no more messages from the inter-deck comms and he wondered what the raiders were up to. Whatever they were planning, it wouldn't do them much good.

A sharp beep from the console caused his eyes to snap open.

"Warning!" the computer blared. "Survival blister hatches locked and ejection sequence disabled."

Terr glanced at Dhar. "Someone down there is thinking and I don't like that kind of thinking."

Dhar dropped his legs to the deck and looked up at the transparent nav bubble. "Coming at us from the outside?"

"Let's not wait to find out," Terr said as he scanned the weapons console. "Computer, report any object approaching the command level."

"Sled-pad with one occupant now at two hundred and forty katalans. Closure rate is six katalans per second."

"Distance above the hull?"

"Thirty-five katalans."

"Raise the primary shield grid and hold at thirty katalans." The shield was designed to extend several talans, not to hug the ship. Would the screen lines form? Terr was about to find out.

"Primary shield grid raised," the computer announced dispassionately.

It worked!

Dhar looked at his brother in open admiration.

"That was quick reasoning, Sankri."

"The guy out there is in for a nasty surprise when he tries to close," Terr said with a grim smile. "Computer, status of approaching sled-pad?"

"Sled-pad in uncoordinated flight mode after contact with the shield grid."

Probably had every circuit fused as its own nav screen reacted with the ship's grid, Terr thought with satisfaction. He looked out the nav bubble, but there was nothing to see except stars and the sheer side of the VLBC beside them.

"I think it might be time we contacted *Turin*, Sankri," Dhar said gravely and Terr nodded. His maneuver bought them time, but how much and would it be enough?

"Warning, primary shield grid deactivated from Engineering."

Terr smiled and nodded.

"A cute trick," the Palean's thin voice came from the comms. "It cost me a crewman, but it won't work again. You guys got eleven minutes before we burn our way in. By the way, if you were planning to call someone, I wouldn't bother. Your comms are down."

"He is right," Dhar said. "All long-range comms are offline."

"Including emergency bands?"

"Everything. We've only got close-range ship-to-ship left."

"Great! And *Turin*?"

"Still thirty-two minutes away."

"Rit!" It wasn't meant to be *this* hard! "They may get us, but they obviously don't care for their pals up here."

"More shares for the others," Dhar said equitably.

"Hah! Computer, activate the emergency transponder, now! Hold for five seconds and discontinue," Terr growled, his face bleak. "That should get *Turin's* attention."

"Emergency transponder activated…Discontinued," the computer said.

"Computer," Dhar prompted immediately. "Begin core dump sequence, hard copy."

"Core dump sequence enabled. Awaiting final authorization code group."

"Remote download from ID tag," Dhar ordered and waited. Would the computer accept the Fleet override codes? It felt like an eternity before the computer responded.

"Authorization accepted. Core dump in progress. Duration, four minutes."

"Good man," Terr said warmly and yanked his tag out of the comms slot. "Now for the hard part." He looked at the cable-tube and pursed his lips. "Let's test your theory about the shares." He swiveled his seat, got up and walked to Kadatar. Bending down, he grabbed the outstretched left arm and unceremoniously dragged the limp body into the tube. He was

43

annoyed with himself. Dhar was right on the ball to initiate the core dump. After all, that's what they were here for. Instead of feeling smug and complacent, contemplating the meaning of life, he should have initiated the dump the minute they disposed of Kadatar. That oversight might cost them the whole mission.

A blue and white color-coded transparent prism rose from the comms panel.

"Core dump sequence completed," the computer announced.

Dhar stood up and reached for the precious thing. Pocketing the crystal wafer, he strode into the tube. He was about to push the crewman's prone body away from the hatch when Terr pulled him back.

"Not yet. Let's see if they really mean to burn their way in. Every minute we delay—"

"Gives *Turin* more time to get here," Dhar added.

"Right."

They waited in silence. What was there to say? As the minutes dragged, Terr kept glancing at the nav bubble. There was nothing out there, but that didn't mean much. The bubble had a limited field of view and anyone could sneak up on them without being seen. He figured the Palean raider was a tad optimistic about his eleven minutes.

"Time's up," the Palean's voice announced suddenly.

Speaking of the devil…

"You guys release the cable-tube and you'll die easy. Don't let the fact that Kadatar is up there with you make you think we won't do what I say. He's got a tough break, that's all. What'll it be? You've got—"

"Raider vessel. This is SSF *Turin*. Report your condition."

Terr looked at Dhar and grinned. "In comms range! The gods have not abandoned us yet," he said and hurried toward the comms console.

"They must have gone to emergency boost when we set off the transponder," Dhar said after him.

Terr pulled out his ID tag and slipped it into the comms slot.

"SSF *Turin*, stand by for my authentication codes," he said and pressed a pad. The comms plate cleared and the Karkan Master Scout scowled at him.

"I figured something was wrong when I couldn't raise you."

"Please close and board. Have your assault marines ready for some close-quarter action," Terr said.

"Things getting a bit warm, eh, Mister?" the Karkan hissed good-naturedly and his tongue flicked.

"Let's not ruin what's been a fun day so far, Master Scout," Terr said dryly and the Karkan chuckled.

"Very well. Can you hold out for six minutes?"

"I'll have to, won't I?"

The screen cleared and Terr let out a long breath.

"Look." Dhar pointed at the nav bubble.

A sled-pad drifted down and stopped. A pressure-suited figure fiddled with something behind him and raised what looked like a modified riot gun.

"I know you guys can see the sled-pad," the Palean raider announced. "You think you've got us boxed in with that M-4 out there? That might be, but you won't be around to enjoy it."

A searing blue-white beam lanced from the suited figure outside and the nav bubble immediately polarized to cut the glare. Terr plucked out his tag and sprinted for the cable-tube. They watched as the transparent hull material began to glow bright red. The center turned white. There was a bright shower of sparks and the hole immediately self-sealed, frustrating the raider's attempt to cut his way through. Sooner or later, though, the self-sealing mechanism would overload and fail.

Dhar was about to push the body blocking the hatch out of the way when an intense pulse of yellow light suddenly lit the deck. There was an immediate and strong smell of ozone as the air ionized. Small blue sparks slithered across exposed surfaces, crackling eerily as they jumped from console to console. The cable-tube interior glowed as though cloaked in Death's shadow. Sparks arced from the walls and struck exposed hands and faces in an exquisite dance of tiny insect bites. Just as suddenly the effect stopped.

When the M-4 fired, Terr caught a glimpse of the suited figure outside, bathed in the deadly glow. The figure dropped the cutting rod and raised both arms to protect his face. The sled-pad's nav screen field lines flared in yellow and green discharges and failed. The vehicle lost attitude, slammed into the nav dome and caromed into space.

The main comms plate cleared.

"Raider vessel, sorry about that, but you looked like you could use some help," the Karkan said, not looking at all sorry.

Terr snorted, glanced at Dhar and shook his head, still smarting from the little burns on his skin. He walked to the comms console and tapped a pad.

"We did need your help, *Turin*," he said. "A somewhat extreme example, wasn't it?"

"Perhaps, but it was effective. Preparing to dock with you now," the Karkan said and cut contact.

Twenty minutes later it was all over. Terr was told that after the marines boarded, there was some spirited, but sporadic fighting. Four raiders were killed and five injured to rifle and needler fire. The rest surrendered. The marines were still rounding up raiders in the VLBC, but no one was about to deny them a bit of fun.

While the marines were enjoying themselves, Terr and Dhar waited on the command deck. When the marines finally came up, Kadatar and the two unconscious watchstanders were unceremoniously dragged off, none too gently. The Karkan Master Scout himself came up then, accompanied by a very young and nervous Second Scout. Standing in front of the open tube, he looked around quickly, then fixed his fishy eyes on Terr.

"Well, young man?"

"There are three or four survival blisters out there," Terr said.

"The VLBC crew? We'll get them," the Karkan hissed and snapped quick instructions to the hapless Second Scout. On receiving his orders the young officer stood to and was about to leave when Terr raised his hand.

"Wait! The VLBC crew will be returned to their ship and the bulk carrier allowed to proceed on its way."

The Karkan frowned. "Procedure calls for—"

"For whatever I say...sir," Terr said mildly and the Second Scout gaped at him. He was obviously not used to seeing his commander contradicted like this.

The Karkan glanced at the young man and jerked his head at the cable-tube. Grateful, the officer fled. Alone, the Karkan glared and stepped to Terr.

"I'm not accustomed to being ordered about like this, Mister! Especially not by some civilian flunkey!" Hiss.

"I regret if I caused you any embarrassment, sir," Terr said, not really giving a damn. He was tired and reaction was setting in. What he needed right now was a long shower and time to write a report to Anabb—a major downside working for the Diplomatic Branch.

"Hah! You take a lot on yourself, Mister. If that's all then—"

"I'm afraid not. Please assign a skeleton crew and have this ship taken to Kalakan. You can transfer the prisoners to *Tahal* and use it as escort."

"And you two?"

"We're going with *Tahal*. If you could arrange to have power restored to the long-range comms, I would be grateful. I need to contact Taltair."

The Karkan gave a soft hiss of displeasure, his tongue getting a workout. Finally, he dragged out his communicator and issued more orders. When he finished, he sighed and shook his head.

"If you were under my command…I have an M-3 closing on *Virana*. They sheered off as soon as I came into range, but that won't help them. We've got them. Happy?" he snarled and stomped into the cable-tube. The hatch closed behind his back.

"A proud man, Sankri," Dhar murmured. Terr looked at him.

"And I could have been more diplomatic, is that it?"

Dhar arched an eyebrow. "Far be it for me to question the wisdom of my superior officer, sir."

"Asshole!" Terr laughed and punched him on the shoulder.

The *Turin* crew didn't waste any time, and moments later the comms console pads lit up and flickered in a self-test. Terr nodded in appreciation.

"We're in business again," he said with satisfaction. "Computer, open a channel to Taltair, Diplomatic Branch, personal for Anabb Karr." Terr remained standing as he waited for the main display plate to clear. He was not sure what time it was back there and he could be coming in for a withering blast. He gave a mental shrug. A moment later the plate cleared and he was looking at Anabb's personal aide.

Ariane had delicate high cheekbones, full lips and a long neck. Her head was narrow with no hair. Her large dark eyes had captivated more than one of Anabb's operatives, including him. She was simply gorgeous and he couldn't figure out how she put up with Anabb's rude and crusty behavior. Outlined against the transparent window screen, Terr could see the Center's towers lit in evening light.

"Mr. Terrllss-rr, the Director will be with you shortly," she husked and batted long eyelashes. It was too bad, really…

"And how is he today, Ariane?" Terr always asked and she always gave the same answer.

"The Director is well, thank you." Ariane never discussed their boss or engaged in office politics. A formidable young lady in every respect. "Putting you through now."

Immortal in Shadow

Prima Scout Anabb Karr was bulky and of average height, but his presence dominated the office. That came from a lifetime in the Fleet. His olive skin wrinkled and dry, etched with deep lines. The chiseled narrow face was stamped into a permanent scowl of disapproval. A ragged blue-veined burn from a phase rifle creased his left cheek. With modern genotherapy techniques the disfigurement was easily treatable, but Terr figured Anabb kept it as an intimidation tool. He knew from personal and very uncomfortable experience, the scar tended to turn a mottled red when Anabb got angry.

The former Fleet flag officer's presence was commanding and all that force channeled through his eyes. Close-set ovals, they were brown pools smeared with flecks of amber. Hidden beneath ridges of narrow white eyebrows, they cut where they stared. Terr had never been intimidated by those eyes, even during their very first meeting.

Six years ago, a young and raw Second Scout, Anabb sent him on a mission to the Four Suns as a military aide to a General Assembly Envoy. His job was to ferret out evidence of alleged slavery and use that evidence to compromise Kapel Pen, the Four Suns Controller. What he found was much more sinister. Kapel Pen and the ruling Family were planning to cede the Four Suns to the Karkan Federation in a bold attempt to win a Commissioner post on Captal for Kapel. The fact that the move could have plunged the Serrll Combine into political and economic turmoil did not bother Kapel at all.

While inspecting the mining world Anulus, rogue M-3s attacked his M-1 and he was forced to flee. They caught up with him over Anar'on, the fabled and secretive world of the Wanderers. Shot up, his blister crashed in the deep desert. Searching for water, slowly going mad with thirst, the Wanderers found him and brought him back to Dhar's village. He was told later that Dhar entered his mind to bring him back from whatever madness he escaped to. Terr was wrenched from the brink of insanity, but in the process, Dhar also left the seed of Death in

49

him. To be fully restored, Terr was forced to walk in the escarpment of Athal Than where the god of Death claimed him, leaving him with a terrible power, one which even now, he struggled to fully come to terms with.

Then two years ago, having unmasked a Palean-sponsored raider base on Lemos, decorated and promoted, Terr was feeling good about himself and life in general. That was when Anabb pounced, talking Terr and Dhar into joining the Diplomatic Branch—a dirty, low trick if ever there was one to pull on two innocents. Terr's first mission, of course, was to track down a second Palean base from which Anabb suspected the Paleans were launching raids against Kaleen shipping. What Terr found was not a base, but a mauling encounter with Kai Tanard.

Anabb cleared his throat and glared.

"You have some good news, I hope?" he growled, his voice low and gravelly.

Terr sighed. There was no way of getting around it. Anabb was simply a pain.

"Yes, sir. We boarded a raider—"

"The computer core dump? You've got it?"

"We have it."

Anabb allowed himself a small smile, which probably hurt his face. "Well done, my boy."

"The M-4 *Turin* was most helpful in securing the raider and its crew," Terr said. "We also have their pilot."

"Excellent! I was beginning to feel you were wasting your time with that cover of yours."

Terr blinked. Evil old fart…

"Where are you now?" Anabb demanded.

"On board the raider, sir, waiting for an escorting M-2 before proceeding to Kalakan."

"Negative! Take *Turin* and the raider pilot and make for Kalakan at max boost. Your M-1 is being ferried there right now. When you land, hold the pilot and make your way to Taltair."

Return to Taltair just when the operation started to pay off? Something else occurred to Terr. He would have to spend several days staring at *Turin* commander's reptilian sour features. Well, it was his own fault really.

"What's the rush?"

"Kai Tanard has escaped," Anabb said in utter disgust.

Chapter Two

"And Khiman-ra?" Ti Inai asked softly and blinked at the Wall. He was not happy at the lack of progress to get the base operational and he fully intended not to be unhappy alone. Patiently, keeping his long fingers from twining, he waited.

Le Maran's jowls sagged as he sighed. The comfortable formchair in which he'd been relaxing only a few minutes ago, feeling pleased with himself, suddenly didn't feel so comfortable anymore. He wanted to look away, but doing it would be to admit guilt, and he had nothing to feel guilty about. He drove everyone to the point of desertion to get everything done to an impossible schedule. Sitting in his posh Captal office, Ti Inai didn't really appreciate the multiplicity of problems associated with a field operation and was too stingy with his praise to give credit where credit was due. The damned base would be running on time.

"We experienced some delays in commissioning the power grid and organizing the maintenance and repair—"

"Friend Maran," Ti Inai interrupted with an oily smile. "All I want to know is, when will you commence full flight operations?"

Fingers twining, Le Maran squirmed. "Ten days—"

"That's what you told me last time."

"I have two ships out now…"

"You were meant to have five ships out by now," Ti Inai pointed out and allowed the silence to linger. He was not unaware of Le Maran's problems. He had his own sources. Personally, he thought Le Maran had done a creditable job to transform an isolated valley into what was for all intents a fully-fledged Field facility. He could appreciate the magnitude of the job, but the select faceless men behind the Alikan Union Party's organizational machine were not as fulsome with their congratulations. After two years of planning and toil, with megaserrlls of capital poured into the effort, the AUP wanted a return on its investment. They wanted to hear of Kaleen shipping destroyed. Well, so did he.

Following Le Maran's disastrous decision to allow Kai Tanard to attack Fleet escorts, which however inauspiciously led to the unmasking of the Tai Mari Line operation on Lemos, the man was fortunate not to have been summarily executed. If the AUP Provisional Committee had listened to Ed-Kani Takao's vitriolic vilification, Le Maran *would* have been executed. As Le Maran's mentor, Ti Inai came perilously close to losing his own head after the Italan debacle. By staying on Captal, his neck would probably have been on the block. Instead, two other Committee's luckless members had gotten the chop for his sins. Still, it was a near-run thing. When his sources told him Tanard was captured, he immediately fled to Palea. The move was not made in panic, but was one of carefully planned contingency options. It was galling really. His plan to attack a liner, supposedly carrying Unified Independent Front delegates to Anar'on, was tactically sound. Had it worked, the UIF would be crippled and he would have been cloaked in glory. How was he to know Tanard was walking into a trap.

Ti Inai preferred not to dwell on that too much. As a planner and strategist, he considered himself equal to anyone on the AUP Provisional Committee. However, as the raid on the UIF delegates demonstrated all too vividly, he was not an operational commander. As Commissioner for the Bureau of Technology and Development, a strategic posting in the Economics Council, he realized he was far more comfortable with the cut and thrust of Captal's oblique politics. All right, he made a bad call. Not that he considered Le Maran a tactical commander either, but the consolation was that Le Maran's role at Khiman-ra was administrative, not tactical.

"Friend Maran," he said tolerantly. "I have supported you when others would have had your head. Should I have cause to be disappointed with your performance, that support could become strained. All manner of unpleasant consequences could flow from there. Do we understand each other?"

Le Maran understood, all right. One word from Ti Inai and he could wake up one night facing the operating end of a large needler. Ti Inai's polished politician's smile sent a chill down his spine and made his skin writhe.

"There is no need for threats, friend Inai," he piped defensively in a high voice, hands wringing.

Ti Inai blinked. "Threats? Oh my. I haven't made any threats. Consider this a reminder of the volatile situation we both face. What else have you got?"

Canal worm, Le Maran seethed. He could read the signs. Ti Inai would drop him in an instant if it meant saving his own hide. Well, *friend* Inai, I have my insurance. What would the AUP Provisional Committee do if they learned Ti Inai and a group of radical Alikan Union Party cells had set up Khiman-ra to wage their private little war against the Kaleen group? Nothing pleasant for Ti Inai, he was sure, but he did not feel it prudent to mention that right now. The fact that those cells also constituted the bulk of his power base within the AUP didn't faze Le Maran at all. As a tactician, he had learned well the lesson that one never revealed all of one's options. The objective was to hang on and survive.

"Kai Tanard and two of his officers were successfully extracted from Feron and he should have landed on Kapoeen by now."

"Excellent! Remember your instructions, friend Maran. Tanard is to be extended all possible support to execute raids in any manner he sees fit without interference. Is that clear?"

"Perfectly."

"Excellent! You will, of course, tell me when Khiman-ra

becomes fully operational, right?"

"Of course, friend Inai."

Ti Inai's small, pinched lips formed a stiff smile. "I look forward to hearing from you, then," he said and cut contact. The Wall cleared and began pooling into tortuous patterns of solid, flowing colors. He ignored it.

Le Maran was an embarrassing liability, which was clear. If it were up to him, he would have Tanard commanding Khiman-ra. Although tactically sound the appointment was an impossible one. The Alikan Union Party cells that sponsored the base would not have questioned the sound military value of such an appointment, but they would certainly call into question its political viability. He knew much of Le Maran's power within the AUP stemmed from their support. The Palean AUP cells were forced to accept Le Maran's demotion from the Provisional Committee, but it did not mean accepting Tanard in Le Maran's place, no matter how qualified. What price does one put on political cooperation? Besides, Ti Inai reasoned, buried at Khiman-ra, how much damage can Le Maran do?

Sitting back, he reflected on the last two turbulent years. After Lemos, the Palean Congress and a significant segment of the AUP were understandably wary of promulgating a merger with Sargon. What happened after Italan made him shudder even now. The overflight by Fleet M-9s over Palea's capital was a humiliating experience for every Palean. Such gall! After the ensuing outcry the government and Congress resigned as a body. That was when Tao Karam and his pro-Sofam-sucking faction pounced. They took full advantage of the public's outrage against Sargon to consolidate their opposition to the merger in the new Congress. It was a masterful display of timing and political cunning. Ti Inai did not begrudge Karam his tactics. The Executive Director for the Bureau of Justice, and Palean's senior representative on Captal, merely took advantage of available circumstances. Ti Inai would have done the same thing had the roles been reversed and had he thought of it. It was simple politics and one took advantage of circumstances as they presented themselves.

But just because the Pizgor gambit went sour in such spectacular fashion did not necessarily mean the underlying reasoning behind the tactic was erroneous. Why not apply the same tactic to Kaleen, he argued. It was an argument the Committee back on Captal liked. It also restored some of his badly eroded standing, something far more valuable if he wanted to exert any sort of influence over the Committee's policymaking process. However satisfied with the plan, he was still not completely happy. He resented Sargon's domination of the Committee and its executive machinery.

If Sargon and the Palean Union were going to be true partners, he wanted the Palean arm of the Alikan Union Party to be more aggressive in setting the merger terms with Sargon. It was fortuitous that Le Maran's AUP cells happened to agree with him. In subsequent policy discussions within the Committee, Ti Inai had not sought to inform them of Khiman-ra's existence and its real role, and saw no reason to change his mind. The Committee was beset with enough problems, he thought comfortably. He was perfectly happy to have the base a totally Palean operation. Of course, should the Committee ever become aware of Khiman-ra, things could become decidedly disagreeable for him. Naturally, there was a simple answer to his problem. He would have to see to it the Committee remained blissfully ignorant of Khiman-ra.

The comms alert beeped and he half jumped out of the formchair.

"Mr. Commissioner, will you accept a call from Executive Director Ed-Kani Takao?" The voice was cool and diffident, befitting an appointee when addressing an elected representative of Ti Inai's stature. Although annoyed at having his train of thought interrupted so rudely, Ti Inai could hardly take out his pique on a personal aide. He *could*, but he didn't believe in mistreating his underlings. He thumbed the comms pad set in an inlaid array on his desk.

"Put him through," he said heavily and swung to face the Wall. He didn't really want to talk to the Bureau of Economics Affairs executive, but he was phlegmatic about it. In life one did many things one didn't like. He took solace from the fact that in some five years, Ed-Kani would be swept away into mandatory retirement after thirty years of service, but five years in Captal was an eternity.

Ed-Kani's narrow bony face looked even bonier than usual. Deep character lines crossed the corners of his eyes and stern mouth. As Captal's senior Sargon representative, it took its toll. He was completely hairless, his pale features were a startling contrast with the icy blue-white eyes. He snapped his delicate jaws, tapped the glossy black surface of his huge desk with a stiff finger and hissed his displeasure. His eyes gave nothing away, as usual. They could have been open ports for all the expression they revealed. In any game of power and ascendancy, emotion was a tool to be used sparingly. After a momentary silence, he deigned a brittle smile.

"I was reviewing raider statistics of shipping mikans lost to Kaleen. Most satisfactory. A few more months and they will be ripe for picking."

"We may not have those months, friend Ed-Kani," Ti Inai said suavely, fingers twining.

"You mean the increase in Fleet activity? That was factored in and is something you already know."

"Then perhaps it's time we went to Phase Two," Ti Inai ventured and Ed-Kani shook his head.

"I disagree. I will recommend to the Committee that we bypass Phase Two and move directly to Phase Three."

Ti Inai stared. "Negotiation? Is that wise?"

"Wise? Expedient. I want those systems in Palean hands before we get into the next round of general elections. They may still be five years off, granted, but these things take time."

"As I appreciate," Ti Inai mused. It made sense and the

psychological blow to the UIF and other independent nona-ligned systems could be considerable and perhaps worth the risk of rushing things. Still, he was wary of hastening into some-thing without first examining it from every possible angle. Ed-Kani's proposal smacked too much of rashness. The Commit-tee took a long time over many laborious meetings to decide on a plan to destabilize Kaleen and he wasn't comfortable with the notion of Ed-Kani dismissing this process so casually. How typical of Sargon, impatient and scornful of the long-term view. Patience was an art they were yet to master and helped to ex-plain a lot of their historical successes and troubled failures.

With Ed-Kani, this impatience was becoming increasingly and annoyingly evident. Ever since his failure to induce Rolan's five systems to cede to Sargon two years ago, he became driven, almost obsessed with consummating the Sargon/Palean merger before the end of the current electoral session. More than one Committee member either hinted or openly remarked that this preoccupation had more to do with securing Ed-Kani's place in history than an objective to be pursued in the fullness of time for the benefit of all.

Ti Inai particularly resented Sargon's five-member domi-nance over the Committee at the expense of the four Palean members. Well, what was about to happen would only serve Ed-Kani right.

"What I really want to talk about, though, is Kai Tanard. You have him?" Ed-Kani demanded without any preamble.

Blunt and to the point, as always, Ti Inai reflected. The man was totally devoid of any refinement or subtlety.

"You are on top of things as usual, friend Ed-Kani," he said and bobbed his head.

"Never mind the flattery. If you're planning to bring him back—"

"Rest easy. I am aware, as are the Palean AUP cells, that friend Tanard is a marked man. Bringing him back into the Committee organization would be foolish in the extreme, and disastrous for us should he be recaptured."

"For once, we are in agreement," Ed-Kani hissed and snapped his jaws. Was Ti Inai being condescending? His irritating sly smirk, how he wished to wipe it off the Palean's face. "But you haven't answered my question."

Ti Inai licked his lips and fixed on a smooth smile, which he knew irked the Sargon representative.

"Kai Tanard is a patriot who has served the cause with honor at great personal cost—"

"Spare me the sterling eulogy. You engineered his escape, didn't you?" Ed-Kani retorted.

"Hardly."

"I didn't mean you personally," Ed-Kani said, irritated at Ti Inai's obfuscation. "But he couldn't have gotten off that Cantor transport without expert help."

"If friend Tanard *did* have help, and I'm not saying anything one way or another, his freedom has allowed us to explore possibilities. As a military commander, it would be wasteful of us not to exploit his talents."

"His talents are already wasted...unless you intend using him outside the Committee's structure?" The little scheming shit was up to something. Ed-Kani could smell it. "If one of your radical AUP cells decides to use him for its own ends—"

"I can hardly be held responsible for what some hothead does out in the field."

Ed-Kani grinned, but it was a cold, threatening thing. "Take this as a warning, *friend* Ti Inai. If any Palean AUP cell decides to operate in a manner contrary to the Committee's objectives, it will be shut down in a most drastic fashion and I'll be after your head."

Ti Inai believed him and an open threat was a naked blade against which he could take steps to guard himself. The man really had no finesse.

"Whatever he does, Kai Tanard will be supporting the cause."

"Just remember the risks."

"Friend Ed-Kani, I am always mindful of risks," Ti Inai said softly, his hands for once still.

Ed-Kani stared at him for several long seconds, then abruptly cut contact.

* * *

Kapoeen was a sleepy little world, one of two ecoformed moons orbiting a ringed blue-green gas giant. Nestled comfortably in the outer K ring, the moon was not subject to ferocious tides and disruptive tectonic activity that plagued its inner neighbors. It took its time circling the brooding parent. The striated rings of rubble, made from moonlets torn up after dragged helplessly into the gas giant's tidal embrace, and debris of water and organic ices, were a spectacular backdrop for the bridge of stars. Every sixty-four days when Kapoeen's orbit brought it into Kandar's shadow, the moon reveled in glory of the rings spread before it like dappled gossamer of a butterfly's wings. Phenomenal lightning displays on the giant's night side added to the glowing, twisting electrical streams that warred with the magnetic lines of the miniature system. The spectacle created haunting and magical visions on which the romantics and poets waxed lyrical. Eleven light-hours out from Kandar, another smoldering gas giant sulked within its cocoon of roiling brown, red and yellow gas clouds, discarded remnants of planetary formation. Far away in the center of the system a sullen yellow star ruled over its turbulent children.

Kapoeen was a rare tourist attraction, but its location off the regular shipping corridors doomed it to be a destination for lovers of the unusual, or those escaping from somewhere, anywhere. Hands clasped behind his back, staring at the enormous bulge of Kandar rising out of a dawning sky, the sight reminded Tanard of Praxa. Although equally spectacular, Praxa had been only a job, one that left him little time for contemplation or appreciation of poetic magic. As a Fleet officer, he thought in terms of tactics, manpower, logistics and costs. Have two years of confinement changed him so much that the vista of a ring belt and the fluffy softness of Kandar shimmering behind bunched balls of white clouds actually stirred some deeply buried feelings within him? No, he was simply daydreaming, he told himself, knowing it to be a lie. The realization brought a wry smile to the left side of his face. Such undisciplined thinking hardly fitted the image of a hard-bitten ruthless commander. No, a raider! There was no need to pretend here. Winn would be shocked at this display of sentimentality. The thought brought another smile, which slowly faded. Winn would be right. Indulgence and wishful thinking were traps against which he must guard himself. If he is to survive, emotion was an indulgence he could ill afford.

Pretty skies notwithstanding, he was beginning to get anxious. His flight from Feron was uneventful enough. The Field checks at Kumran were laughably rudimentary and his new identity was accepted without question. The three-day flight to Kapoeen, made after one stopover and another identity change, were equally uneventful. He appreciated the professionalism and attention to detail it took to get him to Kapoeen, but that appreciation was given grudgingly. Why wasn't the same professionalism used to extract him off Kalakan, instead of letting him rot in a mental asylum for two years? It was an unreasoning thought, he knew, but he couldn't help mulling over it. He was being paranoid again.

When he got into his hotel a Wall message from Le Maran told him to sit and wait. Well, he had waited two days now admiring Kandar and its rings, and he'd had enough. The irony of the situation didn't escape him. He had little option but to wait—and think. He did nothing else for two years. He now wanted action, not more thinking. To raid, he needed a ship and that meant Le Maran. In desperation, he even tried to contact Le Maran using his controller's old comms code. The code was rejected as invalid, of course, which implied several things, none of them promising. It could have been a simple reorganization of comms protocols within the Committee, something more than likely and expected as routine. It could also mean Le Maran was now 'out'. Ed-Kani Takao must have acted on his report that Le Maran authorized attacks on Fleet escorts. Contact Ed-Kani directly? No, that would be foolish in the extreme, even if he knew how.

"You have an incoming message," the housekeeping computer announced.

Tanard turned away from the floor-to-ceiling window screen and scowled at the Wall.

"Connect," he rasped and automatically massaged his mangled throat. The pooling colors cleared and Tanard's scowl deepened. Custom demanded he greet his superior, but he was forever damned if he would do that right now.

When it became clear Tanard was not going to say anything, Le Maran's cheeks colored and he bobbed his head.

"Friend Tanard," he said softly, fingers twining.

His old protégé looked gaunt and the lines on his face were darker and deeper. He could hardly imagine what the last two years were like for his friend. Studying the hard face in the Wall, Le Maran wondered if they *were* still friends, for this was not the same person he last spoke to on Lemos. So much had happened since, for both of them.

Tanard resented his old mentor looking sleek and fat while he endured hell. It was unjustified bitterness, but that's how it was.

"Friend Maran, a long time," he said at last, swallowing his resentment.

It would be childish of him to alienate the one individual who was in a position to help him. It was hard to shake off the feeling he had been abandoned by an organization for which he sacrificed everything. No, what came hard was the fact that he was an expendable asset to be used and discarded by the Committee as they saw fit. Was that the real face of the Alikan Union to be? Cold and unfeeling, devoid of consideration or care for the individual? What kind of a future were they painting for everyone? It was not the first time he pondered the objective of their cause.

"A long time indeed," Le Maran agreed. "You obviously managed to get off Feron without any mishaps."

"My thanks, and for getting me off that Cantor transport. A slick job as I have ever seen."

"My only and keen regret, friend Tanard, I wasn't able to do it sooner." Le Maran meant it and Tanard saw it. "Any bitterness you may feel is understandable, but your capture was a body blow to the Committee, one they're feeling even now. More on that later," Le Maran added briskly and cleared his throat. "After Lemos and Italan, there were some, ah, necessary readjustments, as you have no doubt surmised."

Hah! So, Le Maran *did* get the chop.

Le Maran's fingers twined. "Mind you, our objective has not changed, but with Pizgor out of reach—"

"The effort to suborn them has been abandoned?" Tanard demanded sharply.

"Ah, not entirely. Sargon has taken punitive steps—"

"They have diverted their commercial shipping away from Pizgor, of course. It was one of the original options we proposed and one which Sargon rejected in favor of more direct action."

"Perhaps they have learned patience."

"One can always hope. What are *we* doing?"

"You must understand something, friend Tanard. After Lemos the Palean Union was subject to retaliatory economic sanctions. The new Congress does not want to antagonize Captal by repeating past mistakes."

"You mean, Tao Karam's faction now controls the government and he is too preoccupied with licking Sofam's boots to act in the Palean Union's best interests," Tanard growled in disgust.

"Somewhat harsh, friend Tanard, but essentially correct," Le Maran temporized. "There are many interpretations of what is in the best interest of the Palean Union. Past mistakes are invaluable teachers, provided we heed the lessons. Do not mistake caution for weakness. We haven't abandoned our objectives. It simply means that some in the Palean arm of the Alikan Union Party were forced to look at alternatives as to how those objectives are best achieved."

"Kaleen," Tanard said. "The Committee is raiding Kaleen commerce in order to force some of its systems to cede to the Union."

Le Maran's eyebrows climbed in appreciation. "That was very astute and, of course, quite accurate. This time, however, the Committee went to some pains not to repeat tactical errors made with Lemos."

"Oh?"

"No reflection on you, friend Tanard, but in hindsight, providing direct support for raider ships was a flawed concept. The operation was always vulnerable to betrayal, as we suspect did in fact happen."

"Have you identified the scum who sold me out?"

"Not directly."

Tanard looked thoughtfully at Le Maran. "Do you know of any raider ship captured at the time when Lemos was exposed?"

"I believe *Drakin* was taken somewhere in the Zeller system. Why?"

"It was Re Nette," Tanard snarled. "The bitch betrayed us."

"*Drakin* was lost with all hands, destroyed in an engagement with a sweeper, as far as I know."

"As far as you know."

Le Maran's fingers worked in agitation. "Even if what you say is true, it is no longer relevant and I advise you not to dwell on it."

"I dwelled on it for two years and I'm not about to drop it now. Who was the sweeper's commander, do we know?" Tanard demanded on impulse.

Le Maran frowned. "Why are you pursuing this, friend Tanard?"

"I want to know why I spent two years in hell, that's all."

The words hammered into Le Maran and he flinched. "Very well. Let me check." He leaned to one side and issued commands to the computer. "This will take a few minutes. Now, as I was saying, with Kaleen the AUP Provisional Committee is still using raiders, something that cannot be helped, but with one major difference. They're not supporting them or have any contact with them at all. There is nothing to link their activities to the Palean Union, the Alikan Union Party body or the Committee. They are simply giving them secure access to Kaleen shipping information and relying on the raider's natural greed and avarice to do the rest. So far the tactic is working."

"And…"

"There has been a measure of success. Naurun and Omiron are feeling the pressure—"

"But it's not enough, is it? The Fleet has naturally responded and the raiders are no longer so eager, right?"

Le Maran bobbed his head. "You're quite correct in your assessment, friend Tanard. To increase the pressure on Kaleen, several local AUP cells have decided to mount an independent operation. What I'm about to tell you is strictly confidential. Should any of this leak…"

"There is no need to explain," Tanard said. "I gather this operation is outside the Committee's knowledge?"

"Some of us believe the Committee's policies are too prejudiced toward Sargon's interests, not Palean. We support the merger, but we also believe it should be done on more equitable terms. To that end, we built a staging base called Khiman-ra, whose location you will never know."

Stefan Vučak

"And you want me to conduct raids against Kaleen?"

"Two ships are already commissioned and are operational. Three more are yet to be acquired. If you accept, you'll be given complete autonomy and tactical command over all units. I'll control administration and support facilities."

Tanard was impressed. It would be quite a challenge. The downside, though, was obvious. He would be hunted not only by the Fleet, but by the Committee's own intelligence apparatus should they ever learn of Khiman-ra's existence. That was an unknown. By tomorrow, he could be dead either way. If he was to die, better in a command couch than behind a rock pile on Cantor.

It was also a chance for him to implement his policies on how the AUP should conduct warfare. Two years of thinking had not been a total waste. If the AUP wanted Kaleen worlds, he would see to it that they got them, willingly or otherwise.

"It's an interesting concept," Tanard said. "You realize, of course, as soon as I start active operations the entire Fleet and BueCult intelligence apparatus will be after me and Khiman-ra."

"Of course. You will have to achieve our objective before we're all discovered and obliterated."

Tanard gave a sour chuckle. "I admire your candor, but how do you hide a base from the local population? Unless you're talking about an asteroid?"

"That option wasn't even considered. Discounting the engineering challenges, it would have cost far too much to set up such a facility. The base is in a remote location disguised as an aerospace research complex. It is well guarded to discourage local visitors."

Tanard shrugged. "Not my concern. How you deal with the locals, I'll leave to you. What kind of ships did you have in mind for this? Armed auxiliaries?"

"The tactics we used on Lemos were sound," Le Maran pointed out. Tanard shook his head.

"Sound, I agree, but the ships were hardly adequate for the job. They were bulky and antiquated, and they lacked speed and firepower. You'll need both if you want to tackle Kaleen. On Lemos, when we needed to force the pace, I had to take out my M-3. We don't have that luxury now."

"What *did* you have in mind?"

"We're not after cargo here. We simply want to kill ships. What we need is something compact and fast. Can you get me an M-3?"

Le Maran's large black eyes bulged and he suppressed a snicker. "Friend Tanard, you must be jesting."

"I'm being perfectly serious. You put a sweeper's power plant and a Koyami 9A or 2/F series weapons pod into a small hull, say ten thousand mikans dead weight, and you would have a fighting platform with speed to do real work. We cannot waste power dragging around two million mikans of useless hull. If this operation is to succeed, your ships must be maneuverable and able to stand off anything up to and including an M-3."

Le Maran blanched. "That means attacking Fleet units."

"Not attacking, but fighting off. If you're thinking of Lemos, forget it. This will be a totally different operation. If you want to wage war with Kaleen, you need to do it from strength."

"But attacking Fleet units..."

"This is total commitment, friend Maran," Tanard rasped. "If you want those Kaleen systems, you must disrupt their ability to sustain trade. But you knew that already. Why else raid their shipping? But raiding is not only issuing an order from some nice air-conditioned office and measuring statistics. It means taking a ship against a helpless merchant and sending it and its crew to oblivion. You must be prepared to keep doing it until Kaleen succumbs or, as you said, we're wiped out. If the AUP thinks otherwise, we might as well forget the whole thing right here and now. I will not throw away my life or the lives of my men for a half-assed political gesture."

Le Maran stared, knowing intellectually that Tanard was correct, but the realization did not help soothe his churning feelings. How would the AUP react? How will Ti Inai react? Did Ti Inai really understand what unleashing Khiman-ra meant? He must have or he would never have put Tanard in operational command. But total warfare…

"Friend Tanard, we're not conducting unrestricted warfare here, but applying an ordered amount of pressure. Should this get out of hand the effort could backfire on us and serve to stiffen Kaleen resistance, not weaken it. We don't want to provoke a reaction from Anar'on."

"An ordered amount of pressure, is it? If the pressure needs to be so ordered, why does the AUP want to go outside the Committee's program?"

A very good question, over which Le Maran had pondered hard himself. What *was* Ti Inai's reason for escalating the conflict? He must know that current measures were working, albeit slowly. There was no hurry as long as Naurun and Omiron eventually succumbed.

"I am sure the AUP has valid reasons for pursuing this policy," he said stiffly and Tanard chuckled.

"In other words, you don't know. Never mind. You get me the equipment I want and I'll apply that pressure for you."

"But an M-3? You're talking military hardware here. That isn't something you can order through a catalog. Besides, why take the risk? We have hulls to spare."

The left side of Tanard's face lifted. "Without meaning any offense, friend Maran, to a bureaucrat like you the idea is undoubtedly fanciful."

"To say the least. The repercussions—"

"You're forgetting one thing. I was a Fleet officer before fates reduced me to my present ignoble circumstances. I am right and you know it. You give me the men I need and I'll get you that M-3."

"You will simply walk onto a military Field and pick one up, eh?"

"Your sarcasm is misplaced, but the idea is essentially correct. Don't look so shocked. It's been done before, if you know how to go about it. If I am to go out raiding, I want the fastest most heavily armed ship around me I can get. I'm not anxious to repeat my stay on Kalakan or its equivalent by driving a clapped-out bucket the AUP salvaged from a disposal yard. As for your other ships, I would start by ripping out their Terrasec projectors and mount something more potent. Otherwise you might as well hand them over to the nearest M-4 right now and save yourself the grief of having them destroyed or captured. The ships must be armored, as much as we can make them, and the M-3's plating will give us that armor. Not enough, but it will have to do. You must know that even if one ship is captured, Khiman-ra might very well be compromised. Sooner or later, it *will* be compromised. It's inevitable and you better be prepared. Before that happens, I want to exact maximum toll."

"The pilots have strict instructions to self-destruct—"

Tanard's laugh was bitter. "You really believe that?"

Le Maran pursed his lips in concentration. Would his commanders really execute a self-destruct? If tested, he knew he wouldn't be able to. The human element, it always came to that in the end. As for new ships, Tanard obviously meant what he said, but steal an M-3? It hardly seemed possible. What would they do with the hull once it was stripped down? Getting rid of existing Terrasec pods was bad news as he already had three 8/Cs on order. Ti Inai's words echoed in his head and he made a decision.

"What do you need?"

Tanard smiled. This was insane, but it could actually work.

"A tramp with a tough crew who won't mind mixing it up, and I want Winn and Railee."

"You want a Koyami in every ship?"

"That would be good, but a Terrasec 16 will do very

nicely."

"You're talking about outlawed equipment," Le Maran protested.

Tanard's face turned cold. "Because of that, I'm supposed to believe the AUP doesn't have any?"

The bind was, and Le Maran knew it, the AUP held considerably heavier platforms than a Terrasec 16. Would the AUP part with three or four right now?

"Very well. Sit tight for two or three days and you'll get your tramp…and your Terrasec 16s," Le Maran said, studying his protégé. "If that equipment should fall into Fleet hands…"

"It's all for the cause, right?" Tanard said, unmoved. The cause was only a convenient handle right now. Once he got his ships, he would show Le Maran what total cause was all about. A measured response, eh?

"As for new hulls—"

"Our ships must be small and fast, friend Maran," Tanard insisted and pulled at his chin, looking thoughtful. "There is one other thing…"

"Oh?"

"I want you to secure access to M-3 IFF transponder codes."

Le Maran stared, then burst out laughing. He couldn't help himself.

"I appreciate your sense of humor, friend Tanard. Very amusing. Why not simply give you a Fleet base?"

The left side of Tanard's mouth rose. "I know, it sounds preposterous, right? But think it through. What's the one thing that plagues every raider?"

"Well—"

"I'll tell you. Closing on his target. But if the target didn't know he's pursued?"

"You're serious, aren't you?" Le Maran demanded, no longer smiling.

"Damn right. With the right IFF code, I'm just another M-

3 on patrol asking for an ident dump. All perfectly natural and innocent. I close, throw up a comms interference field and finish him off before he can transmit or engage his transponders."

The comms alert beeped in the background and Le Maran looked away. When he turned, he wore a strange expression.

"The M-3's commander was Second Scout Terrllss-rr," he said slowly.

Tanard let out a low hiss. *Terr, my old friend…*

"How did you know?" Le Maran piped.

"I didn't, but everything you told me pointed to him. Look at the facts. *Drakin* gets taken and a few days later, Terr shows up on Lemos and arrests Ril Seen. It couldn't have been coincidence. Re Nette betrayed us for her life. Count on it. That Terr should be with *Zavian* was preordained. I want a full update of his current assignment," Tanard said and gave a humorless smile. "I have a feeling we haven't seen the last of him, and if we do, I plan to deal with him personally."

Le Maran looked attentively at his protégé and the man he faced was a stranger. He wondered what he was about to unleash, but as with everything, he suspected that fates had already sealed both their destinies.

"I shall see to the Terrasecs and the IFF codes. I must say, it's good to have you back in operation, friend Tanard."

* * *

Behind the hotel, black waters made gentle slaps against a stone quay. The lake's far shore butted into low cliffs with small waves. In the morning, ribbons of mist clung to the still surface. An occasional canoe cast a mirror reflection as it glided silently by. Birds drifted in open waters or poked around shore rushes for tasty tidbits. Boat sheds crowded the single pier that intruded into the lake. Solitary joggers took full advantage of the single track hugging the shoreline.

Tanard did not care for jogging, but he did indulge in long

walks along trails winding around the lake. He would some-times sit on the end of the pier and gaze at rippling copper wa-ters as the sun dipped over the city. It was spring and odd tour-ists wandered about, families with children who ran screaming over gray sands or splashed in the cool water. The promenade tables along the waterfront were usually full and boisterous well into the evening.

Four days after his conversation with Le Maran, he was still waiting. This time, he did not begrudge the wait. He knew how difficult it was to round up a suitable vessel, man it and bring it to Kapoeen. Space was deep even when transiting through sub-space. If it took another three days, he would not be displeased. He also needed time to plan and the break was welcomed. He had narrowed his choice to two minor outposts, both within a two-day run from Kapoeen. The one he favored was Pittar 2-RN.

The information supplied by Khiman-ra only served to confirm his choice. Pittar sat on the edge of a secondary ship-ping corridor and acted as a stopover station for transiting Fleet units. There were rarely more than two or three small craft at the planet's single facility, mostly M-2s. What made it attractive was its resident M-3, the setup typical of such bases. It was so typical, it reminded him of Lemos. If the Field layout was in any way similar, he would be in and out before SC&C or the ground personnel realized what happened.

He also spent a lot of his time reviewing the setup at Khiman-ra, making suggestions, cajoling and threatening. If he was expected to manage the raids, he wanted nothing to be overlooked. Personnel were a problem. It always was. There were a number of good officers and ratings, but the facility lacked senior chiefs. He had no use for zealots or glory seekers. He needed seasoned, tough professionals who were hardened combat veterans and did not mind dying. Le Maran grumbled when Tanard gave him a list of replacements and demands for new men. In the end, he had given in. After what Tanard went through to establish the Tai Mari Line, Khiman-ra was almost elementary. It also became clear why Le Maran's authority extended to administration only. The man knew nothing about command or running an operational base.

The other problem occupying his attention was pouring over the current tactical and strategic disposition of Kaleen commercial shipping, particularly around Naurun and Omiron. The information had to be integrated with existing and past Fleet movements, a much more difficult thing to do. Computers at Khiman-ra were invaluable, but in the final analysis, they were simply machines and lacked the intuitive insight and imagination so necessary in any such operation, no matter how human their responses.

One of his first orders to Le Maran was to recall the two ships currently raiding. Their activities were completely uncoordinated and random, literally hit-and-miss affairs that would almost certainly lead them blundering against a superior Fleet unit than a fat cargo carrier. With only two operational ships, Khiman-ra could not afford to begin its campaign with a disaster. Besides, both ships were slow and underpowered. Le Maran had not been at all pleased, protesting that he was accountable to the AUP and they expected results. Tanard's comment was blunt. If those ships were allowed to stay out, Le Maran would get his results, all right—as Fleet statistics. At least get them properly armed, Tanard argued. The recall was issued.

Tanard was starting to enjoy his walks along the lake. The peaceful scenery and fresh air perfect for thinking. His legs no longer protested and he ate and slept better. He climbed the hotel steps, strode into the back lobby, swept his eyes absently over the crowd and stopped. As far as he was concerned the lobby could have been empty. Grinning from ear to ear, Winn quickly got up off his formchair, pushed himself between two tour groups and strode toward him. Cracking a smile of his own, Tanard regarded his gangly first officer with affection and slapped him on the back.

"It is good to see you again, friend Winn. Where is our fire-eating weapons officer?" he demanded.

"Railee? Upstairs, sleeping it off," Winn said, vastly amused and pleased to see his commander relaxed and smiling.

"Well, have him wrung out, then I want to see both of you as soon as you can make it. Room 34-12."

"Then we're off again? With a ship?"

"We're kind of borrowing a ship," Tanard said dryly and Winn grinned with delight.

"I like it already."

A weary and scarred freighter touched down late the next morning at the far end of the Field. It looked like any of a number of passing tramps who plied the local systems. SC&C accepted the freighter's data pack and that was it. The freighter offloaded empty fuel cells and picked up four fresh ones. No one noticed or cared when a sled-pad with three occupants headed toward the tramp. The sled-pad returned to the cargo terminal empty. Twenty minutes later the freighter lifted. It would take SC&C some time to figure out that the freighter's ident dump had an irregularity; another snarl to be sorted out by sector traffic control.

As Kapoeen fell away, Kandar and its rings were revealed in their full splendor. At an easy one-third boost, it took the freighter thirty-four minutes to clear Kandar's two point-four million talans gravitational distortion limit, which allowed the freighter to transit. Power flowed from the main drive reactor into massive wave-guide coils mounted along the hull's center-line. The delicate geometry contour lines of the distortion field coiled around the ship and the torus firmed. In a brief flash of blue-white light the freighter slipped smoothly into subspace. Brown and yellow gravity waves corkscrewed around the ship, roiling in its wake.

On the small command deck, relishing having a ship around him again, Tanard studied the nav plot and nodded.

"Nice and tight, Mister. I like it."

The pilot, a former Second Scout, smiled weakly, completely intimidated by Tanard's awful face and grating voice. He knew who Tanard was, of course. Everyone at Khiman-ra did. This first encounter still came as a shock. Tanard's intense eyes made the pilot squirm. Could Tanard be a little mad? Probably. Two years on Kalakan would be enough to drive anyone over the edge.

"There is nothing much to do for the next two days, sir. I would suggest—"

"That you shut your mouth!" Tanard snarled, appalled. If this was the best Le Maran could come up with, he hated to see Khiman-ra's worst. "Can you recite the M-3's secondary reactor startup procedure? The main reactor? What's the lift sequence? What do you do if you don't have the command codes? How do you board and secure a hostile ship? Well?"

The pilot wilted under the withering glare, but he had enough courage to look Tanard in the eye.

"I was first officer on an M-3, sir."

Tanard's anger ebbed and he felt foolish. "I overreacted and I apologize," he said gruffly and turned abruptly.

"Sir," the pilot called after him. "We'll get that M-3 for you."

Tanard paused, then strode to the cable-tube. It was not the crew's competence he should be worried about, but his own, he reflected in disgust. He'd been out of it for too long. Had he lost it? Better to find out on Pittar than against a Fleet escort.

The following two days were busy for his small crew. He might have regretted his rash remark to the young pilot, but it didn't keep him from mercilessly drilling the men. Even Winn and Railee felt the sting from one of his caustic bites. This was not an adventure or a luxury jaunt, and the quicker they all realized it, the better he liked it. One slip by any one of them could mean death or worse for all. By the time the freighter dropped normal four light-minutes from Pittar, Tanard was satisfied and the men were relieved.

When Pittar resolved from a bright point to a brilliant green crescent, Tanard nodded to the watchstander.

"Pittar, this is free trader *Oshin*, declaring an in-flight emergency. Request landing clearance for Etar Field." That was the main planetary port and the only one with Fleet support facilities. If SC&C refused permission, there would be no point going down and the freighter would sheer off. SC&C might squawk at this gross violation, but Tanard hardly gave it a thought.

SC&C demanded an ident dump and the nature of their emergency.

"We have an overpressure blowout of the main intercoolant system and the primary drive compartment is contaminated. I have two radiation casualties." A nice touch, Tanard thought. It took special facilities to treat radiation poisoning, and would account for their request to Etar Field.

SC&C cleared them for immediate landing and the old freighter slanted into the atmosphere. Patches of bright light dotted the night side: cities sleeping. They broke through the terminator into a pre-dawn haze. The Field was almost deserted. A suborbital passenger shuttle stood on the landing ring. An access tube held it fast to the terminal building. At the far end of the apron an LBC's, Large Bulk Carrier, blunt nose protruded from beneath the closed maintenance hangar roof. The sight of a solitary M-3 sitting beside the pebble shape of an M-1 filled Tanard with a warm glow.

This will work.

The freighter settled on the supporting landing ring with a gentle bump and the crimson nav screen flickered and died, leaving a momentary after-image of glowing force lines. Two sled-pads immediately made for them from the terminal building. Tanard quickly looked around. Incredibly the Field seemed deserted. He turned hungrily to the towering M-3 not eighty katalans from them and nodded to the watchstander. The youngster jabbed a comms pad.

"Assault teams away."

A console pad turned a solid amber, indicating the landing ramp was down. In the main display plate, Tanard saw eight hooded figures dressed in black assault gear rush for the M-3.

"We're secure and breaking up into our parties," the young pilot's voice came through the comms, not even breathing hard, Tanard noted with a grim smile. They had rehearsed this part carefully. One section would take the M-3's engineering spaces and the other would secure the command deck. Tanard estimated the sweeper would have a minimal skeleton ground watch, perhaps as few as nine men. Unarmed, unsuspecting, they shouldn't be a problem. Getting the ship off the ground could be something else.

"Engineering is secured. We have two prisoners."

"Very well. Hold them at the landing ramp," Tanard ordered.

"Command deck secured."

"Excellent! We're coming over," Tanard said and pressed a pad. "Engineering? Set her for fifteen minutes and get out of there." He gathered the watchstander with his eyes and jerked his head at the cable-tube. "Let's go!"

After the controlled environment inside the ship, Tanard found it decidedly fresh on the freighter's exposed landing ramp. A thin breeze swirled around his legs. He nodded to his crew and everyone pulled down their hoods, needlers held at the ready. The landing ramp groaned and clanked to a stop. The engineers jumped off and ran for the M-3. On the apron the four civilians standing beside their sled-pads gaped in confusion and fear. As his men ran for the M-3, Tanard strode toward them.

"This ship is about to blow. I would run if I were you."

One of them glanced at a hooded marine holding a needler, then looked at the other three and made off. He was slow at first, probably afraid of getting shot in the back, then sprinted for it. The others did not need further urging.

Tanard glanced at his men and trotted toward the M-3. The gentle curve of the sweeper's belly hanging over him was a familiar and comforting sight. Power support umbilicals were locked on hardpoints along the keel. As he scrambled up the landing ramp, he fervently hoped the drive reactors were not cold or this would be one very short trip. Four of his marines stood guard over seven ratings and one very young and very nervous Base Scout. The boy trembled visibly. Tanard didn't have time for him. He grinned nastily behind his hood and looked at the marine chief.

"Shoot them!"

The Base Scout moaned and collapsed. There was a ripple of bright orange lances and seven ratings lay sprawled unconscious on the ramp.

"Get rid of them and prepare to secure for lift," Tanard rasped and strode to the cable-tube. The hatch hissed shut behind him.

"Command deck."

There was a slight, but familiar shift in gravity as the tube surged up. The hatch opened a few seconds later and he stood there, taking it all in: the deck layout, the transparent nav bubble and the console arrays. Even the air smelled familiar—military. Two black-suited figures were bent over the consoles carrying out a preflight check. Two others, needlers leveled, covered a defiant Third Scout and a watchstander.

"He's kind of reluctant about giving us the release sequence for the command codes," Winn said behind his hood, his voice slightly muffled. He was curious how his commander proposed to get control of the sweeper.

Tanard stepped to the young officer and pulled out his needler. He made an adjustment and fired at the deck. The youngster flinched at the sharp crack and smoke that spurted from a charred spot between his feet.

"The release sequence," he hissed, staring into the young man's eyes.

"Screw you!"

Tanard nodded and shifted the needler. The bright beam caught the watchstander on the chest and the air was suddenly thick with the stench of burnt cloth and charred flesh. It was a familiar smell. The watchstander gaped in agonized astonishment, clawed at his chest and collapsed to the deck.

Winn inhaled sharply and stepped back. The Third Scout lunged and Tanard backhanded him on the mouth. The youngster staggered back, straightened and glared, not bothering to wipe the trickle of blood oozing from the corner of his bruised mouth.

"I am prepared to kill every one of your crew," Tanard promised.

"Scum!"

Tanard sighed and shook his head. Brave, but stupid. He leveled the needler and fired. The bolt lanced through the youngster's upper left arm, burning away tissue, nerves, and bone. The boy screamed and doubled up, clutching desperately at the wound with his other hand. Dark blood leaked between the youngster's clamped fingers.

Tanard felt a twitch of sympathetic pain in his own severed arm.

"The release sequence," he repeated.

The Third Scout looked up. Tears ran down his twisted face. He clenched his teeth and shook his head.

Tanard made a small adjustment and leveled the needler at the boy's face. Without hesitating, he fired. The beam speared into the boy's left eye. The eyeball literally exploded and boiling fluid spattered Tanard's tunic. The youngster howled, fell to his knees and clawed at his face. In shock the pain passed quickly, but the numbness would last for only a few minutes before the boy lapsed into unconsciousness. Tanard had to get his information before that happened.

"For the last time, the release sequence," he grated, then grabbed a handful of hair and jerked back the head. Blood spilled from the burned eyeball. He pressed the needler against the other eye.

Trembling, fists closing and opening, the youngster stared at nothing. Tanard knew what the boy was thinking. Without the command codes, Tanard was stuck, unable to move the ship. He could hardwire a bypass from Engineering, but that would take time, and time was one thing Tanard didn't have to spare. Would the boy be prepared to sacrifice his life to see Tanard captured? As it was, Tanard was only a hooded figure to him. Anyway, how far could Tanard manage to get with a stolen M-3 before the Fleet caught up with him? It wasn't worth his life or the life of any more of his crew.

"Bring up two of the prisoners," Tanard snarled at Winn, tired of waiting. The civilian medics could have reached the terminal building by now and raised the alarm. He did not relish a firefight with the base marines.

"No!" the Third Scout gasped. "Computer, command codes release enable. Sequence alpha, bravo, two, zero, zero release."

"Release sequence accepted. Command codes now available," the computer announced calmly.

Tanard swallowed bile, hating what he was forced to do. On impulse, he bent down and patted the youngster on the right shoulder.

"I'm sorry, boy," he mumbled and looked at Winn. "Get him out of here." The boy would be all right, he told himself. They would patch him up good as new, but the mental scars would not be fixed as easily. They would haunt the boy, wake him at night screaming, feeling the needler burn through him, feeling his eye explode…Tanard had nights like that himself.

When the cable-tube hatch closed, he tore off his hood and sat on the command couch. His fingers caressed the familiar inlaid pads set into the armrests. He pressed one pad without looking at it.

"Engineering," a voice answered.

"Talk to me," Tanard ordered.

"You have the secondaries at your discretion. Mains will be up in eight minutes."

"Very well. Prepare to answer for full secondary boost."

"Command deck? Prisoners are released and the landing ramp is secured."

"Very well, Mr. Winn. Get up here and make ready for lift."

Even as the M-3 surged up, on board the derelict freighter a carefully placed shaped charge detonated against the reinforced casing of the antimatter containment vessel where the magnetic torus branched to feed the main drive reactor chamber. A searing flash of heat instantly burned through the casing and sent a stream of molten ceramic and polymer debris into the helium nuclei plasma. The delicate magnetic field lines ruptured and the artificial antimatter convergence point collapsed. A backsurge of energy burned through the fuel feed regulator and ignited the antimatter fuel cell.

A sphere of intense white light that rivaled the surface temperature of a blue star instantly consumed the drive chamber and radiated through the engineering spaces. It wasn't even fire, but raw unstoppable energy that broke down matter itself. Unchecked, the expanding wave front consumed everything in its path. As the sphere burned through the hull, it devoured the landing ring and formed a perfectly concave indentation in the apron. Finally spent, it faded, leaving behind skeletal frames that glowed with deadly heat. Unsupported, the two ends of the freighter collapsed into a tangled, fused heap of slag.

Chapter Three

Sprawled on the central couch, hands clasped behind his back, Terr sat in the darkness of the command deck. He stared through the transparent navigation bubble that ran chest high around the deck, not seeing anything. A mosaic of colored contact pads from the array of sloping touch-sensitive panels played with the shadows. The main display plate before him was a dark slab of gray, like his mood. He liked the sense of intimacy a darkened deck gave him, although he knew Dhar didn't care for it. This time, though, he found it depressing. His obstinate streak did not allow him to do the sensible thing and increase the ambient brightness. So he sat there, sullen and alone. Dhar had came up a while back, but left after a single glance in his direction. The mind sharing experience they went through gave them both a deep insight into each other's personality, which was not always comfortable.

"Approaching Taltair Surface Command and Control insertion point," the computer announced quietly. "Initial interrogative verified. All systems nominal for orbital approach. Preparing to egress transition mode."

Several console pads changed color and blinked; otherwise the ship was quiet. The problem, Terr realized, he was annoyed at being pulled out of an operation that was beginning to work just because Tanard managed to slip through the Fleet's fingers. He and Dhar had spent weeks establishing the civilian infiltration routine and Anabb was scrapping it on an apparent whim. Tanard was a disgraced Fleet officer and Terr was more than happy to let them handle it. What did Anabb expect him to do? Hold their hand while they tried to find him? Hunting criminals wasn't Anabb's business anyway. He gave a long and heavy sigh. He was oversimplifying things and knew it. Tanard was not an ordinary Fleet officer and hunting him would not be much fun for anybody. Absently, he touched the scar above his left eyebrow.

"SC&C insertion in two minutes. Landing configuration procedure nominal. Ship is within acceptable flight parameters."

It wouldn't have been so bad if only he didn't have to return to Taltair. Eleven days of solid boost from Palean space had become weary. And not a peep from Anabb. The crusty old canal worm could have given him *some* indication what to expect once he landed. Except for the bare details of Tanard's escape, there was nothing. Evil old, scheming…

At least his prisoner had not given him any trouble. During their first day out the raider pilot ranted and raved and started trashing the cabin. Terr didn't like any of it and threatened to have him bound and thrown into the hold. In short pithy words the pilot told him to shove it. Before Terr could flatten him, Dhar settled it by taking on his aspect. He didn't have to say anything as he stood before the pilot. When the raider saw the blue sparks slither along Dhar's arms, he simply blanched and backed into a corner. It was possible he never moved from there during the entire trip.

Nightwings…the shadow who walks at night.

Terr did not bring up the aborted discussion they had in the VLBC's hold, and Dhar never mentioned it, perhaps assuming the matter was settled. Well, it wasn't settled, merely postponed. It was a festering sore that needed cleansing. So why was Dhar reluctant to talk about it? Deep down, Terr knew that testing the limits of his aspect ran counter to even the loosest interpretation of the Discipline teachings. Perhaps so, but he was not on Anar'on now and he needed Dhar to understand that. The god of Death in whose shadow he now walked knew who and what Terr was, including his failings, when he laid his hand on him. What happened afterward was hardly Terr's fault. Was it?

He pictured Sidhara, his master. The old Wanderer's face, a mass of wrinkled lines as old as the Saffal and eyes faded and rusty. A plain brown hood of his surtaf robe covered his once ocher hair, now streaked gray, spilled around his shoulders. He would smile indulgently and shake his head.

"Foolish creature, even the presence of power is an influence," he would admonish in his heavy rolling voice.

Terr nodded. *Master, I walk with power now and we shall see what influence it brings.* He had chosen to walk this road and now needed to see where it led. In adversity the spirit grows, isn't that what the *Saftara* said? Then again, if everything was preordained, where then the exercise of free will? Or was that also merely a cosmic joke played by the gods?

"We'll have to talk soon, Nightwings, my brother of the night," he murmured.

"Insertion point. Dropping normal," the computer said.

The distortion field precursor changed polarity and began to collapse. Nav shield flaring, *Sheeva* exited into normal space and fell below lightspeed. Two light-minutes from Taltair the ship engaged full secondary boost. It still took one hour and twenty-eight minutes before Taltair's mottled sphere filled the nav bubble. Without pausing, *Sheeva* dove into the atmosphere.

Barden broke out of light haze and patchy clouds that filled the landscape. Lines of hurrying cargo carriers, communals, combies and private sled-pads crossed each other above the city in never-ending streams of traffic. Towers of ceramic and gleaming alloy clawed at the sky. The Center complex of three towers was distinct and immediately recognizable in a jungle of clustered buildings.

Tal Field lay spread in a pattern of aprons, approach ramps and work hangars. The four civilian terminals, with their landing rings radiating like spokes in a giant wheel, were taken up with every possible type of ship, from private cruisers to giant

Deklan and Sargon liners. Connected by access tubes the ships looked like insects hovering around petals of a bright flower. Maintenance trolleys and cargo platforms sped across the aprons in seemingly disordered confusion. Beside the sprawling inter-star terminus two somber-painted military complexes exuded a more subdued atmosphere.

As *Sheeva* slowed and sank toward its berth, the Field Administration building reared itself against the skyline; a rounded tower supported by a flared base. The tower was a landmark feature, a giant mushroom with two jutting flat platforms mounted a third of the way down its side. The lower larger platform was a landing ramp for transiting combies and communals. The upper level handled the business end of Taltair's SC&C control.

The M-1 settled with a gentle bump and the landing ring field took up the ship's dead weight. Terr could not see them, but he knew that support umbilicals were now attaching themselves to the ship, supplying *Sheeva* with power. An access tube extended from the terminal and connected with a faint clang. He appreciated getting this slot. A lowly M-1 didn't normally rate such treatment. It could also simply mean there was a spare slot or that he wouldn't be around long enough to admire the local scenery. Either deal was okay with him. With a last sweep at the crowded Field, he pursed his lips, polarized the nav bubble, and got up.

Dhar was waiting for him on the main deck, dressed in a nondescript brown one-piece suit. It fitted him well. In contrast, Terr's plain working grays looked drab and utilitarian. He didn't give a damn. Dhar was a silent shadow as they walked down the access tube.

Inside the terminal, the usual crowd of officials, civilians and military types hurrying to and from tube entrances to deaden the sound of footfalls. It was crowded enough that the place made Terr uncomfortable. Everyone disregarded the usual announcements of arrivals and departures. Giant Wall display stations showed the layout of the Field, ship berths, the Center and the city's various attractions. Terr had been on Taltair long enough to ignore the distractions and strode briskly toward one of the rows of waiting communals. The driver noticed them and hurried to open the bubble. Terr settled into the back seat and the upholstery creaked as Dhar slid in his length beside him. The bubble closed with a hiss.

"Where to, buddy?" the driver inquired offhandedly.

Terr leaned forward and prodded the mike pad. "The Center, but first, make a stop at Razzo's Corner." He felt Dhar's eyes on him and turned. "I only want to say hello, in case we're out of here in a hurry," he explained as the ground sagged away under them and the communal climbed out of the terminal.

Dhar lifted an eyebrow, but did not say anything. It wouldn't have helped anyway. At any rate, he knew why his brother was doing this and approved.

The communal stayed in the low lane of the Beltway: bars, restaurants and other establishments lining the road ring approach to the spaceport. It was a popular place for many going out or coming back. Both were reason enough for that one last drink. Below them, old gnarled trees lined the broad avenue. Locals, tourists, people from all over the Serrll, strolled, hurried or gawked as they stood on the moving glidewalks. The communal dropped to port and sank beside a combie parked on the small landing ramp.

"Ten minutes," Terr said as the door opened.

"The meter will be running," the driver replied comfortably. He didn't question why his patrons did what they did. He had become philosophical, resigned to the fates that compelled him to serve his passengers.

"I will wait here, Sankri," Dhar added gravely. Terr looked at him for a second and nodded. The door hissed shut behind him.

He allowed a small group of strollers to walk past him and strode toward the bar entrance. It wasn't an upmarket dive, but few places along the Beltway were. Still, it cost him a significant slice of his savings to buy and renovate the establishment, not that he ever considered the cost. He would gladly have paid much more for a debt one could never truly repay. How does one pay someone for saving his life?

It was Razzo who took the needler bolt Tanard meant for him. The burly marine chief almost lost his left arm when he threw himself in front of Terr. The medics patched him up, but even modern genotherapy could not restore the full use of Razzo's arm. That act of selfless heroism cost the chief his career, Razzo refusing to take a ground assignment. Although Razzo would die before saying anything, Terr knew the old chief secretly missed active service. He was a combat marine and all he knew how to do. When the medics finally let him go, Terr dragged him to this bar and simply pointed at the sign.

"Dumb," was all Razzo ever said. He may have been all choked up, but that didn't stop him from taking the joint. To everyone's surprise, he made the place his own and the Corner ended up a trendy and sometimes boisterous watering hole for all Fleet servicemen. Merchant crew were tolerated, business being business.

Terr pushed the door open with a stiff hand and walked through. It creaked as it swung shut behind him. It always did that. In a pensive mood, Razzo told him once it added character to the place. Terr told him he was too stingy to oil the hinges.

This time of day most of the tables were empty. Tucked away in a shadowy corner the pairs ring was a bare platform. It was too early for that kind of action. The air had a cool refrigerated smell that failed to hide the reek of spilled booze and ripe bodies. A waiter pushed a whispering cleaner between the tables.

Razzo was leaning negligently against the bar, holding up a glass; eyeing it with a deep scowl. His nose was flattened after countless encounters and beyond salvage. His bald head shone a matted pink, all knobby and scarred. Behind him, arrayed on glass shelves, stood rows of bottles and containers filled with variously colored spirits. Set against a mirrored backdrop was a holoview image of a young nude with demure dark eyes lying on a bed of pink flower petals, long hair strategically spilling over her shapely bosom. Terr spent a moment admiring her curves.

He propped himself against the bar and waited. Eventually, Razzo looked at him and his scowl deepened. His moist, innocent-looking blue eyes gave nothing away. He walked over and snorted.

"What can I get you?"

"A belt screwdriver," Terr said promptly.

Razzo had all the modern conveniences for mixing and serving drinks, but he liked to keep his hand in by making his own. After some clinking of glasses and ice, he turned and planted a tall tumbler on the bar top. Terr eyed the thick yellow liquid, streaked with brown spirals. Then he plucked out the little blue umbrella that sat in the froth. A little red berry came away with it. He picked up the tumbler, nodded to Razzo and took a sip. A mixture of burning and freezing sensations assaulted his mouth. When he swallowed, the spirit went down smooth as oil.

"Not bad," he wheezed and blinked back tears. "You haven't been watering it."

Razzo cracked a grin. "I'm keeping a bottle especially for you. So, back in town?"

Gossip was part of the payment.

"Just came in."

"Our friend Tanard, eh?" Razzo said knowingly and Terr stared.

"Rit! How—"

"I got contacts."

"Maybe I should get you and Anabb together."

"Forget it. I'm comfortable where I am, thanks."

"I'm glad to hear it," Terr said softly and an understanding passed between them.

"What the hell. All I had before was dreary routine with moments of scary shit. I like this better." It was a lie, of course, but not a bad life either.

"Yeah, I can see how you're enjoying it," Terr said.

"You be careful with Tanard, hear me?"

"If he tries another shot, I'll call you."

"Hah!" Razzo scowled and leaned across the bar. "I mean it. Whatever he's up to, it won't be good."

"I know."

"Just don't let yourself get caught in a hairy situation. I can't sell booze to a dead hero."

"Not planning to be a hero."

"Good. Cause this hero crap isn't worth the trip."

"I hear you." Terr straightened and slid a Serrll fiver on the bar. "I've got to run, but I'll be in touch."

"You runt! You know how I hate cash!" Razzo complained bitterly. "Screws up my accounting."

Terr grinned and walked out. He was still grinning when he climbed into the communal.

"I take it Razzo is well?" Dhar inquired as the communal got into Barden's control network.

"Razzo is just fine," Terr said, his good humor restored.

* * *

"You've been drinking," Anabb accused, his nose crinkling.

It was suddenly cool in the office and Terr hoped Anabb wasn't in one of his peppery moods. The formchair squirmed as he crossed his legs. Behind the expanse of Anabb's desk a window screen took up the whole wall. The city's slim towers reached into a bright sky. On his right a floor-to-ceiling full-dimensional Wall display station cycled through random color patterns. Staggered solid wood shelving crowded the opposite wall and held an assortment of trophies and campaign memorabilia.

Anabb's ragged scar was its normal veined blue, not the mottled red when he was really ticked off. Terr decided Anabb was simply being peevish.

"I was visiting a friend," he said, shrugging off the barb.

If he knuckled under every time Anabb barked, he would either have to resign, which had happened to some who found Anabb's particular brand of humor off-putting, or punch out the old fart's lights. Although pleasurable to contemplate, that option was somewhat extreme. He could dream about it...

Anabb bit back a smile and glared instead. The boy was impertinent, a scamp and without a drop of respect for his superiors. He was also shaping into one of his best field operatives. As far as he was concerned the other things didn't matter all that much; at least not for now. There was a lot of roughness about the boy that needed polishing and nurturing, but Anabb relished the challenge. Although the boy came close more than once, Terr had never been insubordinate—exactly. It was only a matter of time, he thought comfortably and his eyes shifted to Dhar's silent and imposing form. The Wanderer looked back at him without blinking. In the end, annoyed with himself, it was Anabb who broke contact.

What a combination these two made!

The boy showed promise, but if he were to exploit Terr's Wanderer side, he would have to separate them. Dharaklin's rigid moral code would never permit Terr to stray down Anabb's path. How he planned to harness the boy's unique power did not twinge on his conscience at all. He was quite prepared to use the tools he had to their fullest if it meant getting the job done, even to the extent of using up that tool. New agents can always be trained. Did he really believe that? In his job, he could not afford to believe otherwise.

Thunderation! Brooding will not get the job done.

"We have another development. An M-3 was stolen from

Pittar 2-RN. A five-day flight from Feron at standard commercial boost."

Terr grinned. "Tanard? He actually stole it?"

"He walked on board and took off. Can you believe it? The Fleet is hopping mad, as you can understand. There is no direct evidence to suggest Tanard is responsible for the theft, but it's likely. The M-3 crew reported men dressed in black assault gear. No way to identify them. We have a clue, though. A deck officer, badly injured when forced to release the command codes, remembers a harsh, raspy voice."

Terr nodded, recalling the odd voice when he confronted Tanard aboard his ship.

"If he's resuming his old ways, he could have been after a possible weapons platform to do it with," Anabb said.

"He could also have intended to strip it down," Terr added. "Tooling around in a stolen M-3 would simply be asking for it."

"If we found him and *if* he happened to run against an M-4." Anabb looked unbearably disgusted. "This is all conjecture and irrelevant. Tanard is a Fleet officer and finding him is their problem. You should guess what is my concern."

Terr could guess easily enough.

"It's possible and quite likely he might try to re-enter the AUP Provisional Committee or some Palean chapter of the Alikan Union Party movement. As a known fugitive the Committee may not be too anxious to take him back."

"Can't say that I blame them," Anabb growled without expression.

"Yes, sir. If Tanard *has* stolen that M-3, then he's definitely back in business."

"A rogue raider you think?"

Terr shook his head. "I don't think so, sir. It doesn't fit his profile. He sees himself as a patriot, not a traitor."

"I know that."

"Yes, sir. Exposing Lemos two years ago and breaking up

raider networks was merely a public relations windfall for Capital. It did nothing as far as the Sargon/Palean merger is concerned. It only delayed things and they are on the move again. No, he'll be raiding, all right, but not for himself. He'll be after Naurun and Omiron. That's what I would do.

"The way I figure it, if the Paleans can pressure three or four Kaleen systems to cede to them, the Lemos setback will be nullified. They could affect the merger with Sargon and gain that all-important third seat in the ruling Executive Council, which in turn would result in the breakup of the Kaleen group and destruction of the Unified Independent Front before it is even born. It could also mean the breakup of the Servatory Party coalition, pitching Sargon against the Sofam Confederacy, which would rip the Serrll apart and likely plunge it into economic warfare."

Anabb beamed with pleasure. There was no getting around it. The boy was good when he wanted to put his mind to it, but his thinking was still mission-oriented. Anabb had noticed Terr's cynical disdain for Captal's bureaucratic process. Well, such an attitude wasn't necessarily a bad thing right now. Later, that side of him would need to be worked on if he is to develop a strategic outlook.

"Not bad, if somewhat gloomy. You should keep in mind that Captal would never allow the situation to deteriorate that far. Although they wouldn't mind seeing the Unified Independent Front compromised in the bargain. If one or two Kaleen systems, like Naurun and Omiron, happened to cede to the Paleans, it could make the others skittish and skeptical of Anar'on's ability to clear the shipping lanes, and is the main reason for your undercover mission. Tanard is merely another dimension in the equation."

"But if they push Kaleen too far, the Wanderers might retaliate," Terr pointed out diffidently. Anabb sighed.

"I have enough gray hairs already."

"The Paleans have protested their innocence for any raider

activity against Kaleen," Dhar pointed out reasonably, playing the devil's advocate, and Anabb snorted.

"You expect them to admit it? This is an AUP Provisional Committee operation. I can feel it."

"Sir, if Tanard *is* involved, some of those raids will invariably have a military flavor, lending them to a degree of predictability," Dhar added. "Predictability, that could be used against him."

"To find and destroy him. If we're lucky, his base of operation."

Terr cleared his throat. "Ah, may I ask, sir, why bring me back to Taltair—"

"Instead of jeopardizing your current mission, we could have discussed this through a Wall conference?" Anabb finished for him and the amber flecks in his eyes sparkled.

"Well…"

"Because you don't credit me that I know how to do my job!" Anabb growled and raised a hand. "Don't worry. I've learned to live with your disrespectful attitude."

"Sir, I didn't mean—"

"I told you," Anabb went on unperturbed, "Tanard is a Fleet problem, and I meant it. However, finding him will mean locating his logistics support base, which he must have. He may be good, but he cannot operate alone. Once found, the base will hopefully provide us with a link to his political masters, the real objective of this program and your job. You must remember the Diplomatic Branch is a security agency, not a policing one. Li Aron, a Master Scout in Kalakan's Internal Operations Division, is in charge of the Fleet's efforts to find Tanard. He'll be instructed to extend you his full cooperation to the extent it aids you in your investigations. Finding Tanard's base is far more important than you two playing Simplon engineers. Moreover, until the completion of this mission, you will have full authority to request whatever resources you see fit, including capital Fleet units, to execute your mission. Is that clear?"

Terr stared at Anabb, hardly believing what he heard.

"I'm running this operation?" he asked slowly and Anabb snorted.

"Hardly! You're too junior and this job is too large for any one man. I am pursuing more than one option to locate this rebel base. Hiragawan, one of my senior agents, is a point man for this operation. Coordinate your fieldwork with him, but son, exercise discretion when dealing with Kalakan and the Fleet."

"That's the only part I do understand," Terr said dryly, but his eyes sparkled. "I'll try not to rub everybody the wrong way at once."

"Thunderation! Pissing off a Prima Scout will not enhance your career."

"Yes, sir. Did we get anything from that raider pilot we brought in?"

Anabb was puzzled. He just handed Terr authority equivalent to a squadron commander and the boy hardly blinked. Was it indifference? Looking at him, he decided the boy was simply not overawed by the responsibility or the magnitude of the task. Should he be? Anabb decided not. Worrying about stepping on somebody's feet wasn't the boy's style—just like it wasn't his father's. Irreverent, both of them. He was right in his assessment. The boy didn't have a shred of respect for his superiors.

Anabb locked his fingers and sat back.

"He was understandably uncooperative, which forced us to use unconventional interrogation techniques." He saw Dhar stir and raised his hand. "It was nothing drastic, Mr. Dharaklin, if you're concerned. He'll live to sample Cantor's invigorating lifestyle. Personally, if it were up to me, I'd shoot him." He cleared his throat and locked his fingers again.

"As to your question, Terr, what we got is all negative. This piece of scum seems to have been operating alone. His association with *Virana* was an opportune convenience for both. Unfortunately, we cannot pursue that line as *Virana* was inconveniently obliterated. Scum! Anyway, the pilot had a Wall code that gave him access to secure Kaleen shipping information and was apparently free to use the data or not. I'm hopeful his ship's computer dump is more informative."

Terr digested this bit of intelligence and decided he didn't like the taste.

"The Wall code was tried, of course?"

"And voided, but a public bulletin board it accessed—"

"And a new code has probably been already issued," Terr finished for him. "That's not playing fair. How do the raiders get hold of a new code?"

Anabb grinned, but it was without humor. "It's something the pilot neglected to mention."

Or had it erased from his memory, Terr figured. There was one other small item not quite clear to him.

"If supposing we know the AUP Provisional Committee is supplying raiders with data on Kaleen shipping, why would they want to jeopardize an apparently successful operation by suddenly engaging Tanard?"

This time Anabb's smile was genuine. "Why indeed? But you're assuming it's the Committee pulling Tanard's strings."

"An independent organization?"

"My boy, the Alikan Union Party is not a homogeneous group. Most likely, we're talking about a radical splinter arm."

"Or a Palean black ops," Terr said and Anabb shook his head.

"After Lemos, that's unlikely. Tao Karam's pro-Sofam faction controls Congress and the government now. However, it doesn't mean the Palean Union has abandoned its objective to merge with Sargon."

"Ti Inai's faction then?"

"If it is, we'll never prove it. If Tanard *is* run by a splinter AUP arm, that's to our advantage. It could disrupt the Committee's timetable and spread dissent among allies."

Dhar sat relaxed on his formchair, content to watch Sankri and Anabb play their word game. The Branch Director was clearly a busy man and he wondered why Anabb was indulging himself by discussing the mission personally instead of passing them off to Hiragawan. He looked back on their assignments and the variations in them. Although each was a specific mission, all of them expanded Sankri's awareness of the Serrll, its players and the political, economic and social interplays between them. The answer seemed pretty conclusive. Sankri was being educated, and in turn, so was he. Dhar realized if he survives the process, he would become somewhat of an expert on every aspect of Serrll structure, something that could potentially be of use to the Unified Independent Front. Was this process deliberate or a byproduct of working for the Diplomatic Branch? He could not tell, but it was an interesting line of thought.

"Have we attempted to infiltrate any of the Palean Alikan Union Party cells?" Terr asked on impulse.

The room was suddenly silent and he wondered if he'd said something wrong. Anabb was looking at him with peculiar intensity, the amber flecks in his eyes predatory.

"You ask some penetrating questions, my boy," Anabb said heavily. "I suggest you don't pursue that line of reasoning."

Terr swallowed, not sure what he had stepped into. If the Diplomatic Branch *had* infiltrated an AUP cell, it could lead them to Tanard's base and possibly save everybody a lot of legwork. Why wouldn't Anabb want to pursue that? Unless, of course, the operation was so multi-layered and conducted at such a level it couldn't be touched. Plans within plans…

Glaring at the boy, Anabb felt he'd made his point.

In the aftermath of Lemos, tracking down the AUP Provisional Committee members had become Captal's priority pet project. After one of the most acrimonious Executive Council closed sessions on record, Sargon and the Paleans naturally voted against any attempt to probe into their internal activities.

With the Revisionists holding the government majority, the Servatory Party was rolled. Sill-Anais, as head of the Bureau of Cultural Affairs, Serrll's intelligence arm, got the job and handed it to Anabb.

Anabb was in a difficult position here. By penetrating an AUP cell, he hoped the communication link through its hierarchy would lead him up the chain of command all the way to a Committee member. All he needed was to compromise one of them and the whole organization would be his. As a body, the AUP Provisional Committee represented a threat to the entire Serrll Combine. Uncovering and neutralizing it was a strategic prize far more valuable than capturing Tanard or locating a rogue base, however inconvenient that may be for Terr or Kaleen, or how many lives it cost. There could not be even a hint to the Committee they were being infiltrated. The effort had occupied much of his last two years, as though he didn't have enough to do unraveling raider networks.

Anabb smiled, slapped the desk with both hands and stood up.

"I'm holding a function tonight for a Captal fact-finding group. I want you to attend. Both of you. Twenty hundred. Give you a chance to network with some of your colleagues."

"Sir—"

"Save it. I'm not in the mood for it."

Terr looked glum. He'd been to one of Anabb's functions before. It meant crawling into a dress uniform, having to crank on a smile and being unfailingly polite to every asshole with a no-brainer. It would also be crowded and he so hated the pushing and jostling that went on at these things.

Rit!

* * *

It was not a large gathering as such functions went, perhaps thirty or forty people. To Terr, it felt like the whole Diplomatic

Branch was trying to crowd into the brightly lit room decidedly too warm for his taste. The wash of background voices and sharp laughter was almost painful. At least there was no music playing. That would have been too much. He didn't mind some of Taltair's classical composers, but the modern twanging, acid and raw, got on his nerves.

He clamped on a phony grin and looked around without enthusiasm. There were several young females attractive enough for the night not to be a total loss, but right now, he simply could not be bothered. If everything else failed, he might get around to them after he'd had one or several drinks. Clutching tall glasses for moral support, little groups held animated discussions as if it really mattered. He eavesdropped on one exchange and shook his head. Naturally, the bitching had to be about their day at work, he reflected morosely. Didn't these people have lives of their own?

He glanced at Dhar standing beside him and sighed. "I hate office politics, but we were told to mingle. So, let's mingle."

Dhar sympathized. Crowded places were never his favorite hangouts either. In the open Saffal, it was seldom crowded.

"This is not so bad. We could still be debriefing with Hiragawan," he said and Terr made a face.

"I think I may have pissed him off."

When he first met the senior agent, his resemblance to Kadatar was immediate and striking. Hiragawan had the same bald round head, thick purple lips, a broad nose and small pinpoint red eyes. His skin was also midnight black, but dry and wrinkled. Terr's reaction was spontaneous and must have shown on his face. Apparently thin-skinned, Hiragawan saw it and had taken a natural dislike to him.

"It is difficult to accept that a member of your own race has turned to raiding," Dhar murmured judiciously.

"Well, if you see him about to go for us, rescue me, okay?" Terr said and headed for one of the side tables loaded with snacks and nibbles. It took some agile negotiation around several weaving bodies, but he made it. He picked up a small black porcelain dish from a stack, its gold border reflecting the twinkle off the chandeliers, and scrutinized the spread of crystal trays for likely items. A deep-fried finger thing looked attractive enough and he tried one. Crunching on the golden morsel, he gave a small shrug. Spicy, but not bad. He put several on his plate.

"Ah, there you are, my boy!" a familiar voice boomed behind him. Terr turned and fixed on a smile.

"Mr. Director," he said politely and nodded to Anabb's diminutive companion.

"My boy, I want you to meet Undersecretary Trish, head of Captal's mission to Taltair."

"A pleasure, sir," Terr said, not really interested right now in any Captal mission.

"Mr. Trish, may I present First Scout Terrllss-rr, one of my more promising field operatives," Anabb gushed expansively.

Trish's little brown eyes lit up with sudden interest.

"So this is the young man who did so much during the Lemos campaign. The pleasure is all mine, First Scout." Trish rolled out his standard bureaucratic smile, measured with a vernier, perhaps a degree warmer for Terr's benefit.

"I trust your fact-finding so far has been successful, sir," Terr inquired politely, sizing up the little bureaucrat. Troublemakers, all of them. Sitting around all day thinking up new ways to screw things up.

"Quite. I must make a point to talk to you before I go. With Director Anabb's permission, of course," he said smoothly, his smile not slipping a cetalan. It was clear he considered that no permission was required.

"Of course, of course," Anabb growled and shot Terr a warning look.

"Outstanding!"

"I shall be looking forward to it, sir," Terr said politely.

Trish beamed and went to glad-hand another victim.

Terr shook his head and turned, only to bump against what felt like a round and firm behind. "Excuse me," he mumbled automatically and his voice died as he turned to see the object of his encounter.

Her large eyes seemed to grow as she regarded him with challenge and a touch of defiance. They turned dark green and mysterious, and he felt he could step into them. The fine lines of her oval face, high cheekbones and pert little nose made him swallow hard. She grinned at him and her right cheek dimpled. Her small delicate mouth opened. Generous red lips revealed even white teeth, the top two showing a slight gap. Her long black hair spilled in soft curls across creamy bare shoulders. As she straightened, her deep violet dress shifted, giving him a glimpse of a supple form. A slim strap ran from her left shoulder and crossed the swell of her breasts. His eyes strayed to the gap in her cleavage.

"If you're feeling adventurous, try these," she breathed in a soft contralto, and Terr's skin tingled. Her voice was strong, yet subtle, in control. He didn't see the delicate little finger pointing at a tray. "They're quite good." She glanced at Anabb and flashed him a smile. "Mr. Director…" With a swirl of her dress, she was gone, swallowed between shifting bodies.

Terr blinked, not sure what just happened. A subtle citrus fragrance lingered where she had stood. It made him think of rolling, wind-swept hills, tall swaying grass and fields of purple flowers. He took an intoxicating deep breath.

"If you're still conscious…" Anabb prompted and waited.

Terr jerked and cleared his throat. "Excuse me, sir?" he mumbled, noticing that his boss was alone.

Anabb's expression was one of tolerant amusement.

"I was saying I wouldn't worry about talking to Undersecretary Trish."

"I wasn't," Terr said, completely distracted. "And I couldn't tell him anything anyway."

"Keep it that way."

Terr leaned closer to Anabb. "Who *is* she?"

"Hah! Teena-raye, one of my analysts. A better analyst than you're an agent, I might add," Anabb muttered darkly.

"And all those things you told Trish?" Terr demanded, looking wounded.

"Propaganda, my boy. Enjoy the rest of the party." Anabb chuckled and walked off, beaming hugely. It did his heart good to see the boy on the defensive for a change.

Terr stared after him, not really seeing him. Teena...He rolled the sound in his head, savoring the image of tinkling laughter, happy smiles and sparkling eyes. Those eyes, gods! He had never seen eyes like hers. If he wasn't careful, he could easily lose himself and drown in such eyes. But what a death! And a mouth with lips full and ripe made to be kissed. The image made him shudder. What the hell was going on? His affairs, the two or three that stuck with him, were fleeting, transitory things with no expectations from either party. Even if he wanted to, his duties didn't permit him to consider a stable partnership and he never contemplated one.

Partnership? Terr, my son, you are coming unstuck!

He looked up and found those enormous eyes fixed on him. Everything else faded. The people around him did not matter and their voices made no sense. There was only her, those eyes peering at him and her small quizzical smile challenging him. Throwing caution out the lock, he left his plate on the table and walked toward her. People parted before him and he didn't see them. With each step, his internal alarms clanged louder, but he needed to talk to her. He had to hear that fascinating magical voice again.

He stopped before her, not too close, but close enough to be within striking range of her scent. It went straight to the mark. The top of her head came to his eyes. When she looked at him, her long eyelashes demurely concealed the laughter on her lips. What was she doing to him? Whatever it was, he didn't want it to stop.

"Did you try them?" she asked pleasantly, cheek dimpling, not minding his company. In fact, she found his unpretentious manner rather charming. Field agents having a certain reputation and she was curious to see if he lived up to the myth. A little flirting did no harm and he was a fresh face. She talked enough to her colleagues during the day to be mixing it with them now.

"What? Oh, the snacks. No, I never got around to it. By the way, my name is Terr."

"First Scout Terrllss-rr. Two years with the Diplomatic Branch. Thirty-four years old and unpaired."

Terr frowned. "That's not fair since I don't know anything about you."

"Oh my."

"Except your name, of course. Teena." He liked the rolling sound it made as it echoed in his head. It had a certain enthralling hint of the exotic that fitted her well. Everything about her was enchanting and he felt himself inexorably drawn under her spell.

"Anabb must have told you. I saw you talking to him," she husked, her smile mischievous. "What else did he tell you?"

"Why?"

"They warned me about fast-moving, low-drag field operatives."

"Is that so? And what do they say?" he asked, joining in on the game.

"That a girl should be careful, that's all."

"And do they say anything about a man being careful?"

Her eyes lit and her laugh was a pleasant musical tinkle that sent ripples along his back. It was devil's work, he was sure of it.

"You'll just have to chance it, won't you?"

He chuckled. Was that asking for a leap of faith or what!

"You seem to be low drag yourself. Anabb tells me you're

one of his star analysts. I gather that's how you know all about me."

"Well! I don't know about being a star, but I processed one or two of your reports."

"Ah! But my reports don't normally include personal statistics."

Her eyes rounded. "Oh dear. I've been caught out."

"This is a serious breach of security, you know. The repercussions could be severe."

"Goodness! And there is no possibility of a reprieve?"

Her eyes turned dark green and he stood there, completely captivated by this vibrant, enchanting woman. She was warm without being inviting. She was alluring, yet secretive. There was a depth to her he longed to explore. She was also sharp, but he never expected anything else from one of Anabb's people. He would enjoy clashing wills with her.

"Only if you have dinner with me tomorrow," he heard himself say on impulse. Unaccountably, he was apprehensive that she would refuse. It seemed terribly important that she accept. He *needed* to see her.

She regarded him with a speculative, pretty frown. The point of her small tongue licked part of her lower lip in an unconscious gesture. He was attractive enough, but he was here today and gone tomorrow. She needed more and she wasn't sure whether he could give her that. The whole thing was silly, of course. After all, it was only one dinner. What harm could come from that?

"That would make you party to a crime," she said at length. "One could construe it as willful concealment of a misdemeanor." A hint of a blush colored her cheeks.

He swayed, wanting desperately to kiss her, to feel the softness of her lips, to feel her against him. He stopped himself with an effort. It would be all too easy to do the wrong thing and blow it. He didn't want to appear as simply another skirt chaser.

"I'll just have to chance it, won't I?"

She flashed him a smile and nodded. "Well…dinner it is, then."

"Nineteen hundred okay? I'll pick you up."

She raised an eyebrow and tilted her head.

"I'll find you. I am also an analyst," he reminded her and grinned broadly. She dimpled and gave him a small curtsy.

"Thank you for a most enjoyable time, but I must leave."

"Already?" His dismay was so obvious, she laughed.

"An early start, I'm afraid. Anabb doesn't make allowances for parties, even when they are official. Good night…Terr," she said quickly, turned and was gone. The air swirled after her. Others moved in to fill the space and he was alone, surrounded by gay, laughing people, but he was alone. It was like an ache he never realized was there. Was he falling for the girl after only a single brief conversation? No. No way. He was only having a good time, he told himself. Wasn't he?

Rit!

She never told him anything of herself. If this is to go on, he would have to watch himself. Did he want this to go on? Terr wasn't entirely sure.

Dhar threaded his way between elbows and waving arms when he noticed the striking girl. His eyes immediately swept the faces and found Sankri wearing a peculiar expression. He hoped his brother had not offended the woman. Sankri sometimes allowed his gonads to lead him, with predictable results.

When he stopped, Sankri looked at him and shook his head.

"Did you see her?"

"The young lady in a violet dress?"

"She's put a spell on me, I swear it."

"She was not fleeing then?"

Terr frowned. "Character references I can do without, thank you."

"Sorry. You mean to see her again?"

"Tomorrow night. That's not an invitation, by the way."

Dhar grinned and raised a hand. "I would never dream of intruding."

Terr chuckled and punched him on the shoulder.

"Let's get out of here. One more phony smile and I'm liable to smash the face wearing it."

* * *

Terr wasn't much good for anything the next day. Hiraga-wan knew his stuff, he gave him that, but the man's monotonous dull voice drove Terr to thoughts not consistent with fostering teamwork spirit. There was no escaping it. He'd been mesmerized by the girl. The only thing worrying him was that he would wake up and find it was all a fantastic dream.

It ended up a very long day.

But it did end. He took a connecting tubeway from the Admin building to the residential tower. Transiting operatives, VIPs and senior staff were housed at the Center, which was convenient, much more so than having to commute in from a suburban guesthouse. He had a house in the new Tildera estate east of the hills he'd bought a year ago as an investment flyer, but he hardly ever lived there. While in town, he preferred to stay in the city. His corner apartment had a great view of the metropolis and the steep hills that crowded the outer residential estates. He didn't notice any of it, his concentration focused on getting himself ready. That wasn't as easy as it sounded. Living most of the time in uniform or ship coveralls, he didn't have much in the way of casual civilian clothing. So he went shopping.

With the sun already behind the hills, long shadows hung over the city already glittering and sparkling like scattered jewels. Bright yellow tubeways made a glowing web among the towers of the central district. Above them, combies, communals, and cargo carriers wove tangled lines of light in fleeing streams of traffic.

Sitting in the combie, Terr waited for the seconds to count down. He didn't want to get there too early and perhaps catch her before she was ready. He certainly did not want to unsettle her by appearing eager. Then again, was he *supposed* to be late? With women, one never knew these days. Well, if he came on time, he should be reasonably safe.

Rit!

One can screw things up without even leaving the house!

The wooded hills were deep in shadow as the combie left the low traffic lane and swooped toward the apartment block. Halfway up the sheer side, it hesitated and settled on the protruding landing ramp. Terr took a deep breath and opened the bubble. A light breeze stirred his hair as he stepped out and strode resolutely into the floor foyer. His heart beat a little faster. He checked the apartment numbers of the two branching corridors and turned left. The pale brown-veined marble tile squares did little to muffle his footsteps.

He stopped before a set of double doors and pressed the comms pad. There was a muted click and the right panel slid into the wall.

"Make yourself at home!" Teena's clear voice came from somewhere inside. "I'll be right with you."

He leaned forward and peered in. Rich light green carpet covered the floor, complementing the pale blue walls. Three dark green formchairs surrounded a low glass-topped table. Orange and yellow flowers stood tall in a black rock vase, crowding a single dried purple proteus. Its long conical petals were streaked bright orange.

Teena appeared from a side room and stopped. She wore a dark blue, knee-length woolen skirt and a cream short-sleeved knitted shirt open at the neck, revealing the swell of her breasts. Her hair was tied back into a long ponytail, which accentuated her elfin face. A green filmy thing hung draped around her neck. She had ankle-high black leather boots with loose folded edges. Her large eyes closed slightly as she tilted her head.

"Do I pass?"

Terr laughed. He couldn't help it. "I'm sorry if I stared. You look even lovelier than I remembered."

She nodded in acknowledgment. "Thank you," she said, studying him in turn.

He wore black trousers and ship's boots. His crisp black shirt was partly open and revealed a sprinkling of fine hairs. She wondered what it would feel like to run her fingers through them. He'd probably die if he knew what she was thinking. Her last acquaintance was a rug. She didn't mind the hairs, but the scratching...

He stepped in front of her and whipped his left hand from behind his back with a flourish.

"For you."

Teena pressed her palms before her face and cooed at the sight of a single fresh proteus. They were her absolute favorite. The leaves were brilliant blue and the yellow-white streaks appeared to almost glow. She had no idea how he found out she liked protea or how he managed to get hold of a fresh one. It showed determination and she liked that. She took the long black stem and brought the flower to her nose. The perfume was sweet without cloying, fresh and delicate, with a hint of citrus.

She looked at him over the petals and smiled warmly.

"It's simply lovely. I adore them. Thank you."

Terr grinned in return, pleased and happy to see her smiling.

"It reminded me of the perfume you wore last night."

She fiddled with the arrangement in the vase, making sure the protea fitted just right, then straightened and patted down her skirt. "I'm ready."

Terr gave a small bow and extended his right arm toward the door. She smiled and preceded him out.

"You have a very nice apartment," he said, admiring the

décor.

"It's comfortable."

He escorted her to the combie and opened the door for her. She flashed him a smile. The combie's power plant spooled and the craft lifted. Terr told the computer where to go and sat back. The upholstery creaked as he shifted his weight. The interior was dark. A green safety strip ran along the edge of the bubble. A pad blinked at him from the simple console. He was very conscious of Teena sitting beside him, her small hands folded in her lap. Her fingers were slim and delicate and he wanted to fondle them. Barden was a sprawl of light on their right side that played with the shadows on her face.

"How do you like being an analyst?" he asked on impulse.

She turned her head, her face reserved. Light shone through her hair, making it glow and shimmer. He badly wanted to run his hand through it.

"It's not as exciting as doing fieldwork, I suppose," she said slowly and frowned prettily. "But I like it a lot. I don't have access to everything that's going on, naturally, but what I do see is pretty fascinating."

"Like lifting personal details out of dry reports?" he prompted and she laughed.

"I'm making up for it, am I not?"

There were several openings to that, which he refrained from making; too much room for misunderstanding.

"You are, to my good fortune."

"You're not trying to be fresh, are you?"

"Not tonight," he promised and she giggled.

"And how do you like being a field operative?"

"You know, in all the time I've been working for Anabb, you're the first to ask me that."

"Do I sense frustration?"

"Not at all. I simply recognize my place in the scheme of things."

"My goodness. Are you sure there isn't a teensy bit of frustration there?"

"What kind of analysis did you say you did? It wasn't psychoanalysis, was it?"

She chuckled and allowed herself to relax. His close presence was a bit intimidating and unnerving at first, field agents having a 'right now' attitude, but Terr was unpretentious and she enjoyed sparring with him. There was something else about him that sent her imagination running. Something held in check, too terrible to look at. It was thrilling to contemplate finding that secret.

Hold it, girl! This is only dinner, remember?

"It was a major area of my graduate studies at the Polytechnic."

"Ah ha! I knew it! That's it. You'll get nothing more out of me."

"Oh? That's too bad," she said and sighed. "I guess it's going to be a long quiet night, then."

Terr grinned. She was very easy to talk to. He would have to watch that. He wasn't quite ready to spill everything, not just yet. Maybe tomorrow. Damn! He wasn't going to be here tomorrow. Well, he would have to make the most of it tonight.

The combie slowed as it approached the wide landing ramp of the brightly lit restaurant cut into the hillside. It settled and the power plant spooled down. On their right the city was a lit toy set.

"It's magical," Teena gushed breathlessly.

He opened the bubble and waited for her to get out. Standing beside her, he offered her his right arm. After a moment of hesitation, she smiled secretly and wrapped her arm around his.

She lifted her eyebrows and nodded in appreciation. "I always wanted to eat out at Tiranon's."

Terr grinned at her. "A dream fulfilled, then."

Inside the classy restaurant, the lights were subdued and the décor understated. The waiter took them to a private alcove that overlooked Barden's lights. Soft nondescript music filled the background spaces and mixed unobtrusively with the chatter of other patrons. The rich wall paneling, the comfortable seats and the smell of good food, it all served to put them both at ease.

Terr did not remember ordering or eating the tasty entrée. He was too busy staring at Teena; memorizing the curve of her lips, the way her right cheek dimpled when she smiled, the way her eyes changed from light to dark green when she looked serious or was teasing, the soft lines of her chin and the sway of her hair when she moved. Every now and then a rebellious lock would stray toward her right eye and she would brush it away in a purely unconscious gesture. The little flaw made her real. She wasn't a frigid manikin, perfect and still.

She took a sip of wine and peered at him over the rim of the glass.

"You still haven't answered my question."

"Which one was that?"

"Being a field operative."

"Oh, that one." He spent a moment fiddling with his glass. "I guess I joined the Diplomatic Branch because I wanted to make a difference," he said, afraid he'd made a fool of himself. She only nodded.

"Being a Fleet officer was no longer enough?"

"You are perceptive and correct, of course. I had my M-3. It should have been enough, but after Lemos, it suddenly wasn't enough. Anabb made me feel I could make a difference by joining the Branch. It was a lousy, dirty trick to pull on me. It was also ego and I was full of myself. I don't know whether I have made a difference, but the last two years were certainly eventful." He arched his eyebrows at her. "You would know about that from my reports."

"Hah! You want to go back to active duty?"

"Some day, probably. Unless Anabb gets me killed off in one of his bad deals."

She inhaled sharply. "He—"

"Teena, it's part of his job," he said gently. "You must have come across notes from agents who bought it."

"Well, yes, but…"

"I know. It doesn't seem real in the back office."

"We talk about it…"

He placed his elbows on the table and palmed his chin. "What do you talk about?" he asked to lighten the atmosphere. Her eyes sparkled as she regarded him.

"Girl talk. You wouldn't be interested."

"In that case, you cannot blame me if I draw the worst possible conclusion."

"You're crude and a beast!"

"Low life, I agree," he said and took a sip.

Her giggle was a tinkle of running water, bright sunshine and warm breezes. They spent time pushing food around and Terr spent most of it gazing at her.

"Mr. Dharaklin," she said on impulse. "I know he was your first officer, but you are never apart, even on a mission." Even as she spoke the words, his face changed and he was suddenly someone else. She froze, afraid to breathe. She had opened a door and now wasn't sure it was a wise thing to do.

He put down his fork and his eyes bored into hers. She had touched a raw nerve and caught him off guard. How much could he tell her?

"You know about my crash on Anar'on and that he is a Wanderer? Well, the Wanderers have certain powers. Dhar used that power to save me from a hell where my mind fled after the desert took me. Our personalities merged and we became one. We become brothers…and friends."

Teena sensed a flood of emotion behind the simple words and realized that a lot was left unsaid. Perhaps one day, he would trust her enough to tell her the rest of it. One day? The thought brought a cascade of half-formed possibilities, each one pleasantly tantalizing.

Yes, there will be other days for us, First Scout Terrllss-rr of the House Llss-rr.

She knew all about his family, she had checked up. On Kaplan the House of Llss-rr were old aristocratic blood, space-farers and politicians all of them. Terr's father was a promising young officer and strange that he was killed on Anar'on, of all places. Fates? It was not so strange that Terr should have wanted to follow in his father's footsteps. His uncle, Enllss-rr, was Commissioner for the Bureau of Colonial and Protectorate Affairs, a very senior posting in the Security Council. Despite that, as far as she could find out, Terr had never accepted any kind of nepotism, if it was ever offered, to advance his career.

"I'm sorry. I did not mean to pry."

"Just memories. Never mind. Do you want to be a field agent?" Terr asked, changing the subject again.

She prodded the food with her fork, then looked up. "I'm honest enough with myself to know there is very little glamour or romance in my job—"

Terr raised an eyebrow. "None at all? Oh my."

"Beast!" she said and blushed. He was impossible! "You know what I mean. Nothing I do right now as an analyst means anything without fieldwork."

"You're oversimplifying, but I understand."

"Anyway, it will probably never happen," she said briskly and started eating, the gesture betraying how terribly important this was to her.

"Don't give up. How in the world did you end up working for the Diplomatic Branch?"

She put down her fork. "Oh, that's easy. The Center offers the best internships, and ever since it moved to Taltair, the Branch was seen as the best of the pick. When I got my Scholar's—"

"They picked you," Terr said. He wasn't surprised to learn she held a Scholar's degree. Her intelligence wasn't flaunted, but it was clearly there. He was curious to read her report on one of his missions, but that was unlikely to happen. Still…

He noted her bemused expression and grinned. "What?"

"I know what you're thinking."

"Bet you don't."

"You want to read one of my reports, don't you?"

"Rit!"

She flashed him a broad smile. "They all want that."

His eyes grew large. "And that's all…" He stopped himself in time and cleared his throat. "I am sorry. I didn't—"

She placed a small hand on his forearm and looked deep into his eyes. The touch sent a tingle up his arm that spread through his body in tiny prickles of fire. Gods, what a unique woman!

"I know," she said softly. "I want you to be able to say anything to me, Terr." Her lips parted and the tip of her tongue momentarily peeked out.

Terr brushed her cheek with his finger. Her skin felt warm, soft and smooth.

"You're remarkable," he whispered and she squirmed with pleasure at his touch. This was getting out of hand, but she didn't know how to stop it, and she didn't want to stop it. It was delicious madness and she craved more.

"And you are sweet when you're not teasing."

When she declined dessert, he grinned and pushed back his seat. "You willing to take a little trip?"

Her eyebrows lifted. "We're leaving?"

"I want to show you off."

"Well…" She had enjoyed herself much more than she expected and wasn't sure how to take this sudden interruption.

The night was clear and the stars burned bright. The combie left the brooding hills and headed for the city. It swung to starboard as it entered the service-ring approach to Tal Field. Traffic flowed in thick ribbons around them, crowding the approach and departure lanes of the inter-star terminus. The Field was a blaze of light that rivaled the city itself.

Teena glanced at him. "You aren't kidnapping me, are you?"

He smiled. "I'm tempted, but I'm afraid it's nothing so dramatic, or pleasant."

"Mmm," was all she said as the Field grew before them.

The combie dropped out of the ring and swung into the Beltway. It dropped farther, slowed and came down for a landing. The boulevard was well lit and the glidewalks were packed with locals, tourists, and people in transit. There were lots of uniforms around. Couples strolled casually along the way, sometimes pausing to stare at displays or deciding to stop and sample foods from the numerous vendor stalls that lined the walkways. A gaudy light show here and there advertised other attractions.

Teena pointed a slim finger at one establishment of earthy pleasure.

"When you said you wanted to show me off…"

Terr looked at the sign and chuckled. "Not tonight. I don't want a riot on my hands."

"Beast!" She fisted him on the shoulder and he grunted.

"In there," he said, indicating with his head as he massaged the bruise.

"Razzo's Corner?"

"It's not exactly upmarket, I admit, but you'll like it."

"Mmm."

Terr locked the combie and looked around. A communal driver glared at him, resenting that anyone would provide his own transportation. They negotiated other pedestrians and walked toward the entrance. An elderly couple strode in and the man held the door open for Teena. She flashed him a smile and Terr gave a nod.

It was crowded inside and noisy. The pairs ring was full, arms waving and bodies swaying as they tried to synchronize the lights with the music. There was loud talk and lots of laughter coming from the full tables. Although the crowd may not have had the refinement of the restaurant they just left, Terr sensed a casual and free atmosphere, friendly and easygoing. There was never any trouble at the Corner. Razzo did not tolerate such people or behavior and kept unobtrusive help to make sure of it.

His arm held protectively around Teena's shoulder, he steered her toward the bar seats. One glance at her and people made way. There were enough women there, some quite pretty and well dressed, but Teena seemed to shine among them and attracted more than one speculative glance from the men.

At the bar, a waiter noticed Terr as they sat down, nodded and hurried off. A moment later, Razzo appeared wearing his usual scowl. When he saw Teena, his face cracked into a smile. It didn't do anything for his looks.

"Razzo, be nice and say hi to Teena-raye," Terr said sternly.

Still wearing his broken smile, Razzo gave a small bow. "Charmed, my dear," he growled.

"Teena, I want you to meet Master Chief Razzo, late of the Fleet Marines, the man who saved my life," Terr said.

Teena saw the exchange of glances between them and a sharing of something. She wanted desperately to share and be part of it as well. What a strange evening this turned out to be and Terr was *nothing* like what she thought to expect.

"I am pleased to meet you, Chief," she said warmly. Her eyes brightened and she smiled impishly. "Tell me, was he worth saving?"

Razzo beamed at her. This one didn't look like the usual one-night stand that Terr hung around with. This one was different and he approved. About time too. The boy needed an anchor.

A waiter brought them drinks without intruding. Teena picked up the tall frosted tumbler and tasted the brown mix. It was tart and sweet and left fizzy bubbles in her mouth. She nodded in appreciation. Terr sipped his spirits.

"I sometimes wonder," Razzo said. "He had a good thing

going, then he went and sold his soul to the establishment."

Terr looked hurt. "If you're going to be nasty, I'll take my business someplace else."

"Hah! I've been hoping for that, but you never do."

Teena giggled, thrilled to be admitted into their circle. The casual rapport Terr had with Razzo told her a lot. He was probably an easy commander, provided things ran his way. Of course, he possessed that wild streak marking him a maverick, which got him picked by Anabb. That got her thinking. Did she have that necessary wild streak as well? Probably not, she mused. Her skills were of a different order. Oh well…

"You don't think much of the Diplomatic Branch, do you Chief?" she asked.

Razzo planted his meaty hands on the bar top. "It's like this, ma'am. I try not to think of it at all. In my line of work, they brought me to where the action was—sometimes," he said with a stern glance at Terr. "I was told when and whom to shoot and I shot 'em. This undercover stuff, though…I don't know." He looked at her appreciatively. "But after seeing you, my dear, I could get to change my mind."

"If I throw Terr back, we'll talk," she offered and he chortled.

"I'm almost tempted, but don't give up on him yet. He used to be a fair M-3 driver and might be worth keeping. At least he's developed enough sense to bring someone like you here."

"Chief…" Terr growled in warning, and Teena grinned with delight.

"So, he's a ladies man, eh?"

"I've seen him once or twice with a sweet thing draped around his neck."

She laughed, charmed by Razzo's coarse manner and Terr's evident embarrassment. Terr glared and lifted his fist in front of Razzo's face.

"One more word out of you and you're busted!"

"That'll be the day. Seriously, Teena, work on him. He's

salvageable."

She studied Terr's strong chin, the aquiline nose, and firm, resolute eyes. Something lurked in those eyes, something terrible and frightening. She wondered what those eyes had seen to make them look like that. They were also kind eyes that laughed easily, honest eyes. She loved the unconscious gesture he made of touching a small scar above his left eyebrow when he concentrated on something.

"I'll do that," she murmured and took another sip. There was shouting on the pairs ring and the Wall rippled with wild colors. Everyone seemed to be having a good time. It was a real contrast with Teranon's refined establishment they left earlier.

"How did you happen to get into the bar business, Chief?"

Razzo glanced at Terr. "You might say it was kind of handed to me."

Her eyes rounded. "You mean, Terr got this place for you?"

"He kept busting every joint on the Beltway," Terr explained. "I figured if I gave him a place of his own, he could bust it up as much as he liked and no one would mind."

"The only thing I want to bust is you, runt!"

Teena giggled. Behind the mock banter, it was obvious there was deep affection between the two of them. Was Terr paying off a debt or simply being kind? Perhaps it was a bit of both. Whatever, it was still a very generous gesture. Given the prized location, it must have cost Terr a small fortune to get it.

They finished their drinks and Teena assured Razzo she would be back with some of her friends. The old marine hooted with delight, much to Terr's consternation.

Later, in the combie, she looked at Terr and placed her hand on his arm.

"Thank you for sharing that with me," she said softly. He glanced at her and smiled.

"Razzo isn't much for small talk and tells it the way he sees it. I wouldn't pay too much attention to him."

"Oh, I don't know. Some of the things he said about you sounded pretty good to me."

"You're teasing."

She chuckled, then sobered. "I noticed his scars."

"He's seen some action. When he got his medical discharge, they let him go with the rank of Master Chief. A good man to have at your back."

"You said he saved your life."

"You know about Kai Tanard? When I boarded his ship, he tried to kill me. Razzo threw himself in front of me and took the needler bolt meant for me. He was badly wounded and almost lost his left arm. They patched him up and as you saw, he's good as new—almost."

"But not good enough for the Fleet," she murmured, finding it difficult to even imagine what it must have been like, what it must be like for him now. "He seems happy enough, though."

Terr sighed. "I wonder. Razzo is a combat marine, Teena. How happy would you feel if you couldn't be an analyst ever again, even if you could do the job, and every day you had to listen to other analysts talk about their work?"

It was a startling thought and she gave an involuntary shudder.

"I'd simply die."

"It might have been better for him if he *had* lost his arm," Terr said harshly as the combie lifted.

"You cannot mean that," Teena said, shocked.

"Why not? They'd have grafted on a new one and he would have been back in action within fifteen days. Sometime genotherapy just doesn't work. Anyway, it doesn't matter now."

Searching his face, she felt his pain and there was no way for her to share it with him. On impulse, she reached with her hand and placed it on his. Without turning his head, he took her hand and squeezed. Content, she leaned her head against him. He felt warm and strong and she savored his man smell and was satisfied.

The flight to her apartment was spent in silence. Both had made a beginning and words would have spoiled it. Both were sorry the night had to end, but that did not detract from the closeness they felt. The combie touched down on the landing ramp and the power plant spooled to a whisper.

Terr got out, walked around the craft and opened the side door. She stepped out and the city lights twinkled in her eyes. Then he was in front of her and she lifted her face, her heart suddenly racing. She felt a flush of heat surge through her and her skin prickled all over.

Terr looked deep into her eyes, probing for something, but the shadows hid it all. There was a momentary glint there, then they turned dark again. He felt the warmth of her body and he wanted badly to embrace her. Her scent was almost overpowering and sent his thoughts reeling. Slowly, he brought his mouth down and brushed her lips. They yielded slightly, incredibly soft. When she didn't move, he pressed more firmly. Her lips parted and her tongue touched him, a velvety delicate thing that set him on fire. Then she pulled back and their eyes locked. Staring into their hidden depths, he knew. He didn't imagine it. There would be other nights for them.

"Thank you for tonight," he whispered.

Wild feelings tore through her. She did not want the moment to end, not like this. For it to continue would spoil what might be an even richer promise.

"I had a great time," she said breathlessly in a small voice. "If you want to come in—"

"I'm lifting off tonight."

"Tanard?"

"But when I get back…"

"Until then…"

He brushed her cheek, then turned abruptly and climbed into the combie. It lifted and she watched until its navigation lights faded. After a time, she sighed and smiled.

* * *

Sheeva bored resolutely through subspace, trailing twisted filaments of brown gravity waves in its wake. Small ship noises interrupted the faint background hum of whispering machinery. Seated around a small lounge table, Terr and Dhar waited for the Palean in the Wall to stop squirming.

"You must understand, Agent Terr, there were any number of opportunities for them to get off Feron," Li Aron piped, almost in apology, and bobbed his head. "If, as everybody suspects is the case, the Alikan Union Party network arranged Tanard's escape, they almost certainly arranged for him to get off the planet. He couldn't have done that alone."

Staring at the Palean's drawn features, Terr sympathized with Li Aron's problem. Pre-booked flights, new identities, it was easy to vanish. Passenger lists could be checked—already done. Route stops—already done. Transfers—already done. When a citizen can roam through most of the Serrll with nothing more than an ordinary ID tag and basic security checks, he was almost impossible to track. Some worlds, especially in the Sargon Directorate, made that a bit tougher, but he doubted the AUP would have shunted Tanard to one of those, nominal ally or not.

Okay, if tracking Tanard presented such a challenge, why not track down the clues of his passage? He must have made contact with the AUP to firstly get off Feron, then to stage his raid on Pittar 2-RN. The freighter *had* to have left some clues that might lead the investigation back to the AUP.

The Palean locked his fingers into a knot and smiled without warmth.

"I can anticipate your next line of questioning, friend Terr," he said evenly. "How did Tanard, and we're assuming it was him, get hold of a tramp freighter that got him to Pittar?"

Terr grinned and nodded. "You are right, Master Scout. I was indeed wondering about that."

"And you're not alone. Our only break was the data pack SC&C got from *Oshin* when it declared its in-flight emergency."

"A nice touch," Terr said ruefully and the Palean snorted.

"Very. The M-3 was wide open and security was lousy," he said in disgust. "Well, it won't be so easy to pull that trick again, I can tell you. At least not on a Palean base."

Terr figured the incident was probably a career showstopper for the unfortunate M-3 commander. Tough break, but not his concern how COMPALOPS ran its business.

"And yes, friend Terr," Li Aron continued wearily, "the Fleet did issue an immediate interdiction order on the sweeper, but the damned thing simply vanished, swallowed whole in space. You don't have to tell me what that means if some AUP cell somewhere mounts a Koyami 9A projector or an M-3 power plant into an armed auxiliary. Or both. The very idea has already cost me some sleep, I can tell you."

Terr chuckled, liking the Palean. Whatever Li Aron might personally feel about the AUP or the Sargon/Palean merger, he told it like it was without trying to make excuses for the Fleet. Terr would be happy to work with him.

"You were telling me about the freighter's data pack?"

"I was. Its last port of call was Kapoeen, and very interesting that is too."

"Don't tell me. Feron shuttles transit there?" Terr said dryly.

"It's a three-day flight with one stopover. Coincidence perhaps as Feron has daily shuttles to Kapoeen. The freighter landed ten days after Tanard made his escape. I don't consider it likely it was the AUP's idea to steal an M-3. As you know, Tanard used his sweeper against Pizgor shipping when he was operating Lemos. The first time he climbed into an armed auxiliary, he ran against you and your M-1s. If he's planning to raid against Kaleen, my guess is, he didn't want to repeat that experience."

"And a Koyami 9A under him would make sure of that,"

Terr added softly.

"Count on it. Of course, with the concentration of Fleet units in Kaleen space, catching Tanard, or any other raider he or the Provisional Committee might be running, is only a matter of time. He must know that. His record shows him to be an excellent tactician and he'll invariably seek to limit his exposure. The political question I must wrestle with, and presumably what's also keeping the Diplomatic Branch awake, can Kaleen survive the interim?"

Terr shrugged. It wasn't his problem even if indirectly it affected his operation.

"It all boils down to this, friend Terr. If we want to catch Tanard, we must do it with sweepers working in pairs or introduce more M-4s into the area," Li Aron said, clearly not liking either idea.

"The freighter…"

Li Aron's thin mouth twisted in an ironic smile. "I always like to see a single-tracked mind working. Well, before it landed on Kapoeen, its data pack showed it to be a scrapped hull from Santor. We checked with the yard manager and he confirms he has a hull with that registration. It hasn't moved in months."

"A fake ID."

"Obviously. It happens all the time and sometimes legitimately. A hull is deregistered, refurbished and taken back into flight service by some washed-out operator. By the time the record trail is sorted out, the hull could have been scrapped again and the ID issued to another vessel."

"A dead end, then."

"I know how you feel, friend Terr. Forensic tests may show up something yet."

"I guess you've got to go through the process," Terr mused, knowing it to be a futile exercise. Whoever dug up that freighter would not have left themselves open to a beginner's trick. The operation had been too smooth. "*Sheeva* will be docking on Kalakan in seven days. In the meantime, we'll try and think of something."

"I could certainly use a new idea."

"Thanks for the update, sir."

"I wish you luck. You'll need it."

When the Wall image faded, Terr shook his head and sighed.

"Life can't be much fun for our Palean friend right now," Dhar said.

"And he is not alone in his misery." Terr tapped pads on the inlaid table console. "Computer, show Kaleen and Orgomy. Overlay borders with data received from the Diplomatic Branch."

He pushed back the chair and started to pace up and down the deck. He paused and scowled at the Wall image. A disturbing clustering of bright orange dots represented commercial carriers that disappeared around Kaleen and Orgomy.

"Tanard on the prowl and Anabb sends us this. Just look at it, will you?" he demanded and waved his hand at the display. "If this is not a direct attack, I don't know what you'd call it. What the hell is going on with everybody these days?"

Dhar didn't like any of it either. He understood the application of economic force against Kaleen to destabilize the Unified Independent Front, but using raiders as an expression of political policy was taking a dangerous turn toward chaos.

"The hits along the Deklan border," he said. "They are too systematic to be purely coincidence."

"You're telling me. There is no way they're purely random raider hits," Terr added and rubbed the scar on his temple.

"It's the Deklans then, up to their old games again," Dhar commented glumly.

"Seems that way to me and Anabb was certain enough to have sent us this update."

"Is he suggesting the AUP Provisional Committee is working with the Deklan Republic to destabilize Kaleen?"

Terr winced. "It's *possible*, but I don't buy it. After seeing what the raiders have done to Naurun and Omiron, I'd say the Deklans have seized an opportunity to apply a bit of pressure of their own. I hate to tell you what you probably already know, but if enough Kaleen and Orgomy systems are forced to cede to the Paleans or to Deklan, the Unified Independent Front will be an impotent hollow reed. You can figure the numbers."

Dhar did figure the numbers. Kaleen had eight systems and Orgomy six. Together they formed the core of the UIF: fourteen systems out of two hundred and forty-seven. Two or three independents were likely to throw in their hand and join, but the UIF party machine did not count on that as a given. The margin for success was depressingly narrow.

"Three systems," he murmured. "That's all it would take to bring the UIF below the five percent threshold."

"And that all-important Executive Council seat," Terr agreed. "Another incentive for the AUP Provisional Committee to carve out Naurun and Omiron."

Dhar looked grave. "It's a nasty way to do business."

"Just what I thought."

"Is Anabb expecting us to do anything?"

"He hasn't said so and there is nothing we *can* do. This is way out of our league. No, I would say he sent us this to put our mission into perspective."

Dhar raised an eyebrow. "Perspective? I don't get it."

"Sure you do. He's telling us that in our effort to catch Tanard, we shouldn't lose our objectivity."

"Don't hunt the man, but the threat he represents."

"Exactly."

Dhar pondered a while. "Then our focus will be to search for his support base, not him?"

Terr grinned. "That's what Anabb wants us to do. Eliminate his support and he's stranded, no matter how powerful a ship he might have. He'll be forced to abort his raids and we would effectively have done our job."

"Mmm. It sounds good, but how do we find the base?"

"You tell *me*."

Dhar frowned. Sankri was playing mind games again. Okay…

"A raider is after cargo, first and foremost. Whereas Tanard, and probably other ships—"

"I am glad you mentioned that."

"—will be delivering a message." The implication made Dhar pause. "They will be destroying carriers in place?"

"I'm counting on it. Tanard has no use for cargo. Trying to sell it would be a major overhead and serve only to increase the likelihood of compromising his security. For him, that's a liability." Terr looked wistful. "But if we manage to nab one of his ships…"

"The crew might know where their base is."

"Or provide us with clues to find it. You put enough little facts into a computer and something is bound to come up."

Dhar nodded. It was simple enough really. He might not know where he was, but a night sky can tell him a lot if he bothered to look. Does the place have a moon or moons? Was *he* on a moon? Can he see planets and where? If so, how many and what kind were they? Are there any recognizable star patterns or nebula?

"We could be searching for a long time, you know," Dhar said dryly.

Terr waved his hand in dismissal. "That's what we got the Fleet for. They can check likely sites for us."

Dhar raised an inquiring eyebrow. "A bit of a change in attitude for you, isn't it?"

Terr grinned. "Yeah, and I'd hate it if I was turning into one of those unfeeling bureaucrat types."

"I will remind you when you get too overbearing."

"Thanks. What we must keep in mind are the objectives. The Fleet's may not necessarily be the same as ours."

"They are hunting the man?"

"Right."

"I like your reasoning, Sankri, but there is a catch, isn't there? How do we find Tanard or one of his ships?"

"Ah, you're getting picky again. We certainly can't pull that civilian engineer dodge. Not if an encounter results in our ship being carved up."

"Something just occurred to me. If Tanard isn't looking to secure cargo, we might be making a mistake looking for an armed auxiliary."

Terr looked thoughtful, then nodded slowly. "I hate it when you're right. He needs a fighting platform, not a cargo hull. Lunge, make a kill and withdraw. That means a fast, small ship and heavily armed."

"A ship that could be imitating an M-3," Dhar added softly and Terr blinked.

"You mean, messing with IFF codes? You know, it's just the kind of nasty thing Tanard *would* think off."

"He has done it before. I wonder if Hiragawan has thought of it?" Dhar added. "Tanard could cause a lot of damage with that cute tactic before he was cornered."

"Yeah, but how do we corner him?"

"Remember *Zavian*?"

Terr nodded in appreciation. "Plant a couple of M-2s into a VLBC? Not bad."

"It would certainly give a raider something to talk about."

"I wouldn't mind seeing that," Terr said and chuckled. "But it would be a different story if that VLBC were to run up against Tanard or one of his ships. Even a couple of M-2s won't make much of an impression against a Koyami 9A or a heavy Terrasec, unless they tandem their fire control, of course."

"Anabb did say this job could have tough breaks along the way, my brother."

"Some break if it ended up being terminal."

"A less than desirable outcome, I agree," Dhar said, vastly amused. "Especially now."

"You were not by any chance referring to my current romantic entanglement, were you?" Terr demanded with a glare.

"I had that example in mind. Teena must be special indeed to have made such an impression."

Terr's features softened and his eyes got a faraway look. "Impression? Nightwings, if I'm not careful, this could turn out to be serious."

"Do you want to be careful?"

"Not particularly. When I am with her, I don't want to be anywhere else. I haven't felt like this...I cannot remember. She is...enchanting."

"You have your answer, then."

"Oh? And that's vast experience talking, eh?"

"If you run away, you will never know, will you?"

Terr pursed his lips and sighed. "You're right. I would never know and it's inconsiderate of you to point it out. If only she hadn't come into my life right now."

"You don't plan these things, my brother," Dhar said gently. He sympathized and understood fully the emotional turmoil Sankri was going through.

"Yeah. It's never the right time. It's just—"

"When you think of her, your heart beats faster and your palms go all sweaty. You want to touch her, run your fingers through her hair, explore the hidden curves of her body, feel her against you, never let her go."

Terr could not hide his astonishment.

Dhar gave a wan smile. "I loved once and it was a love that will endure for all time. I hope to love again, but it will never be like that first love."

"What happened?"

"We were both young and she ignited a fire in me that's still burning. We shared a passion that was more than infatuation or mere physical attraction. Or so I thought. Then she was gone, a pairing arranged with someone in another village. The irony of it was that I always knew she could never be mine. It didn't stop either of us from loving a doomed love. Then I was gone to the Academy and that ended it." Dhar's eyes closed and poignant memories chased each other. When he opened them, they were fierce.

"Love your Teena as you love your life, Sankri. Love like there is no tomorrow, because there might not be a tomorrow. Only in the fullness of time will you be able to tell whether that love will be forever, but you should not deny yourself this moment because of that."

Small ship sounds seemed suddenly loud and Dhar's words rang in Terr's ears. He was deeply moved that his brother felt free enough to reveal a side of himself still obviously tender.

"Nightwings…"

"Do not be concerned about me, Sankri. What we share can never be taken away or forgotten and Teena can enrich both of us."

Terr swung one of the couches around and sat down. It was time to get down to business.

"Prepare a recommendation to have M-2s with augmented projectors installed in two VLBCs. Personal for Li Aron with a copy to Hiragawan. We'll have an ops plan ready by the time we get to Kalakan." Arms crossed, he searched Dhar's face. Something else needed to be settled. "We have to talk, my brother."

Moments come to everyone when a cusp is reached that offers a branching of possible paths, each one holding the potential to profoundly change one's life. Dharaklin had faced one such cusp when he ignored his master's warning and entered the mind of a suffering alien creature. What he considered to be an act of selfless altruism had unwittingly transformed the alien into a Saddish-aa Wanderer. The ripples of that action still carried them, inextricably joined, toward an imponderable future, their lives forever changed.

Sankri was a mirror into which Dhar stared in wonder and trepidation, for his brother now trod a path never meant for a

Wanderer and where the words of the *Saftara* were helpless to guide him. Why then was he so outraged when Sankri acted in apparent violation of the Discipline? Did he attribute a failing of character in his brother when in reality it was his own failure? As his master was want to say, 'The shadow is not that which cast it.' He was one with Sankri in spirit, but they were still two separate and distinct beings. Was he so rigid in his behavior and interpretation of the Discipline that he had forgotten tolerance? A demand for conformity and intolerance of difference was a path to darkness and anarchy. Had he strayed onto that path?

Dhar looked deep into Sankri's gray eyes without flinching. They were hard eyes, but they were also honest eyes, and they did not miss much. He had seen those eyes when they were kind and he saw them cloaked in Death. Those eyes were now simply waiting.

"And all those who stand with me in the shadow of Death shall know my power and be comforted," Dhar quoted quietly and paused. "Powerful words...Sankri, my brother. I stand in your shadow, and beneath its hand, we are one until there is no time. No matter what." The words came hard, but he did mean them. Everything else was small-mindedness. He reached out and his hand held the fires of Death.

There was much left unsaid behind those words and Terr knew it would never be said, simply because Dhar didn't know how. He understood and did not hold it against him. A Saddish-aa warrior was a silent presence in the desert, alone, self-suffi-cient, a master of Death. He had to share that mastery with the Saffal. Should he ever forget that harsh reality even for an in-stant the sands would claim him and leave his bleached bones on the dunes. In an environment that was without pity or re-morse, sentimentality and emotion were a liability.

The god of Death may have his hand over Saffal's children, but he also exacted a bitter price for allowing them to stand in his shadow. In a flash of insight, Terr realized the god was also demanding that same price from him, alien as he was. His inner conflict, was it because the mirrors of his personality, one alien and the other Saddish-aa, were warring for ascendancy? In his bargain with Death to test the limits of his power, which side was winning? A terrible truth dawned on him then. There could never be a winner or loser, for they would war always. If he is to have peace, they must become one and he must be himself where the duality of his heritage contributed to a single whole.

Wryly, he also appreciated that simply recognizing the problem did not necessarily mean the process of integration had ended, or that it would be painless.

Reflected in Dhar's orange eyes, he was forced to come back to the one question that had always haunted him. Why didn't his brother war with the heritage he took from him at the moment of their fateful joining? With brutal honesty, Terr acknowledged the jealousy he secretly harbored against Dhar, mocking him for the firmness of his convictions as he resolutely followed the calling of the Discipline. He was jealous that Dhar had so easily achieved peace with his duality when he was struggling so hard to reach his. The words of the *Saftara* rang mockingly in his head. 'A morally superior position will always triumph over a pragmatic and empirical one.' There was no denying the force of those words. His morality and the morality of the Serrll were certainly pragmatic.

That was the problem. Terr had always found wearing the halo to be a tight fit.

With a tingle of ecstasy, almost religious in its intensity, he felt the power ripple through his body. Goosebumps sent a wave of prickles down his back. He felt a qualitative difference as Death settled on his shoulders. He was not one with the god to destroy, but to heal. He reached with both arms and grasped Dhar's hand. As they touched, cold fires sparked and brightened, then joined. In a backwash surge the radiance raced up their arms and cloaked their bodies until both were bathed in a cocoon of blue light.

"No matter what," Terr said in a deep voice that rang with

power. He saw the tension and wariness drain from Dhar's eyes and he gave a small smile. "You have always guided my footsteps when I strayed. Stand with me now, Nightwings, as I carry Death into the Serrll."

"Does it have to be, my brother?" Dhar rumbled and shuddered. Will Sarumajan, the destroyer of worlds, march again? It was a terrible future he saw.

"Tah, the gods will tell," Terr said simply and forces shifted within him. Alone, with Death in his hands, could he right some of the wrongs he saw around him? But the path he was prepared to walk, was it because his was a superior moral position or merely hubris?

That too the gods would tell.

As always, when looking at his strange alien brother, cloaked in power and Death, Dhar felt awed. The ways of the gods were indeed inscrutable. Alien he may be, but Sankri *was* his soul brother and that placed an obligation on him from which he could not turn away even if he wanted to.

Washed in the glow surrounding them, he felt he now understood Sankri better, and equally importantly, himself.

"Wherever that path may lead, let us walk it together," he said solemnly, accepting whatever the gods might decide.

Terr leaned forward and gazed intently into Dhar's eyes.

"I have become Death, my brother of the night. I have to accept that or face obliteration. You must also understand, by accepting what I have now become, I *cannot* stand idly by and watch an injustice without challenging it. To do so would allow an even greater injustice. I stand because I can and because another cannot." He gave a heavy sigh. "I know what you're thinking. The *Saftara* tells us to use the Discipline and develop a capacity and patience to live in harmony with conflict and chaos. In the waiting, most things resolve themselves, right? But how much suffering must pass while we wait?"

Dhar listened to the words and what they implied. The con-

tradiction of having almost unlimited power to destroy or con-
quer, and the moral imperative to refrain, was debated by the
Rahtir over millennia. The *Saftara* was created from those de-
liberations and served the people of the Saffal well. Can it serve
the Serrll equally well with Death loosed on it?

It was a difficult proposition, but he had to accept that sitting before him, he had his answer. Death *had* been loosed on
the Serrll and only the gods knew whether Sarumajan would
walk again.

"No matter what," he said gravely.

Chapter Four

Hidden in the system's outer debris cloud, almost half a light-year from the cool yellow primary, the disguised auxiliary waited for its prey. Nav screen down and secondary reactor barely cycling, a prowling patrol ship would need to be very close indeed to paint an emission signature. Less than two lights from the arterial shipping corridor that led to Kaleen, the auxiliary was ideally placed to make a lunge at any suitable target that might lumber by. However, the auxiliary was not interested in just any target. It was hunting a specific victim. Because of its strategic location, the Turney system waypoint was also a favorite flyby for Fleet sweepers trawling for prey of their own. The raider pilot knew that for the next eighteen hours, he was safe. How Khiman-ra contrived to tap into Sector TACOPSCOM's, Tactical Operations Command, secure data net was beyond him, but he was grateful that they did. In his new line of work, knowing the disposition and movement of Fleet units was an invaluable and life-saving tactical advantage.

Skin wrinkled and dry from decades of watchkeeping and squinting at displays, Ver Dit tapped the armrest of his command couch. The joints of his long fingers were knobby and the pale skin almost translucent, clearly showing dark veins and ligaments. A casual glance would have dismissed him as an aging, brooding figure, but for the eyes. Large and black, they glowed with energy and resolve. They were also bleak, uncompromising eyes that complemented well a thin, cruel mouth.

Passed over twice for Prima Scout, his career doomed, supposedly for holding political views unacceptable to Captal's Fleet Command hierarchy, his humiliation was complete when he lost his command and was given a battered and antiquated M-3. A Master Scout commanding a sweeper? It was not unheard of, but it was an insult for which any honorable Palean would have demanded blood. Being in the Fleet, of course, that was not possible. After thirty-nine years of unblemished and exemplary service to the Fleet and the Serrll Combine, he was rejected as unworthy. There was only one possible course of action open to him. He resigned his commission. What surprised him, he felt relieved at the decision and not at all bitter. He had every right to feel deep resentment and even hatred for a system that supposedly held such lofty moral principles, but was in reality deeply flawed and even corrupt. He had learned early and learned it well, that principles were a first casualty of pragmatism. After all, that was how he lost *his* principles.

No, Ver Dit did not feel betrayed by the Fleet he loved, but he did feel slightly soiled and used. And now, he was used again. He was phlegmatic enough about it to realize that everyone was used in one way or another all the time. It was only a question of willingness to go along with the charade.

After landing on Kalakan for a change of command, he hardly had time to step off the M-3's landing ramp and shed his uniform, when the local Alikan Union Party cell whisked him away. It was only justice in a way. If he could not support the Palean Union by his service in the Fleet, he would support it outside the Fleet. He was not the first or the last to have sacrificed all for a principle or a belief. What amused him, and that was perhaps also a twisted justice, his principles were already sacrificed on the altar of pragmatism. Why else would he be driving a Kaleen registered armed auxiliary, hunting Kaleen shipping—he didn't want to dwell too much on the fate of their crews—for a radical AUP arm whom even the mainstream organization shunned, but secretly applauded. Pragmatism again?

He swept his eyes over the nav plot repeater and rubbed the itch in his nose. There was really no reason for him to be on the command deck and his presence only annoyed the two watchstanders. It was either annoy them or brood restlessly in his cabin. He had been out hunting only once before and caught nothing when the abrupt recall came from Khiman-ra. In hindsight, he considered himself fortunate to have survived that excursion. He'd had no plan, scant information on Kaleen shipping movements and no intelligence at all on Fleet unit dispositions. In his ignorance it would have been all too easy to run up against a prowling M-4. That would have been a shame.

"Plot?" he piped, fingers drumming on the armrest.

The tactical officer looked up, wishing the commander would simply crawl away and let him get some sleep!

"One hour and eighteen minutes, provided *Kalnar* is on time."

"Very well."

More drumming. The engineering watchstander glanced at him and quickly averted his eyes. Ver Dit almost smiled.

Eighty-eight minutes. It seemed a long time when he thought of it like that. Thinking of the approaching VLBC, his thoughts drifted to the moment when he first saw the awful face of Khiman-ra's operational commander. The man was a walking nightmare, but as a professional, Ver Dit did not want anyone else. His natural resentment at having a former First Scout in command swiftly evaporated when Kai Tanard met the eight pilots—four held on rotational leave—of his small raiding squadron for the first time and outlined his action plan.

In a cold rasping voice, Tanard explained why Ver Dit and Hardara were recalled and handed them all a military-style operation: shipping timetables, Fleet movements, threat factors, risk mitigation strategies, comms protocols, logistical and engineering support. In fact, everything needed to keep his ships in one piece for as long as possible in order to inflict the maximum economic and political damage on Kaleen. Tanard reminded everyone they were engaged in general unrestricted warfare. If they forgot that fact just once, they were dead, a fate he did not attempt to hide from them. For they were all dead already in one way or another.

Total destruction with no mercy, that was the order.

Ver Dit saw the concerned look on Le Maran's face at this announcement and guessed the policy did not rest well with the base administrator. It was none of Ver Dit's concern. He was committed and the door that led to this commitment was now firmly shut.

He checked the chronometer readout; six minutes to go.

"Anomaly track identified as a type five VLBC hull," the computer announced suddenly. "Range, two point-four light-years. Speed, point-six lph."

"*Kalnar* detected, sir," the plot officer said, tracking the carrier's course and speed.

The lumbering carrier was early, but not suspiciously so.

"Computer, time to start of intercept run?" Ver Dit asked quietly.

"Three hours and sixty-seven minutes."

"Mmm." The VLBC obviously did not believe in stressing its main drive. "Closest approach?"

"Point-nine-six light-years at present course and speed."

"Designate as target one."

"Acknowledged."

At maximum boost, *Urethar* could cover a gap of point-nine-six lights in less than an hour, provided *Kalnar* did not deviate from its present course, something Ver Dit thought was highly unlikely. Data on the VLBC told him that *Kalnar's* maximum boost was point-seven-five lph. *Urethar* had a point-two-five lph advantage, barely adequate in a stern chase. Speed was one of the things Tanard wanted rectified, insisting that all his ships needed to have a minimum limit of one point-two lph, equivalent to an M-3 sweeper. Speed and firepower, that's what was needed. Anything else, he argued, and the ships were working with a double handicap: slow in catching their prey and slow in getting away. Lack of speed meant death and Tanard found that unacceptable. Ver Dit could not fault his reasoning, especially when he found he would be getting a new ship at his next Khiman-ra stopover. Until then, he would have to make the best of it with *Urethar*.

At least he mounted an excellent sensor suite.

He did some calculations. If he began his run at *Kalnar's* closest approach, *Urethar* would immediately came into detection range of the VLBC's sensor suite, which probably had a range of one point-two lights; standard for a commercial carrier. He knew as he was detected, *Kalnar* would boost maximum in the opposite direction and almost certainly activate its emergency transponder. The transponder signal carried for a radius of eight lights and represented the only serious threat to his operation. He had driven an M-4 for nine years and knew its performance parameters very well.

The M-4 6/A Sofam-built main battle cruiser had a better part of nine tetalans grade C composite armor on top of the four-tetalan-thick polymer hull construct. Even without secondary shields, it could withstand several twenty-four-millisecond bursts of up to one hundred and twenty-eight TeV at close range.

It mounted two Koyami 3/C phased array generators; their power channeled through a single projector dome beneath its belly. An M-4 was capable of pouring almost continuous twenty-four millisecond, 128 TeV bursts to a maximum range of 140,000 talans. It carried a crew of 240. Formed into a triad with two other ships, their fire control systems slaved to the command unit, the M-4 was a formidable weapons platform.

A point-two-five lph difference left Ver Dit a thin margin of speed to catch *Kalnar*. His intelligence brief told him there were no unscheduled Fleet units in the sector. He didn't relish the idea of a transponder blaring away while he conducted a long stern chase. It would be a long stern chase: three hours and fifty minutes. Too bad *Kalnar's* course did not allow for a closer intercept. He appreciated why Tanard wanted more speed for his ships.

So be it. Ver Dit climbed out of the couch and looked pointedly at the plot officer.

"Get us hot in three hours and forty minutes. I'm going below."

"Aye, sir." The plot officer watched as his commander disappeared into the cable-tube and snorted.

"I thought he'd never leave," the engineering watchstander mumbled.

The plot officer glared. This was a gross breach of discipline, but what the hell. They were not in the Fleet anymore. Besides, he understood how the watchstander felt.

* * *

The comms alert beeped and Thoran was instantly awake. Old habits were hard to break, even when you're a commanding officer.

"What?"

"Approaching the Turney system, sir," the First Pilot announced crisply. "Four minutes."

"Closest approach?"

"Point-nine-six lights."

"Anything within detection range?"

"All clear so far."

"Mmm. I'll be right up."

Turney was one of those unavoidable waypoints along this corridor no one liked, but could do little about. To skirt it meant a delay in his schedule and delays cost money, which his hardnosed owners never tired of reminding him. Bastards! Thoran argued they should avoid Turney altogether, but he could have saved his breath. It came down to statistics and what was seen as acceptable risk. Unfortunately for him, his owners had both factors on their side. To date, no ship had ever been lost in this sector, despite being an acknowledged choke point.

To the owners, running close to Turney was an acceptable risk. Besides, their insurer would meet any losses. That was great, but would the insurer bring back dead crews? The owners were unmoved and Thoran continued to run the Turney gap.

* * *

Managing to catch a short nap, Ver Dit returned to the command deck and settled himself comfortably onto his couch. The two watchstanders were bent over their consoles. With a wry smile, he glanced at the main tactical plot, knowing full well what went on. The two would rather not have him around, but this close to his target, there was nowhere else he could be.

"Target one at closest approach," the computer announced.

Ver Dit turned to his plot officer. "Go to secondary alert, but don't raise our shield grid. Commence run."

On the cramped command deck of the converted Kaleen inter-system hauler—Kaleen shipbuilders had no concept of comfort, Ver Dit thought—the order meant manning the weapons and comms suites. In the engineering spaces deep within the central part of the auxiliary, it set off a cascade of events.

Both drive reactors were brought online as the computer increased the level of energy demand management. A trickle of power channeled through the containment field into separate wave-guides and directed into massive secondary bus nodes mounted along the hull's centerline. The computer reported primary and secondary shield grids available at command discretion.

The powerful Terrasec 10/D phased array projector array ran through a status check. The wave-guides allowed some of the energy to flow into a separate reaction chamber, flooding the projector generator. Coils fully powered up, the computer waited for the command to raise the defensive screen grid, enabling it to synchronize the firing pulses with the grid frequency management system.

Using its secondary drive, *Urethar* boosted to clear the gravitational distortion induced by Turney's outer debris cloud, enabling it to transit into subspace. Almost one million talans later the raider's distortion field torus charged and the ship transited in a discharging flash of white light. It boosted immediately to one light-year per hour, but at a ferocious consumption of fuel, strain on the drive system and structural integrity. The auxiliary never designed for such stresses. At Khiman-ra the ship had undergone extensive modification to its frames to ensure it was capable of sustaining such speed runs. Until something failed, there was no way to tell how successful those modifications in fact were.

* * *

"Anomaly track identified as a type five transport hull," the computer announced calmly and the command deck was suddenly alert. "Range, point-nine light-years. Speed, one lph."

"Profile?" Thoran snapped, not liking any of this. The track was running far too fast to be a commercial carrier.

"A Markan May 34-6 hull, manufactured by the May-Tan Group on Anar'on."

Thoran blinked and his tongue flicked from his mouth in a blur. A Kaleen raider? Now that would be a novel twist. More likely it was a Kaleen hull converted into a raider by somebody. If it was a raider. Whoever they were, it wasn't good. Within a shipping corridor, vessels were not normally alarmed at the sight of another ship, but the unexpected emergence of this unknown fast hull was distinctly suspicious. Out here, Thoran was wary of anything unknown.

It also wasn't fair.

After being forced to abandon *Kalnar* to an ambushing

raider some weeks before, then dramatically rescued by an M-4, Thoran felt aggrieved that fates appeared to have singled him for their special attention.

Fair or not, he could make it decidedly difficult for this unidentified ship.

"First? Max boost away from his closing course line and give him and interrogative ping."

The First Pilot nodded and issued orders. A moment later, he looked up.

"No response to our ping, sir."

"Activate the emergency transponder." This could be a false alarm, but Thoran wasn't taking any chances with his crew or his ship; his owners be damned.

The jarring *blurr-reep* shattered the silence of *Kalnar's* command deck. It was an almost comforting sound.

Thoran sat back onto the couch, his smile grim.

"Catch me if you can, you scum worm," he murmured.

* * *

The sudden *blurr-reep* screech jolted Terr awake from a very pleasant daydream about Teena. It was a shame really, because after an extremely promising beginning, he would now never find out how it ended. Especially after Teena had been so cooperative and understanding.

The story of his life. Worse still, he was dozing on watch. He rubbed his eyes and sighed. It would never do.

"Computer, status?"

"Receiving an all-ships signify from VLBC *Kalnar*," the computer said coldly. "Current position, Turney system. Distance, four point-tree light-years."

Kalnar…why, that was Master Pilot Thoran's ship. Ouch! This could be tricky. "Our run time at max boost?" Terr asked and touched the scar above his left eyebrow, automatically scanning the status displays.

"Two hours and thirty-seven minutes at present closure rate."

"Set intercept course and initiate run at maximum available boost."

"Acknowledged."

"Open channel."

The cable-tube hatch hissed open. Dhar strode in, glanced at the main display plate and took the left couch. Terr nodded to him.

"VLBC *Kalnar*, this is SSF M-1 *Sheeva* responding."

The comms plate cleared and Thoran's eyes widened in surprise. Color rippled over the green scales of his head.

"Don't tell me, Mister. Because of your outstanding talents as a fusion engineer, they let you roam around in an M-1?"

Terr's smile was grim. Any ship could respond to an all-ships signify, but Serrll Scout Fleet vessels were specifically tasked and properly equipped to react to an emergency transponder or blister beacon. Unless he chose to ignore *Kalnar's* signal, probably the correct thing to do given his mission, under regulations, Terr was obliged to offer assistance. The thorny part was that despite driving an M-1, he was not officially part of the Fleet and could ignore the alert. By responding, Thoran had blown his cover, something that would have to be dealt with after the emergency. He wondered what Anabb would make of this snarl. Noting pleasant, he was sure. One thing at a time…

"Master Pilot, please state the nature of your emergency."

"I'll tell you my emergency, Mister. I'm pursued by a raider—again!" He looked totally outraged.

Terr had to think about that one. An M-1 was all legs and mounted the most basic weapons suite. Any ship he was likely to come up against would almost certainly be far more capable. Assisting *Kalnar* could be a futile gesture that might only add to the raider's box score.

"Have you received other responses?"

Thoran could well imagine what Terr was thinking and the unpleasant conclusions of those thoughts.

"*Kriva*, an M-4 has diverted, but given its course, it won't be here for another five hours."

Terr did a quick calculation. At one point-six lph the M-4 must be all of eight lights away, right at the limit of transponder detection. In the end, he had no choice at all.

"I am altering course, Master Pilot, and will close on you in two hours and thirty-two minutes."

"Don't be a hero, son," Thoran growled. "There is nothing you can do for me with your little toy ship and I would hate to have your ghost haunting my nights, what's left of them."

"You're right. There isn't much I can do for your ship. I'm truly sorry about that, but I don't intend to be a hero either."

"Smart," Thoran said, surprised that Terr's pragmatic admission hurt him. Pits! What did he expect? The little M-1 blazing away and obliterated for its efforts? Terr was doing the only practical and sensible thing possible. Still…

"What I *can* do, Master Pilot," Terr went on, "is not let him get away with it."

Thoran understood. An M-1 was a scout. No matter how fast the raider might be, it was unlikely it could match the scout's speed.

"And my presence could convince him to sheer off," Terr added. With a speed deficit and a dogged scout on his tail sitting beyond his acquisition envelope, it would only be a matter of time before a more powerful Fleet unit intercepted them and finished off the raider.

"He could still turn on you, son," Thoran hissed and his tongue flicked in a blur. "If his secondary drive is faster than yours, all he has to do is drop normal. That will force you to do the same and he'll have you."

"I'll just have to be careful, won't I?" Terr looked hard at the wizened Karkan. "Master Pilot, you must launch your survival blisters as soon as you're forced to drop normal. I'll try

143

and pick you up."

"If the raider lets you."

"He'll be too busy plundering your cargo to care."

"You hope."

"It's the only way to save your crew and you know it. If this doesn't work out, you might have another blister joining you."

Thoran grinned. "You've got guts, I'll give you that. Okay, we'll do it your way. Good luck, son…Mr. Dharaklin."

"You will tell me if someone else happens to be in a better tactical position, won't you!" Terr shouted as the plate turned gray.

Rit!

"Computer, send all logs from the time we received the all-ships signify, personal to agent Hiragawan, Diplomatic Branch, Taltair. Copy to Master Scout Li Aron, SSF support facility Ka-lakan."

"Transmissions completed."

Dhar listened to the exchange with interest. Although his brother had made light of their danger, he was not fooled. He also knew why Sankri was doing this and it had nothing to do with distress in space regulations or that Thoran was someone they both knew. He had known Sankri long enough to realize his brother almost never allowed emotion or sentiment to sway his judgment. Even with Teena in the equation now, Sankri was totally focused on his mission. He might not have thought of her when he acted, but when he invariably does, what then?

"If he's a genuine raider, you're expecting him to break off, aren't you?" Dhar said quietly. Sankri returned his gaze, the gray eyes clear and unflinching. There was also something else there, a glow of anticipation, a hunter stalking his prey. "And if he does not…"

Terr smiled. "It could be Tanard, or one of his ships. Worth the risk, eh?"

"If it's Tanard—"

"He could have an M-3 power plant and a Koyami projector waiting for us. I know. Shit happens."

"There is something else. If that raider *is* one of his, the ship will probably be commanded by an ex-Fleet officer who will almost certainly be an expert in combat tactics."

"Ah, you're being picky again."

* * *

"Plot? What is our range and time to target?" Ver Dit piped. His fists were clenched to keep his fingers from working. The long run to *Kalnar* was getting on his nerves. He just *knew* that some Fleet unit somewhere must have responded to the carrier's transponder and was waiting for him to get into range before it pounced. His every instinct, honed by decades of tactical experience, warned him to break off. The longer he kept this up, the worse his position would become. He pictured Tanard's scarred face scowling at him and grimaced.

"One point-three-nine lights. Time to run, one hour and twenty-seven minutes."

Ver Dit set his mouth and waited. He knew that making a tactical decision based on emotional blackmail was foolish, but it would not be the first foolish thing he had done.

"Anomaly track detected as an SSF M-1 scout," the computer announced. Heads turned toward each other, faces questioning. "Designating as target two. Target will intercept target one in one hour and twenty-eight minutes at present closure rate."

Ver Dit frowned. What in the pits was an M-1 doing out here when the whole sector was supposed to be clear? The answer was obvious and immediate. It must be a transiting flight and would explain why it wasn't in his movements schedule. Had the M-1 detected him? It was likely. The damned things carried a pretty good sensor suite. Was it a threat factor? Not to his ability to destroy it and the VLBC. However, the M-1's subspace speed advantage could turn into a serious problem if the scout decided to stand off and shadow *Urethar*.

Things were falling apart on him. Pits!

"Do we have an IFF?"

"SSF M-1 *Sheeva* authenticated, sir," plot answered. "First Scout Terrllss-rr commanding. Currently detached to the Diplomatic Branch."

The name meant nothing to Ver Dit. The fact that *Sheeva* was closing on his target did. Terr must know how vulnerable his ship was. The M-1 then probably meant to shadow him until a more capable unit joined them to deal with *Urethar*. He pursed his lips. It was not an auspicious start to his career as a raider. He unclenched his fists and his fingers coiled in relief. His options had disappeared as soon as *Sheeva* came within detection range. He could not hope to hide from the M-1 or outrun it. Therefore, he had to dispose of it; once he dealt with *Kalnar*, he told himself. After coming this close, he would not deny himself the pleasure of a kill. If the M-1 refused to play?

He had learned long ago that asking certain questions was an exercise in futility.

Tension slowly mounted throughout the ship as *Urethar* closed on its quarry. The fact they had an M-1 for company only added to the anticipation. Ver Dit had been a commander for too long not to feel it. It was like winding up a spring and he was holding the release pin. He met every one of his men, ratings and officers, and liked what he saw. Professionals, all of them, for which he was extremely thankful to Tanard. In a fighting ship, there was no room for zealots or malcontents. They were always the first to fail in a crunch. In that, he shared Tanard's philosophy completely. From hundreds Tanard interviewed personally, those that were selected were all disciplined. Belief in the AUP's cause, or any cause at all, was a liability. If Tanard was ruthless in picking flight ratings and junior officers, from what Ver Dit heard, he was savage with the kind of commanders and senior officers he chose to lead them.

He remembered clearly his own interview. Black eyes unreachable, the terrible scars running down the right cheek and throat raw and tender, Tanard asked just one question, his voice harsh and uncompromising.

"Why do you want to command a raider?"

The question itself was interesting in what it implied and what it left out. Patriotism? That was a nebulous and elusive commodity. Besides, the fact that Ver Dit was at Khiman-ra had to prove something. Belief in the Alikan Union Party and the merger with Sargon? That was a coin with two heads. He was about to answer when Tanard's words finally penetrated. Tanard did not ask why Ver Dit wanted to fight for the AUP or the Palean Union. Ver Dit's service record must have told him that. His question was about commanding a raider, being a pirate and an outlaw, hunted by everyone until he was destroyed, even by the very organization now using them. Could Ver Dit commit to that? Pragmatism and principles again.

"Because I am a combat officer," Ver Dit said and relaxed when Tanard allowed himself a small smile as he nodded.

"Then you shall have your fill of it," Tanard rasped.

And that had been it.

Any doubts Ver Dit may have had regarding Tanard's fitness to command the Khiman-ra facility vanished there and then. Tanard would have made a superb flag officer.

Ver Dit glanced at the nav bubble and scowled. It was opaque white. That was one thing he intended to rectify at the earliest opportunity. He wanted to see tactical and other displays reflected in the bubble, something all command deck watchstanders were used to in a Fleet vessel. Years of watchkeeping made the reaction almost instinctive. In a tight situation this reaction could now prove costly. His new ship better not have this crap.

Computer readiness reports made soothing background noises. Touch-sensitive pads blinked to themselves. The watch was fully manned and everyone waited for the end run. Just like a drill, cold and impersonal.

At minus four minutes the exec looked up. "We can try a ranging ping now, sir."

"Very well," Ver Dit said.

The exec nodded and glanced at the tactical display. "Confirm target one course and speed. Confirm target two course and speed."

"Very well. Go to primary alert. Extend secondary shield grid and synchronize."

Urethar's secondary shield extended three talans beyond the primary grid along elongated lines of force to accommodate the rectangular shape of the ship. With both grids in place, an envelope of energy enclosed the raider extending seven talans from the hull. The wave-guides switched to allow energy flow into the weapons reaction chamber, which flooded the single Terrasec 10/D generator. The computer synchronized the firing frequency with the shield grid management system and extended the projector dome. Panels slid away along the belly centerline and the dome eased down from its cradle and locked, glowing dull orange.

"K-band acquisition lock established with target one," the computer stated. "Range, seven point-two-five billion talans relative. Closure rate is 604.8 million talans per second. Effective firing solution in twelve seconds."

Ver Dit nodded to the exec. "When you get L-band lock, match target's speed and fire. Continue firing until target is destroyed."

"Range to target one is 902,000 talans," the computer said.

"Matching speed," the exec shouted. "Stand by weapons…Speed matched…Acquisition…Fire!"

Energy surged from the Terrasec generator into the projector dome and formed and overload point. At the projector's maximum range of 48,000 talans, an orange line of fifty-two TeV pulses bracketed *Kalnar's* stern. The VLBC's nav grid flared in a cascade of yellow and white discharges. It collapsed and reformed around the impact point. A long burst licked the length of the central drive spaces. The entire grid destabilized and went into a cascade of wild fluctuations. As it collapsed, the distortion field precursor failed and *Kalnar's* emergency signal died with it. The VLBC promptly dropped out of subspace.

"Target two will close in one minute and fourteen seconds," the computer announced.

When *Kalnar's* distortion field began to destabilize, *Urethar* immediately dropped normal. The maneuver was well enough timed that it left an acceptable one point-four million talans separation between the two vessels. The raider engaged its secondary drive and boosted back along its track to where *Kalnar* was drifting. At 7,600 talans per second, it was going to take the raider two point-seven minutes to close the gap. Ver Dit appreciated the extra speed of his secondary drive. Running normal, he could thumb his nose at anything smaller than an M-6. The ship may be a lumbering cow in subspace, but it could look after itself at any other time.

After two minutes the exec looked at Ver Dit and pointed at the nav plot.

"The M-1 has dropped normal and is closing. He'll be on us in under a minute; sixty-seven seconds to be exact."

"I see him," Ver Dit said. "I expect him to keep his distance." With both ships running normal, this time it was *Urethar* who held the tactical advantage; a vital five hundred talans per second over the M-1. Terr had to be just a little bit careless, come just a little bit too close, and Ver Dit would have him. Once the M-1 came within his firing envelope, he would simply lunge and finish off the dangerous pest. However, he doubted Terr would allow himself to fall for such a simple ploy. Still, even the best of them can make a mistake. And it only takes one.

"Target one has launched emergency beacons and four survival blisters," the exec added calmly.

Ver Dit could hear the annoying *blurr-reeps*. He turned to

the comms operator.

"Shut that off!"

"K-band acquisition lock established on target two," the computer said. "Range, one hundred and two thousand talans relative…Target two has changed course to intercept the closest survival blister."

Boosting at their maximum of 800 talans per second, it would take the blisters one minute to get out of *Urethar's* immediate firing envelope. With his speed advantage, Ver Dit did not consider this a tactical factor; unless the M-1 managed to close, recover the blisters and transit while he was busy disposing of *Kalnar*.

Then again, did he want to destroy the blisters? He had spent his whole career protecting life in space. This reversal of roles would take some time getting used to. He recalled Tanard's uncompromising words: total unrestricted warfare. Destroying *Kalnar* would fulfill only one part of his mission objective—economic damage. Killing the VLBC's crew would fulfill an equally important, if unpleasant, and perhaps a more vital objective—political damage. However inconvenient and disruptive to ship owners, lost cargo can always be replaced, but how long would crews be prepared to man ships in the face of mounting losses?

Ver Dit understood the logic of his mission. It did not mean, however, that he necessarily agreed with its application.

He glanced around the command deck, wondering if somehow his thoughts were being broadcast. The watchstanders were attending to their duties, apparently unaware of his lapse into moral self-examination. It was a bit late for such thoughts anyway, he mused wryly. He accepted command of a raiding warship, knowing well the implication of that decision. At least he thought he did. Faced with the act itself, Tanard's cold words somehow did not seem enough now.

He wondered what Khiman-ra's operational commander would have thought of all this. Probably shot him on the spot, and rightly so.

Very well. Total warfare it is.

"Range to target one, 138,000 talans," the exec said calmly. "L-band acquisition. Seventeen seconds to firing point."

"Match speed and fire," Ver Dit said. "Keep those reports on target two coming."

Urethar swooped on the VLBC. At maximum range a solid line of yellow ionization stabbed at *Kalnar's* drive spaces. The nav screen collapsed in a sparkling discharge that traveled the length of the huge carrier. Under continuous bombardment of fifty-two TeV bursts the polymer hull construct initially ablated, then softened. Internal pressure blew out a jagged rent in the hull that sent a gush of white atmospheric vapor into space. Lit by the Terassec discharges, the frozen air glittered and winked like a cloud of dancing fireflies. Knives of torn hull plating stabbed in defiance into empty darkness.

With the loss of hull integrity, one discharge from *Urethar* plunged through the tear into the engineering spaces. The sweeping beam licked over the secondary reactor console. The color-reactive pads vaporized instantly, the effect sending a barrage of conflicting signals to the reaction chamber. With the computer down when the VLBC was abandoned, there was nothing to regulate the message stream. The reactor chamber went into uncontrolled oscillation. A fuel surge overloaded the antimatter containment field and the reactor vanished in a sphere of white brilliance.

Kalnar's central section exploded in an expanding cloud of spinning debris, the reaction sending the forward and rear sections tumbling slowly away from each other.

"Target two has locked with one of the blisters. Range, 260,000 talans. The remaining three blisters are closing on its position," the exec said as he dispassionately watched the VLBC remnants drift away.

Ver Dit faced a cruel decision. A drive reactor explosion could normally be relied upon to completely break up a ship, even a VLBC. A carrier was a honeycomb of holds, which acted to neutralize and dissipate the force of an explosion. It was bad luck that this particular detonation resulted in the bulk of the carrier still intact, albeit in two pieces. He would simply have to take the time to finish the job.

"Destroy the stern section, then the forward end," he ordered at length.

Urethar closed to 12,000 talans and opened fire. At a reduced range the ravenous energies carved up the hull until the skeletal frames showed. Lacking explosive cargo the stern section stubbornly refused to break up. After several shots went clear through the hull, Ver Dit hissed in disgust. His fingers worked in agitation.

This was useless.

"Target two has locked with the second survival blister," the exec said. One glance at his commander was enough to convince him they were running out of time. If Ver Dit didn't break off the M-1 would escape. "Range, 286,000 talans. Thirty-seven seconds relative at max boost."

Ver Dit clenched his teeth and nodded. There was nothing to be gained by destroying the VLBC's forward section, even if salvageable cargo remained in the drifting hull. If the owners wanted to go after it, they were welcome to it. He had achieved his objective.

"Break off and close with target two," he said and bobbed his head. He needed to finish off the M-1 pest before it could transit. Once the scout was in subspace, *Urethar* was doomed. If he were Terr, he would abandon the blisters and run, but he knew the M-1 commander would never do that. No Fleet commander ever would and the realization sat heavy with him.

Total warfare...

Urethar swung to its new course and boosted.

* * *

In the tactical plot, Terr saw the raider's energy bloom brighten as it changed course. He saw it close with the carrier at 7,600 tps and didn't like any of it. Staring grimly at the plot, he grappled with the realization that the raider's superior secondary drive would force him to do something that until a moment ago, he firmly believed was impossible. He would have to abandon retrieving the remaining blisters.

With the second blister locked to *Sheeva's* docking port, running at a paltry 600 tps toward a third blister, they might as well have been stationary for all the good it did them. Terr glanced at the range plot and ground his teeth in frustration. The raider was getting awfully close.

"You have a message," the computer announced suddenly and Terr swore. "Do you wish to view message?"

There were only two people who could reach him. Right now, he didn't want to talk to either of them.

"Open channel," he said.

Hiragawan's stern black features scowled in the display plate and his little red eyes glared.

"Agent Terrllss-rr, what in the pits do you think you're doing pursuing a raider?"

"Doing my job…sir."

"Your job does not include engaging raiders!"

"It does when it could be Tanard."

"And you intend to face him with an M-1? Don't be a fool! You will break off and—"

"I am aware of the tactical situation. Do you have anything specific for me? I'm a bit busy right now."

"I gave you an order, Mister! Break off—"

Terr touched a pad and cut contact. Idiot!

"Target one within L-band acquisition lock," the computer said with infuriating calmness. "Range, 137,600 talans. Firing point in eleven seconds." This took into account the apparent maximum firing distance of 52,000 talans.

Terr savagely stabbed the comms pad. "Dhar! Talk to me."

"Survivors aboard. About to jettison the blister."

"L-band lock established. Firing point in eight seconds," the computer said remorselessly.

"Then get rid of the damned thing. We're leaving…Computer, emergency transit, now!"

The cable-tube opened and a second later Thoran thrust his enraged face at Terr.

"What in the pits are you talking about transiting, Mister! I still have eleven men out there."

"And I've got my mission!" Terr snarled. "Which is far more important than your eleven men."

Thoran pulled back in outrage. "I'll have you broken for this, you lousy coward! I never thought I'd live to see a Fleet officer derelict in his duty to men in distress."

"And I'm not a Fleet officer!" Terr snapped, his eyes glued on the main reactor power curve. He'd had enough bureaucratic crap already and was in no mood for more.

Come *on* Nightwings!

"Survival blister detached," the computer said at last.

A precious second was lost while the computer waited for the empty blister to clear. Even this miniscule gravitational disruption induced by the blister's mass was enough to prevent the formation of the distortion torus.

"Initiating transition."

Terr was furious with himself. He should have transited with the blister attached. It would have cost him marginal boost performance, but he would have evaded the raider. Too late for that now.

The transition field wrapped *Sheeva* in a cocoon of energy, but the computer left it a fraction of a second late. As the distortion field torus stabilized, *Urethar* flashed past the M-1 and fired at point-blank range: 26,000 talans. *Sheeva* vanished in a glaring flash of blue-white light and the distortion field immediately failed in a forced collapse as the field overloaded from *Urethar's* burst. The M-1 was in subspace less than a second, but

154

the jump threw them almost twenty million talans from *Urethar.*

Sheeva shuddered as it dropped normal and the restraining field snapped on to protect the ship's frail human cargo. Terr groaned as the field gripped him. It held him for two long seconds of eternity before the computer decided it was safe to release him. His left leg went into a spasm and sharp pain raced up his spine and left side. He slumped forward and massaged his ribs. They didn't feel broken, but breathing was painful. The pain in his leg receded to a dull throb. Nightwings!

Cursing, Thoran grabbed the armrest of the right couch and heaved himself up.

"What happened?"

"The raider fired on us as we transited," Terr said, checking the displays. He wanted to rush to his brother, but there were things he needed to do first.

"And induced a forced collapse. That's great. What now?"

"We find out how bad it is. Computer, status?"

"Operating on secondary reticulation systems only. Reinitializing primary drive reaction chamber. Precursor field test required due to damaged bus nodes induced by the forced collapse. Autonomous repair system active."

"State time to availability of primary drive."

"One hour fifty-six minutes."

"Status of target one?"

"Target one closing at 7,600 talans per second. IP in thirty-seven minutes at forty-one seconds if *Sheeva* doesn't maneuver."

Thoran hissed, his tongue getting a workout. "At least something went right for you. The canal worm cannot transit to close."

Even with computer control, it was impossible to regulate the distortion torus to such a fine tolerance required for a twenty million-talan jump. When transiting it was generally assumed one wanted to get much farther.

"Computer, go to three-quarter secondary boost away

from target one, then raise SSF *Kriva* and transmit my authentication and clearance codes."

"Acknowledged."

"Command deck?"

"That's my First," Thoran hissed.

Terr jabbed the comms pad. "Command deck."

"Better get down here, sir. It's your friend."

A cold lump formed in Terr's chest and he felt a numbing heaviness press on him. He knew something bad had happened down there. There was a familiar rusty, metallic taste in his mouth as a wave of nausea swept through his body. His left leg gave a twinge.

"Stand by," he whispered hoarsely.

The main display plate cleared and a young Master Scout raised an inquiring eyebrow.

"Mr. Terrllss-rr? I am Hvar, SSF M-4 *Kriva*. Pardon me for saying so, but you look like hell."

"That's yet to be unleashed," Terr said bluntly, wanting badly to rush down to Dhar.

"You don't happen to be calling about VLBC *Kalnar*, are you?"

"*Kalnar* is destroyed and the raider is about to do the same to me."

Hvar squinted. "You cannot transit?"

"I was picking up the VLBC's crew when the raider attacked and induced a forced collapse."

"How long do you have?"

"At three-quarter boost, one hour and twenty-nine minutes."

"You *want* him to pursue?"

"That's right. The raider has a power curve advantage over me, but if I go to full boost now, he might lose interest and break off. I cannot let him do that."

"I won't be able to reach you before he closes," Hvar warned.

"You won't have to. In one hour, I am going full gain. That will stretch out his closure time. If he has any kind of sensor suite, he'll detect you when you get within two point-two lights or so. Once that happens, I'll be the last thing on his mind. Even if he transits, with your speed advantage, he'll be yours. And Master Scout? I don't want him destroyed. Is that clear?"

"Copy that. Is there something I should know about this particular raider?"

"It could be Kai Tanard."

"Tanard!" Hvar's lips curled in a sneer. *My old friend...* "I can see now why you're keen to get him. Very well. I will close with you at max boost."

The comms plate turned gray. Terr slumped back onto the couch and rubbed the scar above his eyebrow. He had put on a brave face before Hvar, but if the raider decided to continue his pursuit when *Kriva* came within his detection range, *Sheeva* could be in deep trouble. Well, nothing to be done about that now.

As Terr stood up, Thoran grabbed his arm and spun him around.

"All right, Mister. What in the pits is going on around here?"

Terr was in no mood for explanations right then, but he understood the pilot's pique.

"I guess you deserve some kind of an answer. As you've probably guessed, I am engaged on a mission to track down raiders who are plundering Kaleen shipping lanes and causing a lot of political embarrassment on Captal and not a little concern on Anar'on."

"Hah! I never figured you for an engineer anyway. Is that why you and Mr. Dharaklin stayed behind the last time? To capture that raider?"

"That's right."

"This time, it looks like they have captured *you*. And who the hell is Tanard?"

"You don't want to get involved in this."

"I've had my ship blown up by those scum. I would say that makes me involved. Wouldn't you?"

Terr looked hard at the Karkan. "Okay. Tanard is a renegade Fleet officer—"

"And he is raiding Kaleen shipping?"

"That's our guess, yes. But he's only one part of a much larger operation we're conducting against raiders in general."

"But he is the one causing all the embarrassment, right?"

"Master Pilot, you understand that everything you have seen or heard is subject to the Nondisclosure Act."

Thoran snorted, his tongue flicking. "You don't have to quote regulations to me, son. I used to be a marine."

"Then sit tight. I need to go below."

Terr strode to the cable-tube, leaving Thoran staring after him. The hatch closed with a hiss and he locked his jaw. The fingers of his right hand tapped against his leg. A hollow knot formed in his stomach and he tensed.

Nightwings!

His brother was hurt, he knew it. The thought of Dhar lying on a hard deck, torn and bleeding, was like a spike that throbbed through his body. It was as if a piece of himself had been ripped open. His left leg tingled.

The hatch opened. He stepped out and hurried toward the emergency docking bay. Two of *Kalnar's* ratings blocked the entrance. One of them saw Terr and pulled back his companion. Terr stopped at the hatchway.

Dhar was lying on the deck moaning softly. Dark blood stained his left leg and the deck around it. There seemed to be an awful lot of it. One crewman held his legs firmly pressed down while another was tying a crude bandage around the torn thigh. The stench of congealing blood hung heavy in the air.

Terr hurried toward Dhar and knelt beside him. Dhar's face was pale and glistened with sweat. Terr automatically wiped the drawn, clammy features. Dhar moaned at the touch, but showed no sign of consciousness. Terr looked at the man beside him.

"I was *Kalnar's* medic," the man explained.

"What happened?" Terr heard himself say in a strange voice devoid of all emotion.

"When the raider fired on us, the restraining field failed. It threw us all about, but your friend got the worst of it. He was slammed against the hatchway and suffered a compound leg fracture and broken ribs. The fracture is bad as the thigh bone penetrated the skin, tearing muscle, nerves, and gods know what else along the way. I have a bandage around it, but he is still bleeding." The medic looked at Dhar and frowned. "And there could be possible internal injuries. He could die if he doesn't get immediate expert attention."

The words twisted the inside of Terr's stomach. He gripped Dhar's left hand and squeezed.

Nightwings!

"Have you set the bones?"

"They're back in place, but that's only an emergency fix."

Terr shifted slightly and stared at the bloody bandage. "Take that off," he commanded.

The medic stared and his mouth opened in protest, but he didn't say anything. Slowly, he undid the bandage.

Terr saw the jagged tear in the trouser leg and the ragged flesh underneath. Thick blood welled from the raw wound and flowed freely down the side of the leg. The smell was heavy and cloying and he swallowed heavily. After a moment, he took a deep breath and set his teeth. This was no time to get squeamish. He grasped the edges of the bloody, soaked trouser and pulled. The material resisted, then gave way with a sharp rasp. He wiped away the trail of blood, placed his hands on the wound and waited for Death's touch.

It began with a tingle in his middle that spread through him in a wave of heat and throbbing power. He felt himself grow and the room shrank around him. Detached and above the pain of mortals, he could see himself bent over Dhar's body. The sensation of duality faded, but he still felt the union with the god. It was a heady feeling. He knew himself to be a mere mortal, but in Death's shadow, with the power coursing through him, he felt by reaching out, he could shape reality. He shrugged and heard thunder roll across red dunes. An amber sun burned hot on his cheek.

Dhar's blood pulsed warm under his hands. Small blue lightnings slithered up his arms and he heard startled gasps behind him. The lightnings crackled and his hands were wrapped in blue radiance. He closed his eyes and concentrated. After a moment, he sensed the lightning flash and felt the heat sear blood and open flesh. Dhar jerked under him and gave a strangled scream.

Terr opened his eyes and pulled back his hands. The wound was burnt brown, but it did not bleed. He looked at the medic.

"Take him to the infirmary, next deck up. Third hatch on the starboard side."

"How…" the medic started, but something in Terr's dark gray eyes stopped him. He motioned to two of the ratings who looked at Terr with awe and fear before stepping gingerly around him.

Terr stood to allow the ratings to pick up Dhar. He looked down where the little blue sparks still slithered over his hands and gave a long exhale. With a shudder, he let go and the power drained from him, leaving him hollow and incomplete.

He followed the medic and the ratings to the cable-tube. On the upper deck, he hurried to open the infirmary. The room smelled of antiseptic, medicines and dark memories. They laid Dhar on the single bunk and faded as the medic jerked his head at them. Terr did not see them go. He crouched before the labeled cabinet drawers and frowned, then pulled one open. Stacked neatly side by side were small black and orange vials. He took one of each and held them to the medic.

"Tailored nanobods and genotherapy starter sequencers."

"It will take more than that to save your friend, sir," the medic said.

"They will stabilize him, and that's what he needs now."

"What he needs is expert attention."

Terr knew what Dhar needed without being reminded.

"Look after him," he said and hurried out. In the corridor, he leaned against the bulkhead and absently rubbed the burning in his left leg. When the lightnings touched Dhar's wound, he felt them as if they had touched him. He wondered what his master Sidhara would say about that. Through his joining with Dhar, they shared everything, their memories becoming one. He had not expected that this link would also manifest itself in such an unexpected and physical fashion. Would the effect fade as Dhar's memories were slowly fading, becoming integrated with his own? It hadn't so far.

He recalled how he was shot two years ago on Earth during a clandestine mission to destroy an old C-32 scoutship. Did Dhar feel any sympathetic pain then? His brother never talked about it, considering it perhaps something too personal. Maybe they should discuss it.

It was an interesting symbiosis the people of the Saffal held with the gods of Athal Than.

He straightened and pulled down his tunic. It was only then that he noticed the blood on his hands and working grays. He hurried down the curving corridor and stopped before the hatch to his quarters. He extended a finger and touched the glowing amber pad. A muddy yellow stain smeared the pad when he pulled back his finger. He strode in and headed for the washroom. The ceiling automatically lit as he entered.

He washed his hands, splashed cold water over his face and looked at himself in the wide mirror. The eyes were remote, expressionless and cold. The scar above his left eyebrow was a faint white line. A rebellious lock of black hair teased the right side of his forehead. After a moment, he dried himself and strode out. In the mirror, he saw something he wasn't sure he liked. He had seen determination, a resolution that meant stepping on a path fraught with peril, not only for himself physically, but for his soul. His master would most certainly not approve of this resolution. Right then, Terr didn't care for his master's approval. He had played by the rules and those rules might end up costing Nightwings his life. He had the power to influence reality around him. If that meant unleashing the lightnings to right some of the wrongs, or spill the blood of raider scum, politically motivated or not, so be it, and the *Saftara* be damned. The scum were not worth one drop of Dhar's blood, or anyone else's.

Ponderous forces shifted within him and he accepted the burden.

Thoran swiveled his chair when he heard the tube hatch open. His tongue flicked as he regarded the young officer. Congealed blood stained the front of his tunic and there was a cold determination in Terr's eyes that brooked no interference. They were also old eyes, eyes that had seen things beyond his years. Thoran wondered what made those eyes so old, but he wasn't about to ask. He could be answered and he wasn't sure he wanted to know the answer.

Terr checked the displays and took the central command couch. Only nineteen minutes had passed since he went down, but they seemed like an eternity. Without looking at Thoran, he settled down to wait.

* * *

Ver Dit drummed the armrest, his fingers restless, reflecting his unease. The M-1 was fleeing, but it was only at three-quarter boost. That worried him. Why didn't the scout run at full boost? It was clear his fire had damaged the scout's drive, probably induced a forced collapse. That might account for his reduced speed. Should it? What worried him was the unknown factor. When the VLBC sent an all-ships signify, it was possible that a powerful Fleet unit was even now closing on his position. He was also worried that he didn't know what exchange the M-1 commander might have had, or is having, with that Fleet vessel—if he established contact at all. Too many variables and none of them favorable to him. His tactical instinct told him again to break off. Destruction of the M-1 was not worth risking his command. He had achieved his objective and pursuing the scout may be prosecuting total warfare beyond sound tactical doctrine. His mission was to survive and hunt down Kaleen targets. Then again, was he being overly cautious and suspicious?

And if he couldn't evade the M-1?

His fingers tapped on the armrest. Enough of this!

"Plot! Prepare to transit—"

"Anomaly track identified as an M-4 cruiser," the computer stated indifferently and Ver Dit's blood turned cold. "Range, two point-four light-years. Speed, one point-six lph. Time to intercept, one hour and thirty-five minutes under current flight parameters. Designating as target three."

A ripple of whispered comments raced around the command deck. The exec looked up and Ver Dit saw the resignation in his eyes. *Urethar* was dead. Even if they transited right now the M-4's speed advantage made the brutal end inevitable. He was certain it would be brutal. There would be no mercy shown by the M-4. He only hoped it would be quick. Did the M-1 commander deliberately lure him into a pursuit only to suck him up against the M-4? Ver Did was convinced of it.

Pits!

"Time to intercept target two?" he asked quietly, his fingers frozen above the armrest.

"Sixty-two minutes," the exec responded gravely.

Ver Dit nodded. The M-1 had pulled a sucker's move and he'd fallen for it. He recalled Le Maran's instructions in the event of capture and his mouth shifted in a grim smile. Blowing himself up was simply not an option. He would stand and fight, no matter what. It was a far more honorable end, if honor there was in this. Who knows? A lucky shot could make all the difference between destruction and escape. He wasn't fooling himself. He had commanded an M-4 and knew how slim his chances were of evading the coming deadly embrace.

Two missions, one kill. A fine epitaph for his career as a raider. He wondered if it had been worth it, then decided probably not. He pressed a pad on the armrest control panel.

"Engineering?"

"Engineering, aye."

"Boost to one hundred and ten percent."

There was a slight hesitation. "One hundred and ten percent, aye."

"Comms? File a sitrep with Khiman-ra."

His fingers resumed their tapping.

* * *

"He increased boost the minute I was acquired," Master Scout Hvar said.

Terr nodded. "I saw. Boost to one hundred and ten percent and close on him."

"You're shaving things pretty close, Mister. He could overstress his drive and get to you before I can intercept. He's got nothing to lose now."

"I can still go to full boost myself," Terr said patiently. Wasn't that clear to Hvar? "When you do close with him, remember, I want him disabled, not destroyed."

"That might not be easy to do," Hvar said. The glint in his eyes betrayed the anticipation of a kill. It was only a lousy raider, but it all looked good in a service record. If it *was* Tanard, it would look *very* good in his service record.

Terr leaned forward and glared. "Master Scout, if you destroy that raider, I will see to it that you never command a ship again. I'll break you. You'll be begging your food from a gutter!

Do I make myself clear?"

Hvar's face turned to stone. Who did the little shit think he was talking to? He had checked Terr's service record and knew the boy was only a First Scout, but those authentication codes were formidable and left him little choice. In the end, he gave a jerky nod. There were ways of evening things out.

"I will carry out your instructions...sir! But if this ends up costing the life of even one of my men—"

"I don't care if your ship is crippled! I want that raider," Terr snarled and cut contact. Staring at the gray display plate, he leaned back and sighed. Another macho M-4 driver interested in a kill, blind to the bigger picture. The man was a fool.

Rit!

He smiled then, wondering if his superiors saw him in the same light when he was driving an M-3. It was droll to observe himself from the other side of the table. Had he changed that much?

"Pushing a bit hard, weren't you, son?" Thoran growled and Terr looked at him, his expression indifferent.

"He is a tool. A means to an end, that's all."

"You want that raider bad, don't you?"

"He is only a means to another end."

"Is that all that really matters? Ends and means?"

Terr's face drained and his heart hammered. "My brother is lying on a slab below because of that scum out there—"

"Your brother?" Thoran hissed in disbelief.

"That raider and the people who stand behind him are responsible. They're not worth one drop of his blood, let alone his life. I have a mission, but they didn't tell me how I was to execute it. Pissing off that M-4 driver to do it won't keep me awake at night."

Thoran shook his head and grinned. "It won't do much for your career either."

Terr snorted. "Like I give a damn."

The cable-tube hatch hissed open. The rating hesitated

when he saw Terr, then hurried to Thoran. He leaned over and whispered something in Thoran's ear. Thoran gasped and his head jerked. The rating gave Terr a frightened glance and retreated into the tube.

"Is it true?" Thoran asked after a moment of uncomfortable silence.

"That I walk in the shadow of Death? It's true," Terr said heavily.

"A Wanderer Discipline adept," Thoran whispered and sighed, his tongue running in a blur from his mouth. "I have heard of it, but I always considered it an old woman's fable, but you're not a Wanderer…"

Terr didn't say anything.

"If you have that kind of power, why don't you simply reach out and crush the raider? It would save everybody a lot of angst."

Terr chuckled. "That part *is* an old woman's fable. Even if I could do it, I wouldn't."

"Yes, you mission."

"That's right. My mission." Terr tapped a pad on the armrest console and sat back. The command deck darkened. It was almost a cocoon where he could think and keep the outside at bay, if for but a moment. A pad winked and changed color; otherwise it was quiet. There was a soft background whisper of machinery and life support, but these were comfortable sounds. Only if one of them failed would the fact register consciously.

Terr allowed himself to drift. There wasn't much thinking to be done right now. He was in a set-piece engagement and if everybody played out their role, he would have his raider. Then what? That part was rather vague. One way or another, he intended to get the necessary information he wanted. Take the crew to Kalakan? A waste of effort. Besides, his method of extracting information would save time for everyone. The prospect of using his aspect to intimidate, and if necessary, go further with a raider crewman, left him cold and unmoved. He did not hate. It was more like brushing away an irritating insect.

The road he proposed to walk was filled with shadow and chaos and he accepted the danger. Where the words of the *Saftara* failed him, he would have to write his own.

He tapped another pad.

"Infirmary," the medic answered.

"Any change?" Terr asked and a tingle ran up his left leg.

"He's coming around."

Terr got up and walked into the tube. When the hatch opened one deck down, a few short strides got him to the infirmary. Dhar had a dark blue blanket draped over him and there was color on his drawn brown face. His eyes flickered and he blinked before they focused on Terr.

"Sankri…"

Terr glanced at the medic and the man walked out. He looked at his brother, smiled and moved to the bed. He grasped Dhar's right hand and squeezed.

"Nightwings…"

"What happened?" Dhar rumbled, his voice faltering.

"A hatch got in your way. Don't worry, you didn't damage it."

"I am relieved." Dhar tried to move his left leg and winced, then gasped when he turned his body slightly. "I don't seem to have been as fortunate."

"Rest," Terr said soothingly and patted his shoulder. "You'll be good as new as soon as the M-4 closes with us."

"And the raider?"

"We have him."

Dhar lifted his head and listened to the background noises. "We are running from him?"

"There is nothing to worry about, Nightwings. Really."

"Sankri, I see the fires of Death in your eyes," Dhar whispered fiercely. "Beware of temptation, my brother."

Terr's face was expressionless. "We shall talk later," he said and gently pulled back his hand.

"Sankri…"

Terr paused in the hatchway and looked back. "It is a fitting thing I do," he said harshly and walked out.

Dhar stared at the empty hatchway, his heart heavy with dark foreboding.

* * *

"Target three has increased boost," the computer stated. "Time to intercept, forty-eight minutes at present closure rate."

The M-4 commander in a hurry to get it over with, was that it? Ver Dit allowed himself a moment of sardonic amusement. All in good time, sir.

"Message from *Lahra*, sir," the comms watchstander announced.

Ver Dit nodded and looked at the main display plate. When it cleared, he wasn't surprised to see Tanard's scarred face. They stared at each other for a few seconds. What was there to say that could make a difference, and Ver Dit did not care for empty platitudes or sanctimonious consolations right now.

"Friend Ver Dit, you seem to be in an invidious predicament," Tanard rasped at length.

"I would be happy to exchange places with you," Ver Dit said and Tanard chuckled.

"No doubt. You cannot allow yourself to be taken."

Ver Dit's tongue flicked across his mouth. "I will do what is necessary."

Tanard stared, then gave a jerky nod. "I could order you to break off, but it's far too late for that, even if you could. Can you overhaul the M-1?"

"I'll have L-band firing lock in four minutes."

"Unless he increases boost. He might not be as wounded as he appears."

"The thought had occurred to me."

"Terr is a very unusual and capable officer, friend Ver Dit."

"You know of him?"

"We had an encounter. Two to be precise."

"Ah. He was responsible for your capture?"

Tanard set his jaw. "He has lured you into a trap. Not your fault, of course, but you'll never reach him. Is there any way at all you can evade?"

"I can't," Ver Dit said without emotion. "I'm committed. I cannot even launch my blisters. There is nowhere for them to hide. If I can eliminate the M-1, my destruction will not be a total loss."

Tanard nodded. "You will engage the M-4?"

"I might get lucky."

"You cannot allow yourself to be taken," Tanard repeated, this time with frigid authority.

"The idea doesn't hold much appeal for me either."

"Very well then. Good hunting."

Ver Dit grunted as the plate turned gray. It would be good hunting, but he won't be the one doing it. He waited as the seconds counted down. Had Tanard seen the resignation in his eyes?

"Computer, time to intercept target two?" he asked.

"Three minutes and fifteen seconds."

"Engineering? Boost to one hundred and fifteen percent."

"We're overstressing the drive now!"

"Blast the damn drive!"

There was dark muttering from below, followed by a re-signed sigh.

"Going to one hundred and fifteen percent."

Urethar surged, only to see the M-1 compensate by increasing boost a few seconds later. Ver Dit's smile was grim. So, Tanard was right. First Scout Terrllss-rr *was* an unusual officer. He wondered if fates had destined that they should meet.

They ran in silence for thirty-six minutes. *Sheeva* was so tantalizingly close, yet beyond his reach.

"Target three has dropped normal," the computer stated. "Range, 116,000 talans. K-band acquisition lock established. Target has raised primary and secondary shield grids. L-band firing lock established. Target three's shields pulsing in preparatory firing phase."

Ver Dit glanced at the exec. "Go to primary alert and ready the projector."

Detached from the action, he admired the professionalism and precision of the M-4's approach. Dropping normal within 140,000 talans off *Urethar* had brought the M-4 into immediate firing position. It was a superb example of precision piloting. Even *Urethar's* 200 tps secondary drive speed advantage was useless to help him now.

"Raider vessel. This is SSF M-4 *Kriva*. You are ordered to shut down all drive reactors and assume neutral position or I will fire on you."

"Turn into him," Ver Dit ordered, wanting to present a minimal aspect to *Kriva*. It was futile, but he had to do it. "Make ready to engage."

Even as *Urethar* started its swing, *Kriva* fired. The traversing beam of yellow ionization left by the 128 TeV burst intersected *Urethar's* position and its shields scintillated in a cascade of orange-white discharges. The secondary shield grid failed under the assault, flickered and died. *Kriva* fired again and the burst tore through the primary shield grid, *Urethar's* defensive grid never designed to stand up against a Fleet warship. Jagged back-surges licked along the rear part of the hull and the energy discharge made the thin plating glow. The hull composite was commercial grade, not military, and ablated under the bombardment.

Urethar completed its swing and rushed at its tormentor. It was a wasted gesture. *Kriva* shifted and continued to pour fire into *Urethar's* stern.

A section of the rear hull softened and the material began to flow and bulge from internal air pressure. The plating blew out in a puff of crystals and debris that left scimitars of frozen hull reaching into space. *Urethar* shuddered as the decompression shockwave boomed through the breached cargo compartment. A pressure door failed to close, jammed in its slides by the roaring tornado of air that forced itself from the adjoining section. This only added to the enormous strain on the already weakened structural frames.

With the hull breached, *Kriva's* continued fire devoured the outer plating, vaporized interior bulkheads and melted support frames. Sealed compartments ruptured in cascade failure until the entire rear section of the ship, over one hundred and twenty katalans, finally tore off, trailing cables, hull plating, deck frames, and cargo. The shock rippled through the rest of the hull and the entire ship groaned in protest. Its structural integrity compromised, the delicate balances of the drive reactor assemblies were forced out of alignment. The computer immediately initiated an emergency reactor shutdown.

Urethar drifted, driven by the residual momentum of its dash to close with *Kriva*.

Ver Dit saw the sudden flicker of touch-sensitive pads on the engineering panel turn white and felt the ship die under him. A moment later the deck shuddered and he could hear the agonized screech of tearing metal and hull plating. He didn't have to hear the computer's dispassionate voice to know *Urethar* was mortally wounded.

"No casualties reported from the rear section," the exec said and Ver Dit nodded. "Bruises and broken bones, that's all."

"We've been lucky," Ver Dit mused, if one can consider this as luck. His fingers still over the armrest panel, he searched the exec's face. It betrayed nothing. Regret, perhaps?

"Computer. Initiate the self-destruct sequence. Authorization: alpha, two, two, primary, zero, enable."

Watchstanders gaped at him.

"Self-destruct not functioning."

Ver Dit nodded and pressed a pad on his armrest console. "Engineering?"

"Engineering, aye."

"Mr. Trip, can you disable the safety interlocks on the main reactor containment field?"

There was a pause. "That would initiate a chained failure. The reactor would go critical."

"That's right."

"Respectfully, sir, I refuse. I don't mind dying for the cause, but I'm damned if I'll kill myself for it."

"That's mutiny, Mister!"

"That's right, sir. It is."

Ver Dit tapped the armrest and slowly swept his eyes around the deck. Every one of them told him the same thing. He glanced at the exec, then looked at the comms watchstander.

"Open a channel to *Kriva*."

When the full-dimensional display plate cleared, he didn't hesitate.

"SSF *Kriva*, I surrender my ship." The harsh words were lumps of stone and each weighed on his chest. He had never lost a command before and the unexpected wave of emotion made him swallow hard. There was no sympathy in the *Kriva* commander's stare, only frosty contempt. Ver Dit expected little else.

"Raider vessel, retract your projector dome."

"I cannot do that," Ver Dit piped and bobbed his head. "I have lost all power. Running on emergency backup only."

"Discharge your coils."

Ver Dit nodded in admiration. *Kriva's* commander was sharp. Although *Urethar* was no longer under power, the weapons pod was fully charged and ready for action. It still held a full fifty-two TeV burst that could cause significant damage to an unprotected hull, should the M-4 be foolish enough to close within his firing envelope. Ver Dit nodded to the exec. A moment later the projector dome glowed a dull orange and the weapons pod discharged in a silent crackle of arcing lightning.

"Stand by to be boarded," *Kriva's* commander added. "If you offer any resistance, I'll not hesitate to execute every one of you on the spot. Do I make myself clear?"

Ver Dit never doubted the Master Scout would do exactly that. He didn't particularly relish what he and the rest of his crew faced at the hands of Fleet interrogators, prison on Cantor or even execution, but those were imponderables. Until then, he would still be alive, and that was eminently preferable to the alternative of immediate self-annihilation. His failure to comply with Tanard's last order could now conceivably compromise Khiman-ra, but he accepted that without qualm. In that, he also accepted that he had betrayed Tanard's trust.

His failure was now complete.

"There will be no resistance, Master Scout," he said quietly and settled back to wait as the plate turned gray.

After a tense moment the exec cleared his throat.

"Sir?"

"I know," Ver Dit said. "You may proceed to purge the computer."

* * *

Terr detached from the M-4 and allowed *Sheeva* to drift away from the parked warship and down toward the raider. In seconds *Kriva's* black hull vanished against the background of spattered stars.

He marveled at the awesome sculpture of torn hull as the ship maneuvered to dock with the looming shape. In its way the mangled structure had a kind of terrifying beauty, which the hand of destruction seemed to always leave behind where it touched. The sight repelled him, but he could not help stare at the dark gaping holds as they drifted past him. In a burst of startled insight, he realized that the lust to destroy and the desire to see the frozen pain of its passing could become addictive. It was a sobering revelation.

Was the byproduct of sentience and the imperative to survive automatically translated into warfare? He had no ready answer.

Sheeva stopped and extended an access tube. It mated with the raider hatch and locked. Terr set his mouth and stood up.

"What happens now?" Thoran demanded, not sure he liked what he saw in those gray eyes. Terr looked at him.

"That depends on what the raider pilot has to say."

Three short strides took him to the cable-tube and he stepped in. On the main deck, he opened the access tube hatch and walked briskly along the four-katalan-long tube. At the other end, he thumbed an amber pad. It blinked and the hatch slid back. A marine guard brought his worn rifle across his chest and stood to.

"This way, sir," he growled and Terr followed the tall, imposing figure.

The cable-tube whispered to itself as it went up. Hands clamped behind his back, Terr waited, his face impassive. Like the eye of a storm, his calm was just as fragile and just as deceptive. Poised on a knife's edge of raging emotions, he had to maintain a well of stillness or the forces churning inside him would plunge him instantly into a lust of uncontrolled annihilation. That would be a fate infinitely more terrible than mere insanity.

'In the shadow of Death I walk and do my god's bidding for righteousness' sake.'

He didn't know why those particular words came to him, but perhaps those who wrote the *Saftara* had known someone like him before and recorded the deed.

Very well. *I shall walk with thee, O Death, and let us find some righteousness.*

174

The power settled on him and he stood in its shadow.

The hatch opened and Terr automatically looked around. The layout could have been any commercial carrier. He could be standing on *Kalnar's* command deck. Two Fleet ratings were checking the failed and partially active control panels. Three burly marines, their rifles held leveled, stood guard over five men whom Terr presumed to be the raider's command crew.

The marine beside the hatch stood to as Terr stepped out of the tube. A tall Master Scout walked up to him and nodded.

"Mr. Terrllss-rr?"

Terr looked past him at the prisoners. An elderly Palean slowly lifted his head and they locked eyes. Terr instantly recognized the military bearing and command presence. Another Fleet traitor. Another Tanard.

"Is he the raider pilot?" he asked without looking at Hvar.

"He's not your concern anymore," Hvar said sternly, sensing he was about to lose control of the situation. "Or this hull. Both are now under Fleet jurisdiction. I told you not to bother coming!"

Terr felt a ripple of power course through his body. It felt good and comforting. So, this puny mortal would stand in his way? He turned, his lips a tight line.

"Master Scout Hvar, I am indebted to you for getting me out of a tight situation and for treating my associate. Your professionalism in retrieving Pilot Thoran's two remaining survival blisters shall be noted in my report. I suggest you don't want to tarnish anything I might say in that report through a misguided impression that somehow you're in charge here." Terr's half smile didn't touch his eyes.

The marines barely glanced at each other.

Hvar felt his face drain as Terr's cold words slammed into him. To be humiliated like this before his men was intolerable. He wanted to physically assault the little twerp and have him thrown into the brig. Two things held him in check. The Diplomatic Branch shit had the authority to do what he said. There was no way of getting around those infuriating authentication codes without incurring the full wrath of COMPALOPS. The other thing that held him rooted was the almost tangible power that seemed to surround the young officer. There was something about it that made Hvar very uneasy.

If the Diplomatic Branch wanted jurisdiction, Terr was welcome to it.

"Very well, *sir*. I am at your disposal."

Terr watched the play of emotions on Hvar's face and almost smiled. It was all about career point scoring. In that, Thoran was right. Terr didn't give a damn about playing that game. Still, he could soothe Hvar's wounded pride. After all, he had to work with the prickly bastard.

"I appreciate that and I apologize for my abrupt manner. I've had a tense few hours."

Studying Terr's calm, assured bearing, Hvar didn't believe a word of it, but was smart enough to recognize a peace offering. They needed each other, for now.

"I understand." And he did.

"You can have this hulk and its crew as soon as I'm finished with them," Terr said. "Which shouldn't take very long if they cooperate. You can destroy the hull in place or tow it to Kalakan, your intended destination, I assume?"

"That's right."

"Excellent. If you would care to contact Master Scout Li Aron, I'm sure he will make all necessary preparations to receive you. "

Hvar squinted in an effort to mask his surprise. Li Aron was marked for flag rank some time back and was due to get his promotion and posting to COMPALOPS on completion of his current assignment. Could that assignment involve the Diplomatic Branch and its hunt for Kaleen raiders? Terr was moving in rarified circles indeed.

"This appears to be part of a larger operation, even if we didn't get Tanard," he said cautiously.

"You may get your chance at Tanard yet, Master Scout," Terr said indifferently and pointed at the elderly Palean. "Bring him to me."

Hvar nodded to one of the guards who motioned with his rifle.

The Palean stood before Terr, not defiant, but with poise and assurance. Terr had seen his kind in many places, on many planets. The Paleans wore their uniform like a cloak to protect them from feeling, from seeing the outside, and of course, to keep themselves in. A uniform was also a cloak of power that magnified the image of the one wearing it. Well, this Palean wasn't wearing his uniform now, but then, neither was Terr. As for power, he would show the raider pilot its meaning.

The Palean raised his head and met Terr's gaze.

"Tanard has told me something of you, Mr. Terrllss-rr," Ver Dit piped and bobbed his head. His fingers were still.

Intentionally or unintentionally the raider's simple words told Terr a lot. Tanard *had* set himself up with a base and was running raids against Kaleen shipping and at least one ship was prowling. Used to, he reminded himself.

As if realizing what he said, the Palean grinned and shook his head.

"Formidable."

"And you are?" Terr asked.

"Ver Dit, pilot of what's left of this ship."

"I want an answer to one question," Terr said softly, his eyes boring into the Palean's black pits. "Your base."

Ver Dit allowed himself a small smile. The young man didn't wear a uniform, but he had seen too many men in uniform not to recognize an officer out of one. The boy was Intelligence then, probably the Fleet's Internal Operations Division. He had watched how Terr handled Hvar and was not about to make the same mistake. The boy was naïve if he really expected him to answer.

"Even if I knew where it was, I wouldn't tell you," he said and watched the young man nod.

Terr pointed at one of the raider watchstanders and motioned to the guard. The rating slowly walked over, stopped and glanced nervously at Ver Dit.

"Your station?" Terr asked mildly.

"Comms watch."

Terr looked at Ver Dit. "I'll kill this man where he stands if you don't tell me what I want to know."

"You mean you'll order one of the guards to shoot him," Ver Dit remarked with a sneer. He expected better from the young man.

"I meant exactly what I said," Terr told him and felt the power shift into his arms. "The base."

"I have nothing to tell you," Ver Dit said and clasped his hands behind his back.

Without taking his eyes off the raider, Terr raised his right arm. Blue light crawled over his hand. There were startled gasps around him and one marine shifted his rifle.

"Stand to!" Hvar roared in shocked surprise and everyone froze.

Terr didn't hear him. His eyes still focused on Ver Dit, he grasped the rating's shoulder. Small lightnings danced from his hand and slithered over the startled Palean. He gave a silent scream, jerked once and collapsed to the deck. Terr slowly lowered his arm.

Ver Dit stood in astonishment, not quite sure he believed what just happened. He wasn't shocked that his comms watchstander was dead. Every one of them had known that death faced them when they landed at Khiman-ra. To see it meted out through the hand of a Wanderer, for Terr *had* to be a Wanderer, made his skin prickle. He gave an involuntary shudder.

Hvar stood there gaping at the contorted body on the deck and felt his face grow hot. He grabbed Terr's arm and spun him around.

"What in the pits do you think you're doing?" he roared in outrage. "This is murder!"

Terr shook him off. "You can thank your gods for their mercy, Master Scout, and for your life. Touch me again at your peril. Stand back and don't interfere."

"There is due process, you maniac!"

"And I am exercising it."

Hvar shook a stiff finger in Terr's face. "This is not the end of it."

The marines stood uneasily and looked at each other. They were not sure what just happened, but one thing was clear. The strange civilian had touched one of the raider crew and the man was dead. No one was about to make a rash move until Master Scout Hvar told them to, and it appeared their commander was equally reluctant to be a hero.

"You do what you have to," Terr said, his voice cold and indifferent. He accepted that there would almost certainly be repercussions from this, not the least of him using his aspect. Right now, though, he had a job to do and if he managed to get something useful from the raider crew, the results would have justified his actions. In the end it was always the results that counted, right? Terr pushed back the doubts and the questions and pointed at another raider crewman.

"You! Station?"

The watchstander blanched and stared in panic at Ver Dit.

"Look at me!" Terr bellowed and the lightnings brightened as they moved along his arms.

The rating moaned and his eyes misted as he slowly turned his head. His hands worked in agitation, fingers locking.

"Weapons," he gulped in a tight squeak.

Terr locked eyes with Ver Dit. "Your base."

There was a terrible light in the young man's eyes and Ver Dit swallowed hard as he contemplated the face of Death. He did not doubt at all that he stood before Death and it would consume him and every one of his crew if he didn't answer.

"I don't know—"

Terr lifted his right arm and his fingers pointed at the raider rating. It happened so fast the rating hardly had time to lift his arms before his face and give a strangled scream of terror as a shaft of blue light struck him in the chest. There was a sharp crack of thunder, which made everyone cringe and the air smelled of ozone, burnt cloth and charred flesh.

An almost sexual thrill ran through Terr's body and he bathed in the glow of unleashed power. It was a giddy feeling and he watched dispassionately the mortals who stood before him, awaiting his judgment. He was Death and a shaper of reality. Those who opposed him would feel his wrath, but he didn't expect interference from these feeble creatures. They were nothing.

The rating stood there transfixed, mouth gaping as life faded from his eyes. The cloth in the center of his chest was burned away, the edges curled and black. The flesh around the deep dark hole was charred. Thick blood oozed from the raw wound. The rating took a step back and fell with a crash. The marine beside him twisted away smartly not to be felled himself.

Terr forced himself to swallow slowly and not gag at the cloying stench that hung in the air, his attention focused on Ver Dit. His display of raw power clearly shook the Palean, but was he ready to crack?

"Do I have to go on?"

Ver Dit locked his fingers in a tight clasp to stop them from fluttering in agitation. He no longer doubted Terr's resolve to kill every one of his crew, no matter what the consequences with the Internal Operations Division. Even if there were any, which he didn't believe, he suspected they would be irrelevant. After all, who cared what happened to a raider's life. As for his crew, he had no loyalty toward them. They were mercenaries, all of them, who sold themselves and their principles in order to practice their killing craft. Rejects or not, he could not stand idly by and watch them summarily killed. Did Tanard know what might happen if Ver Dit allowed himself to be taken? It hardly seemed possible.

Then again, perhaps he hadn't felt it necessary to explain.

"I cannot tell you what I don't know."

"Then start with what you *do* know," Terr said mildly, ready to unleash the lightnings. The power was strong within him and he felt detached and invulnerable. He wanted to raise his arms and let loose the hand of Death until there was nothing and no one left. The urge was powerful and his hands trembled. A low rumble bounced from bulkhead to bulkhead. He did not see heads turn to look at each other in awe and fear.

Ver Dit saw the coiled power held in check by Terr and gulped.

"I direct the computer to return to base and it gets me there."

"And you trashed the computer."

"I have."

"Inconvenient, but not terminal. Very well. I believe you. You really may not know the location of your base, but you know something that could be just as useful." Terr turned to look at Hvar and missed Ver Dit's puzzled look. "I want him interrogated, every one of them. Everything they can remember. From the color of the grass to what the sky looks like, night and day. Everything."

"It's not my job—" Hvar began, but Terr cut him off.

"I want timings. After lifting off their base, ask them how long it took to reach their cruising position. Ask about boost rates, anything to help us calculate distance."

Despite himself, Hvar was intrigued. "That won't give you direction, though."

"Not directly, I agree, but this also works in reverse. They had to have returned to their base at least once. If we can get a series of known starting positions—"

"We could run a triangulation plot," Hvar mused.

"That's right. One more thing. Only three people see your findings report. Master Scout Li Aron, agent Hiragawan, Diplomatic Branch, and myself. Are we clear?"

Any thoughts Hvar might have had to get even with Terr evaporated. The image of lightnings tearing through his body made his skin prickle. Terr was playing at a level Hvar didn't understand, and he was happy to leave him to it.

"Quite clear, sir."

"Let's get started." Terr said and allowed the tension to slip away. With an effort of will, he let go and the power drained from him, taking Death with it. It may have gone, but the stench of its presence still lingered over the two still bodies on the deck.

Nightwings, my brother of the night. If you only knew how it feels...

Chapter Five

"He had orders to self-destruct in the event of capture!" Le Maran spluttered in outrage. He was a split second away from slamming his fist against the desk. Instead, he clenched his fingers and glared.

"Even if he were able to, did you honestly expect him to do it?" Tanard remarked coldly. "I told you right away, friend Maran, that yours was a misguided policy."

"He willfully compromised our security!"

"I cannot argue with you there, but he doesn't really know anything. If he trashed his computer the damage should be minimal, unless Khiman-ra is more exposed than I was led to believe. Is it?"

"Of course not! No amount of casual observation by day or night can categorize its location. The facility is secure. Nothing comes in and no one goes out. You set the criteria yourself. The Alikan Union Party hasn't invested millions into this base only to have some simpleton identify it by a recognizable star pattern. The horizon distortion field makes sure of that."

Tanard wanted to agree with him, but no technology was fully secure. When it failed, it could be spectacular.

"Friend Maran, the AUP invested only enough to scrape by. However, I am not insensitive to your concern," he said reasonably. "But given enough information it's possible to locate anything. Granted, finding us might take some time, but time is one factor that's against us. If we lose another ship—"

"You are certain Ver Dit is lost?"

"Against an M-4? What do you think?"

"Pits! Khiman-ra has just gone operational. You cannot expect me to go to the AUP executive and tell them that we're planning to evacuate. I'd get shot!"

Tanard stared at the Wall and frowned. "Tell me, friend Maran. How prepared are you to execute Khiman-ra's self-destruct directive?"

Le Maran squirmed and averted his eyes. "The situation is not the same and you know it."

"Nothing ever is, but if we lose another ship, you better be prepared to issue that command. You must never forget that we're running a combat facility, not some profit-oriented commercial venture. The fact that you've gone operational simply means your survival now is a day-by-day proposition at best. The sooner you and your masters accept that, the easier you'll both sleep."

"You paint a pretty bleak picture, friend Tanard."

"Not bleak. Realistic."

"If you really think that, why did you agree to join?"

"Because you needed someone to do your killing for you," Tanard said bluntly and Le Maran's face colored.

"I deserve that and I apologize. It's just—"

"We've been over this before, friend Maran. I am a tool. So are you and so is Khiman-ra. The best the AUP can hope for here is that they'll achieve their objective before the tools are used up. You must know they'll not hesitate to write you and Khiman-ra off the instant we turn into a liability. The same way the Committee wrote us off after Lemos."

The problem was, Le Maran *did* know it. Ti Inai practically told him so, but pits! Telling the Commissioner a raider was lost with only one Kaleen carrier destroyed and Khiman-ra possibly compromised, would not enhance his prospect of a long and rewarding retirement. Still, Ti Inai didn't have to know, at least not right away anyway. Once he had a few kills to report, he could slip it in then. After all, this was war and losses were to be expected.

"It's a cruel blow nonetheless," Le Maran piped and bobbed his head. "I can only hope you and Hardara will have better luck."

"So do I," Tanard said earnestly.

Le Maran stared hard at his friend. "Your pessimistic assessment makes me feel that you don't completely agree with the AUP's handling of Kaleen."

"I don't!"

"Forgive me for saying this, but that raises a question of personal commitment to the cause."

"I'm out here and you're safe in your cozy office. Don't talk to me about commitment."

"Your attitude could be construed as criticism."

"Criticism? Let me tell you something, *friend* Maran, and you can take it any way you like. The window of opportunity to use force as a political tool is closing. After Lemos, even the AUP Provisional Committee has come to appreciate that. They haven't abandoned their goal to overcome Pizgor. They're simply using different tools. Economic tools. These are now the currency of diplomacy and aggression. You only have to look at Sofam's Paravan Trading Association as a prime example. That hypercorp monster has everyone running scared whenever it happens to look their way.

"We both know the Committee is routing Palean and Sargon commerce away from Pizgor and its handling and refurbishment facilities. If the impact on Pizgor's revenue flow is severe enough, they could conceivably secede to Sargon or the Palean Union, and the Committee would have won without a shot fired. The rub, as we both know, this process takes time. So, why not run this on two fronts? Why else engage raiders to prey on Kaleen? But impatient as Sargon is, even they recognize they have to move slowly or the whole thing could blow up in their faces. In view of such prudent caution, why Khiman-ra? Why antagonize the Fleet more than is necessary? Something doesn't add up here."

Le Maran could not say this to Tanard, but he *had* been thinking a lot lately about Khiman-ra and the strategy to directly raid Kaleen shipping. Ti Inai and the AUP must have known this would generate an equally aggressive response from Captal and the Fleet. In effect the tactic was already proving counter-productive and only served to stiffen Kaleen's resistance rather than weaken it. Instead of accelerating the merger with Sargon, using Khiman-ra could conceivably slow it down. Why would the AUP want to do that?

This was definitely something he preferred not to think about, or voice. It could be so easily misinterpreted—with terminal consequences. He had his orders and he obeyed them. He left strategy to Ti Inai.

"I don't concern myself with such questions, friend Tanard, and I would urge you to do the same."

Tanard managed a wry grin. "Don't worry. I'll do my job, and if necessary, die for it."

"I wasn't implying—"

"Never mind. Just think about what I said. Tell me. What's the progress on the new hulls?"

"We started retrofitting two ships and two more are due at the facility in nine days."

"And the Terrasecs?"

"You will get your four T-16s."

"Excellent. When will you have the first two out and running?"

"Ten, fifteen days."

Tanard shook his head. "Work the crews harder. We need those ships out here, not rusting at Khiman-ra. I want Hardara in a new ship as soon as one is available."

"You're a hard taskmaster, friend Tanard," Le Maran said ruefully.

"I'm a bastard, I know. Just get me those ships. You know I wasn't happy releasing Ver Dit and Hardara in those lumbering hulls. Losing Ver Dit, armed with a lousy Terrasec 10, only proves my case."

"Ver Dit didn't have access to those damned IFF codes, that was his problem," Le Maran protested. "You and Hardara do. That should help."

"We shall see."

"How is your shakedown going?"

"The M-3 power plant is purring and I'm anxious to try out the Koyami," Tanard said with obvious satisfaction and allowed the left side of his mouth to shift into a half smile, revealing a predator and a hunter. His target was only a plodding merchant, but one could never tell. It could have an M-2 escort or even an M-3, although the Fleet movements schedule did not show it. He wouldn't mind running his ship against a sweeper. However savory the prospect, he hoped to avoid such an encounter. He was running with a powerful ship, but he could not afford to forget that *Lahra* was not a true warship built for combat. He wouldn't last ten minutes in a close exchange.

"Keep me advised," Le Maran said and cut contact.

The Wall cycled through whorls of blue, green and purple tendrils. Tanard stared absently at the patterns. Small ship sounds intruded into the silence of his cabin. He scarcely paid them any attention now, having become fully attuned to the ship. It was only a converted courier, its hull and frames strengthened to stand the strain of high-speed runs, but he liked its crisp responsiveness.

Bad luck about *Urethar*. He could ill afford to lose the likes of Ver Dit or his crew. What stung more, the loss could have been avoided if only they had waited until AUP intelligence managed to secured those M-3 IFF codes. Running beneath a stolen IFF, Ver Dit would never have been intercepted. Tanard blamed himself for *Urethar's* loss. He was the operational commander, but he bowed to Le Maran's insistence to have the two capable ships released for raiding. That's what they were for, he was told. Besides, Le Maran pointed out, the new ships were not ready and he couldn't agree to have two perfectly sound weapons platforms sitting idle. Le Maran was a chair-bound bureaucrat more worried about how he would look before his superiors than concentrating on the job at hand, and Tanard had been a fool for listening to him. One should never allow sound operational doctrine to be suborned by political drivers. History was full of such stupidity and he had now repeated the error himself.

The comms alert beeped. He reached across the desk and tapped a pad.

"What?"

"Target identified, sir. Running in the Naurun corridor as per schedule," Winn said. "Range, two point-four lights. Time to intercept, one hour and eleven minutes at current closure rate." Winn hesitated, then cleared his throat. "Sir, it's a Palean ULC."

"So?"

"It's one of ours!"

"You knew we were after an Ultra Large Carrier, Mr. Winn?"

"I didn't know it was Palean."

"Does that make a difference?"

There was a moment of silence, followed by a lengthy sigh. "No, sir."

"Good. You know what to do. I'll be up in sixty minutes."

Winn was understandably squeamish, but the sooner everyone realized what this was all about, the better Tanard would like it. If Winn or anyone else couldn't stomach the job, he wanted to find out now. He wondered what the AUP would say to Le Maran when the carrier's owners came howling to them in protest. Nothing endearing, he was sure of that. Well, as long as they didn't come crapping at *his* door.

Tanard allowed the minutes to tick away, his mind absorbed with the evaluation of *Urethar's* loss and the impact on his raiding tactics. In the end it proved to be a fruitless exercise.

He'd been over this scenario countless times. There simply wasn't any way of predicting the effect of random factors. If he varied his strategy now, it would only lead to confusion and uncertainty. He and Le Maran had made a bad call, that was all.

On the sixty-minute mark, he strode out of the cable-tube and took the central command couch. A glance at the displays showed everything normal.

Winn swiveled in his seat. "Time to intercept, twenty-one minutes. Target hasn't transmitted a ping. IFF is on."

Tanard nodded. With IFF broadcasting, the ULC had no reason to suspect the unknown ship was anything else than a sweeper. The hull type might not be standard Sofam Industries issue, but an M-3 was a designation and there were enough variations to stifle any suspicions—for now.

Ten minutes later, Winn donned his Fleet zip-jacket and glanced at the comms watchstander.

"Merchant vessel, this is SSF M-3 *Saxa*. Please identify yourself."

The main display plate cleared and Winn leaned toward it. The Palean Master Pilot nodded to him.

"This is a Veron registered Ultra Large Carrier, *Fahr*, on route to Naurun. Ready to transmit ident dump."

"Standing by, *Fahr*," Winn piped and bobbed his head.

The ident dump came through, but no one was interested to look at it. Time, they were buying time; time to close. After a few minutes, Winn moved to the display plate.

"Ident received, *Fahr*. You are cleared to proceed."

"Thank you, *Saxa*."

"Time to intercept, two minutes," Railee said, not looking up from his weapons station. "Projector is powered up and we're ready to synchronize."

"Very well," Tanard said. He glanced at Winn and grinned. "You look good in working grays."

Winn tore off the zip-jacket and shrugged. "A poor fit these days."

Tanard chuckled. "Right. Mr. Railee, at minus forty seconds, raise secondary grid and synchronize. Mr. Winn, you will close to optimum range and jam all comms. Begin run."

Lahra accelerated to its maximum one point-two lights and made a gentle swing to port, designed to give the impression it was boosting away. However, the swing also happened to intersect *Fahr's* course. It looked all so natural and innocent. Tanard had made hundreds of such maneuvers commanding a real M-3. By the time the merchant pilot became suspicious, it would be too late.

At 90,000 talans, *Lahra* began jamming the entire subspace comms spectrum. It was a local effect only, but it prevented any emergency transponder signals from getting through.

"Closing to 50,000 talans," Winn said.

"Firing!" Railee shouted and stabbed the commit pad.

A yellow trail of ionization left by the seventy-two TeV discharge leaped for the ULC's nav bubble. The carrier's shield flared and arcing discharges licked the opaque dome. Tearing through a point collapse the beam penetrated the thin dome plating. The ravenous energy melted equipment and vaporized bodies. In seconds the ship had turned from something alive to a mindless hulk.

Railee methodically walked the discharge along the carrier's spine and centered it on the engineering spaces.

"ULC's precursor is failing," Winn warned. "Dropping normal."

Lahra and the ULC dropped normal almost simultaneously as the carrier's distortion field failed. The raider quickly closed the 292,000 talans separation and resumed its business-like bombardment. Seconds later the central part of the hull glowed a brilliant white, momentarily illuminating the enormous structural frames. The light expanded into a sphere of raw energy as the runaway antimatter reaction consumed the huge ship. Secondary explosions hurled jagged sections of hull careening into space.

Tanard watched the plasma cloud cool, turn a mottled orange-red, then dissipate into drifting filaments until they too were swallowed by darkness. He absently scratched the scars along his neck, well pleased with the performance of his crew and ship. The use of an M-3 IFF code not only made the destruction of the ULC possible, but it also ensured that *Lahra's* presence and identity remained unknown; of vital importance if he were to continue raiding. If Le Maran still harbored any misgivings about the tactic, this would be proof positive of its effectiveness.

"Are we clear?" he rasped.

"Nothing within detection range," Winn said immediately.

"Very well. Set course for next intercept." He swept his eyes over the command crew and nodded. "Well done everybody."

* * *

"Happy with the VLBCs, friend Terr?" Li Aron asked with deceptive mildness, his fingers coiling above the desk.

Terr suppressed a smile and nodded. "I'm looking forward to be on my way."

"So am I. It's been fun working with you, but I'll be glad to get you out of my face. The carriers will be lifting later today. That should give you and Mr. Dharaklin plenty of time to get the M-2s to the intercept point. After that, you're on your own."

"I appreciate your help securing the hulls."

"You will not be so quick to thank me when the Diplomatic Branch gets the bill for leasing the two VLBCs," Li Aron remarked dryly. "Still, the plan is simple enough and has a good chance of working. That's all that matters."

The plan *was* simple. The Fleet regularly leased hulls of all types from civilian sources. There was nothing unusual at seeing carriers around a Fleet base, and Kalakan had plenty coming

191

and going. Two more heading out should not excite comment in case anyone was watching. It was more unusual to have them manned by Fleet personnel, but it did happen sometimes and the owners charged plenty for the privilege. It was a standard commercial transaction and no amount of checking could prove otherwise.

The simplicity part kicked in once each carrier took on board its complement of two M-2s. Slow and fat, lumbering along the Kaleen shipping lanes, the VLBCs were ideal targets for any interested raider. Terr hoped Tanard or one of his ships would be interested enough to take a bite. The M-2s would make sure it left him with a sour taste.

"Too bad we cannot equip every carrier with a couple of M-2s. Of course, that's hardly practical. One way or another, Tanard must be stopped. Eleven ships in nine days," Li Aron said in disgust. He picked up his cup and took a sip of the steamy concoction. The cup made a loud click when he brought it down. "Eight of those simply disappeared. Vanished. Not even a transponder peep. Can you believe it? Naurun and Omiron are screaming at Anar'on for sitting on its hands and Anar'on is screaming at Captal because they say the Fleet is sitting on *its* hands. And I'm caught in the middle. If that weren't enough, we're getting raids along the Kaleen/Deklan/Orgomy borders. Probably the Deklans taking advantage of the confusion to muscle in. Someone will have to tell them gently to pack up their toys and quietly go away before they get their hands slapped. At least I don't have to worry about that dimension. We're moving in extra ships into all areas, but I have my doubts it will make a difference. The problem is political, not tactical, as we both know.

"Political or not, this wholesale destruction of merchant hulls has got to stop and stop soon. I'm afraid, friend Terr, your prediction that Tanard would use compromised IFF codes must now be assumed to be a cold fact. There is no other way

to explain why none of the eight carriers issued an all-ships signify. Of course, there's not a damned thing we can do about it.
The thought gives me scant comfort."

"If I may, sir, that's not quite true," Dhar said quietly and
the room suddenly chilled. The window screen was closed and
the Wall cycled through wisps of twisting mauve colors.

Li Aron slowly turned his head and stared at the Wanderer.
"Oh? I don't claim to be omniscient, Mr. Dharaklin. Pray then,
enlighten us."

Terr cleared his throat to hide a smirk and shifted on his
seat. The formchair squirmed under him. Li Aron was yet to
learn of Dhar's penchant for sardonic verbal sabotage, and it
was good to see his brother in high spirits again. He still limped,
favoring his left leg, but Nightwings was well on his way to a
complete recovery.

Dhar was unperturbed by Li Aron's intimidating stare. He
sensed Sankri's amusement and paused before dropping his
verbal grenade.

"You should issue all merchant hulls transiting to and from
Kaleen with IFF codes of every Fleet unit in the sector."

"And how would I do that?" Li Aron demanded sarcas-
tically. He'd had five very long days, longer than his usual eighteen hours, especially after Terr turned up with *Urethar's* captured crew, and did not relish having his time wasted with asinine ideas. Still, this could be amusing.

"SC&C could upload the codes to the ship's computer at
point of departure," Dhar said, unperturbed by Li Aron's abrasive attitude. "Kaleen if going out, or last port of call if coming
in. As positional information changes, SC&C can provide up-
dates in real-time."

Li Aron snorted. "Mr. Dharaklin, a flash of revelation. Merchant hulls already have a list of all active IFF codes. How else
do you think we respond to an interrogative ping?"

"Yes, sir. But those codes do not contain positional data.
It simply tells a merchant the code represents an authentic Fleet

unit. As Tanard so vividly demonstrated, the ship itself could be anything."

"Okay, friend Dhar. You've got me intrigued. Walk me through this if you please. Let's pretend I'm a lumbering merchant. I send out a ping and I get an IFF return showing me an M-3 that's supposed to be twenty lights someplace else. My suspicion is aroused and I set my emergency transponder squirting, but the way I see it, I'm still screwed. How am I doing?"

"It might not prevent you from getting destroyed, I admit that, but the tactic will nullify any advantage Tanard is getting right now from using the IFF codes."

Li Aron gazed thoughtfully at the Wanderer. "Which is to prevent or delay me activating my transponder, thereby keeping any nearby Fleet units ignorant of my predicament." It was a brilliantly simple and devastatingly effective idea. Someone on his team should have thought of it.

"That is correct," Dhar said. "Tanard will be forced to use an IFF code of a Fleet unit that might be uncomfortably close, or abandon their use altogether. Either option will curtail his ability and the ability of his other ships to prosecute their targets. It should take some heat off Kaleen."

"There are holes there, Mr. Dharaklin, but I'll pursue this. It's better than some notions I've heard and holds at least a chance of us nabbing Tanard." Li Aron locked his fingers to stop them from weaving. "And I apologize for my attitude."

Dhar merely nodded.

Li Aron sighed and turned his attention to his other problem.

"You realize, of course, friend Terr, the storm you created through the use of your, ah, unorthodox method of interrogation has sent ripples all the way to COMPALOPS. Master Scout Hvar doesn't think much of your approach, although it has yielded us some very valuable information. Since technically you're not subject to Fleet regulations, the Diplomatic Branch will determine any disciplinary action that might be taken against you. Given their silence on the matter, I have my doubts there will be a reaction." Li Aron suddenly grinned. "After all, they were only raider scum. I would have shot them on the spot." He chuckled and shook his head. "Wish I could have seen it. Must have scared them shitless."

Terr allowed himself to relax. When Li Aron started, he wasn't sure where the Palean was taking it, but his impression of the Master Scout had proven correct. Li Aron was focused on the mission objectives and wasn't bothered or sidetracked by irrelevancies. Not that Terr considered using his aspect an irrelevancy, but it was something Li Aron clearly preferred not to get involved with. He was somewhat uneasy that neither Anabb nor Hiragawan bothered to raise this with him, but he was happy to defer any confrontation that might ensue. At any rate, he hadn't heard the last of this, he was certain. That was tomorrow and he could be dead tomorrow.

"It got them thinking," he said with a wry grin. Li Aron laughed, a thin piping sound that shook him.

"I don't doubt it. We haven't finished with them, but what we learned so far has enabled us to initiate careful investigation of several likely systems that could be harboring the raider base."

Terr squirmed and Li Aron raised a hand.

"Rest easy, friend Terr. I am not insensitive to the fact that this falls under your jurisdiction and the Fleet is merely one of the tools the Diplomatic Branch is using to uncover Tanard's base."

"Sir, I did not—"

"When I said careful, Agent Terr, I meant exactly that. In the event of positive identification, I shall not initiate any action without prior consultation with you and Agent Hiragawan. I too must answer to my masters."

"I can live with that," Terr said. "However, I am also mindful of the fact that your job is to apprehend Tanard. It's possible that some consideration could have been given to merging our mutual objectives. Such as positioning shadowing Fleet units along the VLBCs route, in case Tanard happened to take a nibble at our bait." Terr looked hard at Li Aron and allowed himself a lazy grin. "If someone *has* thought of doing this, I earnestly hope you will dissuade him, as I would have to resort to using all those tiresome clearance codes of mine, which would make me very unhappy. Nothing would please me more than to see Tanard enjoying an extended vacation on Cantor, but we need to be conscious of our priorities and broader objectives."

"Friend Terr—"

"The Kaleen shipping corridors are crawling with M-3s, yet Tanard still destroyed eleven carriers. I can only read that one way. Whoever is supporting Tanard and his ships has very good intelligence. They probably know the disposition and movement of every Fleet unit around Kaleen. The only way for them to know that, is if Sector TACOPSCOM has been compromised. If shadowing units are sent ahead of me, my guess is, Tanard will know about it and I would be wasting my time. That would also make me unhappy."

Li Aron listened to Terr's words and nodded to himself. The boy was good and there was no getting around it. He would have to countermand the order to the M-3s and have them pull back, much to his keen disappointment. It was such a perfect trap, but he also understood the need to focus on unmasking the rebel base. Jeopardizing Terr's mission to remove a Fleet embarrassment wouldn't be playing fair, or wise. Terr was probably correct about Sector TACOPSCOM; another to-do item to add to his already lengthy list.

"I shall see to it that nothing stands in your way of being happy, friend Terr," he said and smiled. Terr returned his smile, but neither was fooling the other.

"I am relieved to hear it, sir," Terr said seriously. He really couldn't blame Li Aron for trying that beginner's trick. He would probably have done it himself.

"The downside, Agent Terr, is grim, as you no doubt al-ready know. Should you happen to run up against Tanard or one of his ships, you could be facing an upgraded Koyami 9A or a Terrasec 16. Even with two M-2s, he'll carve you up."

"If it was easy, it wouldn't be fun," Terr said with relish.

"Your butt," Li Aron piped and shook his head, wishing he were going instead, but he couldn't. That was the downside of *his* job. He stood up and the meeting was over. "I wish you luck and good hunting."

"Thank you, sir. If I do happen to run into Tanard, I'll keep him warm for you."

* * *

"He closed to 84,000 talans and threw up a comms inter-ference field. I launched the M-2s and he simply gave up."

"Just another enterprising raider, after all," Terr mused.

"Except it was the end of his enterprising," Dhar said with a chuckle.

"And the hull?"

"Taken to Omiron. The local Diplomatic Branch Resident wants to have a chat with the crew."

"I feel sorry for them already."

Dhar's face clouded. "I don't. Seeing them made my flesh crawl. There is not a pit deep enough for what they're doing, no matter what the motivation."

Terr nodded. "It gives me no pleasure the hear you say that, Nightwings, but some things need to be scoured out of exist-ence."

"What troubles me, Sankri, and I admit it freely, the *Saftara* seems helpless to guide us here."

"You need to remember that we're not on Anar'on, my brother of the night," Terr said gently.

Dhar lifted his hand, palm open. "Safe journey, Sankri," he said and cut contact. The Wall cycled into pooling colors.

Terr sighed and leaned back onto the couch. The thing molded itself around him. Dhar's words echoed in his head, but they gave him no comfort. His brother had finally confronted the ghosts that haunted his days and now Dhar had to deal with them in his own way. Terr wished him better luck.

But it wasn't all bad news. Dhar may not have caught Tanard, but it was still one less raider to plague Kaleen shipping. Critically, though, the tactic to use M-2s was vindicated. To weave the net complete, all Li Aron needed to do now is implement the revised IFF codes to totally ruin Tanard's day. What if they did plant M-2s in other carriers? Terr did not doubt the initiative was sound and should be pursued. The thing might not be as impractical as Li Aron thought. What would probably derail the notion were the ships' owners. An M-2 took up an enormous amount of space, valuable space to a carrier, space that could otherwise be filled with cargo. Would the owners be prepared to entertain the idea if Captal were to lease that space? Running patrols was okay, but it was a hit-and-miss proposition. Nothing like having some teeth of your own when entering into aggressive negotiation with a raider. Admittedly, not every VLBC or ULC could be so accommodated, nor would that be possible. If done to enough hulls, and if the tactic put a serious dent into raider numbers, it would be cheap for the price. Perhaps something to discuss with Hiragawan.

Luxuriating the feel of the soft leather formchair, he reflected that merchant pilots did well for themselves. Rich gray pile covered the deck. The size of his sleeping quarters! A Prima Scout would not have frowned at them. He also had a separate dining/entertaining area and a private study. He could definitely get used to this.

He turned to look through a large section of transparent hull. Thin filaments of brown and yellow gravity waves twisted and roiled outside as the VLBC distorted the local subspace continuum. Teena…the thought came unbidden. He concen-

trated on her face, the enormous green eyes and her pert up-
turned nose. Her full lips parted and she smiled. He reached for
her with an open hand and she was there, her form a shimmering ghostly outline. He gasped in startled wonder and the magic
faded, taking her with it.

"Rit!" he whispered, not sure what had happened.

Did he imagine it? No, she was here, real. He stood up and
held out his hand. No matter how much he strained, she didn't
come. He was trying too hard. After a while, he allowed the arm
to drop to his side. Was this a byproduct of his aspect? Why
hadn't his master ever mention it? He would have to talk to
Dhar about it.

Are you peeking into another of my reports, he wondered with a
grin.

Her smile still haunted him when the comms alert went off.
He tapped a pad in the inlaid console on the desk. "Yes?"

"Command deck, sir. We received an interrogative ping
from an M-3 sweeper."

That in itself was not unusual this close to Naurun. Terr
pulled at his chin.

"Is he transmitting IFF?"

"SSF M-3 *Maya*. She is valid, sir."

All it meant was, the ship out there had a valid Fleet code,
but what lay behind that code? It was disturbing that the one
symbol of trust and integrity that helped glue the Serrll into a
whole could no longer be trusted. This side effect of Tanard's
operation was perhaps the most destructive.

"Mmm. What does the computer say?"

"Type four hull, a bit large for a modern sweeper."

A bit large? The exec wasn't kidding. The thing could easily
accommodate an M-1 with space to spare. Still, it wasn't beyond
the realm of possibility. Some of the old I/14s got to be pretty
big in their day. If someone is driving an I/14, he was driving a
museum piece.

"Has he asked for our ident dump?"

"Not yet."

"How long before he closes?"

"Eleven minutes at current rate."

"Very well. I'll be right up. And Mister Rowland…"

"Sir?"

"Get the M-2s manned and warmed up."

"Aye, sir!"

Terr grinned. Bloodthirsty lot, all of them. Well, that's what they volunteered for. Humming, he strode toward the hatch.

Everything was quiet when he entered the command deck. He automatically glanced at the nav plot. *Maya* was now five minutes away. He missed the detail a tactical display could give him, but this was good enough for the job at hand.

The exec swiveled his seat, looking concerned. "We downloaded our ident dump for him. Both M-2s manned and ready. Sir, I really think that I—"

"Mr. Rowland. If we engage, I'll take one M-2 and that's the end of it, okay?"

The comms watchstander looked up. "*Maya* has opened a channel."

Terr nodded and pressed himself against a sloping console, out of the display plate's pickup range. He could not risk being recognized.

Scowling, Rowland waited for the plate to clear.

"Bulk carrier, your ident dump has been verified and you are cleared for Naurun. Please stand by for a sensor flyby."

"Acknowledged, *Maya*," Rowland said and nodded to the comms watchstander. The display plate immediately changed to nav mode and Rowland frowned. "What do you make of that?"

"It has been done before and could mean nothing," Terr said thoughtfully, "but I don't like it. I'm going below. Should *Maya* turn out to be something else, you'll let me know, won't you?"

He turned and hurried toward the tube hatch.

Hold four was huge: two hundred katalans by one hundred and fifty, and ninety katalans high. Still, the M-2 made it a tight fit. The patrol ship looked gigantic in the confined space of the hold. Terr ran under the curved belly and up the landing ramp. It retracted even as he punched a pad for the tube.

The command deck was instantly familiar and fully manned. Faces turned and gave him a speculative stare. Terr didn't mind. He automatically scanned the displays and sat on the center couch.

"Our status?" he asked. The Palean in the right seat turned.

"Primary drive reactor is down, but it's warm and will be brought online in two minutes. Standing by on secondary drive and ready to engage. Projector array is ready to be energized. Fire control tandem link is enabled. Ready in all respects, sir."

"Very well. Comms? What's happening with Force Two?"

"Force Two reports ready in all respects, sir."

"Excellent. Tell him to watch his energy profile. We don't want to alert the M-3. That goes for us as well," Terr said with a grin at his exec. The Palean merely nodded, stiff and formal, and Terr silently cursed. The watch didn't know him and he didn't know them. That could be telling when a fast response was required. They were a unit, confident they could do their job. It was up to him to show them he could do his. Perhaps he should have listened to Rowland and stayed aboard. Too late now.

"Comms? Link us with the command deck," he ordered.

"We're up, sir."

"Command deck, this is Force One. Talk to me."

"*Maya* is still closing. Fifty seconds."

"Depressurize holds four and six."

"Acknowledged…*Maya* has extended its secondary grid and is synchronizing."

"Drop normal!" Terr ordered. "He'll be targeting the nav bubble hoping for a quick kill." He glared at the exec. "Power up! As soon as we drop normal, prepare to launch…Weapons?

When we're clear, extend both shield grids and synchronize. Keep them tight. Ready to engage under tandem control."

Both officers acknowledged. They were tense, everyone was tense, but they were ready. With an untried crew, Terr couldn't ask for more than that.

He felt the gentlest of ripples run through his body as the VLBC dropped normal. The effect barely faded when he saw the ponderous hold hatch split and roll away to expose the harsh stars. It seemed to take forever. With a silent clang the two sides at last locked into place. The M-2 retracted its landing skids and hovered, then slowly glided toward the gaping maw.

All doubts vanished as the M-2 cleared the carrier and rushed for its quarry.

* * *

On the raider's command deck, Hardara was told of the sudden change in the VLBC's energy profile, but he was committed. M-2s…He shook his head in rueful wonder. After losing *Urethar*, the fates appeared determined to toy with him. His position did not look good. From being a predator stalking an easy kill, he was unexpectedly the one getting stalked. He couldn't even run.

An M-2 could boost at one point-four lph to his paltry one lph. His 7,600 tps secondary boost when running normal gave him a tactical advantage over the M-2's 6,960 tps, but his ungainly hull was a wallowing tub in any close action, which the M-2s excelled at. They were fast, nimble and powerful, probably mounting a Koyami 7/F or eight-series integrated phased array projector. He could look forward to fifty-six TeV bursts from each. If they tandem their fire control? He didn't want to think about that. In his past life, he had driven an M-2 and knew well its capabilities.

Pits! He expected to make at least one kill before being run down.

But if he could take out the VLBC before it could launch the pesky M-2s, he might still walk away with his skin intact.

The raider swooped on the VLBC. The powerful Terrasec 10/D array unmasked and the projector dome lowered, glowing dull orange. At 35,000 talans, invisible against the backdrop of stars, the raider fired. It was only a fifty-two TeV burst, but more than adequate to rip through a carrier's feeble nav grid. It was only a civilian after all. In the tactical display, Hardara saw the distortion field flare in point collapses. He must kill it before it dropped normal, but it was an exercise in futility. It would take a lucky shot indeed into the drive spaces to induce a runaway reactor event before the precursor failed, automatically dropping the ship into normal space.

Another burst tore at the nav bubble as the distortion field depolarized and the VLBC simply vanished. It didn't even bother activating its emergency transponder, Hardara mused. But then, this was not a normal victim. If he couldn't take on two M-2s…He ordered a sitrep dump to be sent to Khiman-ra, just in case.

The raider dropped normal and boosted toward the stationary target.

* * *

"K-band acquisition established with target," the computer announced. "Range, 216,000 talans. Closure rate is 14,560 talans per second. Effective firing solution in twelve seconds." This permitted the M-2s to engage at their maximum range of 40,000 talans.

"Tandem fire control enabled," a very young Third Scout weapons officer announced.

"Target entering L-band acquisition."

At five thousand talans separation the two M-2s raced toward the approaching raider.

"L-band firing lock established."

But it was the raider who got in the first shot. At maximum range, overstressing its projector array by ten percent, it fired a sustained sixty-two TeV burst at the port M-2. The raider had little to lose. It was a race between projector meltdown and disabling the M-2s, with horrible consequences either way for the loser.

The M-2's primary shield arced in point discharges under the assault, which sent brilliant sheets of blue-green backsurges against the primary grid. Tandem fire control was lost for several vital seconds.

On acquisition, both M-2s fired as one. Their ionization tracks slanted toward each other and merged into a bright rod of yellow death that slammed into the raider. The augmented 112 TeV discharge tore through the raider's shield grid in a visible display of arcing and impacted the hull. The raider reared and slued to starboard under the physical blow, its shields flaring. The M-2s fired again as the raider flashed past them at less than 15,000 talans, the augmented beam raking its starboard side. Hull plating ripped open and atmosphere vented. Wounded, it still managed to fire back.

It was a fluke shot. The beam rippled along the bottom of Terr's ship and slashed across the projector dome. The shield grids failed momentarily, then reformed, but in that instant of failure, vivid backsurges licked over the projector dome.

When the M-2 shuddered under him and the weapons console flared in a display of white and green flashes, Terr knew they were in trouble.

"How bad?" he asked gently. The stunned weapons officer looked up and shook his head.

"Tandem fire control link is down and we're at thirty-five percent projector capacity."

"Very well. Comms? Direct Force Two to engage the raider independently."

"Sir, the raider has blown through our line and is heading

for the VLBC. He'll be in firing position in twenty-eight seconds," the exec said looking grim, but calm.

"Force Two acknowledges."

"Get us turned around, Mister," Terr ordered. "Go to one hundred and fifteen percent boost."

The exec stared at him, then nodded. Orders were orders, even if they didn't make sense.

Terr touched the scar on his temple. He could order the VLBC to transit, but he needed to capture the raider more than he needed to save the carrier. His M-2 was useless as a weapons platform. What if the other M-2 couldn't finish off the raider? One-on-one, it was more than an even match as the raider's larger hull could absorb much more punishment. The exercise could turn into a prolonged slugging exchange with needless loss of life.

In the end, it was really a very simple decision.

He locked eyes with the exec. "Order everyone into survival blisters."

The exec gaped and the command watch exchanged worried glances.

"Now," Terr prompted.

"Sir—"

"I don't have time to debate this. Execute my order!"

The exec was about to protest, then changed his mind. "Computer, issue a general abandon ship and enable blister launch on command."

"Acknowledged…Abandon ship! This is not a drill," the computer blared. "Everyone to their assigned survival blister!"

Two hatches, one on each side of the cable-tube, snapped open, the entrance outlined by a pulsing yellow stripe. The command deck watch did not need two blisters, but redundancy guarded against failure.

The crew slowly got up, everyone looking anxiously at Terr.

"It has been a pleasure serving with you, and one we might share again," Terr said pleasantly and flashed a grin. "Right now, I need you out of here."

"Target entering L-band lock," the computer announced remorselessly. "Firing solution in fourteen seconds."

"Evacuate the deck!" the exec bellowed in a thin voice and everyone jumped.

The weapons officer looked at Terr, stood to, and then calmly stepped into the left blister. The remaining two watchstanders followed him. The exec didn't budge and Terr frowned.

"I meant everyone, Mister."

"You're going to ram that raider, aren't you?"

"I'm running out of time talking to you."

"The computer could—"

"No it couldn't and I may need to maneuver. For the last time, Mister, you're out of line."

"Or what? You will charge me with insubordination?"

"Firing solution in seven seconds," the computer said.

"You fool!" Terr snarled. "You're jeopardizing my mission and everyone else's life with your theater heroics. I gave you an order!"

"Sir!" The Palean nodded and dove for the left hatch.

"Computer, state blister status," Terr demanded.

"All personnel accounted for. Ready to launch."

"Enable launch and slow to half boost."

The left blister hatch clanged shut and Terr felt six mild jolts as the blisters evacuated the launch tubes. He sprang for the exec's couch, cursing him all the while, and scanned the tactical displays. The M-2 gave a violent shudder and the restraining field snapped on as the raider fired. Terr grunted at the pressure that held him frozen and clenched his teeth. The field released him and he flexed his shoulders.

The raider was within acquisition range of the VLBC, but it could not afford to engage the carrier with Terr's M-2 bearing down on him. It was probably wondering why the M-2 didn't return fire.

"Warning, target on collision course. Impact in eleven seconds. Recommend immediate evasive," the computer stated.

"Disregard! At minus one second, drop all shield grids and apply reverse thrust. Direct impact at target's stern section." Time to be getting out of here. Terr stood up and quickly checked that the M-2 was on course.

"Acknowledged...Impact in eight seconds."

The M-2 reared under him as the raider fired. Terr somersaulted over the couch and slammed against the cable-tube hatch as the restraining field grabbed him. It was a fraction of a second late. He felt his left shoulder go and the snap of breaking bone was loud and sharp. He screamed at the blinding burst of pain and his vision blurred. In a moment of clarity, he knew it was too late to reach the blister.

Rit!

Almost in slow motion the M-2 penetrated the raider's shield grids in a brilliant discharge of coiled lightings, shuddering violently. A second later, it plowed into the rear port side. The raider staggered and rolled to starboard, carried along by the momentum of the collision. Huge sections of hull plating tore away as the M-2 embedded itself into the larger hull. Debris flew spinning in all directions. The secondary drive of both ships shut down instantly and the two hulls drifted, locked in their fatal embrace.

Terr felt more than heard the enormous thump as the M-2 struck. The restraining field held for one vital instant, then failed. He grimaced at the tortured screech of tearing metal and stared in mild surprise as the console bulkhead in front of him crumpled. Display plates shattered, sending scything fragments sleeting in all directions. He didn't feel the impacts on his chest and legs as his body slammed into the central console panel. There was numbing shock and darkness brought merciful relief from noise and pain.

* * *

The M-2s were absorbing his fire and, for a moment, Hardara could say the same. For once, he was thankful to have a massive hull around him. Even if it could not maneuver worth a damn, it could certainly absorb punishment. Still, being under fire from 112 TeV bursts was not pleasant. His ship may be bulky, but under sustained assault it would be only a matter of minutes before he was carved up. Tandem fire control was a brutal way to fight.

He blew past them and headed for the VLBC wallowing dead in space. Twenty-eight seconds and he would dish it up. The port M-2 broke away and accelerated after him. Hardara was curious why the M-2s were nullifying their superior tactical advantage by breaking the tandem fire link. Did they mean to bracket him? The starboard M-2 came at him then at one hundred and fifteen percent boost and overtook its consort.

When it got into range, he took it under fire. It absorbed three shots before his ship came within its acquisition envelope. When it did not fire, he felt a mild foreboding. By the time he realized its intention it was too late. He could not maneuver out of its damned way and it would take too long to initiate emergency transit.

Hardara could only watch in morbid fascination as the M-2 ejected survival blisters. Seconds later the ship heaved under him as the scout struck. The command deck suddenly went dark while the computer sounded the collision alarm.

* * *

Enllss-rr watched the two white translucent panels slide shut after the dejected figure and kept his face impassive. The forbidding image in the Wall silently returned his gaze. He tried to stare it down, but in the end, Enllss had to break eye contact. Those eyes...

"I regret the necessity for such a demonstration, Mr. Commissioner, believe me, I do, but circumstances left me little choice," Marrakan said gravely.

Enllss believed him. He also believed in the awful inevita-
bility of the alternative. After what he just witnessed, he had no
doubt the horrifying alternative would ensue if steps were not
taken, and quickly. The Security Council must be made to realize the seriousness of the situation. His eyes strayed to the deep
coral tray on his desk, streaked through with violet filaments. It
held a small stone plant, its stem dull russet and the delicate
leaves were wings of flimsy red. An extraordinary transformation. His blood ran cold simply watching it.

A live plant like it stood in another tray beside it.

Behind him the window screen allowed soft light to per-
meate the office. Bunched clouds hung over the Center. Endless lines of communals, sled-pads and combies crossed the sky
in controlled patterns. Tubeways linked the towers that reached
for the clouds. Captal never slept. It could not afford to. Far
below, the avenues were alive with the throng from nameless
worlds all over the Serrll. He didn't see any of it.

After a moment, he reached across the desk and touched a
pad. "Ree-Lee? Please show Commissioner Sill-Anais in."

"Yes, sir."

A moment later the door panels slid away. Sill walked in
wearing a bemused smile. He hooked a thumb over his right
shoulder.

"What did you do to Ti Inai? Ach! He looked positively
ashen," the Deklan piped in high treble and thrust out a massive
barrel chest, his gaunt features split in a wide grin. He combed
his fingers through long white hair, streaked with twin bands of
gray of a mature male. His clear wide-set eyes arched beneath
white eyebrows. The olive complexion only accentuated his
pinched, dry face.

Enllss thrust out his square jaw and jerked his head at the
formchair in front of his desk.

"Sit down, Sill," he said firmly.

Sill looked sharply at his powerful, muscular friend and silently settled himself into the yielding chair. Enllss had a clear, penetrating voice that commanded attention. His aquiline nose stood out sharp above a firm mouth. Dark gray eyes regarded Sill without blinking.

"How long have we known each other?" Enllss demanded, painfully aware of the figure in the Wall.

"Some fourteen years now, I guess," Sill said slowly, not sure what Enllss was getting at. When asked to come at once, he demurred. As Commissioner for the Bureau of Cultural Affairs, he had little time for idle chatter. Couldn't they settle this through a Wall?

His eyes caught the stone plant and he leaned forward almost as if to stroke the delicate leaves.

"What an astonishing specimen. Ach! Something you got from Anulus?" The Four Suns mineral-rich world famous for producing extraordinary crystal items.

Enllss ignored him. "In fourteen years, have I ever thrown you a curve?"

Sill frowned and sat back. "We've had our moments, but I cannot say that you have ever deliberately mislead me."

"Keep that thought in mind," Enllss said and looked at the Wall.

Sill automatically followed his gaze and gaped.

"Sill, I want you to meet Marrakan, Controller of Anar'on and Prime Director of the Kaleen group."

"Ach! And head of the Unified Independent Front, I know," Sill added with a wary nod. "We have met, sir."

Dressed in a dark business suit, Marrakan smiled.

"Indeed, and I welcome this opportunity to talk to you again, Mr. Commissioner," he said, his voice deep and mysterious, like the drifting sands of his world.

Sill studied the Wanderer with keen interest. Two point-three katalans tall, thin, honed by the desert. The face a mass of deeply wrinkled lines that had been worked on by time. The heathen might be old, but an indulgent sparkle glittered in his orange eyes. The thin membranes that protected the eyes against abrasive sand were retracted. Long ochre hair, streaked gray, spilled across his shoulders.

"Since we're the only ones here, I gather that this meeting has something to do with us?" Sill inquired politely, somewhat apprehensively. After seeing Ti Inai, he had a sneaky suspicion what this was about. He warned Anall-Marr personally. Damn! Antagonizing Anar'on so blatantly was a stupid policy, and he suspected time has come for an accounting. Wanderers on the warpath? Fiends from the pit! He shuddered at the horrible thought.

"Not with us, Mr. Commissioner, but with the Deklan Republic," Marrakan said. "As your coalition partner, Commissioner Enllss-rr has kindly consented to act as an informal mediator on behalf of the Sofam Confederacy in this matter."

Enllss shifted and the formchair squirmed under him, suddenly hard. "Sill, Director Marrakan has requested that I ask you to convey a warning to the Ecumenical Synod on Deklan."

"A warning? Ach!" *Father, keep me on the Path.*

"The Synod should reconsider the use of a very questionable tactic against Kaleen commerce along the Kaleen/Orgomy/Deklan borders. This tactic could endanger the mutually profitable relationship that Kaleen has enjoyed with the Deklan Republic to date, and with Sofam," Enllss added.

Sill looked at Marrakan. "Mr. Director—"

"It is possible that I may be mistaken," Marrakan said equitably. "The Synod could have been led astray from the Path after witnessing difficulties facing Naurun and Omiron, helped along by Palean adventurism. This might have emboldened them to speculate on the opportune use of similar methods to achieve similar ends. If that is indeed the case, highlighting this error of judgment to them could avert much potentially serious unpleasantness for everybody."

Sill bridled and set his teeth. The infidel would quote the

Path to him? Deklan would grind…With an effort, he slowed his breathing and fixed on his best diplomatic smile. He trod dangerous ground, and getting emotional now could be disastrous. It might already be disastrous.

"If you're referring to the unfortunate loss of hulls to raiders, sir, the situation, of course, is deplorable. Ach! But I hardly see how Kaleen can possibly suggest any involvement by Deklan in such barbaric acts."

After a silent moment, Marrakan nodded. "Barbaric, yes. Eloquently put, Mr. Commissioner, and very striking in your choice of words. You see, sir, they were almost exactly those used by the Palean Union. In Commissioner Ti Inai's case, I was forced to present Kaleen's case somewhat more forcefully before he fully appreciated the weight of my argument. I see that you need to be similarly convinced."

"Mr. Director!" Enllss cried out. "Must we? I promise you that Sofam will bring all its influence to bear on our coalition partner. Has Captal not brought the full resources of the Fleet and its intelligence services to bear in resolving the problem?"

Marrakan gave a small bow of acknowledgment. "I have nothing to reproach the Captal government with, sir. Or Sofam. Your actions have been commendable and I have no doubt that in due time your efforts will be successful. The problem that Kaleen faces, Mr. Commissioner, is the ongoing and senseless loss of life while you prosecute the issue. We don't have time to wait, sir," he said and turned his attention to Sill.

"I have noted your admiration for the stone plant, Mr. Commissioner. It is indeed a lovely thing, but it's dead now. If you will permit me to demonstrate." Marrakan raised his right hand. Small blue lightnings crackled as they crawled over his arm. Sill blanched and pressed himself into the formchair. Could this to be his end? The heathen wouldn't dare!

"Look at the live plant, if you please," Marrakan rumbled and Sill slowly turned his head, his face draining with the dread of certainty.

212

Living sparks suddenly writhed over the plant. It happened slowly. The leaves lost their yellow color, turned red and sagged. The stem quickly transformed into deep russet, the effect traveling from top to bottom. Sill fancied he could hear a faint protesting crackle in the air as the sparks faded. Such power in the hands of unbelievers! Blasphemy! Blasphemy or not the plant was now stone.

"Consider this as tangible expression of my warning, Mr. Commissioner," Marrakan said heavily. "Please convey my personal message to the Synod. Kaleen will take steps to protect its ships and those of our ally Orgomy. What I have done to that plant can just as easily be applied to a raider...or to Deklan itself. Please don't tempt us to demonstrate. Good day to you, sir."

"Sill, Primate Anall-Marr must take steps to stop this madness before things get out of hand!" Enllss hissed. "When you speak to him, add this. If he does not act, Sofam will introduce unilateral trading sanctions and blockade your shipping corridors. Consider this *my* warning." He pressed a pad on the desk console and the translucent door panels slid away. Ree-Lee appeared and waited patiently.

Sill stared at Enllss in a daze and opened his mouth, but the words would not come. Would Sofam really take action? Probably, and relish doing it. Sinful idolaters! Anall-Marr was ill informed, that would be his argument. Perhaps a formal apology would be in order. The thought of Wanderers let loose against Deklan a nightmare out of the pit. He slowly looked at Marrakan and swallowed.

"I shall convey to the Synod the full gravity of your message, Mr. Director," he mumbled and heaved himself up. With a last glance at Enllss, he shuffled out, an old worn-out man. The panels clicked shut behind him and Enllss beamed with pleasure.

"A most satisfactory outcome, I believe," he said brightly and gazed at the two stone plants. "Remarkable."

Perhaps he would offer one to Sill after his friend had collected himself. In all likelihood, he would probably get the damned thing thrown at his head. The other, he meant to keep for himself. It really was extraordinary and possibly unique. He wanted to keep it that way.

"As was your suggestion, Mr. Commissioner," Marrakan murmured and allowed himself a ghost of a smile. Enllss was a truly gifted individual, but did he really appreciate or understand the full impact of his proposal?

"Of course, sir, Ti Inai's faction and Deklan may not believe that you will carry out your threat," Enllss said, suddenly serious.

He knew that a Wanderer who had undergone his three trials was fully capable of projecting force at a distance. That Marrakan, standing on Anar'on, could turn a plant to stone on Captal a chilling demonstration. What else they might be capable of, he hesitated to ask. Turn an entire planet to stone?

Marrakan gave a tight smile. Enllss understood, all right, but one always had to be wary of assumptions.

"In that case, my friend, we shall have to make real our threat. It is a dangerous thing we do here, but I shall not hesitate to carry it out. Too much is at stake for all of us. For you, the stability of the Serrll Combine, and for us, our very survival."

"Indeed," Enllss said slowly and nodded several times.

Loss of Naurun and Omiron to the Paleans, loss of more Kaleen and Orgomy worlds to Deklan, the breakup of the Unified Independent Front, followed by an inevitable Sargon/Palean merger and the equally inevitable open warfare. Sofam would never tolerate a situation where Sargon would attempt to put its dictatorial version of freedom into effect. Moreover, Anar'on would retaliate before things got that desperate. Then what? Cold, stone worlds, drifting monuments to misguided dreams? It did not bear thinking about.

As for Deklan? He didn't give a soggy Serrll fiver for Ti Inai, but he regretted that Sill had to be hit like that. Well, that's what the job was all about. Deklan had overreached itself and must be slapped down. To believe that Sill didn't know what the Synod planned beggared belief. Well, better with a stone plant now than warships later—or worse. They should have known better.

"Mr. Commissioner," Marrakan prompted quietly. "I must ask this. Will Sofam carry out its part of the bargain?"

Enllss looked up and thrust out his jaw. "Like you, sir, Sofam doesn't make idle threats."

"And Commissioner Sill-Anais? I am mindful that as head of BueCult, he is responsible for tracking down raiders—of all persuasions. Given his Deklan bias…"

Enllss' smile was grim. "Does he have a conflict of interest? It's possible, but it is the Diplomatic Branch who is running the operation. Believe me, they'll cut it the way they see it."

"Ah, the redoubtable Director Anabb Karr. I have had an occasion to speak with him."

"Without being offended, I trust."

Marrakan chuckled. "The Director relishes plain speaking, but he is also very adept in the exercise of diplomatic nuances when the occasion calls for it." He paused and regarded Enllss closely before making his decision. "Tell me, Enllss…May I call you that?"

"Why not? Everybody else does."

"With sometimes disparaging remarks, I don't doubt," Marrakan said and laughed. A deep, rich sound that lit his face. Enllss felt privileged to see this side of the formidable Wanderer, which he suspected few ever saw.

"Of course. It goes with the job."

"Enllss, the fact that this meeting took place at your level, and no offense meant, suggests the Executive Council was reluctant to act directly against its own members—"

"Because some of them might be associated with the AUP Provisional Committee?" Enllss finished for him and grinned.

"Our intelligence tells us, as yours has told you when you interrogated Kai Tanard, that Ed-Kani Takao is almost certainly a member. As is Ti Inai."

"Do you have proof?"

"What we have is circumstantial only. The problem is that as a body, the Committee hasn't really done anything illegal."

"As far as you are able to determine."

"Correct."

"You mean to infiltrate their chain of command then?"

"We must and it's one of Anabb's principal tasks. Once our efforts unearth a link with even one raider and the Committee, they can look forward to some soul-searching time on Cantor."

"You must know, Enllss, that such men never soil their own hands. They will be unimpeachable."

"Breaking up the organization will be a good enough outcome."

"May I ask why did Sofam wait so long to act?"

Enllss enjoyed this rare moment of intimacy with Marrakan. The Wanderer had a lot on his mind, yet prepared to engage in chitchat. Was it merely idle talk? Looking at those eyes, he found it hard to read what lay behind them. Sill was right to fear those eyes. Should the Wanderers ever decide to venture into the Serrll, death for many would be but one of the more milder ends. Marrakan was wise to urge caution when Enllss first presented his suggestion.

"Your words, sir. I couldn't have summarized it any better. Although we're making progress and in time the Palean/Deklan threat will be contained—"

"In time…I am pleased that you qualified your statement."

Enllss chuckled. "Captal is not arrogant, sir. We recognize that not every problem will have a single elegant solution, or a solution at all. A workable compromise will do fine. What Kaleen is facing right now is an excellent case in point, which will no doubt be the subject of much learned analysis for some time to come, but I digress. Politically, Captal had to act to discourage this, ah, adventurism of using raiders as an instrument of interstellar policy. That's how business is done here. However, you made the telling point. While we pursue a workable solution, raiders continue to take unnecessary life. Sofam recognized this and sometimes you must jumpstart the process."

"So, a single life is important then?" Marrakan prompted.

"To me it is. Once Captal, or any government, for that matter, forgets that, we're headed toward anarchy. While we pursue our grand schemes, perhaps even for the noblest of reasons, telling ourselves that what we do will benefit everyone, it's all too easy to overlook that single human element. After all, are we not all men?"

"Under whatever god stands over us," Marrakan murmured, impressed despite himself. "Mr. Commissioner, I look forward to the day when we can mutually congratulate each other's efforts today."

"Until then, Mr. Director," Enllss said and the Wall image faded. He leaned back and smiled. However agreeable this particular outcome turned out, it would not stop him from making sure the Unified Independent Front toes the Sofam line, and another game yet to be played. He would relish the challenge.

He tapped the comms pad. "Ree-Lee? Fresh tea! And tell Gershowan I want to see his report on ecoforming stats right now."

He swiveled his seat and looked out. The cloud cover had thickened and he could see slanting sheets of rain obscure the city towers. During the last two years, his First Assistant had developed immeasurably. Time he tried his hand at managing a Branch. Enllss would hate to lose him, though.

By damn! A fine day...

* * *

"That's it! That's it! That is exactly what I'm talking about!"

217

Ed-Kani Takao raged and pointed a stiff finger at Ti Inai. A ripple of concerned murmuring swept around the table as members leaned toward each other, exchanging hushed whispers. The three-dimensional Wall images were perfect and to a casual observer everyone could actually have been in the room. Given the distances involved and the security risks, it was hardly practical for the Committee to meet as a body.

"Order!" The Sargon Pro-Consul banged his gavel. "Let us keep this formal, shall we? Address your comments to the Chair. You may continue, Mr. Director," he growled and nodded to Ed-Kani.

"Thank you Mr. Chairman." Ed-Kani pursed his lips and carefully noted the reactions around him.

Even the Palean members gazed at Ti Inai with concern. It could have been a programmed ploy to remove suspicion from themselves, but he doubted it. No, this was something Ti Inai had hatched all by himself. Ed-Kani was prepared to stake his pension on it. What he couldn't understand, why do it? It didn't matter. *I've got you now, you piece of worm slime!*

"Forgetting the damage the Palean member caused by staging that disastrous attack on the Unified Independent Front delegates two years ago, thus exposing the Italan—"

"Just a minute!" Ti Inai snarled and jumped to his feet. "You cleared me of any involvement—"

"Order!" The chairman banged his gavel. "I shall have order in these proceedings, is that clear?" He glared at Ti Inai. "You'll get your chance to rebut. Now, sit down!"

"He cannot simply accuse me—"

"I said, sit down! And you!" He pointed his gavel at Ed-Kani. "We're interested in facts only, not personal suppositions. Do I make myself clear?"

Ed-Kani bit his lip and nodded. "Your pardon, Mr. Chairman."

"Facts!" the chairman repeated. "Let's get on with it."

"Very well," Ed-Kani said with a nod. "I shall give the

Committee facts. One. Someone in the Palean Alikan Union Party machine engineered Kai Tanard's escape. He certainly could not have gotten off that prison transport without expert help. The Committee did not sanction his rescue. Who then? A rogue AUP cell? Two. Shortly afterward, a raid was staged on Pittar 2-RN and an M-3 sweeper commandeered. I believe Tanard engineered it, but I acknowledge it as only a supposition. Three. Within weeks, merchant shipping along the Naurnun and Omiron corridors started disappearing. Not only looted, but presumably destroyed in place. To date, twenty-three hulls in all. That's not characteristic of any normal raider, and I don't feel that Palean religious zealots have suddenly escalated their activities. Four; and my most telling point. A special investigative Fleet unit on Kalakan has captured two raider ships that turned out not to be raiders at all, but part of a special force commanded by Kai Tanard!" This time the wave of comments around the table rose in an uproar. The chairman furiously pounded his gavel.

"Order! Order!"

Ed-Kani suppressed a smile of satisfaction. This wasn't exactly news to the Committee, but strung out like this, it presented a damning body of evidence.

"What's more," he added quietly, "Ti Inai not only knew that radical AUP cells intended to employ Tanard to raid against Kaleen, but he condoned it, knowing this could only undermine the Committee's own efforts. Why, I ask the member! Why?"

After that it took a while for everyone to settle down.

The chairman stared at Ti Inai. "I am sure all of us are keen to hear from the Palean member," he said sweetly, but it represented a veiled threat nonetheless. The Committee had little tolerance for internal dissent once a policy was made, and treated with terminal harshness.

Ti Inai looked around the table in defiance. This appeared bad for him, but in his haste to bring him down, Ed-Kani had unwittingly thrown him a lifeline. The man had no sense of political subtlety and was yet to learn that a flanking attack could sometimes be far more effective than a direct charge. No finesse and utterly predictable, typical of everything Sargon. Surprising really, given their tactical mastery in battle.

He calmly looked at the chairman. "Can friend Ed-Kani enlighten the Committee as to how he knew that I allegedly condoned such a tactic by this fanciful unknown element within the AUP?"

"Because you told me!" Ed-Kani snapped and immediately kicked himself. *Oh, you cunning bastard! You worm!*

"We spoke about possibilities, yes. Scenarios. I don't deny that. We all do in idle conversation, but that can hardly be taken as condoning the act itself." Ti Inai said softly and smiled with satisfaction. His fingers worked and he locked them into a knot. *Eat shit,* friend *Ed-Kani.* "Mr. Chairman, if I may draw your attention to a memo addressed to the Committee warning of the possible disruptive effect to our program if radical AUP cells employed Kai Tanard?" Calmly, he tapped a pad on the desk console and the incriminating document flashed in the Wall. "In this memo, I urged the Committee to issue a stern directive to all AUP cells not to take unilateral action against Kaleen. I'm now understandably disturbed by friend Ed-Kani's allegation that I am somehow responsible for Tanard's activities and the loss of twenty-three merchant hulls."

He was disturbed by far more than cheap rhetoric from Ed-Kani. The image of blue sparks turning that plant to stone still sent chills through his body.

"Director?" The chairman looked pointedly at the senior Sargon member.

Ed-Kani acknowledged Ti Inai's clever reversal with a flickering smile. Instead of appearing the villain, Ti Inai had twisted the truth into wounded indignation, leaving Ed-Kani looking like he conducted a personal attack on the Palean, which he was. He *knew* the Palean worm had both his hands in this mess. If only he could get proof!

Another time then, *friend* Ti Inai.

"Mr. Chairman, I ask the Committee to indulge me in a moment of reflection. Supporting raiders to attack Kaleen was a carefully orchestrated policy to put maximum pressure on Naurun and Omiron with negligible risk of exposure for us. The objective, of course, is to force those systems to cede to the Palean Union. Once accomplished, pressure could then be brought to bear on two other systems, and so on, until we had enough to successfully consummate the merger and take up that all-important third Executive Council seat. Our tactic designed not only to splinter the Kaleen group, but collapse the Unified Independent Front movement as well; an eminently desirable outcome in itself.

"Despite the predicted Fleet buildup to counter the effect of raiders, we were on track to peel off Naurun and Omiron—until Kai Tanard began his operations. His involvement generated too much pressure and produced an equally forcible response from the Fleet. We all know that the Palean Congress, although supportive of the merger despite opposition from Tao Karam and his faction, feels that the merger terms unfavorably advantage the Sargon Directorate. Because of this mistaken belief, it's possible that misguided Alikan Union Party cells have decided to take matters into their own hands.

"It is impossible for Tanard to be working alone. Someone must be supporting him with intelligence and logistics. His efforts, however successful, threaten to disrupt the entire Committee agenda. Instead of filing down Kaleen's resistance to the point where it's simply easier for it to give up, Tanard has managed to turn this into open warfare, which served only to stiffen Kaleen's resolve and Captal's determination. It's now questionable whether the Committee will in fact achieve its objective. Inexperience has cost us Pizgor. This time it is misguided zeal by a few.

"I'm not interested in pursuing a personal vendetta against

Ti Inai. What I do ask of him and other Palean members is this. If they have any influence over the AUP cells which are running Tanard, they should urge them to desist from this madness before the Committee itself is hopelessly fractured. For that would surely be a greater tragedy, one that could very well poison the entire merger effort and result in untold unpleasant consequences for everybody."

The chamber was deathly quiet. No one wanted to make a noise or draw attention to himself.

Ti Inai kept his fingers locked, but Ed-Kani's clearly passionate words rang in his ears. He almost glowed with happiness. Everything had evolved exactly as predicted, and Khimanra turned out to be extraordinarily successful. Everyone accepted that Naurun and Omiron were hurting, but Anar'on had rallied and the Fleet was closing in on the base. Only a matter of time before they attacked. It would be a regrettable loss of manpower and materiel, but as far as he was concerned, the AUP's objective would have been achieved. Ti Inai supported the merger, but he and a significant section of the Palean mainstream Alikan Union Party believed that things were progressing too quickly. Lemos still a vivid image of failure and humiliation for the Palean Union, one the AUP was not anxious to repeat in the service of Sargon's ambitions. No, not Sargon's, but Ed-Kani's!

Something in Ed-Kani's speech made his blood run cold. Should Sargon tire of the Committee process, it could very well decide to invade the Palean Union directly. Unlikely as the scenario was, Ti Inai did not like Sargon's impulsive military tendencies. They were simply too unpredictable. If Sargon did invade? It would be messy, very messy. No one wanted that. Unlikely to happen, though. Sofam would never allow the situation to deteriorate to that point.

After yesterday's dramatic warning from Marrakan, a word to Le Maran to slow things down might be in order to relieve the political pressure a little. Le Maran may find this directive strange, but Ti Inai did not believe that subordinates should be aware of everything.

Perhaps he should have another discussion with Tao Karam. They had their differences, but in the end, they were both Paleans.

The chairman banged his gavel, the sharp crack making the members start.

"An eloquent rendition, Mr. Director. You have given all of us something to deliberate on. I move that we adjourn for one hour."

"Second," Ti Inai piped and his head bobbed.

Bang!

"Carried!"

* * *

Terr heard hushed voices, but couldn't make out the words. The air soft and warm, filled with faint hospital smells. He didn't care. It felt good luxuriating between crisp sheets, without cares or responsibilities. Sunlight tickled his eyes and he squinted.

An elfin oval face hovered over him, framed by long black hair. Large dark green eyes looked at him with concern.

"I'm in heaven and you're an angel," he mumbled in a croak. She grinned at him and her right cheek dimpled.

"You're not in heaven, but the angel part is right," a gruff voice said and the magic shattered.

Terr turned his head. Anabb scowled at him, but the amber flecks in his brown eyes danced with amusement.

"Now I know that I'm not in heaven," he said more easily and sighed. "But if I'm not in heaven, where am I?"

"At the Center's medical facility, convalescing, which you've been doing long enough, I might add," Anabb said.

"I'm on Taltair? The last thing I remember—"

"You were badly hurt when you crashed the M-2 into that

raider," Teena said gently, clearly distressed.

"And a damn stupid thing to do," Anabb growled.

"If we got the crew, then the return has been worth it," Terr said wearily. Anabb was only being an asshole.

"We got them," Anabb conceded and patted his shoulder. "Rest. We'll talk later."

"Was it one of Tanard's?"

"It was." With a nod to Teena, Anabb walked out.

"He really was very worried about you," Teena apologized for her boss.

"Evil old fart," Terr muttered.

"Oh, Terr!" she said and giggled.

He drank in her face and brushed her cheek with a finger. "Teena…"

Eyes bright, she reached for his hand and squeezed. "Everything is all right now," she whispered.

He wiggled his toes and twisted. It all seemed to be working and he felt no twinge of pain in his shoulder.

"What happened out there?" he asked. "I remember being slammed around a bit…"

"Your exec came back for you. You were a mess. It was awful," she said and shuddered. "I get nightmares thinking about it. Anyway, they got you to the VLBC in time to put you into a medicare crib. An M-4 picked you up and took you to Kalakan. You were in induced stasis for nine days while they worked on you. When you started to regenerate, they shipped you back here. You've been on Taltair for two days now."

Terr mulled that over. With modern genotherapy most body damage could be fixed in a few days or so. He must have been really beat up.

"And how long have you been here?" he asked with a mischievous grin. Teena blushed and shifted her feet.

"What makes you think I would waste my time watching a corpse?"

"Oh, nothing. It's just…"

"Yes?"

"Do you think I'm well enough to get out of here? I would much rather discuss this over dinner."

Her nose wrinkled and she frowned prettily. "You shouldn't be rushing things, you know."

"Holding a spoon isn't going to kill me! Besides, being with you will definitely help me get better."

"Beast!"

Just then the door panel slid into the wall. An elderly medic walked in and automatically glanced at the sensor readout plate above Terr's bed.

"Humph! Everything seems to be in order. I suppose he wants to jump up and rush out of here, eh?" he complained and looked accusingly at Teena.

"It was my idea," Terr protested. "She had nothing to do with it."

"I doubt that. Well, the exercise will do you good, but I wouldn't overdo it, understood? And I want you back here before midnight."

Terr looked disgusted. "Are you my mother or something?"

The medic glared at him. "You listen to me, young man. You may feel great lying in that bed, but you're still weak. I won't discharge you until you've had a few days of rehabilitation. You give me a hard time and that rehab program could get real painful. Do we understand each other?"

Terr nodded and sighed. "Yes, mother."

"Humph!" The medic looked at Teena and waved a hand at Terr. "Take him out of my sight, but dinner only! Got that?"

Teena blushed and nodded.

The medic shook his head and strode out, but not before Terr saw a small grin crease his face. Terr locked his hands behind his head and spent a moment looking at Teena. She absently pushed back the sleeves of her surf-green shirt, glanced behind her and sat on the formchair. A rebellious lock of hair strayed over her temple and she blew at it from the side of her mouth. She wore dark green slacks with a broad black belt. She crossed her legs and peered at him.

"What?" she demanded when he didn't say anything.

"Oh, just admiring the scenery."

"Beast!"

He grinned. It really was fun being with her. She was open, unpretentious and her smile made his breath catch. Her eyes, enormous and soft, totally captivated him. They were warm and full of laughter, and when they clouded with concern, her face serious, she was fascinating.

"You're beautiful," he said softly and she looked at her lap. When she lifted her head, her eyes told him what he wanted to know.

"Will there be time for us?" she asked slowly, fearful of stepping on a path that lay open before her, yet excited at the sweet prospects it promised.

Her stomach tensed and she felt a flutter of alarm. He looked so confident, alive and ready to take on anything. Even when he lay unconscious, his face relaxed and vulnerable, she sensed his strength. An almost invisible glow of power she wanted to tap into, to share. Yet despite his strength, he could be hurt, his body torn like any other man's. Next time they brought him back, would he be as fortunate? Could she give herself to this man knowing that her heart could be broken tomorrow?

But that was tomorrow and it not need be so.

Terr sensed her mood and thought he understood some of the doubts that must be running through her mind. It might be glamorous and romantic to flirt with a real live field agent. All the girls have the hots for a dashing hero, right? But was it practical? A girl wanted a man in her bed, not a fantasy or a memory. What did *he* want? A satisfying flirtation every time he returned to Taltair? Did he have room in his life for Teena or someone like her? Can he commit, knowing that thinking about her, wor-rying about her, could affect his judgment while on a job?

Stupid!

His job was not his life! He reflected on what he shared with Nightwings. He would not turn back time even if he could, even for a chance to wipe away all the pain he had endured and probably would still face. What could be more meaningful and lasting than to share himself with another person and enrich himself with that person's experiences, loves, hurts, sorrows and joys? To be there for her, like she would be there for him.

"We can have all the time that's offered us," he said simply and watched in fascination as her eyes turned soft green. She stood up and patted down her slacks.

"I've got to rush," she said briskly.

"Hey! I thought—"

"I do have a job, you know," she said primly. "Unlike some."

"Now, that's not fair."

She leaned over him and patted his cheek. A faint citrus smell lingered around her.

"I'll pick you up this evening. Nineteen hundred."

"But—"

"Later." With a flutter of fingers, she was gone, taking the sunshine with her.

Rit!

That afternoon, two grim-faced orderlies collected him and hauled him off to the rehab center. After a bone-wrenching workout, they relented and let him go. Weak, dripping with sweat, legs wobbly, he silently cursed all medics. After a sauna and a massage, feeling somewhat mellow and more kindly dis-posed toward his fellow creatures, he grudgingly admitted that he needed the strenuous exercise. Still, he hoped that over the next few days the sadistic monsters looking after him would show some mercy.

Snagging his motherly medic, Terr pointed out reasonably,

since he was at the Center, he could be relocated to the visitors quarters. Nothing doing! The medic wanted him right where he could find him. He would not chase Terr all over the city if he had a relapse. What about clothes, Terr protested? He planned to go out that night. Look in the wardrobe, the medic said and left Terr gaping after him.

Evening shadows were staking out their corners when Teena came for him. He paced, pestering the computer for time checks with increasing anxiety, afraid she wouldn't come. He behaved like an adolescent, he knew, but couldn't help himself. Then she was there and he broke into a huge grin. She wore the same outfit she had on earlier and he suspected she had come straight off work. He was immediately concerned.

He took her hands in his and searched her eyes. "We don't have to do this if you're tired," he said gently and she giggled.

"Silly. Just a long day, no worse than others. And you?"

"I'm a prisoner!" he complained bitterly. She laughed and tossed back her hair.

"Poor Terr. Let me rescue you, then," she chirped and dragged him out by his hand.

"I am all yours, my pet."

It was warm outside and the avenue filled with strolling people, the whisper of overhead traffic and shuffling feet. They took the glidewalk. Terr craned his head at the surrounding towers, lit by their reactive panels. The connecting tubeways were yellow ribbons of light high above. It felt good to be alive, to feel, to see. He looked at Teena and squeezed her hand. She flashed him a smile and pointed.

"This is where we get off."

The Slee Club faced the boulevard, its entrance well lit without being gaudy. Wide black doors slid away as they approached. The attendant inside smiled and bowed.

"Dama Raye, your usual, I presume?"

Subdued lighting kept the large floor in shadow. Comfortable tables lay scattered in seemingly careless disarray, but the arrangement left plenty of room between them. Tall potted plants added to a sense of privacy. The place smelled of fine cooking, rich wines and expensive spirits. Heads turned as the attendant led Teena toward a corner table.

Terr allowed the upholstery to mold itself around him and nodded in appreciation.

"Wow."

Teena dimpled. "It's close and the girls have lunch here when we get tired of the Center's plastic issue meals."

"Not bad. I could get used to this."

The attendant unobtrusively brought two short, narrow-necked glasses filled with a thick red liquid. Teena picked hers up and scrutinized Terr's face.

"I am glad to see you recovered," she said softly.

He touched his glass to hers. The crystal rang with clear purity.

"And I am glad to see *you*," he said and smiled into her eyes.

The red liquor fiery, but silky smooth as it went down, leaving a lingering fruity aftertaste.

"Excellent," he said and took another sip.

"Terr, I don't want to talk about your mission, not tonight, but I have to understand something."

"Why I rammed that raider?"

She nodded, her eyes cloudy and dark.

"I couldn't let it get away," he said simply, and then chuckled. "I know. It sounds silly saying it like that, but it's true. This wasn't any raider, but one of Tanard's, although I did not know that at the time. Capturing its crew means we're possibly closer to finding his base."

"But you could have been killed!"

"Hah! I certainly didn't plan it that way. I had a survival blister all ready to blast me off the ship before I cracked in. I simply never got around to using it," he said with a shrug and smiled.

"How can you take it so lightly? Your life is not worth

229

Tanard's or anyone else's. I mean—"

"I know. I *have* to take it lightly, Teena. I cannot worry about what might happen to me or I'll not be any good at what I do."

She looked at him, shook hear head and sighed. "What made you take service in the Fleet?"

He did not mind the questions. It forced him to think about some of the answers where there were no real answers. Sometimes things simply happen. He hadn't intended to ram that raider, but it was the only solution that minimized the risk to his crew and the other M-2. Perhaps the other M-2 could have disabled the raider. Then again, perhaps not. Would he do it again given the same circumstances? But circumstances are never the same.

The attendant brought them hot dishes of thick steaming noodles swimming in rich brown gravy. Terr bit into one and his eyebrows lifted. The noodle pieces were filled with fine minced meat and vegetables. The sauce tangy and hot and he blinked at its bite. Teena seemed to relish the tidbit. Okay, she liked hair-curling hot food.

"Almost didn't," he said around a mouthful. "Join the Fleet, I mean. My father was killed when his ship crashed into Anar'on. Now isn't that a twist of fates? He was Anabb's first officer at the time. I was still a boy. My mother didn't want me to follow in my father's footsteps. She had lost a partner and presumably didn't want to lose me in the bargain. Irrational, I know, but these things don't have to make any sense to still rule our lives. Go into the diplomatic service, she urged. Your uncle will look after you, she said. Enllss would certainly have looked after me, but I didn't want that kind of patronage."

"You wanted to make it on your own?"

"It's a macho thing, you know," he said and she rolled her eyes. "Had I listened to her, I would probably be a stuffy bureaucrat on Captal right now. But I had stars in my eyes and went to the Academy instead. My mother never forgave me. To this day, she doesn't speak to me and I have no shadow." He shrugged and forked another piece of noodle.

Teena swallowed and watched as Terr attacked the noodles. He made light of his mother's rejection, but it was clear it still hurt. She placed her hand on his.

"I'm sorry," she whispered and was rewarded with a warm smile.

"Tah, the gods will tell," he said in Saddish-aa without thinking.

She stared at him. "What did you say?"

He looked sheepish. "Sorry. It's a Wanderer saying. It means that our fate is held in god's hands. It also means that sometimes the god needs a little help."

She giggled. "You are irreverent."

"The *Saftara*, it has words for every occasion," he explained.

"Your brother Dharaklin. You sometimes call him Nightwings."

"The shadow who walks at night. When a Saddish-aa youth undergoes his first trial—"

"Trial?"

"Faces the god of Death."

"You mean a *real* god?" Teena stared at him in wonder.

"That's still a matter of intellectual debate, but to the Wanderers, the gods are manifestly real. Anyway, when he faces the god, a presence really, not a real being, he is judged to see if he is fit to receive the god's blessing. If found worthy, the youth is in a manner reborn. He walks away with the power of Death itself. He can kill at a touch or at a distance, the effect manifesting itself as lightning."

"It's true then? The legends?"

"It's true, all right."

"But with that kind of power—"

"Why don't the Wanderers march in holy war across the

Serrll? They could and there would be terrible carnage and misery before they were stopped. And the gods have their own way to prevent abuse of their gift."

She was silent for a moment. "What if the youth is found wanting?"

"Ah! Sometimes nothing. Sometimes, he is driven mad or loses his soul, or both. If the affront is great enough, he's never seen again."

"So why do you call your brother Nightwings?"

"Well, once a Saddish-aa Wanderer successfully undergoes his first trial, he is a warrior and entitled to bear a new name. No one may call him by that name other than another warrior."

Terr suppressed a hiss of annoyance. That one had slipped out and he cursed his loose tongue.

"But you call him Nightwings."

He could read the unspoken questions in her eyes. He had forgotten what she was, conceivable that she could work out the connection. Behind those beguiling eyes and melting smile lay an excising intellect.

"Well, ah, it's the thing we share. After joining, we were one, like brothers. It entitles me to a measure of tolerance." He hoped it wasn't as hollow to her as it sounded to him.

"Mmm." Her small mouth concentrated in a pretty frown.

Something occurred to him then and he paled. If Teena had access to his reports, she presumably could access Dhar's, and sometimes his brother called him Sankri. What if Dhar used that name in one of his reports? Gods!

"Are you all right?" Teena asked, obviously concerned.

"It's nothing. Only a twinge."

She looked chagrined. "Perhaps it was a mistake bringing you here. I'm a fool!"

He grabbed her hand and squeezed. "Teena, I'm fine. Believe me. Besides, we're not leaving until I find out all about you."

"Compared to yours, my life has been dull."

The dishes were cleared and replaced with the main course: an assortment of different fried meats, filled savories, mashed vegetable balls and fresh salad. The attendant also brought a carafe of rose wine, icy cold and delicious, its bouquet fragrant and inviting. It took some time to make an inroad into the serving and they spent it in idle chatter.

Terr found it hard to eat, talk and stare at Teena all at the same time. She noted his dilemma, of course, deriving much amusement from his predicament. In the end, he gave up eating, pushed his fork around the plate, and concentrated on looking at her.

"Why hasn't someone already run away with you?" he asked on impulse.

Glass halfway to her lips, she paused. "I guess my work consumes me as yours consumes you."

"Thin." He shook his head. "That argument wouldn't stop a determined stud from snatching you."

"Well, there is no way that *you* will snatch me, if that's what you were thinking."

"The thought had crossed my mind once or twice."

"You're terrible!"

He laughed, comfortable in her company, finding her easy to talk to, and she did not judge. He felt that he could tell her anything and she would keep the trust. He folded his hands under his chin.

"And…"

She took a sip of wine and placed the glass down with a click. Her fingers played with the stem.

"There were moments when I thought it was love," she said softly, afraid he would laugh. His gray eyes looked at her with understanding and compassion. That was important. "I had fun. I won't be a hypocrite and say I didn't, but it had no meaning even while we loved. I guess I clung to my image of a perfect man knowing that there is no such thing."

She challenged him with her eyes.

"Were you afraid to commit?" he asked softly.

Her fingers twined around the glass stem. "Afraid of failing, I guess. Afraid of getting hurt. It's much safer to keep things at arm's length."

"Yeah. You avoid the hurt, but you also miss out on being close," he said seriously, because he was talking about himself. He wanted to draw her to him then, to comfort her, to keep her safe from any hurt. He wanted to tell her that he would never be the cause of her pain.

Her heart skipped a beat. He did understand! Her eyes sparkled as they searched his. A doubt popped into her head and exploded. Did he really mean it or was this a polished come-on job? After all, he was a flashy agent and all the girls knew what they were like and what they wanted. Looking at him, she didn't believe it. Not of him.

"It takes time to get close," she said. "And you?"

Looking at her, he smiled. It takes time, all right.

"What was it you said once? That I'll just have to chance it?"

"Oh, you're impossible!"

He chuckled, then sobered. "Locked in a ship, there are not all that many chances, even with a mixed crew. When you're a commander, there are none. A commander cannot allow himself that if he is to lead. When I hit dirt, I am still a commander. There is maintenance, reports, meetings with brass, endless things. When I did get a free moment, I spent it with Nightwings. One-night stands never really appealed to me."

"That's not what Razzo said." She grinned impishly.

"And I told you not to believe everything he said."

"Ah hah."

After a fine brandy for him and a liqueur for her, they strolled hand in hand down the boulevard toward the blazing lights of the Center. Taltair's capital city never slept. Despite the late hour the stores and restaurants were filled and the glide-walks crowded. Lots of people chose to stroll along walkways simply for the hell of it.

Terr had no idea what they talked about, but they suddenly found themselves in front of the Center's residential tower. Teena patted back her hair and gave him a small smile.

"I had a wonderful time," she said demurely, suddenly nervous and apprehensive.

"Me too." Terr brushed her cheek. "Tomorrow?"

"I cannot in the morning, but I'm free in the afternoon," she said brightly. "We can go sightseeing."

"I would like that." He leaned close to her and she stood very still. Her lips were soft and yielding when he touched them with his. Her scent sent tingles of fire down his body. "Thank you," he whispered and pulled back.

Looking into his eyes, Teena brought up her arms and wrapped them around his neck. Her breasts moved against him and his arms encircled her, drawing her hard to him. Her lips parted and she closed her eyes.

When he brought his mouth over hers, he could taste the liqueur on her lips. Everything dissolved as her velvety tongue timidly felt him. The effect electric and his skin prickled. He explored the sensuous softness of her tongue and mouth and she moaned. He pulled back and kissed her cheek.

"Of course you know, this will send me into a relapse," he whispered into her ear and she giggled.

"Beast! Now let me go, please, before this gets out of hand." She touched his lips with her fingers and almost ran toward a row of waiting communals.

He watched the driver close the bubble behind her. The power plant spooled up and the communal lifted straight up. She fluttered her fingers at him, and then she was gone. He stared long at the spot in the sky where she had vanished.

Teena…

And she still hadn't told him anything about herself.

Rit!

The next two days were moments of magic stolen out of

time. His mornings were spent in rehab and tests, but the afternoons were all theirs. Terr had never seen much of Barden and Teena delighted in showing him around. The first evening, they hopped from place to place, sampling foods and entertainments. As the capital, the city attracted the best from all over the planet.

Teena was laughter and she was sunshine and happiness and irrepressible energy. She was innocent and wise and wonderful. It was like getting hit by a whirlwind and it left him both exhausted and bemused. Being with her was also very satisfying. She had managed to pry open that part of him he'd kept shut for a long time. The hinges creaked a bit at the effort, but she finally contrived to work her way inside. Only then he realized how lonely he'd been. Dhar would always be his shadow, but there were things Terr could not tell even his brother. With Teena, she had peeled him open and he wondered if he would withstand the scrutiny.

Should he tell her about himself? One day, he would have to. Right now, though, things were still too delicate, too uncertain. He needed her to get used to him as himself first.

The second night, she invited him home for dinner.

When the door to her apartment opened, Terr stood there and simply stared. Her hair piled high in a twisted bun. The effect highlighted her elfin face and long slender neck. She wore a necklace of small white pearls, contrasted elegantly by a large central black orb. Her simple black dress fell to her ankles. Around her waist, she wore a loose narrow yellow belt that slanted across the curve of her hips. The top of the dress went straight across her chest in a startling contrast with her perfect creamy skin. Misty green eyes regarded him with curiosity and challenge.

"Rit!" he whispered in awe.

Her nose crinkled and she dimpled. "Was that a compliment?"

"You look stunning, but I wouldn't go out in an outfit like

that."

"Oh? And why not?"

"You'd cause a riot."

"Well! At least I'd be noticed."

Terr pulled his hand from behind his back and held out the flowers. Surrounded by orange and yellow orchids was a single purple proteus.

"For you."

Her eyes glowed and she took the bouquet and gently fingered the proteus. "Thank you. Come in while I put these in a vase."

Teena patted the flowers just right, straightened and nodded at the dimly lit dining room. A floor-to-ceiling window screen showed the city beginning to light up against an orange background of a darkening sky. Rich green drapes were pulled back on either side of the window. Only an electronic screen, but the drapes made it look like a real window. In the center of the room, two high-backed chairs were positioned on either side of a glass-topped table. The place mats were light green, contrasting the black napkins.

Terr pulled back the right chair and sat down. The ceiling above the table brightened slightly. Teena came in with a tray of dips and assorted crackers. When she sat down, he picked up the open bottle and poured for both of them. The black wine light, rich, and left a faint berry aftertaste.

Teena looked at him above the rim of her glass. When he glanced up, she dropped her eyes.

"Try the dips," she urged, unaccountably nervous. "I've been dying to make them, but I never seem to find the time."

Terr took a rectangular cracker that glistened with shards of rock salt and dipped it into a small bowl of red paste. He popped the whole thing into his mouth and was assaulted by a mixture of meaty tastes, hot spices and various vegetables.

"It's terrific," he said seriously and tried a mix of what looked like several ground beans. It tasted cool and creamy and he nodded in appreciation.

Encouraged by his reaction, Teena sampled all three dips, very conscious of his presence. The last two days had worked a transformation. There was a solidity about him, a presence that dominated the room. His eyes were in shadow, but she could feel them on her, and felt slightly intimidated. Something melted in the pit of her stomach and she gave a small shudder.

"How much time do we have?" she asked on impulse, afraid to shatter the moment.

He looked at her. So…

"I don't know," he said. "I'm getting discharged tomorrow as fit for duty. I doubt that Anabb will simply let me wander about."

"Then you'll be going after Tanard again?"

"His ships and his base, probably."

"More M-2s, more ambushes, more firefights?" She didn't mean it to come out like that, bitter and reproving, but too late to take back the words. Oh, this was going all wrong!

Terr felt his heart tear at her silent misery. As soon as he walked in, he sensed a tension in her, a reserve so unlike her. He put it down to anxiety that he might not like her cooking. Clearly, much more lay behind her moodiness.

"Teena—"

"Don't!" she cried and raised her hand. "I shouldn't have let you get close. It's just…" She felt her eyes fill and her chest was suddenly tight. She placed a protective hand across it, fingers splayed.

Her distress struck him like a blow and he felt his own chest squeezed. He reached across the table and clasped her hand. She looked at him tragically and hot tears spilled down her flushed cheeks. She did not sob or say anything. She sat there and cried.

In one fluid motion, he pushed back his chair and stood up. Then he was beside her and lifted her up. She let out a wrenching moan and clung to him. He wrapped his arm around her and held her tenderly. As she shook against him, he lowered his head and pressed his cheek against hers.

"It's all right, pet," he whispered and stroked her back. "It's all right."

She sobbed and he murmured soothing words to her. After a while, she sniffed and pulled back. Her eyes were swimming as she looked at him.

"I'm sorry," she mumbled. "I've spoiled everything now."

He kissed her eyes, tasting the salt of her tears. A lump formed in his throat and he swallowed hard. He pressed his lips to hers. She pushed against him and her mouth opened. It was a sweet union that left him full of tenderness and confused feelings. He was quite prepared to take on her hurt if she would only smile again.

She leaned back and sniffed. He wiped away the wetness under her eyes with a gentle finger. She flashed him a small smile and mouthed a 'thank you'.

He stroked her arm and caressed her cheek. Feather light, she rested her head on his shoulder.

"Being with you is hard," she whispered brokenly. "I cannot bear to see you hurt again."

"It's not something that I'm planning on either," he said gruffly.

"But death and destruction follow where you go. I don't know if I can handle that."

There was very little he could say. Whatever he said would only sound trite and patronizing. How can he possibly reduce the essence of what he was and why he did what he did into a few simple words that would make sense?

"I do it, Teena, for all those who cannot."

"It's not fair," she mumbled into his chest.

"Perhaps not, but that's how it is."

She lifted her head and her eyes glistened. "I know. I'm being silly and I've ruined your evening."

He smiled into her eyes. "You're my angel and as long as

you say my name, I shall always be there for you."

"Always?"

"For all time." He let her go and cleared his throat. "I had better go…"

She held his hands and leaned toward him until her fore-head touched his chest. "Don't go," she said faintly. "Stay with me."

He could feel her shiver and his arms went around her.

"I need a little loving and some comfort right now," she said in a small voice.

Gently, he picked her up and her arms circled his neck, her sweet breath hot against his cheek. He carried her out of the dining room and headed for the only other door he could see. It opened as he approached. The room was dark and he sensed large. A green safety strip ran along the bottom of the walls. He could barely make out a wide bed as his eyes adjusted to the gloom. She shifted against him when he stopped beside the bed. With a kiss to her forehead, he leaned forward and slowly laid her down. Without saying anything, he kicked off his shoes and lay beside her. He gathered her in his arms and held her close to him. Trembling, she buried her head in his chest. He stroked her back, paused, then repeated the gesture. She continued to tremble.

"You won't mind if I cry a little?" she asked softly. "I won't make a sound."

He continued stroking her as she shook with silent sobs.

Time took on a fuzzy quality and seemed to stand still. Terr held her and blinked into darkness. He sensed her breathing slow and become even. He did not move for fear of disturbing her, happy to be merely with her. He felt complete and more joined with her than he ever felt with another being—even Nightwings. With Teena, the bond was physical, tangible and real. Nightwings filled his soul and would always be there, but the love they shared was at a different level.

Did he love her?

Right now, right at that moment, he had no doubts whatever.

She stirred and her head lifted. He could sense her eyes on him. Her lips touched his cheek.

"Love me," she whispered into his neck.

Terr's heart pounded and his mouth went dry. How he wanted to taste her sweetness, abandon himself in her, but right now? When she was so soft and vulnerable?

"Are you sure?" he asked, not daring to breathe.

She moved against him and her head rested on his chest. "I have been sure from the first moment I saw you, my Saddish-aa warrior."

When Terr hesitated, she pushed herself up. Kneeling on the bed, she reached up and loosed her hair. It fell in a cascade around her bare shoulders. One hand behind her back, she undid the clasp and the dress parted along the seam. She slowly lowered her arm and the dress slid in a rustling heap around her hips. Her breasts tightened in the cool air and she waited.

In the dim light, Terr could make out her form, the small breasts and slender arms. He knelt before her and gently touched the bare skin of her shoulder. She shivered and bit her lip. Her skin felt smooth and cool and he ran his hand down her arm. He brought up both hands and cupped her breasts. They were soft and yielding and he gently pinched her nipples. She swayed toward him and pressed herself against his hands, her breath hot on his face, then arched her back. He kissed the swell of each breast, lingering over the feel of her satin skin. She gave a little whimper of pleasure. His mouth went up her neck and cheek before his hungry lips found hers.

"My sweet," she mumbled and his tongue twirled around hers.

Still joined, she fumbled with the front of his shirt while he unclipped her belt. She swept her palm against the soft hairs on his chest and pulled the shirt down. Her arms went around his neck and she pressed herself into him. Locked in an embrace,

241

Terr pulled her to one side until they were both lying down.

He leaned over her and tugged at the bunched material around her waist. She lifted her hips and he dragged the dress down. She kicked it free. He placed his palm on her left breast and slowly stroked the soft mound. Traveling to the other breast, he kissed it and moved his mouth to the flatness of her belly. His fingers slowly sought the edge of her black panties and tugged. She lifted her hips again and he slid the flimsy material off her.

It took only a moment to take off his trousers and pants. Lying beside her, his hand moved gently across her body, feeling the curves, the swells, reveling in her smoothness and warmth. Her thighs parted and he positioned himself between them.

"Teena…" he whispered and slowly pushed into her.

"Uh!" she moaned and mashed his head against her breasts.

Terr felt a wave of joy and warmth ripple through his body. Teena had given herself completely to him and he was gentle, their lovemaking slow and satisfying. There was no need for urgency. Passion with love, which made it very special. Her body moved under him. The effect sent tingling needles along his back. Their mouths sought each other in desperation and hunger.

Afterward, they rested, her head nestled against his shoulder. Her sharp fingernails marched playfully through the small hairs on his chest. She grinned when he winced.

"I am so glad your chest is not a rug," she murmured. Wearing an impish smile, she traced patterns along his skin.

His arms encircled her. One hand caressed the delicate smoothness of her back.

"Have you been playing around?" he demanded in mock outrage.

"Oh, I've been taking samples."

"I knew it!" He pinched her rump.

"Ow! That hurt!" she yelped and bit his shoulder in retaliation.

He tightened his grip on her and she let out a soft growl of satisfaction. She felt safe with him, protected from what lay outside. She had been upset and uncertain about pursuing this relationship. She could not forget seeing him all hurt and broken when they brought him in. It had torn her apart and she slept badly thinking about it. Faced with a painful decision, she had ruined their evening together. But he hadn't taken advantage of her moment of vulnerability. Instead, he was there to comfort her, asking for nothing. She valued that. Tomorrow could bring pain and hurt, but right now, she knew what she wanted.

"Tell me more about Anar'on and the Wanderers," she purred dreamily, her fingers marching across his chest.

Terr's thoughts were a whirlwind of images.

"In the morning," he said in a low voice, "when the sun is about to break and the sky is all red, the desert slowly wakes up. Colors become alive. Yellow dunes stretch as far as the eye can see. Brown sand streaks their steep sides. On the flats, the sands gently undulate like waves in a heavy swell and they go on until they touch the sky. The air is rich with the fresh scent of burnt rock, tarad grass, and oily peelath. In some places the dunes are covered with spiky tarad and you can sometimes see tendrils of fog drift above the grass fields. The silence is all pervasive and it feels like you are standing in a cathedral. The Saffal has a terrifying beauty that's enchanting while it's killing you if you're not prepared to face it on its terms."

Teena listened to his words and the hairs on her arms stood on end. She had never seen a desert, except in a Wall, and could not understand how something so alien can also be so captivating. Clearly, Terr felt a mystical attachment, which she wanted so much to be a part of, to share.

"And you love this land?"

"The Saffal is a cradle of rock and sand and fantasy and it took me when I crashed. Whether I want it or not, it's now part of me. In a way, I am most complete when I'm there. Life for the Wanderers is hard there, but it's not without beauty, culture and sophistication. It's not the sophistication of our lives, but we would be enriched if we treated ourselves and others the way they do themselves."

"How do people live if there is no water?"

"There are shallow aquifers everywhere and over the centuries the Wanderers have developed skills to tap into them."

"But where does the water come from if it's all desert?"

Terr grinned at her perceptiveness. "The gods provide."

"Mmm."

"They say the polar caps drain into the desert and feed the aquifers. Others say that evaporation could never sustain the drainage process."

"In other words, they don't know."

"That's about the size of it."

"Yet the Wanderers thrive there."

"Anar'on is a large world and there are not all that many Wanderers. They live in scattered villages, tribes who have carved out a harsh life in an even harsher environment. They have the oark; hairy lumbering animals that provide them with milk, hair for weaving, skins and on rare occasions, meat. They grow legumes and forage. When the tarad becomes scarce, they seek other pastures. A single village will occupy hundreds of talans of territory. Harsh as their life is, they have the Discipline and the *Saftara* to guide their lives."

"With death in their hands," she murmured.

"And they do unleash it on each other sometimes," he admitted. "They cling fiercely to their way of life and resist the change that had been imposed on them by having to deal with other worlds. Yet deal with them they must."

"So they created the Unified Independent Front?"

He grinned into darkness at her perceptiveness. "Clever girl. They first unified the eight systems around them, which now makes up the Kaleen group. Now, with Orgomy's six systems, they're seeking independence. As a political force with a voice in the Executive Council, the other powers will have to deal with them more warily."

"But how representative is the UIF of the ordinary Wanderer who has perhaps never heard of us, or even seen an offworlder?"

"I cannot say. Having lived with them, though, having experienced the rich texture and density of their lives, I would also fight to preserve what they have. Their lives appear simple, but they have a culture that is rich and complex and the teachings of the Discipline rivals any set of moral tenets anywhere. Cloaked in Death, their morality has to be strong or they would have wiped each other out."

"I would like to walk your desert sands and see a red sunrise," she said wistfully.

"One day, maybe that too."

Terr could feel her eyes on him as they lay in silence, surrounded by the desert. He sensed her questions, but she did not ask them, for which he was grateful. He had said far too much already.

"Thank you for tonight," she whispered after a while. "After ruining everything…"

"Love you, Teena-raye," he said tenderly and brushed hair off her face. She nuzzled his neck.

"Would you mind terribly…"

He sat up and she straddled his hips. He gasped when she took him in. She leaned forward, placed her head on his shoulder and gave a long sigh of contentment.

* * *

"You're fully fit for duty?" Anabb growled kindly.

"I have a workout program I must follow for a while, but I feel fine, sir," Terr said guardedly. He couldn't say anything else. Anabb had his medical report and knew exactly his condition.

"Good…good. I want you to take a commercial shuttle to Kalakan. The reservation is already made. Check with Ariane. Your M-1 is still on Kalakan," Anabb said, not at all pleased as he looked sharply at Hiragawan. "Once there, touch base with Master Scout Li Aron and resume your mission."

"Aye, sir. Anything new from the raider's crew?"

"We're following several promising leads. It takes time to properly check out every likely location, my boy. However, I feel the net is slowly closing on Tanard. Or his base at least, which for me is far more important."

"Agent Terrllss-rr," Hiragawan said sternly. "Disregarding your insubordination when you broke off contact with me—"

"I was in the middle of a firefight, sir," Terr said patiently.

"One that you had no business being in. You have also blown your cover to Master Pilot Thoran!"

Anabb cleared his throat in warning. Hiragawan bit his lip and fumed in frustration.

"Very well. We'll leave that one for the moment. There is something else far more serious. I have been reviewing the report made by Master Scout Hvar. By using your aspect during that highly controversial interrogation of your prisoners, you violated—"

"That subject is closed!" Anabb snapped and glared.

"But, sir! Once we start adopting—"

"Enough! I don't want to hear it."

"Yes, sir," Hiragawan mumbled, not looking very happy. Clearly, the Branch Director held his protective arm over Terr and he was smart enough to know when to stop pushing.

Terr carefully avoided looking at Hiragawan. The man carried a chip on his shoulder the size of a combie, when he should have had more sense than to take things personally. Oh well. You cannot have everything.

"May I ask, sir, how Dharaklin is doing?"

"Took three more raiders," Anabb said with satisfaction. "None were Tanard's, but that was expected. He somehow knew you were wounded and wanted to rush to your side, but he had a job. At any rate, you seem to have someone else looking after you."

Anabb knew that Terr and Teena were seeing each other and was pleased. The boy looked relaxed, confident and obviously ready. There was something else there, a new resolve, and Anabb suspected how that came about. Young scamp!

"You have time to say goodbye to Teena before catching that shuttle," he growled in dismissal.

Terr stood up.

"Son? Good job so far."

"Thank you, sir." Terr stood to and walked out.

Anabb grinned and shook his head. "A talent that boy has for getting himself into trouble."

"Sir, I must protest at being dressed down in front of a subordinate," Hiragawan complained.

"Thunderation! That wasn't a dressing down. I told you before. Terr's approach, unorthodox it may have been, but effective. Right now, that's all that matters."

"It may have been effective, but he has broken the law! Instead of protecting him, I would have him charged."

"You can tell it to all the merchant crews those scum have killed and ships destroyed," Anabb said wearily. "How many now attributed to Tanard?"

"Twenty-eight."

"Twenty-eight," Anabb repeated. "And we're not counting losses to zealots and simple opportunists. After ramming that raider, instead of prosecuting him, I'm recommending him for a decoration."

Hiragawan clamped his mouth in stern disapproval. Anabb sighed and sat back.

"Look, I know that technically, he has broken the law, but we're faced with a virtual war scenario—"

"Even in war—"

"Thunderation! How many men have you personally liquidated since you've been with me?"

"Ah, well…"

"Care to analyze the legality of those acts?"

"The circumstances—"

"Different they were, granted. They always are, but I won't sand for a holier-than-thou attitude. Not from you or anyone else in this Branch. Is that clear?" Anabb said harshly, the warning in his voice unmistakable. "As for revealing himself to that merchant pilot, he was focused on the mission objective. He gambled the raider was Tanard or one of his ships. Besides, Thoran is bound by the Nondisclosure Act." For some reason he could not fathom, Hiragawan had adopted a singular dislike for Terr. Chemistry, he figured and gave a mental shrug. "Whatever is going on between you two, get over it."

"Yes, sir."

Hiragawan was stung by Anabb's remarks and realized that he had allowed himself to get emotional over something Terr probably didn't even know he had done. Still, to have one of his own race a raider…What burned was the boy's irreverent and casual attitude to authority and discipline. That Anabb tolerated such behavior was beyond him.

"Now, you have anything else for me?" Anabb demanded.

"Terr's suggestion to mount M-2s in other carriers—"

"I'll talk to Sill-Anais. Is that it?"

"Two raider hulls were intercepted drifting off the edge of the Kaleen/Deklan shipping corridor."

"So?"

"When examined, the crew were found dead where they sat. Both ships had a single burn hole that ran right through the hull. The exit damage suggested something like a projector burst, but there were no detected emission residuals. The Fleet investigators cannot account for it."

"Crew postmortems?"

"They exhibited evidence of neural disruption, every one of them. It's almost like they were electrocuted."

"In a manner of speaking, they were," Anabb mused. "How much do you know about the Wanderer Discipline?"

Hiragawan stared. "Are you saying those ships were taken out by a third level Discipline adept?"

"I received a memo from Sill-Anais, advising me that Prime Director Marrakan has authorized deployment of Wanderers into their merchant fleet. Hah! It looks like Anar'on has grown weary of Palean and Deklan antics and decided to take affirmative action."

"We are in an end run then?"

"Hardly! You must remember that for now, Anar'on is looking after its own. There are plenty of carriers coming into Kaleen space that could still have their ass shot off. We'll have to concentrate on them. As for this being an end run, I'll sleep happy once Tanard is on Cantor and his base a slag heap," Anabb commented dryly. "But they're only a symptom. We won't rid ourselves of this nonsense until the AUP Provisional Committee itself is silenced. They are far more dangerous than any raider."

Chapter Six

Blurr-reep...blurr-reep...

The emergency transponder signal seemed inordinately loud in the confines of the almost silent command deck. Tanard glanced at the comms watchstander and nodded. A second later the signal cut off.

"Talk to me, Mr. Winn," he rasped and absently ran his fingers along the scar tissue of his neck.

The touch left a painful trail of fire in its wake. At night sometimes, his throat felt like it was closing in on him, preventing him from breathing. He would jolt awake panting, having to consciously tell himself he was having a psychosomatic reaction. Knowing what was happening did not exactly alleviate the discomfort of the symptoms. He really should submit himself for treatment before he *did* choke!

Once this mess was over, he told himself.

"A type nine Tadrak hull, Deklan design. It's powered down. Detecting eleven survival blisters."

Tanard frowned. Eleven blisters? Was the ULC carrying passengers? Not unusual and wouldn't stop him from doing his job. In fact, the ensuing public outrage may work to his advantage.

"Are we clear?"

"Nothing within tactical range. Our Fleet movements schedule is now fourteen hours old, but we should be safe if we clear IP within two hours. The second contact scooted off at one point-one lights."

It looked like they had stumbled across a raider in the act of picking over his victim. Well, bound to happen sooner or later. Not sure what *Lahra* was, the raider wisely chose to be somewhere else.

"Time to intercept the ULC?"

"Eleven minutes at current boost."

"Go to full boost and set primary alert."

"Full boost, aye. We're attacking the ULC?" Winn asked without emotion. "Including the blisters?"

"They are also targets, are they not?" Tanard said without feeling.

"Some of them could be carrying passengers, sir."

The command deck became suddenly quiet, everyone waiting. Tanard touched his throat.

"Perhaps, but they're still targets, is that clear?"

Winn simply nodded. Everything out here was a target. Really very straightforward when he looked at it that way. There was nothing to discuss, nothing to decide. Life reduced to its basic primordial level: hunt and flee. Questioning only raised doubts and doubts threatened his efficiency to hunt and flee. He had trained himself to think in terms of targets only, hulls. If he strayed once from that and started thinking about crews, he knew he would lose a vital edge that kept him sane. There also lay darkness.

ULC or blister, just a hull...just a hull.

At least the raider saved them the trouble of running down the ULC. Its pilot probably pissed at having such a rich prize snatched from his grasp. Winn grunted. Tough shit. He glanced at Railee.

"Get us warmed up...Engineering, going to full boost."

"Command deck. Recommend ninety percent only. With all the speed runs we've been doing lately, you're pushing the primary drive way over its recommended limits."

Winn mashed his finger against the comms pad. "Engineering, are we in all respects flight capable?"

There was a perceptible pause. "Aye, sir."

"Then execute the order."

Tanard listened to the exchange and nodded. As first officer, it was Winn's job to know the status of every system aboard *Lahra* and deal with them. Engineering was out of line and Winn had rightly jumped down their throat. Tanard could not fault Winn's performance. If they lived, Winn would turn out to be a very fine commander—in whatever service they might find themselves.

Lahra surged.

Railee brought the Koyami to full readiness and extended both shield grids. Synchronized, he was ready to engage. He didn't care about the why of it. As far as he was concerned, Tanard and Winn could handle that part. All he needed to know what target and when to fire. As for fighting the AUP cause? Fighting for a cause meant dying for a cause. In his book, a mug's game. Don't get emotionally involved. Stay detached and live. They were going to get him sooner or later, he knew that, but he'd been living on borrowed time ever since Feron. Right now, every day being free a bonus.

Winn dropped normal 180,000 talans behind the stricken ULC. A masterful piece of piloting. At full secondary boost, it took seventeen seconds to bring the ULC within 60,000 talans. Without waiting for orders, Railee fired two long bursts at the engineering spaces. Plating blew out as the hull was penetrated and air gushed in frozen streamers. Railee walked the beam along the hull, seeking out the reactors. One burst must have caught the secondary drive reactor, for a sudden explosion ripped the giant carrier into several spinning sections, each larger than *Lahra* itself, accompanied by a cloud of smaller debris.

At a leisurely one-third boost, they methodically hunted down the eleven blisters.

When *Lahra* attacked, the sensors in each blister must have told them what was happening. They sent frantic pleas for mercy on the emergency band. From the screams, women and children appeared to be on board some of the blisters. Tanard sat on his command couch unmoved, his mouth a tight line. For Railee, it was ordinary target practice. One burst usually enough to overload the blister's power cell containment field and the thing would brew up in a flash of white light and flying junk. At least it was quick.

"All targets destroyed, sir," Winn reported at length. Hulls, just hulls.

"Very well. Stand us down and clear the datum point. Transit and set three-quarter boost along designated bearings."

"Transiting along designated bearings, aye, sir."

Lahra vanished in a burst of blue-white light.

Tanard was about to pry himself up when the comms watchstander looked at him.

"Sir, personal from Khiman-ra. It's Administrator Le Maran."

"Very well. I'll take it in my quarters."

The screams were loud in his ears as he rode the cable-tube down.

In his cabin, he took off the zip-jacket and ran a hand through his hair. He flopped on the formchair with a sigh and turned to the Wall.

"Computer, enable comms link."

The Wall cleared and Le Maran bobbed his head. "You look exhausted," he said without preamble.

"Ghosts, friend Maran," Tanard mumbled. "And you can add one more to our score."

"You have the ULC?"

"Interrupted a raider in the process of gutting it."

"I doubt he was very happy at seeing you," Le Maran said and chuckled.

"Probably not. Scum! I hope you will tell me that *Griga* is operational."

Le Maran's fingers twined and he looked distracted. "For the moment, I'm holding *Griga* back," he piped and prepared himself for the inevitable blast. It came quickly enough.

"Holding it back! For pit's sake, why? We have Naurun and Omiron in a sling. Kaleen freight costs across the board have gone orbital. Insurance premiums are edging close to hull values and some carriers are refusing to take on Kaleen trade. I've been watching the newscasts. Another month, I tell you, and they'll fold. Can't the AUP see that?"

"We don't have another month!" Le Maran snarled. He hated these sessions. Tanard always made him feel that he had missed something, making him look foolish, but not this time. "Anar'on has started manning Kaleen and Orgomy carriers with Discipline adepts. You know what that means? One of those heathen creatures can destroy you before you can get into range."

"Worm crud!"

"Is that so? Well, it wasn't worm crud for the two raiders caught off a Deklan/Kaleen shipping lane. Pierced like insects and left drifting, they were. An example to others, no doubt."

"Okay. They may be able to protect their own hulls, but they cannot protect the hundreds of carriers coming into Kaleen. It's impossible."

"Friend Tanard, listen to me. All they have to do is scare off enough raiders and they will have won. The Fleet will then be free to concentrate on you. How long do you expect to last if that happens, eh? After your aborted attack on that VLBC the other day, it should be clear even to you that we need to rethink our tactics. Until we do so, *Griga* and the other two ships are grounded. You are the operational commander and you can overrule me, but you must know that I'm right. In view of recent developments, I would urge you to recall *Trasher* as well."

Le Maran was about to add he had orders to scale things down, but refrained. It wasn't the time to start yet another argument.

Tanard glared and fumed, but his anger not wholly directed at Le Maran. He still thought the administrator was a cowardly woman, but he conceded that this time, Le Maran had made some telling points. Unpalatable as it was, he *had* been forced to abort an attack on what looked like easy prey. When he transmitted his IFF the carrier immediately activated its emergency transponder. It surprised the hell out of him and he had been too far off to press an attack, uncertain as he was of the exact position of Fleet units in the area. He knew that at least one M-3 was within six lights. Not an immediate threat, but his data on two prowling M-4s was over a day old and those monsters could have been anywhere. He chose to run.

Later, he thought he knew why the VLBC had sounded off. COMKALOPS and Sector TACOPSCOM must have changed the IFF code designators to include positional data. Even with a stolen IFF code, however real, as soon as he returned a carrier's ping, it would show him way out of position where the code said the real Fleet ship should be. Rather than risk being wrong, the carrier would naturally activate its transponder. It was a dirty, low down sneaky trick to pull on him and he had to admire the cunning of whoever dreamed it up.

But placing Wanderers in Kaleen hulls? That was nasty. Worse still, and he hated to admit it, Le Maran was absolutely correct in his situational assessment. Tanard's activities were manageable only because he prowled in a cloud of other raiders, either working on their own or supported by the Committee. It didn't matter which. If the Wanderers destroyed enough of them, the rest would undoubtedly flee and lay low or go elsewhere. That would indeed enable the Fleet to concentrate on him and *Trasher*. With Hardara gone, losing *Trasher* would not be good. Moreover, Khiman-ra itself could now be seriously vulnerable. Pits! Nobody told him this would be easy, but did it have to be this bloody hard?

"There is another thing to consider, friend Tanard," Le Maran went on, trying to be conciliatory. "You're overdue for maintenance and resupply. I dare say your crew could use a break as well."

No matter which way Tanard sliced it, Le Maran was right. After all the speed runs lately, *Lahra* badly needed maintenance, as did his crew. He also wanted to change his power plant emission signature again. Disguised as a fast courier, it accounted for him having a large main drive, but *Lahra* still radiated too closely to M-3 specs. He would not be happy until he could vary that signature at will. If he were ever boarded for an inspection the game would be over. The only way to prevent that was by not giving a prowling M-3 a reason to board him.

"Very well," Tanard conceded. "I'm coming in. *Trasher* will remain on station until I have completed my turnaround."

"I look forward to seeing you," Le Maran said earnestly, genuinely relieved.

"Friend Maran, I am very serious about activating your evacuation procedures. If Khiman-ra is taken, I don't want us to lose the ships as well."

"I shall keep it in mind."

"There is one other thing I want you to do," Tanard said. "Set up an automated ping to be transmitted by Khiman-ra's SC&C on a two-hour interval."

"Is that really necessary?"

"It cannot hurt."

* * *

The shuttle angled into the thin atmosphere with barely a shudder. Below, Kalakan lay in a mosaic of browns, greens, and azure oceans. Whorls of white clouds stretched from the southern polar cap almost to the equator in one enormous weather system. In full phase the daylight glare made Terr squint.

After eight days and three shuttle transfers, he'd had enough of smiling hostesses, bowing waiters and dreary cocktails. Even the few eligible women attractive enough to have peaked his interest and who may have been similarly inclined were out of reach. With Teena occupying his mind, he simply wasn't interested. He spent a lot of time working out, getting himself back into shape, but he couldn't keep that up for a whole day, every day. Not inclined to join the ship's organized entertainment programs, dull affairs anyway, it made for a tedious flight. The time he did have, he spent most of it thinking.

His last night with Teena in particular, occupied a lot of his thoughts. It was not the consuming intimacy, which only made him hungry for more, that disturbed him. What surprised him were the soul-fulfilling moments of tenderness, compassion and understanding he felt for Teena's pain and uncertainty. The physical love they shared could not hope to compare with the satisfaction he felt by just being with her, holding her, comforting her when she was open and torn with tragic indecision. She had become part of him and the realization left him very sobered.

Clearing customs was one of the things he hated when taking civilian flights. When upward of eight hundred passengers, all scrambling to be first, dragging squalling brats and luggage, poured out of the shuttle, he felt trapped. He plain didn't like crowds. There was one compensation. With his Diplomatic Branch clearance, he bypassed normal protocol and was out of there quickly.

Once outside, Terr dropped his travel bag and exhaled. The passenger terminal was a hive of activity: people pushing baggage carts, strolling, gawking at shop displays, hurrying to catch that flight, or simply looking bewildered and lost. Giant Wall screens showed flight information: arrivals, departures and landing ring data. Others cycled through glittering ads of city attractions and things to be had there. As a premier Fleet base, the Field required considerable infrastructure and personnel support, all of it needing accommodation. The terminus well lit, modern, and noisy. The constant hum of background voices never let up.

Well, you cannot have everything.

About to pick up his bag, he spotted a tall, gangly figure

dressed in a plain brown suit on one of the numerous glide-walks traversing the terminus.

"Nightwings!"

Dhar broke into a smile and stepped off the moving glide-walk. Terr hurried toward him and they embraced. That earned him a few curious looks, but he didn't notice them.

"As always, I am happy to be basking in the warmth of your shadow, Sankri," Dhar said, his deep voice rough with emotion. It was good to be together again.

Terr stepped back and swallowed. "And I am filled with peace now that you're here, my brother. What *are* you doing here?"

"Are you well?" Dhar's eyes clouded with concern, searching his brother's face.

"You know about that?"

"When I felt your pain tear through my body, I knew something terrible had happened."

So, their bond indeed transcended the physical barrier between them. They would have to talk about that—later. He grinned and stretched his arms.

"Everything is working again as you can see."

Dhar frowned and shook his head. "A reckless thing to do, Sankri. Brave, but reckless."

"Now you're talking like Anabb," Terr growled and punched him in the arm. "Lighten up. What I did poured more sand into Tanard's machinery. They cannot shoot me for that. You haven't told me what you're doing here."

Dhar picked up Terr's bag and ignoring the glidewalks, they sauntered toward the military end of the terminus.

"Five days ago, I was intercepted by an M-1 and brought here. The frightened little Second Scout driving the thing wouldn't tell me anything. I think he was intimidated by me."

"Hah!"

"We got in last night."

"And?"

"They told me to pick you up and go to the military terminus."

"That's it?"

Dhar smiled. "Just following orders."

Terr snorted. "It's Li Aron playing his little games. Well, since I have nothing better to do right now, we might as well humor him."

"Did you enjoy your convalescence?" Dhar asked casually and Terr grinned at him.

"I enjoyed it very much, thank you."

"And Teena. How is she?"

"She's fine, you randy old man."

"Sankri—"

"Just kidding." Terr paused and looked deep into Dhar's orange eyes. "I love her."

Dhar stopped and placed his palm on Terr's chest. "I delight in this, my brother."

Terr gripped the hand and squeezed. For a few timeless seconds they looked at each other in silent communication, then resumed their walk.

"She has a problem with what I do—"

"I have a problem with what you do."

"—but we'll work it out."

"Does she know—"

"About my aspect? No, not yet."

"You will have to tell her sometime," Dhar pointed out gently. "And show her. Otherwise…"

"I know."

"But she suspects?"

Terr chuckled. "Somehow the little imp senses that there is something strange about me. She is surprisingly perceptive. What's worse, she has this insatiable curiosity—"

"The mere presence of power is an influence," Dhar quoted from the *Saftara*.

Terr cocked an eyebrow at him. "Looking into those green

eyes of hers, I found that out. There was a moment once on the transport…I thought of her and she was there! It startled the hell out of me, but no matter how hard I tried, I could never bring her image back. What happened, Nightwings?"

Dhar nodded. So…

"When someone becomes close to you," he murmured in a deep, resonant voice, "that you feel joined, you can reach out for that person. Part of the other's essence if you will, or soul, can manifest itself as a real image. Although unusual in someone who has undergone only the first trial, the ability is more prevalent in a second level adept. It appears, Sankri, that your attachment to Teena is indeed more than mere infatuation."

"It is, but why haven't you ever appeared to me then?"

"We are always together, my brother."

"Yes. Something to think about." Death stirred and Terr had an urge to lift his hand and conjure her image, but this wasn't the time. He looked up at Dhar's gaunt features and smiled. "What of you? How did you like your time in command?"

"To tell you the truth, it was easier than I imagined it to be. Even during moments of action chasing a raider, it came effortlessly to me."

"And fun, no?"

Dhar grinned. "I admit to enjoying the experience. Of course, I only had a handful of men—"

"Handful or two hundred, it's only a matter of degree," Terr said. "It's a feeling of being in control and free, with everyone ready to respond to your every whim that makes command tolerable."

Dhar frowned. "It was not all fun. The experience was also humbling. The weight of responsibility, the knowledge that my mistake could cost a life or everyone's life, sometimes rested heavily on my mind."

Terr nodded with understanding. "You cannot dwell on it or it will crush you. You can only take it as things come and rely on your training and judgment. You cannot fear making a mistake. Everyone does so sooner or later."

"Even you?" Dhar asked with a cocked eyebrow and Terr chuckled.

"I never make a mistake."

Dhar looked up and shook his head in resignation.

At the security checkpoint into the military terminus, a grim looking marine guard passed them through. On the other side, the hall smaller, but just as crowded. After all, Kalakan *was* a major military base.

Terr looked around and glanced at Dhar who shrugged.

A stocky First Scout emerged from the left departure lounge, spotted them and hurried toward them, his ship's boots soundless on the polished marble floor. He stopped before them and tugged down the zip-jacket of his working grays.

"Mr. Terrllss-rr…Mr. Dharaklin?"

"You've got us," Terr said amiably.

"I am Vibar, first on *Udav*, an M-6. If you two will follow me, please."

About to ask what this was all about, Terr refrained. Someone was bound to enlighten them eventually. It always happened. When they got to the lounge, the two figures sitting around a small table broke off their animated conversation and stood up. Terr gave a wry smile.

Li Aron bobbed his head, his fingers working and hands fluttering. "Agent Terr, I am pleased to see you again and in one piece."

"Thank you, sir."

"Allow me to present Master Scout Yia Rdan. You have already met his first officer."

"A pleasure, sir," Terr said and nodded. The short Palean gave him an appraising stare.

"Your reputation precedes you, Mister, if I am to believe friend Aron," he piped and puffed out his chest.

"It's all true, except for the bad parts."

"A man of humor. I like that."

"Friend Terr," Li Aron interrupted. "You are no doubt curious at your change of orders."

"The thought had crossed my mind."

"Yes. Well, we found Tanard's base. At least we think it's his base."

Terr broke into a grin. "Now that *is* good news."

"Information supplied by Hardara and his crew proved crucial and filled gaps in our intelligence. To that end, your action in ramming the raider was justified."

"If you were under my command, Mister," Yia Rdan hissed, "you would be facing a general court for losing the M-2."

"So I've been told already," Terr said indifferently, wondering what the hell was the matter with the man. Compared to the empty hull value of even a type four hauler, he could get two fully outfitted M-2s with crews thrown in as change. If Hardara had gotten away, what would have been the cost of more lost shipping and lives? Compared to that, the idiot worried about one lousy M-2. Disappointing to see such a narrow attitude from a senior officer who should have known better.

Yia Rdan colored and was about to deliver a blast when Li Aron raised a hand.

"Friend Rdan, we've been over that," he said with quiet authority that brooked no argument.

"Humph!" Yia Rdan cleared his throat and shot Terr a cold glare. "We'll get along, provided you don't plan on scrapping any of *my* assets like that."

Terr looked at Li Aron. "Then my assignment here is not over?" The thought of some joint operation with the prickly Master Scout did not exactly set his hair on fire.

"Not quite." Li Aron gave Terr an appraising look and smiled in sympathy.

The boy would go far unless some superior officer somewhere didn't shoot him for insubordination first. Perhaps in his line of work that is what it took to get the job done. Terr was brash, irreverent of authority, clearly confident in himself, and Aron was a little envious.

"Master Scout Yia Rdan commands an M-6. *Udav*, with its two M-4 escorts, will proceed to Galia, a Palean system eleven lights from a major Kaleen shipping corridor, and secure the Khiman-ra base located on Ophir, the system's fourth planet. Its job is to validate that it is in fact Tanard's base. As this is a Diplomatic Branch mission, you will be in tactical command," Li Aron said woodenly.

"Damned bureaucratic nonsense!" Yia Rdan fumed.

Terr understood then what bothered the senior officer. Yia Rdan probably saw this as an all-Fleet operation, and justifiably resented political interference. Having Terr in overall command came as a final insult.

"Friend Rdan will do his duty as per orders, Agent Terr," Li Aron said firmly. "I have received additional instructions from Director Anabb Karr regarding the handling of this mission. The file is in *Udav's* computer. Access code is niner, two, alpha, alpha, enable."

"Do you know the substance of those instructions, sir?" Terr asked.

"The message is personal coded to you," Li Aron said, allowing a touch of pique to creep into his voice.

"I see. The fact that we're all here means we're to get underway immediately?"

"At your convenience, Agent Terr," Yia Rdan snapped.

"I wish you luck in tracking down Tanard," Terr told Li Aron warmly and stood to.

"We'll track him down, friend Terr," Li Aron said with obvious relish. "One thing. If the Diplomatic Branch has any more chores of this kind, I would be obliged if you could tell them to keep me out of it?"

Terr grinned. "I'll do that."

Li Aron looked at Dhar. "Mr. Dharaklin, try and contain

your friend's predilection for ramming ships, okay?"

"I shall see to it, sir."

"I wish you good hunting, then." Li Aron nodded to everyone and walked quickly out of the lounge.

A tense and silent group made its way to the access tube. Terr didn't particularly care if Yia Rdan was somewhat ticked off, as long as the Palean did his job. Simply glad it was over. At least, he hoped so. Not over for Li Aron, though, but none of Terr's business. Would Li Aron catch Tanard? From what he came to learn of the renegade officer, he was sure Tanard would have left himself with an out. Well, that was Aron's problem and he was welcome to it.

Yia Rdan wasted no time with preliminaries and lifted as soon as they boarded. Given the Alikan Union Party's intelligence network, it was conceivable the operation was already compromised. If true, by the time they reached Galia, they might very well find a gutted installation. Another imponderable not worth worrying about. Cleaning up Khiman-ra sounded simple enough and he liked that. The sooner the messy business was done, the sooner he would be on Taltair with Teena. The thought gave him a warm glow of anticipation.

Terr had never been on board an M-6, but from inside, it could have been anything. Stiff and reserved, Yia Rdan invited him to the command deck, but Terr excused himself. He wanted to view Anabb's instructions. He and Dhar had adjoining cabins, which was convenient. His quarters were spacious and comfortable and reflected the M-6's size.

He dropped his travel bag on the carpeted deck and sighed. Wearing a wry grin, he tilted his head at Dhar.

"The end of the hunt, my brother."

"I am not sorry, Sankri."

"But I'll bet that Tanard will be."

"If Khiman'ra *is* his base."

"There is that. Right, then. Let's see what Anabb has to say."

They walked into the study and Terr turned to the Wall.

"Computer, access coded file personal, niner, two, alpha, alpha, enable."

The wall cleared and Anabb stared at them from his office.

"You should be on your way by now, Agent Terr. Master Scout Yia Rdan may not be happy that you're in tactical command, but he'll carry out his duty. Any problems that you may have with him, deal with them. I have supplementary instructions for you that go beyond the mere mission brief given to Master Scout Li Aron.

"You know that Tanard's operation is a dangerous method to exercise interstellar diplomacy. As such, it could serve as a destabilizing example to others, whether promulgated by Sargon or anyone else; like the Deklans. I don't have to tell you the effect if others take it into their head to emulate the practice. BueCult and the Security Council cannot allow this. A clearest possible message must be given in warning. If you manage to locate the rebel base, you are tasked to totally destroy it by saturated bombardment from orbit. I don't need prisoners. I have enough already. How you deal with them, I'll leave that to you. Hand them over to Yia Rdan if you like, but no one is to escape your net. That must be clear. On execution of your orders, return to Taltair for an assignment debrief."

The Wall turned to images of pooling colors, all flowing into each other in never-ending patterns. Terr leaned back and looked at Dhar.

"Well! What do you make of that?"

Dhar allowed the silence to linger for a long time before his eyes lifted.

"Total destruction with no mercy? Even pirates deserve due process before the law, Sankri."

"But these are not pirates, Nightwings," Terr said gently, fully aware of his brother's misgivings. "They are worse than that."

"Can one injustice be cleansed with another?"

"I wonder how much justice Tanard and his ships showed to the merchant crews *they* slaughtered."

"That was not what I asked."

"I know."

"Then you intend to carry out these orders?"

"I do, and what's more, I agree with them. The question of morality and ethics doesn't even arise. Don't worry. The rebels will receive a measure of mercy from me, even if it's not de-served."

"Sankri, my brother, this action goes against the teachings of the Discipline, but I also understand its need. Sometimes an evil must be simply burned away. I stand with you, no matter what."

"I know," Terr said gently.

* * *

Black clouds raced above a slick apron. Ribbons of jagged light danced in their dark bellies. A rolling low rumble shook the window, hesitated and moved on. A sheet of white lightning licked the earth and a hideous crash bellowed in defiance. The sound rolled ponderously across the heavens. Low on the hori-zon the wall of broken clouds bathed in blood. Then the rain came, slanting walls of hissing water that obscured the hills and the buildings: cold, heavy, and gray.

Le Maran stared out the window screen and sipped his tea. He could almost hear the thin whistling of the wind as it worked its way through the trees at the end of the landing field. The base looked forlorn and deserted in the fading light. Even the gray shapes of his two refitted raiders nestling on their landing skids looked weary and abandoned. Fully provisioned, they would be leaving tomorrow. *Griga* was already on its way to Ratalan. The new base far from complete, but serviceable enough that he didn't have to use the temporary staging facili-ties at Manargee, with all its security implications, and he felt happier knowing that one of his assets at least was safe. Besides, it got Tanard off his back. He resented having to hold down two jobs. Tanard far too senior to be piloting a raider himself. Time for his operational commander to pull his weight.

Despite his pique, Le Maran was satisfied. Khiman-ra had proven itself, as had he. The AUP hierarchy was very pleased at the damage inflicted on Kaleen's commerce, and there was a hint of being moved to headquarters once Naurun and Omiron were secured. Even Ti Inai was complimentary, albeit grudgingly, and did not comment on the loss of two ships. His order to scale down the attacks not altogether a total surprise. In fact, Le Maran welcomed it. Everyone needed time to collect themselves and recuperate.

The comms alert beeped. He frowned, placed the cup on the table with a loud click and pressed a pad in the small inlaid console on his desk.

"What is it?"

"Long range scans show an M-6 with two shadowing M-4s entering the system. Their course places them on an intercept with Ophir, sir," Levan said breathlessly.

Le Maran stared at his assistant and felt his face drain. His heart began to pound. Could this be a simple innocent flyby? They had Fleet units routinely running through the system, but not in such force.

"How much time do we have?" he managed a strangled squeak.

"Seven minutes before they drop normal. One minute after that, if they're after us and going full boost, they'll be in orbit. Orders, sir?"

Le Maran was in a bind. If he authorized a general evacuation and the Fleet ships only transited through, he would look like a panicked fool. On the other hand, delaying a call to evacuate could cost needles lives. In the end, there was really no decision to make. Installations can always be replaced. Personnel were far more valuable. If this was for real, some of them could conceivably make it to Manargee, where the local AUP cell would process them.

"Can we get the two ready ships off?"

His assistant shook his head. "We could get them away, but their primary reactor is cold and it would take too long to prep it. They wouldn't be able to transit."

Le Maran frowned. That was too bad. "Set general code One FQ, friend Levan," he ordered and cut contact.

A moment later the sirens sounded.

"Evacuation order now in effect!" the computer announced. "Evacuation order now in effect! This is not a drill!"

Outside his office, Le Maran heard startled shouting and a thud of running feet. Everyone was supposed to be familiar with evacuation procedures for their section, but he wondered how many actually bothered to study them. He'd held only one drill two weeks ago and knew it wasn't enough. Too much to do and too little time to do it in.

"Computer, connect personal with Commissioner Ti Inai."

After forty agonizing seconds the Wall cleared.

"You fool!" Ti Inai snarled. "I told you never to contact me. Do you realize the risk I'm running if this transmission is intercepted?"

"I regret the inconvenience, friend Inai, but I thought you would want to know this."

"Know what?"

"It's likely that Khiman-ra is about to be attacked."

Ti Inai's face remained impassive. "You're right. I did want to know. You are evacuating?"

"Even as we speak. Forgive the rush, but I have to cut this short." Le Maran touched the comms pad and the Wall faded into pooling grays and strings of blue. Depressing, like the whole day.

"Computer, if the base comes under direct fire, initiate core purge."

"Acknowledged. The Administrator is reminded that

standing instructions call for general self-destruct."

"Disregard."

"Acknowledged."

Setting off the base reactor would level the whole area in a ten-talan-radius, effectively removing most of the evidence that something had ever existed here. The blast would also kill many of the personnel fleeing into the countryside. In an ironic twist of fates, Le Maran now appreciated better why Ver Dit failed to execute his last order.

He tapped another pad on his console and a camouflaged door slid into the wall. With a last look around the office, he hurried into the small cubicle. The door clicked shut and he felt a tug as the cable-tube accelerated. It seemed to take an eternity for the tube to reach the underground launch bay. When the door finally opened, he exhaled in relief and ran toward the landing ramp of an already hovering transport. A shadow fell across him and he looked up. Another transport was clearing the overhead doors, its nav screen bright against a dark sky. Cold rain slanted into the hangar and the wind howled in protest. The transport climbed into low clouds and disappeared. Le Maran scrambled up the ramp even as it lifted beneath him. Knees weak from tension, he sagged against the bulkhead. After a few deep breaths, he straightened and touched the tube hatch pad. A moment later the hatch hissed open.

"Command deck," he piped as he walked in and the hatch closed behind him.

When it opened again, he automatically glanced at the transparent nav bubble. Nothing to see but thick overcast. Seconds later the ship broke through. The western sky a smear of reds, yellows and orange reflected off towering cloud columns. Above them, evening stars winked back.

"How many do we have, Mr. Levan?" he demanded. The figure on the central couch swiveled around.

"We picked up thirty-four and the other transport has forty-five. I don't know how many the first transport carried off."

Probably another fifty or so, Le Maran reflected. Not at all bad—two-thirds of the entire base complement. Some were outside, in workshops or otherwise unable to reach a transport in time. If they managed to bleed into the surrounding hills, they should make it. Unless, of course, the Fleet sends out search patrols. He pitied the poor devils.

"Sir, the M-6 has dropped normal," the tactical watchstander said. "It has an L-band lock on the first transport. They are firing! The transport…it's…it's gone."

There was shocked silence as everyone grappled with the horrible fate of their sister ship.

Le Maran looked at his assistant. "What do you intend?"

Levan grimaced. "We cannot run for it, that's clear enough." He glanced at the plot watchstander. "Take us into low orbit and head around the other side of the planet. When we break their sensor lock, drop down."

"Aye, sir…The M-4s have dropped normal and are closing to bracket Ophir."

"Once we're down," Levan added, "we'll disperse into the countryside. Some of us might get lucky."

"Your optimism is encouraging," Le Maran murmured sourly. "How long before the M-6 gets into range?"

"Fourteen seconds."

"Can we make it around before then?"

"Sir! The second transport has dropped its nav grid and is powering down."

"Cowards!" Le Maran snarled. Levan gave him a pitying stare.

"I would drop my shields now if the alternative meant certain death," Levan said.

"Idiot! They are dead already. What do you think the Fleet will do to them?"

"Better a corpse on Cantor than one out here."

"Orbit achieved, sir," tactical said. "Going to one-quarter

secondary boost."

A brittle black sky stared down at them. The transport canted slightly and Ophir's white crescent filled the nav bubble.

"Unidentified vessel! You are ordered to power down and assume neutral status," a cold voice announced over the emergency band. "This is your only warning."

"L-band lock established by the M-6. Firing point in five seconds...four—"

"Take us down now!" Levan screeched.

It took two precious seconds for the ship to slow for orbital insertion. The transport stood on its beam and slanted down. Then that the M-6 fired. It must have been at extreme range, but the 218 TeV beams from its twin projectors still struck the transport with a physical blow that made the ship shudder and groan. Control panels flickered wildly. A moment later the ship slued and flipped over under another powerful strike. The main deck lighting went out and someone screamed as the restraining field gripped them. The air filled with the sharp smell of ozone. Bright blue sparks slithered across exposed surfaces from the near-field effect.

"Computer, issue a general abandon ship and enable survival blister launch," Levan shouted.

Nothing happened. The restraining field let them go. Color-reactive pads blinked into darkness. Levan met Le Maran's gaze as the ship moaned to the thin sigh of the upper atmosphere. Someone scrambled for the nearest survival blister hatch and slammed his palm against the large brown pad beside the hatchway. The hatch immediately clanged open, its edge outlined by a bright yellow stripe. The figure disappeared inside and the hatch slid shut. Before it could launch, the M-6 fired.

Le Maran always wondered if he would know what it was like to die. Curiously, he was not afraid. He could see bulkheads glow and deform as the hull melted. Sparks jumped and arced from point to point, eating everything they touched. He felt

himself stabbed by hundreds of burning needles, the pain ex-
cruciatingly sharp. The air burst into flame and he finally managed an agonized scream. A flash of yellow light vaporized the
bulkheads and his cry suddenly died as his body turned into
plasma.

A shower of scattered debris trailed orange fire as it
plunged into the atmosphere.

* * *

The command deck reflected the huge size of the M-6 warship. Eight watchstanders manned the various stations in addi-
tion to the command and executive couches mounted on a
small platform. A two-katalan holoview node rotated in the
center of the deck. The equally large nav bubble reflected tactical plot data from the main display plate.

"We're getting painted by a long-range sweep, sir," the exec
said without a trace of emotion.

"Galia SC&C?" Yia Rdan demanded.

"Negative. It's coming from Khiman-ra on Ophir."

Terr watched the byplay between the watchstanders with
interest. He had come to learn this was not a happy ship. Not
that Yia Rdan was cruel or vindictive in any way. He just exuded
an atmosphere of gloom and rigid discipline that left little room
for informality or levity.

"Thank you, Mr. Vibar," Yia Rdan replied with equal cool-
ness. "What is our transit time?"

"Seven minutes."

"All the ABPs told off?"

"Ready to launch on command, sir."

"Very good. Go to primary alert, but don't raise the secondary grid. Advise the M-4s."

"Aye, sir."

Terr took a deep breath. No use putting it off any longer.
He should have raised this earlier, in private. It was merely one

of those things. Well, they were never going to be pals. So…

"Master Scout," he said deliberately, knowing that the next few minutes could be somewhat uncomfortable.

Yia Rdan turned. "Mr. Terrllss-rr?"

"If confirmed, you will not interdict the rebel base, sir. When you get into low orbit, subject the installation and its perimeter to saturated bombardment. Is that clear?"

"My orders are to identify the base and then secure it, Mister."

"Those orders are now countermanded."

Yia Rdan gave a sour smile. "I have no idea what constitutes normal operating procedure in the Diplomatic Branch, but in the Fleet, we carry out orders. I don't play by your rules, son."

"Sir, you're aware of my authentication and clearance codes? Please don't force me to use them."

"Damn your clearance codes! What you're asking for is murder!"

"I'm not asking for anything, Master Scout. I have given you an order."

"Under protest, Mister!"

Terr felt his face flush and his skin prickle. He swung himself out of his seat and stood over the Palean. The silence around the deck thick and uncomfortable, everyone waiting in tense anticipation at the unfolding drama.

"What the hell do you think we're playing at here, eh?" Terr shouted. "Some elaborate game? Honor and glory? Well, there is no honor in this and damned little glory. If your refined sense of morality is a little rattled, you should have stayed where it was comfortable. While you wear that uniform, sir, you take whatever is dished out. Copy that?"

Not exactly the most endearing speech he had ever given, but right now, he didn't give a damn, heartily sick of Yia Rdan and the whole dreary business. He only wanted to get it done and over with.

The Palean turned white with fury. He pushed himself up and glared. "You dare talk to me like that on my own deck? I could have you shot!"

"But you won't," Terr said, his smile grim. "Those clearance codes, remember?"

"To the pit with your clearance codes! I wonder how you sleep at night, you cold-blooded bastard."

"I sleep just fine…sir."

"I shall carry out your orders, Agent Terr, but I tell you this. I don't like any of it."

"Nobody gives a shit whether you like it or not, Master Scout. I don't like it either, but I have my duty."

"The shield of duty can hide a multitude of sins, my boy," Yia Rdan said wearily.

"And dirt. It sure can, but right now, we've got a job to do. Let's get on with it!" Terr hissed and clenched his fists, eyes blazing.

Yia Rdan turned to Vibar. "Make an entry in the log noting my official protest at these orders and cite Mr. Terrllss-rr for gross insubordination. Charges and specifications to be entered later."

The exec glanced at Terr and bit his lip. "Ah, sir. Technically, he is not part of the Fleet TO and cannot be charged under regulations."

"Just make the entry!" Yia Rdan bellowed and scowled around the deck. "Stations!" Everyone was suddenly very preoccupied.

"Sir, a small transport has cleared the atmosphere envelope above Khiman-ra," the tactical officer advised. "Another is lifting off."

"Dropping normal," Vibar announced.

"Challenge it to stand down," Yia Rdan ordered.

"No response, sir."

"Dispatch *Skira* to head it off—"

"Master Scout," Terr said as he sat down again, his face

expressionless. "You will destroy that transport in place as soon as we have lock."

Yia Rdan glanced at Terr, then looked steadily at Vibar. "Execute his order."

The main display plate showed the orange blip of the transport surrounded by a pale yellow ring of its nav grid. The transport suddenly accelerated. A red line extended from the M-6 when the warship fired. The blip flared under the impact. Another burst and it became a fuzzy cloud and disappeared.

"Target destroyed, sir," tactical said.

Terr glanced at Dhar standing beside him. "They were only raider scum, Nightwings."

Dhar did not say anything. He didn't have to. Disapproval plain on his stone face.

"We have an interrogative from Galia's SC&C," the comms watchstander prompted. "They want to know what we're doing over Ophir."

"Not now!" Yia Rdan snapped. "They'll just have to wait."

"Sir, *Skira* is in range and has challenged the second transport," Vibar said.

"A third transport has now lifted off," the tactical officer added.

"Range?" Vibar demanded.

"We will have lock in sixteen seconds. Sir, the transport has established a low orbit and is heading around the planet."

"Hoping to evade. It looks like Khiman-ra is our target after all," Vibar mused. "Sir, the second transport is powering down."

"Instruct *Skira* to launch two ABPs and secure the transport, then challenge the third transport," Yia Rdan ordered. "Unless Agent Terr has an objection?"

"No objection."

"No response from the third transport," the comms watchstander said.

"Fire into it," Yia Rdan ordered.

"L-band lock established. Firing in three…two…one!"

"Target destroyed, sir," Vibar reported after the third burst.

"Very well. Ready to deploy the ABPs. Notify the M-4s. Then bring us into position over the raider base."

Udav and the M-4s slowed as they approached Ophir. At one hundred and twenty talans altitude they stopped. Almost immediately, a cloud of Assault Battle Penetrators emerged from the three warships and dropped into the atmosphere. Their job was to interdict the immediate base perimeter and snare any escaping personnel.

Angular pebble shapes, the twenty-two-katalan-long platforms were designed to carry a six-man assault team, attach itself against a target ship, burn its way through the hull and board it. Heavily armored to withstand limited bursts from an M-4, the little ships could penetrate a vessel's secondary and primary shield grids, making them particularly deadly in any close-quarter encounter. They were also handy for carrying assault troops.

"Sir, we're in position," Vibar said and Yia Rdan glanced at Terr.

"On your order."

"Commence fire," Terr said, his voice impassive. Coward! Didn't want blood on *his* hands.

Twin tracks of yellow ionization stabbed through the atmosphere that instantly vaporized the cloud layers below. In the tactical plot, the display showed the target ring pulsing under direct assault. It was impossible to see the effect of the bombardment. Terr didn't have to imagine what it must be like. He had seen it before and the images burned in his mind.

They were only raiders, he told himself. Worse than raiders, scum of the lowest order and not worthy of any sympathy. Society had already tried and judged them. He was merely being the black hand of an executioner.

On the ground, the projector fire sent whirling geysers and disassembled particles shooting into roiling clouds, themselves torn apart by the ravenous energy streams coming down. Structures literally dissolved as atomic binding forces were overcome to reform into lighter elements. The very air burned.

Twin beams hit the raider ships sitting on the apron and the unprotected hulls vaporized almost instantly. It happened so swiftly that both drive reactors in one ship flashed into plasma before they could go critical. However, that was not the case with the stored fuel cells. The fraction of a second it took for the heavy casing to degenerate was enough to disrupt the containment field and set off the volatile antimatter pellets. In a searing white flash the cell vanished. Its sphere of expanding energy added to the conflagration. This set off two more cells and the reaction burned a hole into the underground facility below the apron. A wave of consuming plasma devoured everything it touched—and reached the main fuel storage chamber. The resulting blast produced a crater eight hundred katalans wide and almost two hundred deep. The effect seared the storm clouds above it, letting through the cold stars of night.

When the bombardment started, there were still many who were scrambling to find a means of escape. There just weren't enough sled-pads, combies or cargo lifters to accommodate everyone. Inevitably, bitter fights broke out between what minutes ago were comrades, sometimes with deadly effect. For most of those outside, the end came quickly. Caught under direct fire, their bodies simply vanished before they could feel anything. For others, death took them more slowly.

When the air burst into living flame, there were seconds of mindless terror as garments, hair, eyeballs and flesh melted before the body itself vaporized. Outside the immediate near-field effect of the projector beams, people simply burned, screaming, running, tearing at clothing and charred strips of skin in an attempt to relieve the agony as blue sparks flowed over their bodies. As the underground fuel depot flashed, it brought merciful relief.

The ABPs came then to sweep for dazed survivors, stumbling in shock, horror reflected in their vacant stares.

Terr lived it all and his soul hardened.

On the command deck the watchstanders monitored their stations. Only computer status reports interrupted whatever they were thinking. They had no hesitation firing on fleeing raider ships, but this cold-blooded extermination left some with mixed feelings.

The weapons officer looked at Vibar.

"Detected a secondary energy bloom, sir," he said somberly. "Probably a reactor core breach or a fuel cell reaction. Target is destroyed."

Vibar nodded and turned to Yia Rdan. "The ABPs have deployed and are conducting a grid search around the base perimeter, sir."

"Very well. Secure weapons and stand down." Yia Rdan swiveled his seat and looked at Terr, disgust and loathing plain on his face. "Satisfied?"

"Yes, sir," Terr said, his voice hollow and indifferent.

"In that case, Mister, you have no more business on my command deck."

Terr immediately stood up and strode to the cable-tube. Dhar's heavy footfalls were loud behind him.

Chapter Seven

The comms watchstander blinked and suppressed a yawn. The graveyard watch almost over and his thoughts kept drifting to images of a soft bunk and six hours of uninterrupted sleep. Besides, his duties did not exactly keep him busy. Waiting for the computer to tell him that he had an incoming, then him telling Mr. Winn, or whoever happened to be officer of the deck, that they had an incoming, he might as well not be here. The computer could handle the whole dreary thing, but would command listen? Oh no. They wanted the comms station manned at all times. Stupid. All officers were nuts, created for the sole purpose to make a rating's life a misery. He'd been stupid himself to be here with them. Well, that's what he got for volunteering.

Napping, he was caught unawares when the top left corner of his full-dimensional display plate suddenly blinked bright orange. A soft chime accompanied the blinking. Following procedure, he told the computer to send an interrogative ping. Nothing.

"You've got something?" a pleasant voice inquired behind him.

The watchstander looked up. Mr. Railee was all right. He didn't fuss and never got excited over the small things. Watches under him were easy and relaxing.

"It's Khiman-ra's ping, sir. It hasn't come through at the designated time slot. Neither has my interrogative. It's like SC&C isn't there."

Railee nodded and strode to the command couch. He pressed a pad on the armrest console.

"What?" a harsh voice demanded.

"Command deck, sir. We lost Khiman-ra."

There was a moment of silence.

"Advise *Trasher* to make for Manargee, then get us moving in the same direction."

"Aye, sir." Railee turned to the comms watchstander. "Raise *Trasher* and issue code blue enable."

"Code blue enable. Aye, sir."

"Plot? Turn us to Manargee on designated bearings. Three-quarter boost."

"*Trasher* acknowledges, sir."

"Very well."

"Answering three-quarter boost on designated bearings, sir," plot said. No one would know a thing until the change of watch. Some would miss the action, but most would not care one way or another.

Railee nodded and closed his eyes, comfortable with the computer taking them to their destination. No more targets...

He settled himself onto the couch and pursed his lips. His long fingers slowly tapped the armrest. Was Khiman-ra really lost? It would represent a very costly investment for only three months of raiding. Not that the thought would keep him awake. If the Alikan Union Party were happy with the deal, so was he. Would this mean an end to their raiding? Probably, at least until the powers that be decided what to do next. That was all right with him too. He could use a break. Everyone needed to get out of this tin can, taste fresh air and put some distance between themselves. He only hoped that Manargee's entertainment facilities had more to offer than merely Wall flicks. Once they reached Ratalan, he suspected that entertainment would be hard to come by.

He leaned back and closed his eyes, his thoughts dwelling on shapely targets other than ships.

His sleep broken, Tanard clasped his hands behind his head and stared vacantly at the dark ceiling. Soothing background noises broke the thick silence that blanketed the cabin. The green safety strip along the bottom of the walls failed to keep dark shadows at bay. He found the small ship sounds comforting. A reminder of stability and permanence, however fleeting. In his present circumstances, stability and permanence were definitely a contradiction.

Khiman-ra fallen, Anar'on dishing it to the Deklans, and the Fleet finally able to mitigate the general raider threat. It was depressing. AUP intelligence briefs told him of M-2s placed in carriers and he had to smile. *Friend Terr, why am I not surprised?* After his own bruising encounter with Terr's M-1s two years ago, he had no doubts whatsoever that his old adversary was behind this latest devilish idea. Not only a cunning maneuver, but also one impossible to counter. Too bad that fates have denied him his moment to face off against the M-2s. With his Koyami, the M-2s would have been a boring shooting exercise. Perhaps it was just as well the two of them never met. Tanard would have hated to lose another arm.

He was phlegmatic about the loss of Khiman-ra. It had simply been a matter of time and Le Maran paid the price for his blind belief that technology and denying everybody the location of the base would be sufficient to maintain security. The attitude typical of Maran's bureaucratic approach to operational problems. The man had no feel for the human element, more comfortable with processes and numbers, and that was his undoing. Had he thought it through, he would have realized the dramatic flaw in his logic. Tanard's crews didn't have to know Khiman-ra's location in order to compromise it. What the Kalakan interrogators probably sought from their captives was not information on distance, but on time. Tanard himself didn't know Khiman-ra's planet, but he knew that it took his ship running at standard boost two days to reach his cruising station. Given enough such bearings, simple triangulation would have given the Fleet a fairly accurate fix on the system. It was then only a routine matter investigating individual leads.

If he carried that reasoning to its inevitable conclusion,

Ratalan would also be vulnerable to the same process, unless he ensured that none of his ships were taken. He did not place much stock in a pilot willing to atomise himself in a self-destruct, but he had lots of faith in computers obeying carefully worded instructions. The twisted irony of the situation not lost on him, and he gave a wry grin. By the time they learned all the tricks, it would probably be too late. To him, that sentiment typified a lot of the AUP's effort—too late.

The fact that the AUP went to the trouble to build Ratalan suggested they wanted to continue applying pressure on Kaleen or some other target. With the loss of Khiman-ra, would that be wise? Naurun and Omiron may be crying out for relief, but destruction of Tanard's force would do nothing for the cause, if anyone cared. He recalled his conversation with Le Maran on the dubious value of applying force to resolve a political problem or prosecute an objective.

The use of military power not a hollow reed, though. As its practicing student, he only had to look at history, anybody's history, to see the value of skillfully engineered application of military tools, or disasters where the practitioners had blundered. He was citing Serrll history, a period when individual ambitions and territorial conquest still formulated interstellar relations. Those days of glory, if there was ever any glory in a battered ship drifting cold in space with bodies torn and minds broken, were now merely romantic fiction. Economic tools; these were the weapons of choice today. Even the mighty Serrll Scout Fleet was merely just one of those tools in that arsenal, and Kaleen a prime example. What was the Fleet doing if not protecting vested economic interests?

Would the AUP continue to raid?

For Tanard the question was irrelevant. He was damaged goods. Discarded by the Fleet, discarded by the Provisional Committee and now, probably by the splinter AUP arm that had used him. Nothing more useless than an out of work killing machine. Crawl into a glass case to be sealed until needed? Not an amusing image.

He knew how to kill and he did it well. So why did the thought of more killing leave him with a decidedly sour taste? In war, someone always had to die. Although it did not wage war, were Captal's methods any more honorable? Admittedly, they didn't kill, but their economic weapons also left a trail of shattered and broken lives. Perhaps an even more terrible end? The hypercorps played their games, uncaring of the little investors who ended up mangled in the process. Who could judge was the worse fate: a mercifully quick end in a projector beam or a lifetime of mental anguish when an investment deal went horribly wrong?

The sounds of screaming children, weeping mothers and frantic pleas before death consumed them were loud in his head. He could cloak his actions under a banner of patriotism, but he was also honest enough with himself to see the difference. Making an investment decision a person exercised choice, whatever the outcome. When Tanard fired on helpless survival blisters, no one in them had a choice. Simple extermination.

When his end came, he figured that hell would have lots of room left for him and the hypercorps.

After three days of boost, *Lahra* dropped normal and allowed SC&C to bring him in. In full phase, shining blue and white, Manargee looked pretty, shepherded by its two orange moons. Three major land masses girthed the eastern hemisphere. The rest, ocean that helped moderate the otherwise harsh winters, compensating for Manargee's relatively long distance from its primary. It also had rich soils, tall snow-capped mountains and a sweet atmosphere. An attractive world, it drew its share of tourists, just what *Lahra's* crew needed before they headed for Ratalan.

The AUP transit facility was located at a real commercial Field that handled passengers and cargo. As a Karkan registered hull, Tanard explained to SC&C he was in for perishable cargo transfer and routine maintenance, all of it true. He dumped his data pack and that was it. SC&C brought him in to a private facility berth his registry said housed Trimuran Shipping, but really an AUP front. The setup bore such a striking resemblance to Lemos that he had to grin. He only hoped the similarity hadn't been carried too far, and the base wasn't used to stage actual clandestine operations. As he found to his cost, mixing civilian and military objectives was a disastrous combination.

There was a moment of poignant silence when *Lahra* touched down on its landing ring. It powered down and waited for the access tube to connect from the terminal complex.

Winn allowed himself a long sigh and turned.

"Sir, we're grounded and the ship is on external support."

Tanard nodded. "Very well. Everybody is to stay put until we sort things out. Pass the word that dirtside security protocols are now in effect."

"Aye, sir."

The comms watchstander looked up. "We have a company rep and two customs officers on the main deck." Only a slight emphasis on the 'company'.

"Mr. Winn, take care of our customs guests and escort the other visitor to my quarters. Nobody from outside is to set foot in Engineering or the command deck." He did not have to explain why. Not that he expected trouble from customs, the Manargee government owned by the AUP. Still, he could not openly flaunt the status of his ship.

"Aye, sir."

Tanard stood up and strode to the cable-tube. The hatch slid out of his way and he got in. Inside, he clasped his hands behind his back and stared vacantly at nothing. He admitted it was good to be down again, not having to stand watches or worry whether the next contact was a Fleet unit or a target. Maybe his ghosts would give him a moment of peace to sleep again. Maybe…

He just had time to splash cold water over his face when the door chime went off.

"Come in!" he rasped and neatly folded the towel.

The door slid back and a rating stood to.

"Sir, Dame Narina Deva, representing Trimuran Shipping."

Tanard nodded to the tall, shapely woman. "Welcome aboard." His eyes flickered at the rating and the man faded.

"Thank you, commander," Narina said softly. She wore form-hugging dark gray trousers and a black jacket. Short brown hair framed a handsome, elongated face that showed character and resolve. This was no blushing youngster to be overawed. She regarded him with bright yellow feline eyes, showing no revulsion at his scars.

Tanard led her to his lounge and sat down. Narina glanced around the plain cabin with curiosity and took an offered form-chair.

"Not too many frills aboard a warship, Dame Narina," Tanard said rather heavily and brushed the scars on his neck. The damn things were hurting again.

"I suppose it's necessary," she said with a small sigh.

"That remains to be seen. No offense, but I expected a senior AUP official."

A curious smile played across her sculptured features. "Commander, I *am* a senior AUP official and president of the Manargee chapter."

"My apologies."

"Now that we know who I am…" She reached into her jacket pocket and placed a black rectangular wafer on the table. "Ratalan's nav coordinates. Encrypted, of course, with a one-time random pad cipher. Before you ask me, I don't know where it is. The chip also has your authentication and authorization codes which will give you unrestricted access to the base computer core." She allowed herself a small smile. "You'll need them as Ratalan's commander."

"Ratalan's commander?"

"There is a downside. You will not pilot a ship again. Your

285

talents as an organizer, administrator and tactician are badly needed and are wasted aboard a ship. We've got plenty of pilots. If we are to face off the mainstream Alikan Union Party machine and the AUP Provisional Committee, we desperately need those talents."

"To conduct more raids?"

"Hardly. Khiman-ra was a throwaway. You must have realized that by now."

Tanard searched her face, then looked into her yellow eyes. This was one formidable woman and not to be underestimated. She knew what she wanted and how to go about getting it.

"Khiman-ra was never intended to succeed, was it? You never wanted Naurun and Omiron, did you?"

"Oh, we would have taken them if they wanted to secede. You just made sure they never would."

Tanard grinned with the left side of his mouth and shook his head.

"All those hulls, all those lives, just to derail the Committee's efforts?"

"Sounds harsh, but that's about it, commander. Don't get me wrong. We believe in the Sargon/Palean merger and a unified Alikan Union Party. Without sounding like a fanatic, it is our destiny. What we do not believe in is the Committee's urgency to consummate the merger."

"Or formation of a Greater Sargon at our expense," Tanard added softly.

Narina gave a small nod. "Exactly. If this is going to be a partnership, then it has to be done on equitable terms. Done clumsily, we could end up with the Palean Union split and in civil war. Not the most desirable of outcomes, even for Sargon."

"If you feel that way, and without stating the obvious, why don't we make sure that our Committee members reflect your concerns?"

"They do, believe me. Sargon holds a five-four voting majority and our cries are lost in the process."

Tanard chuckled. "If the process sucks, Dame Narina, scrap it."

"Or influence its direction through other means," Narina husked with a warm smile, looking pleased.

"Like Khiman-ra."

"That's right. If you harbored any doubts about your fitness for the job, commander, this conversation should have dispelled them. Your incisiveness is exactly what we need to forge new initiatives. Sargon must not take us for granted."

"Flattering, Dame, but you'll have to forgive my cynicism. You realize, of course, unless your views become mainstream AUP policy, you will always be regarded as a radical splinter group, hunted by all. How many Khiman-ra's can you afford to lose before that sinks in?"

"I appreciate your candor, although some would not. Like any organization, we have our share of zealots and extremists. Fortunately for us, they don't control what we do. Let me say that we enjoy considerable support in the Palean Congress. Considerable support. Take it from me. Khiman-ra cost us nothing and it served its purpose. We won't need another."

"If that is so, why Ratalan?"

"Just in case, commander. Just in case."

Tanard let that one ride. "Getting Ratalan to military readiness will not take up too much of my time, Dame Narina. What am I supposed to do then?"

"Isn't that obvious? You will start contingency planning for raids on Sargon shipping."

Tanard almost laughed, but for her expression. She looked at him with her feline eyes, perfectly serious. In an insane way, when he thought about it, the idea not as crazy as it sounded. If Sargon chose to ignore the Palean Committee members, they'd be bound to take notice if the point was illustrated more forcibly. If Sargon retaliates? He doubted that they would. Centuries of comfortable living had diluted their martial culture to mere rhetoric. They'd bluster and threaten, but in the end, they would negotiate; a far more preferable outcome for all concerned. Besides, Captal would crush them if Sargon attempted open hostility. Still, there were other ways for Sargon to even things out.

His initial assessment was accurate. This was indeed one formidable lady.

"Yes, it is obvious," he said slowly.

* * *

Terr desperately wanted to see Teena again. He had so much to tell her, renew what they started and build from it, but a dark shadow hung over his happiness. Tanard, Khiman-ra and raiders were the last thing on his mind. After a tortuous debriefing session yesterday with Anabb and Hiragawan, he went looking for her, only to find she couldn't see him—work. When he asked if he could see her that evening, she begged a previous engagement, which sent his heart fluttering and alarms clanging. What was going on?

Today, he didn't intend to let her get away and made an arrangement to meet her after work, only to be running late!

He walked out of the Admin building, paused and looked around. The evening sky gray and heavy, and the air had a chilly freshness that promised more rain. Even the brightly lit boulevard, filled with strolling, hurrying citizenry, the inviting stores and enticing smells, could not dispel his feeling of gloom. It was that kind of day.

Teena spotted him, flashed him a small smile and waited. Her orange knee-length skirt and dark brown jacket clung to her alluring figure. Like an ornament, she looked delicate and frail, meant to be cherished, not used. He knew her soft exterior hid a toughness of mind that could be determined indeed. He broke into a grin and hurried. Gods, how he missed her!

"Sorry, I just couldn't get away," he said and pecked her offered cheek. It felt cool and soft and he wanted to sweep her off her feet right there and then. Her large green eyes regarded him with curiously detached scrutiny.

"It's not important," she said in a tight voice and slipped her arm under his. "Let's walk."

Her reserve sent a flash of renewed foreboding through him and he was at a loss how to break through this barrier she had thrown up between them. A swirling gust stirred her long hair, but she didn't seem to notice as they walked, together, yet apart. Did he say something to set her off?

His heart trembled and he didn't know why.

It could be one of those women things, but he suspected not. He didn't know what was going on and hated it. Perhaps it was time to let it out in the open and face whatever bothered her.

The evening shadows deepened and he shivered. He only wore a shirt and it was decidedly too cool for that. Ahead of them a restaurant looked warm and inviting, and he steered Teena toward it. She did not seem interested one way or another. The attendant opened the door for them, nodded to Terr and bowed to Teena. He snapped his fingers and a youngster appeared as if by magic, wearing a beatific phony smile. The attendant gave them a speculative look and decided on something.

"Table fourteen, I think," he mused and bowed again. "Gentle lady…"

The place not large, but its deep red décor made it appear bigger while still managing to retain a certain intimacy. Small tasteful lamps discreetly lit the tables, bright enough to eat off without dominating. Comfortably crowded and filled the empty spaces with sounds of animated chatter and occasional laughter. Terr saw little of it as the youngster guided them to a corner table at the back of the room.

He seated Teena and they ordered drinks. He pushed the lamp to one side. She picked up a finger-thick breadstick out of a glass and played with it, avoiding his eyes. It crunched as she bit into it. In the background, soft and enthralling, a song played from the latest hit chart. A song filled with regret, pain and poignant memories; a ballad of youth, beauty, and lost love. The melody moody, tragic, and tender. It was also about war and death, of terror and pain. As Terr listened, the words resonated and touched him in a way uncomfortably personal. The song ended and when he looked up, Teena's eyes were fixed on him. He recalled their night of intimacy and the words could have been his.

He cleared his throat and gave a nervous smile. "Interesting song."

"You wrote the words," she said coolly.

"I'm not a disillusioned youth drowning his sorrows in abandonment of war," he reproached her gently.

"No. You know exactly what you're doing all the time. Your every move is perfectly calculated." She lowered her head and fiddled with the breadstick. When she looked up, he saw pain and sorrow in her eyes, and he felt himself tense. "Remember the night we met?" she asked.

He stared at her, wondering where this was leading and somehow knowing. "I remember," he said at length.

"You were alone, lonely, and lost. In a crowded room, you had no one. I was amused, and I guess attracted as well. You were so unlike my image of a gregarious, extroverted field agent that I was intrigued. You were a mystery, you and your Wanderer shadow. Only later I came to learn who you really were. Whether in your ship or surrounded by desert sands, you are always alone and you prefer it that way. But how was I to know?"

A waiter brought their drinks and Teena flashed him a smile. She took a sip and Terr felt the warmth of her eyes spread through him in a rippling tingle. It was painfully pleasant and he stared at her with deep longing hunger.

"You have so much love to give," she went on slowly, "it's overwhelming sometimes, but you've kept that part of yourself fenced off, afraid that if you let go, you would lose yourself. When you finally allowed me to get close, I treasured that because I knew it was real and not a standard line you spin for every pretty thing that may fill a day or a night. Knowing that, I forgot myself and I let you love me as I came to love you in return. After that night we had together, I thought I worked it all out. Then…"

She played with the breadstick.

Terr gulped down his fiery drink. It burned as it went down. "It's Khiman-ra, isn't it?" He did not mean it to sound cold and accusing. It just came out that way.

She flinched and shook her head. "No, of course not. It's—"

"Ship, base, what does it matter? They were nothing but raiders, worse than raiders. They wanted to tear down everything we treasure and replace it with chaos."

"Don't, Terr," she begged, but he ignored her.

"I take my duty very seriously, Teena. Sometimes that means doing what is necessary, however unpleasant."

"I know," she said in a small voice. "I love you because you're strong, unshakeable and full of purpose, but your path takes you through the worst that life has to offer and I cannot follow where you go. That's why I cannot see you anymore," she said in a rush.

He looked at her in disbelief. His world crumbled around him and he was lost. He clutched his tumbler and felt his heart hammer. His ears buzzed and he had difficulty breathing.

"That doesn't make any sense!"

"Terr—"

"What about the moments we shared, the dreams we made? All the sorrows we conquered? Are all those things lost now? Write them off to experience?"

She reached with her hand and placed it on his. "Those things can never be lost. I sit here and feel the pain tearing at your heart, but I have to do this."

"Love me, Teena," he pleaded in desperation. "I'll resign my commission and we'll be together. No more missions. There is nothing more I can do." He begged and it came hard. He was not used to pleading for anything.

Her eyes glistened, bright with tears. They spilled and ran down her cheeks.

"I would really lose you then," she choked. "Every time you saw a ship go up, a little bit of your heart would go with it. After a while, there would be nothing left. Nothing for me, nothing for you. Where would that leave us?"

Painful as it was, he admitted she was right. He could not change what he was and she knew it, but she'd known that all along. There had to be something else. Follow where he walked? She knew what he did. She read his reports…A deadly calm settled over him and his face turned to stone. Slowly, he pulled back his hand and she tensed. He wanted to tilt back his head and cry out in agony.

Teena! Why couldn't you have left it alone? You should have left it alone!

"Ver Dit. That's it, isn't it?" he whispered in a strained voice.

Her eyes turned deep green and her demeanor changed. From teary and sorrowful, she was now the accuser.

"Your report was restricted—"

"But you couldn't resist, could you?"

"I—"

"I would have told you!"

"Told me what? That with Death in your hand, you were free to dispense your own particular brand of justice?"

It was like a slap against his face and he winced. He groped for the right words, knowing that there were no right words.

"Under law, I could have ejected them summarily into

292

space!"

"I'm not talking about law! I'm talking about you!" She stood up, wiped her eyes and sniffed. "If you still don't understand, search your *Saftara*. Goodbye, Terr."

"Teena…" he started, probing her eyes in vain. For what? Forgiveness? But they only held loathing.

She gave a strangled sob, placed her fingers across her mouth and hurried away. Faces stared at them, but he didn't see them.

In shock, Terr gazed at the emptiness where she had been. The room seemed darker and colder now that she had taken the sunshine with her. Throat tight, he blinked rapidly and swallowed. The world had slammed its door in his face and he hated it for it. He looked into his empty tumbler, empty like his heart. She had taken it all.

He did not know how long he sat there. After a while, he stood up, threw money on the table and strode out. Another song played, but he did not hear it. Teena was right. She was not strong enough to follow where he walked. She would only be in his way, be his conscience. The last thing he needed in his job was a conscience.

All a lie, of course.

Rain fell outside, soft, cold and caressing. The avenue glistened and puddles danced in reflected light. There was hardly anybody about.

He waited for a moment, then hunched his shoulders and stepped into the rain.

* * *

Gentle as a snowflake and just as transitory the breeze tugged at his hair. He did not feel it. Below him, Barden a glittering, flickering vista of patterned lights, reflected in the soft glow of low clouds. He did not see it. Above him the stars winked cool, indifferent to the way of mortals. It was better that way. Not to feel, not to see. There lay torment, anguish, sorrow, and an aching heart. Looking at them, he wondered if the stars were happy with the images they made, alone and uncaring. They blazed with a brilliance of internal fire, but that also made them unapproachable.

In the shadow of Death within which he burned, did that also make him unapproachable?

He could love, and he did love, proved that notion a lie. 'Though you walk in his shadow, a god you are not and mortal you still are.' The words from the *Saftara* rang loud in his head. That's what the words said, but were they true? Cloaked in Death, he *was* immortal, a destroyer of worlds. The gods must have understood that before they bestowed their blessing on the very first nomadic Wanderer who happened to stray into the escarpment of Athal Than. If they had not, or if Athal Than and others like it, was indeed merely an inexplicable physical phenomenon, then wherever the gods really resided, they had played a cruel practical joke on the Saddish-aa—and on him.

Whatever the truth, it didn't matter. His power was manifest and real. He walked in its shadow and whether it chose to show its face as justice or hubris, he was Death loosed. He had his failings, but on that fateful day when he walked into Athal Than, the gods forgave him his trespasses and given their blessing. He became reborn and allowed to wield Death in their name.

Has he stepped over some invisible line that separated restraint from blind power lust?

He needed to find out.

It came at his bidding and he stood fulfilled in its shadow. There was no outward manifestation, no blue glow or crackling lightnings, yet the surge of power coursing through him made him squirm and he held out his arm. She appeared before him, a pale ghostly outline, delicate, fragile, and beautiful. Her eyes turned and stared at him. He gazed longingly at her, his need a physical throb in his chest. She opened her mouth to say something, but he didn't hear her. Then the image shimmered and dissolved and he watched as her spirit returned from wherever it had come.

The breeze whispered to him as he walked to the combie. It lifted, humming quietly and sped toward a dark line of hills hugging the pool of city lights. Far in the west, lightning rippled among the clouds as the gods talked among themselves. He could not hear the thunder of their voices. Tempted to seek out Nightwings and his quiet, gentle understanding, but it was not his brother's understanding that he needed right now.

The hills drew near.

Brightly lit the apartment block loomed before him. The combie made a sweep and descended on the landing ramp. When it touched down, he listened to the whisper of the power plant for a moment, and then shut down. He opened the bubble and stepped out. Face expressionless, he walked into the foyer. There was no one about to disturb his thoughts.

He stopped before her apartment and paused. Mouth set, he pressed the comms pad, took a step back and waited. What if she wasn't home? What if she didn't want to see him? Then he would wait until she showed up and did see him, however long that might take.

After an eternity the lock cycled and one of the door panels slid back. She stood there; cool, aloof, and his heart tore at the sight of her. Her eyes were puffed from crying, but she held herself with regal pride, untouchable in the shell she had thrown up between them. How he needed to break down that barrier!

"I told you. I cannot see you anymore," she said in a brittle voice.

"I need to show you something," Terr said woodenly. "Afterward, if you still don't want to see me, I won't bother you again."

"Show me what?"

"You'll have to come with me."

She hesitated, then stepped into the corridor. The door slid shut behind her. He led her to the combie, walking close, yet so far apart. She got in and sat rigid, her hands clasped tight in her lap. He walked around the other side and climbed in. The plant spooled up and the combie lifted and climbed rapidly. He didn't look at her, painfully conscious of her presence, her scent, and her unhappiness.

They hurtled through the night.

Feather-light the combie dropped and touched down into the small clearing, the clearing he had left what seemed now a lifetime ago. The bubble lifted and he stepped into the cold wet grass. He walked to the edge and the city lay at his feet. When he turned, she stood beside him.

"Peaceful, isn't it?" he said softly. "They don't care about Tanard, raiders, lost ships, and dead crews. Why should they? As long as they are fed, housed, and kept warm, they shouldn't care. If they do, it's probably with detached curiosity, like having to pick up groceries tomorrow."

She stood beside him, wary and silent.

"But whether they know it or not, they are confronted with a monster of many faces and each is different, depending on where you look. My job is not to cut off its head, but if I can poke out an eye or two, I sleep fine, and it has nothing to do with law. It was about me, it always was, like you said. For you to understand, it's time that you did see the real me."

He stepped back and lifted his arms.

"I shall walk in the shadow of Death," he chanted. "And it shall be with me all the days of my life. With shadow shall I smite my enemies and with thunder shall I purge their land." His hackles rose and small blue lightnings slithered and writhed across his hands. Teena gasped and clamped her hands to her mouth to stifle a scream. "And all those who stand with me in the shadow of Death shall know my power and be comforted. With shadow and thunder shall I walk their land!"

He tilted back his head and reached for the stars. Two sheets of blue light stabbed at heaven and a peal of thunder shook the ground at his feet. Strong with the power, he stared at the cowering woman before him, mortal, puny, yet worthy of nurturing, worthy of his love. About to unleash the lightnings again, reality shifted and he held out his arm.

"Take my hand," commanded the voice of Death.

Badly frightened, Teena looked with terrified fascination at this stranger bathed in a faint blue glow. This was not Terr. This was…something unearthly. Yet, seeing Death unleashed, she also recognized Terr beneath its cloak. She had sensed this power in him from the very beginning and drawn by its mystery. That she had now gotten more than she bargained for was, after all, only deserved.

Did she dare give this…being, her hand? What she knew of Wanderer adepts, to touch him meant death. Was that true? Whoever this person standing before her might be, he was also Terr, and she knew without hesitation that he would never hurt her. Was this a test of faith then? But fates can be so cruel sometimes.

Timidly, she reached out with her hand. When she touched the blue glow surrounding him, she felt a slight tingling and small sparks crackled and snapped as they slithered up her wrist and elbow. She bit her lip and stifled a whimper. Then they stopped. Her heart thudded loud in her chest and she stared with terrified fascination at the radiance encircling her arm. Fleetingly, she touched his open palm and felt a rush of heat surge through her arm and body. She gave a small moan when he closed his hand and held her tight.

"What do you feel?" Terr demanded.

"I…I feel your hand," she said in a whisper.

"And that's all you feel! Warm flesh! Not a god, only a man. You judged me once and walked away because I wasn't pure in your eyes. I shattered your illusion of honor and righteousness because I dared exercise a power you felt had somehow become tarnished by my act. Would you have felt differently if I had pulled my needler and simply shot them? Tell me the difference?"

Listening to the distress in his words, she struggled with her own concept of right and wrong. Why was she so outraged by what he had done? Try as she might, she couldn't get the words of the *Saftara* she had read out of her mind.

'Though I am Death, they who walk with me will not fear me, but shall have peace in my shadow.' Powerful words, but did she understand them? Whatever they meant, she felt that somehow, he had violated that trust. Then again, could she judge a god? And why this particular phrase when the *Saftara* was full of words emphasizing restraint, not abandonment? Suddenly, she wasn't sure of anything. Except...

"But you didn't use a needler," she said and pulled back her hand.

"And that would have made it all right?" Terr insisted, but her words burned in his soul.

"I only know that somehow, what you did was wrong."

Terr stared helplessly at her. How can he fight emotion, prejudice, and the weight of preconception? She lived in a safe, warm cocoon, removed from strife and pain that filled his days. Comfortable, she was outraged that her sensibilities were shattered so rudely.

"Because I dared play a god?"

The words hammered at her. She lifted her eyes and looked at him. "Above all else, a god must have mercy."

"But I'm not a god, Teena."

"I know," she said and hung her head in misery.

Terr chuckled, a hollow, empty thing and he wept inside. "Because I failed to act like one? You're disappointed that with all my power, I'm simply just a man?"

"I expected you to act with honor and integrity. Instead, you abused it."

"I used what I had to purge an evil! How does that stain

me and diminish me in your eyes?"

Bitter tears slid down her cheeks. When she first read his report, she felt awe and a tingling in her belly. Terr was a god and he would make her immortal. A silly idea, of course, but it haunted her. Still, a god *had* touched him, so he must be more than simply a man. Did she resent him because he could not make her immortal? Because he *was* only a man? Everything else then, was it simply an exercise to hide her bitterness at being cheated out of something he could not give her?

"I'm sorry," she mumbled.

Terr swallowed and it went down hard. He was sorry too. He had not failed her as a man. He failed her as a god. His arms dropped to his side. After a moment even Death deserted him. He blinked back the sting in his eyes. Only the cool breeze, he told himself.

"You were right when you said my path takes me through the worst that life has to offer. Pretending it's not there won't make it go away. I'm afraid we live in two different worlds. You are entitled to live in yours and I'll take you back to it," he said wearily and turned.

There was a different quality about him; a darkness, and she knew that whatever power he wielded had left him. Yet, unaccountably it was still there with him. She could feel it. She could also feel his loss, his pain, loneliness, longing, and love. She knew he did not love easily. That was why it had an intensity that burned and made her feel alive. It made her feel it would last forever. Did she want immortality or a love that would never end? Was there a difference?

With every step he made, she felt growing panic.

She sensed that at this very moment, she could doom both of them because of a silly and superstitious notion—and her pride. She could let him go and he would not bother her again as he said, but his presence would always torment her. Yet she could not turn back time, undo what she had said, what had been done and lost between them. For a lot was lost, she acknowledged that. Could she put back the pieces? Would he want to?

But how was she to put back that first vital piece? She could lose it all so easily with a wrong word, a wrong gesture. This was so confusing! She should never have gotten involved with him!

"Wait!" she cried and he stopped. God or man, she only knew that she couldn't live without him. "I love you," she said with a catch in her breath. It was all she could think to say and it sounded so lame. A tremor swept through her body as she waited for his reaction.

He stood there for what seemed like an eternity. Perhaps it was an eternity. Then he turned, his face in shadow and she couldn't see what he was thinking.

"Even though I am not a god?" he said at length in a voice that seemed to come from somewhere else, some other place not real.

"I don't want a god, just you."

Did he dare lay himself open again? To go through all that pain? What if he was wrong and she meant it? He would walk away, back into his life, but it would be a life without her in it. He hesitated, then took a step toward her and she was in his arms, her head pressed into his chest.

"I only want you," she mumbled and clung to him with desperation and relief. "The god will have to stand in line."

He buried his face in her hair and closed his eyes. Her body warm against him, he held her tight and a great weight lifted off his heart.

"Love you, Teena-raye," he whispered brokenly and she moaned.

He did not pretend that having her close again had wiped everything that now stood between them. In one form or another, Death would always stand between them until he learned to make them all one. He didn't know how to do that now, but he was willing to make a beginning.

He cupped her cheeks in his hands and looked deeply into her dark eyes.

"For all time."

A shiver ran through her. He meant it, she was sure of it, and the intensity of his words sent ripples of desire down her body. She had been a fool, and because of it, almost lost this man. How she ever thought she could give him up, to live without him, was incomprehensible. If it was to be for all time, she wanted to spend it with him.

She lifted her face and his mouth crushed her lips. His velvety tongue wound around hers in a dance of abandon. His closeness, smell and strength were overpowering and she pressed herself closer to him, wanting to become a part of him, always joined.

His cheek against hers, Terr held her in a tight embrace, never wanting to let her go. Gods, how he loved this woman! And she came so close to taking it all away. Life without her would have been such an empty, fleeting thing. What use power and immortality that was without love? Even a god needs love.

"Take me home," she said with resolve.

They walked to the combie and he brushed her lips with his fingers before she stepped in. It lifted into a clear sky and the power plant purred their contentment. A short flight later the apartment block grew before them and the combie came in for a gentle landing. Both sensed the urgency of their need and hurried. The door to her apartment barely closed behind them and they were tearing clothing off each other. It left an untidy trail that led to the bedroom.

It was a frenzied union, intense, demanding, and explosive. It was also a release, a release from pain, anguish, uncertainty, and torment. Like any violent storm, it passed quickly, leaving them exhausted and drained, but happy. Bathed in a glow of their lovemaking, they simply held each other, reassured by the other's touch.

She rolled on her back and Terr entered her again. Her eyes

screwed shut in painful ecstasy and her fingernails left red streaks down his back as her arms held him to her. This time slow and tender, the urgency spent, but just as satisfying. He could think of nothing more important in his life than to cherish this woman.

Finally satiated and at peace, he lay propped against the pillows. Teena rested her chin on his chest while one hand stroked his side. Her skin cool and silky and he loved the feel of her body against him. Slowly, he ran his hand down her right thigh, marveling at the wicked innocence of her passion. Like her eyes, he had to fight to keep from drowning in her consuming abandon.

"Do you bear a warrior name, my Wanderer lord?" she asked dreamily.

He smiled into darkness. "Sankri."

She lifted her head and looked at him.

"It means the strange one," he explained.

"Sankri…" she repeated slowly, letting the sound roll in her head. "They named you well."

"Am I really that strange?"

"Sometimes."

"Because I walk in the shadow of Death?"

"And that's not strange?"

"I guess."

"What's it like…when you join with your god?"

He locked his hands over the small of her back.

"It starts as a warm tingling that spreads from my middle, slowly at first, then with a rush until my skin feels like it's on fire. It passes quickly and there is a presence around me, in me, and I feel detached, as I seem to grow. I can see myself, arms upraised and I hear the creature chant the litany that has invoked me. He is puny, insignificant, but when he calls my name, he also gives me life. I live for all time, but that small creature is also me and he enables me to see through his eyes, to feel what he feels. I am Death and everything that lives is mine and

I breathe my essence into the one who called me and we are one."

Terr paused, relieving the memory, the sensations…

"In that moment of duality when Death comes to me, I indeed feel like a god and creation stands at my feet. If I were to will it, everything would return to the nothingness from which I brought it forth. After all, reality only exists as long as I hold its image in my mind. Right then, I feel that nothing is beyond me. It's a powerful and giddy feeling. I know I'm only a man, mortal and frail, but while I stand in god's shadow, I am also more than that. I am the god manifest, his presence, and those who stand with me have cause to fear my wrath. I am Death, the destroyer of worlds, and blood is my sacrifice."

He was so caught up in reliving the experience, he did not feel the touch as it cradled him, or see the small sparks coil and writhe in his hands, or hear the deep resonance of his voice. Only when Teena tensed and gave a panicked gasp that he was jolted into reality.

"Do not fear, my pet," he said soothingly and brushed her cheek with his fingers. A trail of blue sparks danced in his wake.

"Terr!" Her whole body tingled and she was terrified and fascinated. She wanted to find out, but not like this! This was far worse than the first time. He ran his hand down her shoulder and fire set her body alight. The fire did not burn. It felt cool and somehow cleansing. She could hardly breathe, frightened for her life, but her mind could not stop questioning, awed at what was happening to her.

He embraced her and held her to him. After a while, her tremors stopped and her breathing became even. The fires died and the god lifted his hand. Terr didn't feel loss at his passing, but an understanding, a promise that they were one and would always be one.

"I'm sorry," he whispered into her hair. "It just happened."

She lifted her head and glared. "Beast! I almost died of fright."

"Well, you wanted to find out," he said with a wry grin and grunted when she fisted his ribs.

"Evil man!" She wrapped her arms around him and rested her cheek on his chest. "That was the most awesome experience I ever felt."

"Even…"

She gave a tinkling laugh. "You're crude and beyond salvage."

"You've got something to work on, then."

Her eyes searched his. "I thought that to touch you when you assumed your aspect meant death."

"It does unless I censor my will."

"I can see how this power can be intoxicating. After being a god even for a moment, who would want to be a mere man?"

"The temptation to indulge is always there," he agreed. "That's why the Wanderers have the *Saftara* and the Discipline to enforce it."

"You say Wanderers like you don't believe to be one."

"I am not, exactly. What happened to me was an accident."

Her eyes questioned him.

"When I crashed on Anar'on, I wandered the desert for two days looking for water. A fool's trek, of course, but I had to try. What little I carried didn't last long and I never really expected to survive. Even while the desert was killing me, I could not help being fascinated and enchanted by its vastness, emptiness and silence. Something about it filled my soul and satisfied a yearning I never knew was there. That land has a terrible magic, and in the end, that magic took me."

"And Dharaklin brought you back?"

"Unknowingly, he did more than that. When we joined, we literally became one. Unfortunately for me, the joining was only partially successful, or maybe too successful. No longer mad, but I wasn't myself either. I couldn't speak and I had no memory. It wasn't until I stood before an old Wanderer, torn inside and lost, that I managed to utter a cry for help in a language not my own. Sidhara took me under his wing and taught me survival in the Saffal and about the Discipline."

"Why?"

"Although I couldn't sense the latent power Dhar left in me, Sidhara could. Touched by the god of Death, the only way for me to be complete was to face his judgment."

"That's why he taught you the Discipline? To prepare you?"

"You got it. Had I known what waited for me at Athal Than, I would have preferred to remain insane."

She was shocked. "You have a gift others would kill for and you don't want it?"

"Ah, my pet. If only you knew. When I am Death, the god lives through me, and who doesn't want to be a god? You were right when you said that the power can be intoxicating. It can also be addictive. For who could stand before me should I loose the lightnings? There is so much evil out there that needs cleansing and the temptation to sweep it away is an ever-present urge. That's why we have the *Saftara* to restrain us. The gods were wise to stay on Anar'on. They know that unleashed on other worlds, misery and horror would follow where the Wanderers marched. Some things are simply too terrible for man to use. The problem is that I *have* been unleashed and the realization haunts me. By what right do I set Death on another? But who is to stop me? And who is to say I didn't have justice on my side?"

"Ver Dit's men..." Teena said slowly and understood.

"I do because another cannot. To stand idly by in the face of evil and do nothing would in my mind be an even greater evil. I made a bargain with my god. I am what I am, which he knew before he made me whole. What followed was his own fault. Given free will, even a god can stand helpless before his creation. If by using what I have been given can right some of the wrongs, then Death shall be loosed and I will be answerable only to that god."

"Isn't that a little arrogant?" she ventured, sensing his resolution and determination.

"An exercise in morality doesn't depend on the weapon used. Be it a needler or Death's touch. It's lucky for everybody that I'm a kindly soul," he said with a straight face.

She stared at him, then giggled. "Oh, Terr! You're impossible!"

He stroked her hair. "You are wrong about one thing, my pet. It's not a gift, but a burden. Perhaps it's something meant to test me. The gods have a whimsical side to them, you know. Like the *Saftara* says, in adversity the spirit grows. The problem is that there is too much adversity."

Listening to his words, she realized that he indeed labored under a burden. Playing the god was easy. Learning restraint, deciding who would die and who would live was not. And he *had* to decide. Being what he was, what he had become, he couldn't walk away even if he wanted to. A part of him obviously did want to walk away, to be free, to be like anyone else. But the god part of him demanded payment for his gift. It demanded retribution in his name, and because of it, Terr could not rest.

She cradled his head and held him to her. "Let there be peace in your soul tonight, my god of Death," she whispered soothingly. "Nothing will disturb you here."

Her chest lifted and sank as she breathed, and her breasts were warm and soft against his cheek. Terr let it all slide away and he did feel at peace. He could stop caring, if for a moment. He did not think anyone would begrudge him that.

"You must know," he said slowly, "that tomorrow or the next day, I may have to raise my hand against another."

"Shh. Don't talk now."

He closed his eyes and the sands were warm beneath his feet.

Sometime during the night, he was suddenly awake. Head

resting on her folded arm, Teena regarded him with large, somber eyes.

"Did you know that you glow when you're asleep?"

"Do I? I haven't noticed."

She smiled. "You do. Why is that?"

"It's the god watching over me."

"Even when you're with me?" She sounded hurt.

"Women can be dangerous, you know."

She giggled. "Beast! Seriously…"

"Have you been watching me all night?"

"I had this feeling, a prickling sensation, and when I opened my eyes, I saw a faint blue glow around you. I became startled when the effect touched me. It seemed alive like it was feeling me. If anything, it felt kind of erotic."

"Death is confused. You're not me, but we're joined. It's trying to work out what you are."

"And if it decides that it doesn't like me?"

He gave a mournful sigh. "Ah, it's too bad, then."

She pushed him playfully. "Really…"

"There's no choice. I'll have to give it up, won't I?"

She was silent for a moment. "And can you? Can you become an ordinary mortal?"

"Afraid not."

"That's good," she murmured and snuggled close. "I kind of like the idea of having a real god at my bidding. There are two analysts at work, real bitches. They'll never be missed."

"Just point them out, my pet, and they're crisp."

"I'm kidding, you know, but I can see how I could be tempted. Were you ever tempted?"

"Once or twice. I've got a better-dead list of my own, but the exercise of power, any power, has its own restraints against excess."

"Has it ever happened? Wanton destruction?"

"Not in living memory, but when it did happen, worlds died."

She lifted her head. "You mean an actual planet?"

"Blown to dust."

"Wow. To have such power…Can you—"

"Only a third level adept, someone who had undergone his three trials, has such mastery. I have two to go."

"How can a god let such power loose? I thought the trials were a test to see if you were worthy?"

"They are, but once endowed, the individual is answerable only to himself, and sometimes one turns out to be less than worthy."

"How do you stop someone who can destroy a whole world?"

"By using another adept, of course. Or the gods call him, a pull that is irresistible, and they deal with him in their own way. Free will, remember? A god cannot tell in advance how his creation will turn out."

Teena shivered. "The thought of Wanderers marching across the Serrll, it's frightening."

"It would be a nightmare out of chaos. Because of that, Captal has been watching the current events very closely."

"You mean, Anar'on destroying Deklan raiders?"

"Should Anar'on ever get irritated enough to retaliate seriously, the Fleet would be helpless before them. The Wanderers could rule the Serrll if they were ever that way inclined. The *Saftara* and the Discipline are the only things standing between order and utter destruction. I wouldn't worry. It will never happen. Captal knows that. It may be galling for them, but you don't trifle with Death."

"You said that you wanted to right some of the wrongs. Are you the god's vanguard against the Serrll?"

Ponderous forces shifted inside him and for one terrifying moment, there was clarity. Then it faded.

"I don't know."

It seemed that the gods were not ready to reveal their purpose—just yet.

* * *

"There it is again," Winn said and pointed at the three-dimensional waveform pulsing in the display plate. The complex pattern peaked and waned against a solid blue background.

Tanard pulled at his chin and frowned. The energy bloom looked uncomfortably familiar.

"Mmm."

"The profile matches the startup sequence for a main drive reactor," Winn added. "We have an M-3 out there."

Tanard shook his head, but not with amusement. Why in the pits would an M-3 be waiting around here for? The movements schedule showed this area clear and *Lahra* was not in a shipping corridor. They were in an out of the way intersystem lane, of no possible interest to a raider or a sweeper. A random event then? The fact that the damned thing sat there suggested otherwise.

"Do we evade?" Winn asked.

"Too late, I'm afraid," Tanard rasped. "A real merchant wouldn't have a sensor suite capable of detecting his startup. If we change course now, it's as good as telling him to come and get us."

"He'll get us anyway."

"Not if he accepts our ident dump."

Winn looked skeptical. "I guess we'll know in eleven minutes when we overrun his position."

"Get *Lahra* ready, Mr. Winn. Just in case, but mind our energy profile."

"Aye, sir. Computer, designate as target one."

"Acknowledged."

"Mr. Railee? Get ready," Winn said and Railee nodded.

Tanard's fingers drummed on the armrest. Could the M-3 be deliberately stalking him? Possible, but unlikely. The only way for the sweeper to know that *Lahra* was moving would be if Trimuran Shipping was compromised. If it had been compromised, he figured that BueCult or the Fleet would surely have moved in already; unless it was a deep penetration designed to break down the AUP network. If BueCult knew he was on Manargee, they may not have wanted to expose their operation by going after him while still on the ground. Placing an M-3 along his transit route made sense then, but that would mean Ratalan was also compromised. How else would they know where to place the sweeper?

Tanard chewed his lip, not liking any of it. He could not accept that Trimuran Shipping was penetrated. Besides, placing a lousy M-3 along his route violated every tactical doctrine of force management. You always confront an objective with superior force, never a lesser one. If this was a planned maneuver, he'd have had an M-4 sitting out there. Then again, he could be making too much out of pure coincidence; basic bad luck.

One thing kept worrying him. Why didn't the movements schedule show an M-3 along his route? If only a transiting flight, why stop?

"All stations manned and ready, sir," Winn reported.

"Weapons pod status check completed. Ready to deploy," Railee added from his station.

"Very well," Tanard acknowledged.

"Sir, the M-3 has powered up and is moving," Winn said.

"Merchant vessel, this is SSF M-3 *Scania*. Please identify yourself." The voice on the reserved emergency channel deep, muscular and business-like. Tanard and Winn exchanged wry glances. It looked like *Scania's* commander would not give them the courtesy of a visual link.

Tanard nodded to the comms watchstander.

"*Scania*, this is Karkan registered fast courier *Lahra*, on a run to Pizgor. Ready to transmit ident dump."

"Transmit ident."

The comms operator touched a pad on his color-reactive console.

"Ident received. Stand by, *Lahra*."

It was quiet as the seconds dragged themselves by. Only the inter-deck and computer status reports disturbed the mounting tension. Winn glanced at Railee who shrugged. There was really nothing to be done but wait it out. They had been intercepted twice before and stopped once for a sensor flyby. Only to be expected, given the clustering of Fleet units along the Kaleen shipping corridors. This waiting in the middle of nowhere got on everybody's nerves.

However uncomfortable, it presented Tanard with an opportunity to study his command crew under stress again. Railee as usual looked cool and collected, seemingly unfazed by the moment. His fingers tapped against the fire control console, apparently to some tune, judging by the swaying of his head. Tanard gave a lopsided smile. His weapons officer had given up on life. Consequently, he was able to live each moment to its fullest. Who could say that he wasn't right, when their future was a veil of darkness. If anything, Tanard was a little envious of Railee's ability to distill life to such simplicity.

Winn, on the other hand, wore his responsibility on his face. He was tense and it showed, but it was tension borne of responsibility, not fear or destructive soul-searching. Winn weighed options, running through scenarios, as a good first officer should. Anyone looking at him would be reassured, knowing that he would never quit, never give in. If necessary, Winn would die without making a fuss. He might not be the most brilliant tactician or strategist, and he wasn't, but he had a quality Tanard valued far more. He had loyalty, but was it to him?

As for the watchstanders, they took their strength from the officers. It was up to Tanard and the rest not to let them down. What of his strength? The thought came unbidden and he dismissed it. He had faced far worse and always managed to survive. If forced, he would do battle with the M-3 and some would die—in both ships. That this time he could die, he faced with equanimity. Death was a price everyone had already paid when they stepped aboard.

"*Lahra*, this is SSF M-3 *Scania*. In two minutes you will drop normal and stand by for a sensor flyby."

Tanard gave Winn a single nod.

"Do we have a problem, *Scania*?" Winn demanded; emulating what he thought was a merchant pilot's truculence at this unwarranted interruption.

"Acknowledge your instructions, *Lahra*."

"Charming personality," Winn muttered. "Sector TACOPSCOM shall hear of this, Mister! *Lahra* out."

"Sensor flyby? I don't think so," Tanard mused. "He means to board us. Count on it."

"We cannot let him board, sir," Winn said flatly. "One look at Engineering or the command deck and that would be it."

"Tell me, what would *you* do?"

Winn frowned. The commander probably had it all sorted out and a plan of action decided. He was playing what-if games, then. Okay…

Railee looked up from his console and grinned. He enjoyed these sessions, however uncomfortable for the recipient. He'd had several himself and sympathized. Uncomfortable or not, they were valuable lessons in tactics, something beyond price. This time, though, the price could be rather heavy if the lesson turned out to be wrong.

Winn took a deep breath. "If we run, he will simply call for support. He may have done so already. There are no threats shown in the movements schedule within a six lights radius, except for *Kriva*, an M-4. Master Scout Hvar commanding. Her last known position places her nine lights from us and five point-two lights from Vornan 2."

Hvar! And a Master Scout. Tanard nodded to himself. Well, well. Unfortunately, friend Hvar, this time it's not a Fleet exercise, but he didn't envy his old rival this moment of coming victory.

"How far is Vornan 2 from here?"

"Three point-eight lights."

"Excuse me, sir," the plot watchstander interrupted. "We're approaching the two-minute mark."

"Very well. Drop normal on the mark, Mr. Winn."

"Dropping normal...mark!"

Lahra slipped out of subspace and waited.

"Talk to me, plot," Tanard rasped.

"*Scania* just dropped normal. Range, 294,000 talans. She's closing at max secondary boost. Time to intercept: forty-two seconds. Firing solution in thirty-three seconds."

Tanard allowed himself a frown of grudging respect. The M-3 did very well to close the gap between them with less than a half-minute margin before coming into maximum range of 64,000 talans. Whoever drove it knew his business. That meant he could not rely on its commander making a mistake. All right, he would have to do this the hard way, then.

"Comms, contact Ratalan and give them a sitrep," Winn ordered. "Tell them we'll coordinate with Manargee."

Tanard sat back onto his couch. "Computer, set transition coordinates for Vornan 2."

"Designated bearings set."

"You intend running for Vornan?" Winn asked diffidently.

"We may have to. By waiting for events to unfold, an opportunity may present itself. If one doesn't, then it will be up to us to create one."

Winn stared at his commander and realized that Tanard didn't know everything. He obviously couldn't. What he did was project an aura of confidence in himself and his crew, regardless of what he may personally feel or think. He projected a command presence for everybody to see and draw on to bolster their own confidence. Winn recognized the value of his insight—if he survived to profit from it.

"I suggest, Mr. Winn, that you order all crew away from outboard compartments," Tanard said mildly. If they engaged the sweeper and the hull breached, it wouldn't cost a life.

"Aye, sir." Winn turned to the comms watchstander. "Issue the instruction."

"Warning, K-band acquisition scans detected from target one," the computer announced. "Closure rate is 6,960 talans per second. Effective firing solution in fourteen seconds."

"Mr. Winn, if he intends to board, he'll probably send across an Assault Battle Penetrator. That's six men, not counting the pilot. We'll let them lock on, but I want them neutralized before they can step aboard. Once we've got the ABP secured, I want you to load it with a fuel cell and send it back to *Scania* at max boost."

Winn grinned, liking it. Why wouldn't the sweeper allow its ABP to return? It would look normal if fleeing from a hostile ship. Not suspecting anything, *Scania* would draw it in and get a nasty surprise once the ABP brewed up. He tapped a comms pad on his console and issued instructions to the assault team below.

Disabling a marine decked out in full armor and protective suit was tough. Gas, low-yield explosives and even close range phase rifle fire would not make much of an impression. There were ways to balance things out. Outlawed nanobods designed to break down complex and hazardous industrial wastes worked just fine on polymer construct battle armor. With a half-life of only seconds, contained in a dispersion grenade, more than enough time to reduce the tough armor to a brittle sponge. Any longer and the little things would eat out their surrounds. As it is, the ABP was likely to sustain some damage, hopefully not enough to disable it.

"Warning. L-band firing lock established by target one. Range, 62,000 talans and closing," the computer advised.

Tanard nodded. The closer *Scania* came the better. Winn looked at him.

"Sir, the men are in place."

"Very well."

"Sir, *Scania* is holding position at two hundred talans,"

Railee said. "She has both screens extended and synchronized."

"He is also inside our distortion limit," Winn added.

"That's his first mistake," Tanard murmured. The gravitational distortion induced by *Scania's* mass would prevent *Lahra's* field precursor from forming. If the M-3 meant to stop him from transiting, it was a flawed tactic.

"*Lahra*, this is SSF M-3 *Scania*. Stand by to be boarded."

"Acknowledged, *Scania*," the comms watchstander replied.

"Sir, she has launched an ABP," Winn reported.

"That was his second mistake," Tanard said. "He won't need another." The M-3 should have ordered him to power down. It looked like *Scania's* commander was not so capable after all. Well, that was all right too.

Boosting at fifty talans per second, the ABP closed in nine seconds, allowing for deceleration and approach.

Winn stood up. "If you will excuse me, sir, I have some unfinished business below." He walked into the cable-tube and the hatch hissed shut after him.

Tanard thought he heard a faint clang when the ABP attached, but it was probably his imagination. He looked through the nav dome. Cold stars stared at him.

"Command deck," Winn came in on the inter-deck channel.

"Talk to me," Tanard said.

"The ABP is secured, sir. We have one casualty. He got too close to the hatch when the nanobod grenade went off. Fast little suckers."

"Get the fuel cell on board and launch. Leave the bodies in the ABP."

"What's left of them," Winn said and chuckled. "I never saw those things work before. The marines literally fell apart."

Tanard had seen nanobods in action and the results were not pretty. Where a man once stood, there nothing remained except broken armor, pieces of white bone, bleeding flesh and stinking guts. It was a very tough way to die.

"Sir, the ABP has launched," Railee announced.

"Raise both screens and synchronize. Keep them tight. Four talans," Tanard ordered. "Deploy the projector dome. Comms!"

"Interference field engaged!"

If *Scania* had sent in a sitrep, this was a futile gesture. If she hadn't and he managed to cripple or destroy her, he could proceed on his course and no one would be the wiser. If he must run, then those were the breaks and nothing would be lost.

"We're synchronized!" Railee snapped.

"Fire as soon as you achieve lock," Tanard commanded.

Three seconds after the ABP launched, *Scania* opened fire. A seventy-two TeV burst raked the primary screen along *Lahra's* starboard side. The shield matrix scintillated and the force lines glowed in brilliant discharges.

"Firing!" Railee hooted and stabbed the commit pad. *Lahra's* burst dissipated itself against the M-3's forward screen.

"The ABP is through *Scania's* nav grid," the plot watchstander announced calmly.

Tanard nodded. At least the first part of the plan had worked. Safely through the M-3's debris deflector grid, the ABP only needed to get close now. He'd been right about the M-3 commander's lack of experience. He should have opened fire the moment they detected *Lahra's* defense grids coming up.

"Mr. Railee, give it a grazing shot. Make like we're trying to kill it. Plot! Pull us away."

"Engaging quarter secondary boost."

Railee fired and the ABP jerked as its defensive screen flared under the impact.

Tanard wondered how long it would take *Scania's* commander to realize that something was wrong. He must have tried to establish contact by now. Like Tanard, he was busy and running out of time.

"Sir, the ABP will impact in two seconds," plot advised.

As if sensing disaster, *Scania* at last fired on the ABP. The stumpy assault craft shuddered, its tough hull able to withstand bursts from an M-4. The fuel cell inside not designed for such robust treatment. After another burst it cooked off. Less than four hundred katalans from the sweeper, the ABP vanished in a searing white flash that sent a hail of hypervelocity debris toward the M-3. After experiencing blister explosions that Terr sent against his ship, Tanard could very well picture the dismay and confusion aboard the sweeper when glowing shrapnel peppered the hull. Plating would be torn and penetrated, atmosphere vented, explosive decompression, frantic screams as crew were cut off when emergency hatches slammed shut on failed compartments. Maybe they got it in the nav dome and everybody in there had bought it.

That hope faded when *Scania* fired. *Lahra's* secondary grid failed in a point discharge as the beam tore through the force lines and struck the primary screen. Sheets of green backsurges licked along the hull. Although reinforced, it was still commercial grade polymer construct. It melted and distorted. There simply hadn't been enough plating from the M-3 to cover the entire hull.

"Sir, we've got nine hundred talans separation," plot declared.

"Transit!" Tanard snapped. "Full boost!"

Winn strode out of the cable-tube, swept his eyes over the displays and took his station.

"Answering full primary boost along designated bearings," plot confirmed.

Lahra jumped at one point-two lights per hour, trailing a wake of boiling gravity waves.

One casualty, Tanard mused. Cheap at the price.

"Comms? You can disengage the interference field."

"Aye, sir. Disengaged."

Winn looked up. "We have pressure leaks between frames forty-two and fifty. Compartments are sealed off, but repairs not possible until we land somewhere. All crew accounted for."

"Very well. What's *Scania* doing?"

"She has transited and is pursuing, doing one lph only."

"Very well. You can stand down weapons, Mr. Railee," Tanard said and gazed at Winn. "Call all officers. Main lounge in ten minutes." He stood up and walked to the cable-tube. Winn looked thoughtfully at the retreating figure.

"What do you think he has in mind?" Railee ventured.

"I wouldn't have a clue," Winn murmured.

"As long as we walk out of here with our skin intact."

Winn tapped a comms pad. "All officers, report to the main lounge in ten minutes."

"We should have finished off that M-3," Railee piped.

"Then you would have been dead!"

"I wouldn't have minded. The problem with me, friend Winn, I've seen too much death, too much killing, and I'm tired."

Winn's lips turned up in a frown. "When we get to Ratalan, I'm getting a command—"

"I know. Tanard told me."

"I had in mind asking you to be my first. Now, I'm not so sure."

"A kind gesture, but he offered me a ground assignment. Executive assistant."

"You? A dirt hugger?"

Railee chuckled. "I know. It has a strange ring to it, doesn't it."

"Will you take it?"

"I'm thinking about it."

"You'll miss the action."

"Probably, but staying alive will make up for it."

"Let me know what you decide."

"I'll do that."

"We better get down," Winn said and turned to the comms watchstander. "You have the con, Chief."

In the main lounge they were confronted by a rowdy discussion between four officers. The group barely noticed the two arrivals. Winn looked bemused and shook his head. Railee rolled his eyes, shrugged and settled himself on the formchair.

"I tell you we should have run when we detected *Scania* powering up," a former Second Scout engineer hissed furiously and dared anyone to challenge him.

A burly marine scowled at him. "Buried in Engineering, what the pits would you know about it, Usur?"

The wizened engineer gave the marine an intimidating stare. "I know this, sonny. We would have lived longer."

"You were on the command deck, Mr. Railee," the marine said. "Why didn't the Old Man slug it out with the M-3? We match his firepower."

Railee swept his eyes around the room and saw the same thing in every face: uncertainty, resentment and relief.

"We match his firepower, all right, but we're not built to take it. Some of you saw the damage we took from only one backsurge. A direct strike would have gone right through us. We wouldn't have lasted ten minutes."

The marine was about to protest, but thought better of it. Railee was the weapons officer and ought to know. He looked at the first officer.

"Should we have run, Mr. Winn?"

"I don't second guess the commander's decisions, Mr. Krill."

The marine snorted. "You're not on the command deck now. This is between us."

"And you're out of line, Mister!"

"He might be out of line and insubordinate, Mr. Winn," the familiar rasping voice said from the doorway, "but I cannot fault his curiosity."

Everyone hurriedly stood up.

Tanard walked to the head of the table, looked at them and sat down. They gingerly followed suit.

"Gentlemen, *Lahra* is good as lost. We lost her the minute *Scania* rejected our ident dump. Should we have run when we first detected her? Absolutely not. We were stopped before and this could have turned into another routine encounter. By running, we would have damned ourselves. When *Scania* attempted to board, we had no choice but to offer her battle. In battle, gentlemen, only death is a certainty. *Scania* could have been mauled or destroyed. When we opened fire, *Lahra* was dead. It is up to all of us now to make sure we don't join her. Mr. Winn, what can you tell us about Vornan 2?"

"It's a blue B3 star three point-eight lights from us," Winn said firmly. "It has two inner planets, both uninhabited, and three outer gas giants. The first planet, Titus, is mostly heavy metals and is mined. All the gas giants have a complex system of moons, some large as regular planets. Kanaris, the inner giant, has three inhabited moons and is 463 million talans from the primary. Seros and Petri are the most heavily populated. Mirna, the outermost moon, has a Fleet base, a complement of two M-2s and an M-3."

"It could be worse. Has anyone else anything of interest?" Tanard prompted and waited.

The engineering officer cleared his throat. "It gets worse. As a B3 star, Vornan 2 has an infernally large distortion limit, almost twenty-one million talans. You get too close and we slag our main drive in a forced collapse."

"We won't be doing anything that drastic, Mr. Usur," Tanard said comfortably. "We know that *Kriva* is almost certainly heading for Vornan. *Scania* must have made a sitrep when we broke off action. *Lahra* will reach Vornan in three hours. It will take *Kriva* about ten minutes longer. Those ten minutes are important to us because I don't want either ship seeing what we're doing."

"You intend heading for one of the moons?" Winn asked.

"Not directly. What I intend is to position *Lahra* so that we're occulted from Kanaris, *Kriva* and *Scania* when we swing

around Vornan. We drop normal and take to our survival blisters. The star's radiation flux should mask our maneuver from
their sensors. While *Kriva* is busy following *Lahra*, we shall make
for Kanaris."

Winn squirmed in his seat and frowned. "Let's say we make
it out undetected. Kanaris is a five-day flight for a blister and
we'll be running exposed the entire time. One M-2 and that's
all it would take to mop us up."

"If we were running in a gaggle, yes," Tanard added softly.
"But what if we flew tight formation and made like we were a
ship? SC&C will not be able to tell the difference until it's too
late for it to matter. There are plenty of private cruisers trawling
every system on secondary drives. This one should be no different."

Winn could not believe what he was hearing. Tanard must
be nuts if he thought this would work.

"And if SC&C asks for an ident?"

"Then we'll have to give them one, won't we."

There was a ripple of incredulous murmurs around the table. Tanard raised a hand.

"When *Kriva* destroys *Lahra*, Kanaris won't be expecting
us. All the excitement will be over by the time we reach the
planet. Manargee can check registries and give us a valid ident.
It only has to last long enough for us to close on Seros or Petri.
Once down, we disperse and make it out of the system using
whatever transport is available, with Manargee as the end destination."

"What if SC&C is not happy with our ident and an M-2
decides to check us out?" Railee pointed out, unperturbed by
the stares directed at him.

"Then things will become rather difficult," Tanard admitted. This was greeted by smiles and nasty chuckles.

Usur cleared his throat again. "I hate to spoil the fun for
everybody, but things are difficult already. The plan calls for
running *Lahra* dangerously close to Vornan's distortion limit.

Once we drop normal to launch blisters, the ship might not be able to transit again from the interference."

"Run simulations," Tanard ordered. "I want to launch and get *Lahra* to transit in six seconds or less."

Usur gaped. "Drop normal and reengage all in six seconds?"

"Or less."

"It cannot be done," Usur said flatly. "It takes three seconds for the distortion field to depolarize. Once down, it takes up to seven seconds for the precursor to recharge."

"Six seconds," Tanard said flatly.

Usur shook his head. "I'm telling you—"

"And I am telling *you*! If *Kriva* or *Scania* sense that we've dropped normal, or we take too long getting around Vornan, it's the end game. We've got to make sure that *Kriva* will follow when *Lahra* swings around. I don't care how it's done, just do it!" Tanard stood up. "Given our insertion profile, I want a target check on Seros and Petri. Once we have that, I need a list of major Fields and available flights. Manargee can get that for us and make bookings. Each blister is to be programmed with a designated destination and crews properly assigned. Once we're in orbit, there won't be time to fool around with details. Mr. Winn, see to it.

"I want everyone properly clothed, with money, IDs and ready to take his assigned flight. Everybody must be in their nominated blister five minutes before launch. That includes the command deck watch. The computer will issue a seven-minute warning. Ejection will be automatic. Anyone left behind is dead. It's simple as that."

Chapter Eight

Hvar glanced at the nav plot, scowled and gave a low hiss. He was confused. *Lahra* still bored straight for Vornan 2 like it was some sort of haven or something. He simply didn't get it. Although he hated the son of a canal worm, Tanard's record showed him to be a superb tactician. He ought to know. This maneuver was out of character. So what was he up to?

"Plot? Are we occulted from the target?"

"Yes, sir. We entered target's loss of signal cone two minutes ago."

"Mmm." Could it be that Tanard was simply attempting to outrun *Scania* and detected *Kriva* too late for it to matter?

There was no doubt it *was* Tanard. *Scania's* commander reported receiving fire from a Koyami projector and everyone knew about the stolen sweeper. Tanard must know that *Kriva* would head him off. Making for Vornan didn't make sense. Hvar chewed his lower lip. If he were in Tanard's shoes, he would have scooted in the opposite direction after engaging *Scania*. There were no M-4s within range to stop him and *Scania* would have been forced to break off pursuit due to damage received from the ABP explosion. Of course, Tanard could not have known that. His lips curled in a rueful grin. Using an ABP as a missile? It was absurd. Energy weapons had made missiles obsolete for more than two thousand years. No comparison was possible. Yet, that is exactly what Tanard dared…and it worked.

Did Tanard intend to land on one of Kanaris' moons, hoping to lose himself in the general population? Possible, but he didn't think so. SC&C tracked *Lahra* even now and would pinpoint its landing position once it went into orbital insertion. The authorities would be waiting. Hvar could not accept that *Lahra* would land. Once down, its projector masked, it would be vulnerable to aerial attack from Mirna's M-2s. Tanard wouldn't be so foolish. Pity the stationed M-3 wasn't around. With *Scania* not fully combat-capable, he could have used it right now.

"What is our closure time?" Hvar demanded.

"Twelve minutes. If *Lahra* is trying to swing around, she has left it very tight."

"Is she within Vornan's distortion limit?"

"Just about. If she makes it, we should see her any second…Ah, there she is. Going to full boost."

"Intercept," Hvar snapped. "Go to primary alert."

"Primary alert, aye, sir," the exec repeated and issued orders.

"Target one is boosting to one hundred and five percent…now at one hundred and ten percent," plot said.

"Too late, *friend* Tanard," Hvar murmured.

Kriva remorselessly closed the triangle leg. At one minute separation, *Lahra* raised its defensive grid and powered up the projector, a futile gesture. *Kriva's* superior range meant that she could pound its hapless victim without getting under fire herself. Hvar wondered if Tanard would surrender rather than have his ship destroyed around him. He didn't care one way or another.

"K-band acquisition lock established with target one," the computer announced. "Effective firing solution in eighty-four seconds."

"Her distortion field is depolarizing!" the exec snapped and Hvar grinned.

Probably wanted to drop normal and launch survival blisters, he mused. That wouldn't do him much good. The blisters had nowhere to go.

"Match and drop normal with her. Ready to fire."

Both ships went normal almost simultaneously.

"L-band firing lock established," the computer said. "Range, 186,000 talans. Effective firing solution in two seconds."

Hvar glanced at the comms officer. "Challenge her."

"Raider vessel, this is SSF M-4 *Kriva*. You are ordered to surrender your ship and assume neutral status. This is your only warning."

The comms plate cleared and Tanard's scarred features turned into a sneer.

"Hvar, you were an incompetent driving an M-3, and you're an incompetent now." The plate turned gray.

The watchstanders exchanged amused glances, but Hvar was far from amused. His face burned. In a Fleet exercise when they were both M-3 drivers, Tanard had whipped his butt and got a commendation for initiative. Tanard had never let him forget it. Well, they would see whose butt gets whipped now.

"Fire on acquisition," he hissed between clenched teeth.

"Acquisition! Firing!"

A yellow lance stabbed at *Lahra* from 134,000 talans. Its secondary screen rippled in wild discharges. *Lahra* fired back, more in a gesture of defiance than any real hope of reaching its target.

Hvar sat impassively and watched as *Kriva* continued to fire. The tactical plot showed *Lahra's* secondary grid fluctuate, blink, reform, then fade. They were too far off to show actual damage, but Hvar didn't need to see it. He could imagine it: hull plating breached, atmosphere venting, screams from the wounded and empty stares from the dead. He saw it all and prayed that Tanard was one of the mutilated dead.

"Sir, we're showing a power spike. It's the main drive reactor," the exec said calmly. He had seen Hvar's reaction at Tanard's taunt and wondered what frightful secret they shared.

"*Lahra* is launching survival blisters," plot said. "Two blisters launched."

Almost immediately the plot display flared as *Lahra* was consumed in a plasma bloom. Hvar looked at the nav bubble in time to see a sphere of white brilliance turn blotchy red as it broke up. Darkness swallowed the remains.

He glanced at the plot officer. "Survivors?"

"Both blisters were caught in the explosion and destroyed, sir."

Hvar sat back and nodded. It was over. Tanard dead and he could look forward to a nice entry in his record. A most satisfactory outcome.

"Comms? Contact *Scania* and order it to Kalakan. Then make to Sector TACOPSCOM and Master Scout Li Aron, SSF support facility Kalakan. Quote. Alikan Union Party raider vessel *Lahra* intercepted at Vornan 2 and destroyed. Kai Tanard commanding. No survivors."

"Transmission completed."

"Very well." Hvar turned to his exec. "Resume our base course, Mister."

* * *

"Seven-minute warning!" the computer blared. "Everyone to their assigned survival blister. Seven minutes to launch!"

Two blister hatches popped open, one on either side of the cable-tube. There were nine blisters aboard, but two were reserved for special duty. For the ship's complement of forty-six, seven was more than enough.

Dressed in casual clothing with travel bags scattered around the couches, the command deck looked more like a departure lounge than a warship control center.

The comms watchstander stood up, gathered the other two ratings with his eyes and made for the port side blister. The cable-tube opened and four crewmen entered. Winn pointed at a blister and they filed in. The comms watchstander looked at Tanard.

"Good luck, sir," he said and climbed into the blister.

Tanard nodded and jerked his head at Winn and Railee. They picked up their bags and made for the starboard blister.

"Four minutes to launch!" the computer warned.

It was suddenly quiet. There were no inter-deck comms, no computer status reports or the comforting presence of watchstanders. Standing alone in the middle of the deck, Tanard felt an aching loss. Most of all, he felt the waste and futility of it all. Somewhere out there, he had changed. He thought he could shape destiny at the point of a projector, and perhaps he did. He had seen too much, and now, as well as losing his ship, he had lost his faith in the cause. Ironic that he of all people should come full circle after selecting crews who had no faith.

Dame Narina was right. He no longer belonged on a command deck. Maybe not such a bad thing after all. Narina…

Despite only minutes from the system, Vornan 2 still only a blue speck in the nav plot. At maximum boost, *Lahra* was doing more than two point-nine billion talans per second—an inconceivable velocity. Thick ropy strands of yellow gravity waves whipped around the ship, curling in its wake. The wave density would progressively increase as the ship approached the blue star, placing an ever-greater strain on its drive. At the star's distortion limit the drive would not be able to overcome the stress induced by the proximity of such a mass and fail. It was up to the computer to see that the ship did not get too close.

"Two minutes to launch," the computer said.

Tanard shook off his lethargy and strode for the blister. He climbed in without looking back. It was like a door closing on a part of his life.

"For a while there, I thought you had gotten lost," Winn said comfortably, the strict formality momentarily forgotten.

"Just sidetracked, friend Winn," Tanard rasped and settled

onto the left couch. "Like old times."

"Except this time, we can expect a different sort of reception." Railee added, relishing the experience.

"Better hope not," Tanard said.

"Five days in this bucket…" Railee mused. "A lot of evil things can happen in five days."

"I hope you being gloomy isn't one of them," Winn warned.

"One minute to launch," the computer declared.

"Here we go," Railee muttered.

From a ferociously bright point, Vornan 2 suddenly expanded into a visible disk as *Lahra* plunged through the system and braked savagely. At her speed, twenty-one million talans was a desperately thin margin of safety. An error of two percent the wrong way and she would suffer serious drive and structural damage—and ruin everyone's chance of getting away.

"Five seconds to launch," the computer announced. The hatch clanged shut and the restraining field snapped on. Everyone grunted as firm pressure froze their bodies in place, protecting them from wrenching inertial shearing forces.

There was nothing subtle about the way *Lahra* dropped normal. The computer simply shut off the distortion field. The ship groaned and frames popped at the sudden stresses pulling it apart. Tanard felt a wave of dizziness at transition point and the blister immediately surged down the launch tube, accelerating to clear the IP. Seven blisters in close proximity to the ship would prevent her from transiting. It took them three long seconds to clear the distortion limit induced by their combined mass. Its precursor field at point of collapse, *Lahra* vanished in a burst of white light. There was no one aboard her to see the twisted bulkheads, torn frames and ruptured compartments caused by the abnormal transition.

The restraining field released and Railee doubled up, gasping for air. When he looked up, his face had a sick, waxy sheen.

"Gods! Let me die."

Tanard massaged his ribs, not feeling too hot himself. "Call them in."

Winn took a deep breath and shuddered. "Unit One to all units. State your status."

They all called in, but there were casualties: two broken arms. It could have been worse. The blisters powered down and drifted. Boosting at one light-year per hour, *Scania* was fifty-six minutes behind them. Tanard did not want the blisters under-way until he was sure she cleared Vornan 2. It was a tense wait. Occulted, they could not tell what was happening. Just as well. Sensor blindness worked both ways. *Scania* and *Kriva* were not able to detect them either. Tanard ordered everybody to rest and sleep. No one was going anywhere for a few hours yet.

Tanard closed his eyes and relaxed against the seat. Soft onboard noises kept his thoughts company. He tried to empty his mind, to drift, to accept each moment as it came. It was impossible. How did *Scania* happen to lay in wait for him? Like an aching tooth the thought kept worrying at him. At any rate, a less than memorable start to his new command. His lips twisted in a half smile.

The blister whispered to him.

"Sir! Sir!"

He came instantly awake. He leaned forward and winced, his body stiff after being in one position.

"How long have you let me sleep?"

"Five hours. You needed a break," Winn said, not at all apologetic.

"I ought to have you shot," Tanard snapped and Railee grinned.

"I called everybody in and we're formed up, nice and tight. One katalan separation."

Tanard gave a grudging nod of approval. "You have our course plotted and laid in, I presume?"

"I even have an alternate."

"Titus?"

"The first planet is only thirteen million talans from us. We could make a close approach in three hours, and it takes us away from a direct and predictable course to Kanaris."

"The place is a lump of metal occupied by mining camps," Tanard reminded him. "Who in their right mind would want to visit a dump like that?"

"A resupply transport," Winn said promptly, sure of his ground. "One of the ident dumps Manargee gave us was for a transport, which happens to be on Titus right now. It is due to lift in five hours."

"And you know that how?"

"I called Manargee while we were closing on Vornan 2."

"So?"

"We board her. If it doesn't work out, we can always fall back on our original plan."

"Don't tell me. In order to get close enough to board, we would have to pretend to be something else. Like a passenger life pod for instance?" Tanard mulled it over. Riding in a captured transport, they could approach Kanaris with impunity. The only drawback he could see, if the transport alerted SC&C that they were picking up a life pod from a stricken liner. SC&C would ask what liner and that would be it. He could hardly ask Manargee to blow up a ship for them just to create a plausible cover story. The longer he thought about it the less appeal it had. Introducing variables into a plan also introduced risk factors.

"Let's keep things nice and simple, Mr. Winn. Your idea has merit, but it has one major problem. If things go wrong, Kanaris will be alerted and we've nowhere else to go."

"I thought of that," Winn admitted. "I also think it's worth taking the risk now for an easier approach to Kanaris."

"If we were alone, one blister, I would say, let's go for it. But we're not alone. We have forty-three other people to worry about and it is our responsibility to give them the best chance possible of making it. Your plan would make that chance very marginal."

Winn swallowed his irritation and nodded. He had lost focus of their objective, carried away by the cleverness of his idea. There was obviously a lot more to being a commander than handling weapons and tactics. Was he ready?

"Let's get us moving, Mr. Winn," Tanard ordered, also wondering if his first officer was ready.

* * *

Head propped up by his left arm, Terr gazed dreamily at Teena's face. Her mouth had a slight pout, unconscious disapproval? He wanted to touch her creamy skin, trace the outline of her eyebrows, her nose and soft lips. He was totally captivated by this vibrant woman and life without her would have no meaning. A lock of hair fell across her forehead and he brushed it back. Her eyes opened, large and mischievous and he grinned.

"Morning."

"Spying on me?"

"Absolutely. I have never seen an angel before and I am fascinated that I have one all to myself."

Her cheek dimpled. "This angel has horns, buster."

"And I felt them." He snuggled close to her. "Will you watch over me, my angel?" he whispered and her eyes turned misty.

"Always, my lord of Death."

He kissed the tip of her nose and she buried her head against his shoulder.

"You have a message," the housekeeping computer announced and the magic shattered. Teena sighed and rolled on her back.

"What's the message?"

"Terr!" Anabb's voice boomed. "Get your butt to my office! Something important has come up."

"Rit!"

Teena smiled and brushed his cheek. "That evil old man wants to take you away from me?"

"Doesn't the guy ever sleep?"

She pulled the blanket to her chin and sat up. "How did he know where you were?"

"Not hard to guess."

She pouted and punched his shoulder.

He reached for her and she squealed as he dragged her down. Her breath sweet as he nuzzled her neck and cheek, searching for her mouth. All the while, her small fists pounded his back. He found his target and in a moment of sweet surrender, she melted and wrapped her arms around his neck.

"Love you, Teena-raye."

Her eyes shone. "You can show me how much later."

"I would rather show you now."

"Later. You have to go, remember?"

"It's a conspiracy," he muttered darkly and swung his legs out of the bed.

Her eyes turned dark and some light faded from her face.

"I'm sorry about yesterday," she said softly.

He touched her lips with one finger. "There is no yesterday. Only now."

She sighed. "Good. I'll see you tonight?"

"Do you want me to move in with you?"

"That would be convenient," she said with a lazy grin. "You can tell me more about being a Saddish-aa Wanderer."

"So you can kick me out once you get to know me better?"

She shrugged. "It could happen."

He threw a pillow at her face. Looking at her, he smiled.

"You know, you could move into *my* place. It's big and much roomier."

"Mmm. Let's see how this works out first," she murmured and stretched lazily.

Clear skies greeted him outside and he breathed deeply of

the clean, rain-washed air. Long shadows peeked around corners as the sun grinned down on the world. He climbed into the combie and nodded to himself, pleased with life. The plant spooled up and he lifted straight up. The combie paused as it waited to be slotted into the control network, then surged into the traffic stream heading for the city. The sky was crowded, but he didn't notice. He felt relaxed, fulfilled and at peace. He would make Teena happy, no matter what it took.

Even if he was not a god.

The Admin tower loomed among the lesser buildings of the Center. Communals, sled-pads, and combies circled the complex like scavengers, some dashing down for their share of the spoils. Terr waited patiently as traffic control released him and the combie swung into a slanting descent.

Once down, he left the parking system take care of the combie and took the cable-tube. Ariane looked up when he strode into the reception area and flashed him a brief smile. She looked cool and beautiful, and one day, she would break somebody's heart.

"The Director is waiting for you," she said primly.

"I don't want to see the Director. It's you I'm after!"

"I'll tell Teena you said that!"

"You're not playing fair." He shook his head in resignation and turned as the translucent doors slid into the walls. He walked through.

"You took your time getting here," Anabb growled. The window screen showed the sprawl of the city and the winding traffic lanes.

"I was distracted," Terr said indifferently, noted Hiraga-wan's perpetual scowl and winked at Dhar. His brother gave a small shake of his head in warning. Terr took the only spare formchair and sat down. Judging by the gathering, it looked serious.

Anabb bit back a smile. He could well imagine who the distraction was. Over the last few days, Teena walked around

333

moody and preoccupied, and Anabb was concerned. She was capable and emotionally strong, but still a very young and impressionable woman, and he did not want to see her hurt. Judging by Terr's confident poise, whatever was troubling her apparently reconciled to everyone's obvious satisfaction.

"Now that we're all here at last," Anabb shot Terr a pointed look, "I have some good news. Eleven hours ago, M-3 *Scania* engaged an armed auxiliary. There was an exchange and *Scania* suffered considerable damage. Not from projector fire, but an ABP explosion."

"Tanard?" Terr asked with a grin.

"Tanard it was. He must have overpowered the ABP's party when they attempted to board and sent the ABP packing back. When it failed to respond to calls, *Scania* fired on it. He probably planted a fuel cell, for the resulting explosion peppered the sweeper with shrapnel. Unbelievable."

Terr chuckled. Tanard had clearly learned from their encounter two years ago when he launched survival blisters at Tanard's ship in a desperate attempt to shake him off. He leaned forward.

"How do we know it was Tanard?"

Hiragawan shot him a cold look. This was not the first time where in his opinion the junior agent showed a marked lack of respect and deference to the Director. That Anabb tolerated this behavior was beyond understanding.

"*Scania* reported receiving fire from a Koyami 9A projector," Anabb said, amused by Terr's train of thought. "That's not normal equipment, but it gets better. Although evenly matched, Tanard's ship was not a warship and he wisely broke off action and boosted for Vornan 2. Presumably to lose himself somewhere in the system and make good his escape. Unfortunately for him, *Kriva* was waiting. Tanard must have detected her and chose to swing around Vornan, but that didn't help him. *Kriva* intercepted and Tanard's ship was destroyed. We know it was Tanard because he sent a visual to *Kriva*. Master

Scout Hvar provided the identification." Looking pleased, he leaned back to watch the fireworks.

"But was Tanard in the ship when the message was sent?" Terr said quietly and heads turned. "With an M-4 waiting for him, why swing around Vornan? Tanard must have known he couldn't outrun the cruiser. Heading for one of Kanaris' moons would at least have given him a chance. The option he took gave him none. It was too easy. Everything I know about Tanard tells me that this is out of character. It doesn't feel right."

Hiragawan barely controlled his irritation. "Mr. Terr, you are questioning testimony from *Kriva's* commander, evidence from his log and Kanaris SC&C. Tanard is dead and that's the end of it."

"His ship might be dead, I'll accept that. I ask again, was Tanard in it?"

"For pit's sake, man!" Hiragawan snorted, exasperated. "What will it take to convince you? He had *Scania* trailing him and a sweeper stationed on Mirna ahead of him. For your benefit, that's one of Kanaris' inhabited moons. As it turned out, the sweeper happened to be someplace else, but Tanard couldn't know that. With *Kriva* blocking his path, what did you expect him to do? Step off and walk?"

Terr looked pointedly at Hiragawan. "That is exactly what I think he did."

"You're raving! In case you missed something, Agent Terr, Tanard's ship didn't drop normal or launch blisters."

"And we have evidence of that?"

Hiragawan bit his lip. Damn the man. "Ah, not exactly."

"Let me guess. Tanard was occulted and SC&C couldn't see him."

"I give up!" Hiragawan said and raised his hands in resignation. "Mr. Dharaklin, talk some sense into your friend, okay?"

At first, Dhar thought that Sankri was pushing a hopeless

335

cause. Thinking about it, he admitted there was room for doubt. He did not have to dwell on the repercussions of Tanard alive and on the prowl.

"After listening to Terr's argument, I am not totally convinced that Tanard would have headed for Vornan 2 and allowed himself to be boxed into an end game without at least a marginal chance to get away," he said with deliberation. "Tanard is too good a tactician."

Hiragawan stared at him and shook his head. "You're both insane."

Anabb watched the exchange with delight. Terr's idea may be full of worm crap, but he was defending his position with sound, logical points. In the process, he was winding Hiragawan into a knot. Terr could be a bit more diplomatic, but as someone more experienced, Hiragawan should be more tolerant. Chemistry…

Chemistry or not, Anabb was not about to dismiss Terr's hypothesis out of hand.

"Tell me what you're thinking, my boy," he prompted.

"I suggest, sir," Terr said, "that Tanard wasn't running blind toward Kanaris at all. I think he knew about *Kriva* all the time. Dhar is right. Tanard would never have gone in unless he figured there was a chance of getting out."

"How?"

"In order to raid, Tanard had access to some very good intelligence on Kaleen shipping movements as well as disposition of Fleet units…" Something occurred to him. Why didn't Tanard know about *Scania*?

"And?" Anabb prompted.

"He used M-3 IFF codes to get close to his targets, and you don't get those merely for the asking. To me, it all adds up to one thing. Tanard's move for Vornan 2 was deliberate. He counted on his ship getting destroyed as a distraction while he made his getaway."

"Agent Terr, you paint a farfetched but plausible scenario,"

Hiragawan conceded, "but the plain fact is, even if Tanard did launch blisters, Kanaris SC&C hasn't detected any!"

Terr sighed. "Sir, the ship was occulted! All I'm saying, we shouldn't assume Tanard is dead because the Fleet is anxious to remove a political embarrassment."

"Well, we'll stir up a stinger's nest if their celebration is premature," Anabb mused and nodded to Hiragawan. "Advise Master Scout Li Aron of our concerns and suggest an increased surveillance posture around Kanaris."

"Sir, surely—"

"Thunderation! It does no harm and it's a prudent precaution."

"Yes, sir."

"Excellent. In that case, I won't detain you."

Everyone stood up and Anabb raised a finger at Terr. "Stay a moment."

Terr glanced at Dhar. "We'll talk later." Dhar nodded and followed Hiragawan out.

Terr sat down and wondered if Anabb was about to ream him out. His behavior hadn't been altogether exemplary. It was just that Hiragawan was such a pain.

Rit!

When the doors clicked shut, Anabb leaned forward and crossed his arms on the desk. He scowled and shook his head.

"You should polish your interpersonal skills," he growled.

"I regret if my behavior has caused undue friction, sir."

"Not all your fault, of course. He has a burr in his pants, but Hiragawan is your superior and you should treat him with respect."

"I'll work on it."

"Do that." Anabb cleared his throat. "Tanard...I wonder if he is really dead. A nice piece of reasoning, my boy, but you left something out."

"Yes, sir. *Scania*."

"With all his intelligence, why didn't Tanard know she was

there, right? That is curious," Anabb said and studied his wayward agent. You can order a man to do many things, but you cannot order him to stop thinking. In Terr's case, *Scania's* unexpected appearance was causing the boy to think along lines better left alone. Still, he deserved at least part of the truth. "If you're tempted to ask the next question, don't. I can tell you, though, that any operation this Branch may be running to penetrate the Alikan Union Party cells would not be compromised simply to catch Tanard. A political embarrassment he may be and he's caused frightful carnage, but I must be focused on broader objectives."

"Is the AUP Provisional Committee really such a threat?" Terr ventured, inviting a rebuke.

"You know the answer already. You should keep in mind the alternative. If Tanard is a political embarrassment for us, he could also be a liability for the Committee or whatever AUP splinter cells were running him. With Khiman-ra destroyed, he no longer had a job. A dangerous tool to be left unattended."

"So they set up an ambush?" Certainly possible, but it meant that *Scania's* commander had two masters. Terr did not like that.

"I cannot say, but you should leave it. It's not our problem. Our job was Khiman-ra, and that's been dealt with. Talking of problems, you're fully recovered?"

"Everything is working, sir," Terr said with a straight face and Anabb's eyes glittered.

Impertinent scamp!

"I haven't asked you before, but are you satisfied working for the Branch?"

For the Branch or Anabb? A moot point.

"You have allowed me a degree of latitude, sir, which otherwise would be difficult to exercise as an M-3 driver."

"I'm not surprised!" Anabb grunted, amused.

"It has certainly changed my perspective on many things."

"Mmm. You have a commendation in your record for ramming that raider, seeing how it was instrumental in locating Khiman-ra. However, I wouldn't recommend that you consider doing it again."

"I don't plan to add it to my repertoire, sir."

Anabb chuckled. The boy was impossible.

"Ver Dit, on the other hand, is another matter."

Terr tensed. *Here it comes…*

"What you did, was it right?"

It was such an unexpected question that Terr blinked. "Under law—"

"I'm not talking about law. Did *you* feel it was right?"

It always came to that, Terr thought. There were laws and customs, but in the end, individuals supported those laws and customs—or not. If enough individuals decided to abandon the rule of law, that act threatened the very fabric of society and it would turn on them, no matter the justice of their cause. Order under an oppressive regime still preferable to the chaos of anarchy until compliance became intolerable and the populace revolted.

"I violated the strict teachings of the Discipline, but it felt right."

"You could have waited until *Kriva* reached Kalakan."

"And we could have lost more ships and more lives if Ver Dit escaped. If what I did saved even one life, I wouldn't hesitate to do it again. You don't have to tell me the moral and legal tightrope I walk saying that."

Anabb gazed thoughtfully at the boy's troubled features. He could hardly imagine what it must be like for him, possessing almost unlimited power with only the Wanderer Discipline and his own morality to keep him in check. Was it a gift from the gods or a burden? Was there a difference?

"Were you ever tempted to unleash Death on those you felt less deserving of life?"

Terr grinned. "The list is lengthy, sir, but there is always room at the bottom."

"I don't doubt it," Anabb said slowly and hesitated, knowing that once he took the next step, there would be no return, no reprieve, for either of them. So be it.

"What if you were ordered to remove somebody and I didn't ask how you did it?"

Terr stared. "Is that how you see me, sir? A paid killer, an assassin?"

Blunt and to the point, but accurate. Anabb searched the boy's eyes. He did not see the gleam of killing lust, only concern, and he felt relief. He hated the thought of harboring an avenging angel in his nest.

"A dose of reality, son, in case you were wondering. You're a tool like everybody who works here. You happen to be mine, just as I am Captal's, and both of us have a job to do. Sometimes we don't like it, but we must believe in the value of our work. It doesn't mean servile obedience to orders. There are those who enjoy brutality and the act of killing. There are always such men to be found. When I see them, they're weeded out, but like a malignant growth, they can return and we must be always vigilant. The Diplomatic Branch, while I am running it, will adhere to its charter as Serrll's intelligence arm, without prejudice or passion, regardless of which political party holds government in Captal.

"I don't need to tell you the forces that seek to replace order and law with tyranny by whatever means available. Tanard was such an individual, but naïve and misguided. For all his brilliance as a military commander, he had a flawed character. He believed he fought for a Palean future. In reality, dark and twisted that future would be if they succeed. He was a cancer and others who supported him, and you were instrumental in cutting it out. That task was honorable and just. I like to think that you'll find honor at cutting out other cancers should the need arise."

Terr wondered if Anabb really believed everything he said,

or simply spinning a sales pitch to an idealistic agent. He could not forget that Anabb was a master manipulator and a user. Perhaps that's what the job called for. Nevertheless, a lot of misery remained in their brave and seemingly just existence. He had an opportunity to right some of the wrongs, but was it an opportunity or sanctioned indulgence?

"Who decides if someone should die?"

"In your hand that is, literally. I cannot decide that for you. I'm not that arrogant."

"I would need to know why."

"Of course."

Forces shifted in him and Terr saw the face of his master frown in disapproval. Terr really had no decision to make, because he had already walked this path when he confronted Ver Dit. If the presence of power was an influence, he would see what exercising it would do. He might be Anabb's tool, but that cut both ways.

"I will consider it."

"It means that Dharaklin may not always be with you."

"Some things are better done alone, sir."

Forgive me, my brother…

Anabb regarded his protégé and wondered whether he had done the right thing. Unfortunately, the door through which they just walked only swung one way.

* * *

Ti Inai strode to the liquor cabinet and reached for the stubby dark blue bottle on the upper shelf. The person staring back at him in the mirror did the same thing. Ti Inai lifted the bottle in a silent salute. There was a satisfying *plop* when he pulled the cork. He poured two fingers of clear spirit into a small hand-cut tumbler. Tiny bubbles of gas frothed the edge of the glass. He replaced the bottle and raised the glass to his nose. The twenty-four-year-old rakija had a subtle honey fragrance that invoked images of tall mountains, deep valleys, rolling meadows, and cut hay. He took a sip, savoring the smooth, rich flavor of the spirit and swallowed. Right then, Ti Inai would not have minded trading the reserved opulence of his office for an opportunity to sit in a grassy glade and watch fluffy clouds gather in the silent valleys.

Four strides and he was back behind his desk. He sat down and the formchair squirmed as it contoured itself around his body. The crystal tumbler made a loud click when he put it down. On his left the floor-to-ceiling window screen showed a red evening sky and glowing city towers. Not an image of mountains and valleys of his boyhood, but he had become reconciled to that loss. To reach for power involved sacrifices— for everyone.

Well, no use putting it off any longer.

He took a sip and tapped in a special comms code. The Wall cycled through pooling colors for several seconds, and then cleared.

"Dame Narina, well met," Ti Inai said easily, ignoring her arched eyebrows of surprise. He clasped his hands to stop the fingers from twitching.

She had just walked into her office. The little Palean shit must have timed it.

"Mr. Commissioner, an unexpected pleasure." It really wasn't, but she could not very well say so.

"That remains to be seen. Are we secure?"

"Of course. To what do I owe this call?"

"Unfinished business, my dear."

"Oh?"

"Your faction has been very supportive of Le Maran when some in the Committee saw him as a liability. Unfortunately, he didn't make it when Khiman-ra was obliterated. A regrettable loss, but his will not be the only sacrifice demanded and paid before we realize our objective."

"Your point being?"

"You should be able to guess," Ti Inai said with an oily smile.

Narina stared at the repulsive man and chewed her lower lip. An opportunistic Captal slime, but dangerous nonetheless. It would not be wise to cross him. Their approach to tactics might differ, but she could not fault his focus on the common goal. In the end, that was all that mattered. Personalities merely got in the way. With a hollow in her stomach, she realized what Ti Inai meant.

"Tanard," she said softly.

"That's right, Tanard. As a military commander and strategist, there is none better. What he did at Khiman-ra was remarkable. It gave the movement time to pause and reflect on Sargon's headlong rush to secure the merger. It will happen, but not yet, and we both know why. Despite his invaluable contribution to the cause, he is nevertheless a serious liability. Frankly, I had hoped he would have met his end against an M-4 somewhere in Kaleen space, doing what he believed was right. End as a hero. Despite the odds, he was lucky and survived. Then you threw him a lifeline, against my gravest objections."

"We recognized talent when we saw it, Mr. Commissioner," Narina snapped, suddenly wary. Where was he taking this?

"Under different circumstances, Tanard would have been an excellent choice to command Ratalan. Regrettably, he is damaged goods and a major security risk not only to Ratalan, but to you as well."

"How?"

"Use your head. All it would take is some disgruntled fool on Ratalan or in your own organization to betray him to the Fleet. We would face a disaster that would make Lemos look like a mere distraction. As long as he lives, we are vulnerable."

It dawned on her then. "*You* planted *Scania* to intercept him?"

"I would have preferred something heavier, but an M-4's movements are much more closely directed. As it turned out, Tanard managed not only to shake her off, but elude *Kriva* as well."

"You cannot keep good talent down," Narina said with obvious relish.

"Evidently not, but when he reaches Kanaris—"

"How do you know about Kanaris? The information is only hours old."

"Allow me some privileges of my office," he said with a sly grin. "As I was saying, when he reaches Kanaris, and I have no doubt that he will, his luck will run out."

"What do you mean? Do you intend to tip off Mirna?"

"Nothing so crude, my dear. I only want Tanard. His crew will be free to make their way out of the system as best they can. They are skilled and we can use them. What I have in mind is simplicity itself. One of his officers is a sleeper—"

"You had this planned all along?" Narina said incredulously, disgust clear on her face.

"As far back as Lemos."

"Just wipe him out when he becomes an embarrassment?"

"Don't look so shocked, my dear. This may sound callous, but it's my responsibility to cover *all* options. Now, as I was saying. When Tanard reaches Seros or Petri, he will undoubtedly contact you to confirm his intentions. Sooner or later the sleeper will also contact you. When he does, you will order him to remove Tanard."

"Just like that. And if I refuse?"

Ti Inai stared at her for a few silent seconds, not bothering to answer. His silence did that for him.

Narina got the message, all right. A rhetorical question anyway. Too bad, really. If sacrifices have to be made, well, that was the cost of doing business.

"How will I know who the sleeper is?"

"The file is in your computer. Access code is bravo, indigo, echo, two, niner, enable."

Narina sighed. "Is this really necessary, Mr. Commissioner? There are other ways to resolve this problem, less wasteful for everybody."

"But not as permanent. Tanard is a patriot who sacrificed everything. He'll simply have to sacrifice a little more."

"That little is all he has left," she said bleakly.

"My dear, sometimes even that's not enough," Ti Inai said and cut contact.

The Wall pooled in a swirl of thick colors. He took a sip and turned to watch a darkening sky. After a while, he leaned back and gave a satisfied nod.

"Comsec, query if Director Ed-Kani Takao is available to take a call."

A few moments later the Wall cleared and Ti Inai bobbed his head.

"Friend Ed-Kani…"

The senior Sargon representative regarded the suave Palean with a mixture of revulsion and admiration. He did not know how it was done, but Ti Inai's smooth smile reeked of complicity. The renegade Palean Alikan Union Party cells have successfully sabotaged the Provisional Committee's effort to annex Naurun and Omiron. With Anar'on manning some of its ships with Discipline adepts, the window to secure the two systems now firmly closed. Why had Ti Inai done this?

"Commissioner," he hissed and his clear blue eyes glittered. "I was waiting for you to call. You've got some good news for me, I hope?"

"Only to confirm what you already know," Ti Inai piped and his hands twined.

"Khiman-ra? I am aware of the Fleet's action over Ophir."

"This is not about Khiman-ra, friend Ed-Kani. At least not directly."

"The problem of renegade AUP cells—"

"Please! Don't patronize me." Ti Inai was annoyed that Ed-

345

Kani still refused to see the obvious. Was the man really so pre-occupied with his destiny that he could not see what was happening? "Both of us know what this is about."

"Perhaps it is time you told me what this is about," Ed-Kani said evenly.

"Friend Ed-Kani, the mere existence of Khiman-ra and the AUP structure that underpinned it must tell you something. If it doesn't, then perhaps Sargon should seriously re-examine its tactics in securing the merger."

Ed-Kani's fingers tapped against the desk. "This is about the Committee's five-four voting structure?"

"The imbalance must be redressed if we're to move forward."

"We've been over this ground before," Ed-Kani said wearily, holding back his irritation.

"And left it unresolved. We need to resolve it now, before the next Committee meeting."

"Sargon's fifth vote is there to break deadlocks and you want to remove it?"

"Ask yourself this. If there is a four-four deadlock, surely the issue is of such gravity that merely achieving a quorum majority does not constitute agreement. Sargon has used its majority too many times to push through policies that clearly favored your interests. This has caused resentment and dissent."

"Khiman-ra," Ed-Kani said, impressed despite himself.

"Precisely. If Sargon cannot move from its parochial position, you risk fracturing the Committee and the entire merger process for an illusory short-term gain."

A lot remained unsaid behind Ti Inai's words, which Ed-Kani suspected would never be said. He could see the value of the argument; it wasn't new. If Ed-Kani did mastermind Khiman-ra, he had just made a vivid demonstration that directives issued by the Provisional Committee did not necessarily translate into automatic compliance by the Alikan Union Party movement; at least not by the Palean arm. Whether Ed-Kani liked it or not, he recognized that the merger must be accepted willingly by all. Any attempt to force it, for whatever reason, would abort the process. Was Khiman-ra a lesson in statesmanship?

"What do you propose?"

"Sargon cannot make a casting vote," Ti Inai said simply and Ed-Kani clenched his teeth.

"We would spend our time bickering and the Committee would never achieve anything."

"I disagree. A deadlock represents a position that has not been properly thought through, otherwise it would never have arisen. If that means further discussion and more meetings, then so be it. I cannot make this point any more forcefully, friend Ed-Kani."

"Are you threatening the Committee?" Ed-Kani asked softly.

"I am merely pointing out the obvious corollary."

Ed-Kani noted that Ti Inai's hands were not twining and the polished smile was missing. The Palean may look shifty and sly, and probably was, but it would be dangerous to underestimate him.

"I shall put it to the Committee."

"I want more than that, friend Ed-Kani."

"Oh?"

"I want your endorsement before the Committee sits again."

* * *

Against the backdrop of a brooding gas giant lit in full glory, its surface a swirl of soft yellow and orange pastels, the tightly bunched survival blisters approached Petri. An enormous ice sheath sent tendrils of white toward the moon's equator. Deserts girthed the middle latitudes. Tropical storms dragged pretty streamers of brilliant clouds around the central eye, hiding most of the southern land mass. Petri looked pretty and peaceful nestled in Kanaris' shadow. Largest of three inhabited moons with a population of almost three billion. It had enough room to hide forty-six more.

Surface Command and Control acknowledged their approach and cleared them for landing at Ulbator. With dozens of available ports, Tanard did not intend to come down there. They were incredibly lucky to have made it this far, and he gave silent thanks to the gods. A day ago it could have been all over when an M-2 closed to less than a million talans in a sensor flyby. It swept past them and continued into the inner system. Why it didn't ask for an ident dump, no one could say.

"What do we have in immediate orbit, Mr. Winn?"

"Two VLBCs and a passenger liner. No threats indicated."

"How far off is the liner?"

"Two hundred and eleven talans."

Tanard made a decision. "Head for it. We'll make a courtesy call."

"Sir?"

"Is it transmitting IFF?"

"SCL *Raster*, Palean registry."

"When we are in its shadow, we'll break formation and make our way to designated cities. If SC&C squawks, we're simply tourist parties coming down for a look."

Winn scowled and Railee grinned. An absurd idea, but better than boosting straight in and making a run for it once they were in the atmosphere.

Whoever kept watch on *Raster* could not have been very concerned. The blisters approached without being challenged. Even from three talans, dark against the backdrop of Petri's swirling clouds, the liner loomed huge; a stubby flattened cylinder. An aesthetic embarrassment with all the grace of a shopping bag. Inside, though, its ostentatious luxury catered for every whim a discerning passenger could want to relieve the tedium between the stars.

Winn released computer control and the blisters slowly drifted apart. Everyone knew what to do. They had rehearsed it often enough over the last five days. Tanard wished them luck and nodded to Winn. The blister immediately boosted. For a moment it looked like they would scrape the liner's bottom as they flashed under it, but it was only an illusion. If SC&C noticed the unusual maneuver, it didn't say so. The fact the blister was in controlled flight heading straight for Ulbator may have reassured it. There was no alarm.

Once inside the atmosphere, the blister changed course.

For the first time since they abandoned *Lahra*, Tanard allowed himself to relax. His decision to make for Kanaris had been vindicated. Despite all the modern tracking facilities and Fleet support, it always came down to the men using them. Vornan 2 was a quietly prosperous system tucked away on the edge of Palean space, unconcerned about raiders, politics or fleeing fugitives. If forced, they would make the minimum necessary effort and appear busy, but nothing so strenuous as to disturb the ambient tranquility of their placid lives.

The blister slanted down toward dazzling towers of clouds that looked solid enough to walk on. It seemed to pause, then plunged into a bank of featureless gray. Turbulence made the little craft shudder and dip. As they slowed, rain smeared the transparent forward part of the hull. Wispy streamers whipped past them, then the blister broke through. Nadar a smudge of glowing columns and glinting suburban sprawl far on their starboard side. The country below them: rolling hills, streams and virgin forest, looked bleak and lonely. On the port side a mountain range thrust icy peaks into black clouds in a gesture of defiance. The high northern latitudes did not look very inviting. To Tanard, Nadar was a perfect choice. No one would raise a troubled eyebrow if three passengers decided to board a shuttle in search of a more hospitable world.

They landed on a deserted stretch of shoreline that pushed

against tall timbers. The lake's milky waters were thick with glacial sediment. Short choppy waves slapped on the pebble beach. Winn shivered just looking at it and Tanard grinned.

"You didn't forget your coat, did you?"

"I don't think it would help," Winn muttered, his long face anticipating the misery outside.

"On Kerna Three, we would consider this summer," Railee said with malicious glee. Winn glared at him.

"Then why don't you go there!"

"I aim to…one day."

"Right, let's get this done," Tanard said and dragged on a heavy synthetic fur-lined coat. Winn touched a pad and the hatch cycled open. A biting wind swirled in and Tanard grimaced. It was not too cold if you were used to it. He picked up his bag and stepped out. Railee and Winn were right behind him.

Winn was still zipping up his coat when the blister rose and glided toward the water. It looked awfully large even though the trees along the far shore appeared little more than toothpicks. It stopped and the hatch opened. Without warning, it plunged into the water, sending up sheets of white spray. The lake boiled around the hatchway and there was a furious hissing of escaping air as the blister filled. It canted up, rolled and was gone.

"Is it too late to change my mind about this?" Railee mused as he stamped his feet, his breath a white fog. Winn gave him a nasty grin.

"Summer, eh?"

"The road should be beyond that bend," Tanard said and nodded in the general direction. "Let's see if we can make it into town before dark."

* * *

Teena's arm wrapped comfortably around Terr's hip, she

gave a little tug as they neared the brightly lit entrance. He glanced into her misty eyes. They sparkled with fleeting reflections; reflections from nav screens of passing communals, sled-pads, store displays, flickering signs, people, of a city alive.

"Are you sure this will be all right?" she said urgently, concern etched on her elfin face.

They stopped and the strolling, hurrying crowd parted around them. A distracted girl, her eyes on her companion, bumped into Terr and mumbled an apology as she was swept along the walkway. He hardly noticed her. The evening soft and warm, filled with sounds of nameless voices, shuffling feet and enticing odors, and he relished the moment.

A moment of clarity when everything stood still and time a painted tapestry of all possibilities. He shared everything of himself with her, except for one thing. Time for her to join with everything he was.

"Nightwings has seen you, he knows you."

"On business, at the Center. This is different."

He brushed her cheek. "Think of him as my brother, not a Wanderer."

"That's the problem," she said and winced. "He is both."

He chuckled, trying to make her relax, realizing it was impossible. Whatever unease she felt at the prospect of meeting Dhar socially, something she would have to deal with on her own.

The Slee Club was crowded, wrapped in a haze of alluring perfumes, smells of rich food, the buzz of incessant voices, clinking cutlery and unobtrusive, harried waiters. Unrestrained laughter broke out from a group somewhere behind him. Heads turned to check on the source of merriment, giving rise to indulgent smiles and morbid speculation.

Terr glimpsed several familiar faces from the Branch, enjoying the evening just as he was. For once, he didn't mind the crush of people around him with their unrestrained and stifling spirits. He simply didn't see them. Teena and Dhar were his world, and right now, it was enough. More than enough.

He did not want to admit it even to himself, the silent dread that Nightwings would somehow resent having to share Terr with another person. Not just anybody, but a soulmate, with all the implications that lay behind it. An unreasoning fear, he knew, but that's how it was.

The beginning moments, when they seated themselves around the small table and made abortive starts at conversation, were predictably awkward for everybody, but Dhar opened himself to her and she was perceptive enough to see it. In turn, she responded in kind. Looking at them, alive and animated, Terr felt relieved, chiding himself for having doubted the strength and depth of the bond that bound him to his Wanderer brother.

Terr sat back, a faint smile creasing his face as he watched his brother deep in animated conversation with Teena. He had nothing else left to share, pleased at Dhar's efforts to draw her into his world, to make her belong, to let her know there was room for her.

Deep in conversation, Dhar sliced off a morsel from a vegetable patty and popped it into his mouth. He chewed hurriedly, leaned toward Teena and smiled a skeleton's grin.

"So he slides down this dune and straight into a patch of drum sand—"

"Drum sand?" Teena asked with a raised eyebrow, fork poised above her plate.

"A layer of very compacted sand that floats on a grainy soft base," Dhar explained. "The vibration set off by walking or something landing on it makes a hollow booming sound."

"And I jumped out faster than I got in," Terr added wryly, playing with his tumbler, the image all too clear in his mind.

Teena chuckled, clearly picturing Terr scrambling to get out of there.

"It is a favorite haunt for rock rays," Dhar said with a

straight face, but with a mischievous, sardonic glint in his orange eyes.

She grinned, not sure what a rock ray was, but it didn't sound good. "What in the world were you two doing in the open desert?" Teena demanded in disbelief. "I would simply die in all that heat."

"Contemplating the fundamental relationship between being and the environment that shapes us," Terr said ponderously, looking smugly pleased with himself. He'd had a drink or two and felt kind of buzzy, but what the hell. It was a great party and he figured he owed it to himself to indulge.

Teena rolled her eyes and glanced at Dhar who nodded wisely.

"It was an opportunity to bind our spirits into a cohesive whole from the chaos of nothingness," Dhar added pedantically. Terr nodded and pointed a finger at him.

"That's it!"

Teena shook her head in surrender. "You're both nuts."

"If you're going to spill it all," Terr grumbled, "tell her how I got stuck in the peelath tree."

"He was after the berries, you see," Dhar said with obvious relish. "They were just coming into season."

"The best ones are usually high up," Terr explained with a shrug.

"And of course, you had to get the best ones," Teena added and giggled, seeing what was coming.

"The problem is," Dhar said dryly, "the peelath has thorns."

"I can already guess what happened," she said in delight.

"He got impaled," Dhar agreed. "Everyone in the village thought it hilarious."

"It wasn't funny," Terr complained with a grin. "I got savaged right in the side and I have a scar to prove it."

"You poor thing," Teena cooed and patted his arm.

"He couldn't wait until the berries fell off their own accord," Dhar added.

"But they don't taste as good then, see?" Terr looked imploringly at Teena and she laughed.

"After getting up there, he couldn't get down. The thorns," Dhar deadpanned and Teena broke up. Dhar's face did not show much emotion, but his eyes sparkled. "There was only one thing to do. He jumped and landed on top of one of the huts. Unfortunately for him the commotion must have interrupted a delicate moment. The next thing, there was Sankri racing over a dune with a frustrated youth tearing after him."

Teena gave a little shriek, which caused the onlookers to smile indulgently or frown with displeasure.

"I got away only because the guy was preoccupied holding up his pants," Terr added with a chuckle, the memory vivid in his mind—as was the wound in his side.

When Teena regained control, she wiped her eyes and shook her head. "You two must have terrorized the place during your visits."

"We sometimes failed to blend in," Dhar agreed and looked fondly at her.

Teena wasn't self-conscious. She did not fuss over herself or tried to be the center of conversation. She had the easy personality of someone confident and intelligent. He approved of Sankri's choice. Or was it his choice? The way his brother told it, he might not have had much say in it. Either way, Sankri appeared happy about it. He turned his head and found his brother staring at him. Dharaklin gave a small nod.

Terr picked up his tumbler and raised it.

"To us."

Teena lifted her glass and solemnly clicked it against the others.

"To us," she echoed softly and took a sip, warmed in her soul that she was permitted to share a glimpse of something deep and profound that bound these two men together.

At first, she was intimidated by Dhar's towering and forbidding presence. Even though not cloaked in Death, the latent power was clearly there, ready to be unleashed. She could sense it even now. Dhar's stern appearance concealed a ready and dry sense of humor. He accepted her without reservation and she was relieved, concerned that he might see her as a rival, obviously not the case. The two of them could not be more different physically, but they were clearly kindred spirits. Whatever connection held them, it gave them a unique understanding of each other.

She hoped that in time, she would also be accepted into their circle of understanding.

Terr met her eyes and they reflected the quiet contentment of his own thoughts.

Epilogue

Thick, heavy flakes drifted down out of a leaden sky. There was no wind to disturb the majestic silence. Along broad, brightly lit avenues, bare trees waited patiently, their branches creaking beneath a burden of snow and hanging icicles. Katalan-deep drifts huddled in corners and protected crannies. For once the sky appeared clear of traffic, but only because the cloudbank was so low. Despite the cold and the ice, the walkways and glidewalks were crowded with people. Pedestrians swarmed the length of the boulevard, alone or huddled in twos or threes, all heavily outfitted. The department stores liked the inclement weather; it brought in more customers.

Gazing down from the eleventh floor, Tanard did not particularly care one way or another. After confirming their flight, they spent the last two days locked in a hotel. Any unnecessary exposure meant an increased risk of discovery. You cannot be found if no one saw you. Better not be seen at all than be a topic of idle conversation. If the local security forces were looking for them, the Wall gave no hint of it. Tanard expected nothing so crude as an open manhunt with sirens wailing and people rushing about. Crude or otherwise, in three hours they'd be out of here, safely he hoped.

Only one thing left to be done.

The door chime went off and Tanard turned to face his visitor, his heart heavy with foreboding.

"Friend Winn. Restless?" He could not quite keep the irony out of his voice. His first officer had come a long way, but to have taken this path? A tortured soul, obviously.

Winn glanced quickly around the room. It could have been

his. They were all alike, stamped from the same mold. The only consolation, he didn't have to live in his any longer. He wiped his right hand against the trouser leg and reached into his zip-jacket. The needler came up and he centered it on Tanard's chest.

"I am sorry, sir," he said and meant it. He tried to rational-ize it, way back when things looked simple, but things were far from simple. In the end, he accepted it. Nothing personal, he told himself. Survival, that was all.

Tanard hoped Narina was mistaken. After more than three years together, that Winn could do this…

"Can I ask why?"

"Sometimes you don't want to know why," Winn said. "This is one of those times, but I suspect you know that al-ready."

"I can guess. Sooner or later in our game, we outlive our usefulness. It happens to all of us. We are simply tools to be used and discarded. You were a good first officer, friend Winn," Tanard said and squared his shoulders.

"I had a good teacher," Winn said and tightened his finger on the contact. "You understand, I must do this."

"I know," Tanard said gently.

A lance of white light flashed through Winn's chest and his face contorted in surprise at the sharp stab of pain. He tried to fire, but his finger would not obey him. His hand opened and the needler fell with a soft thud against the carpet. He looked down at the burnt cloth and charred flesh around the hole in his chest and his eyes glazed. It didn't hurt anymore, not really. Darkness brought relief, wiping out the regrets.

Winn crumpled to the floor, his outstretched hand still grasping for the needler. Railee emerged from the bathroom, the needler held limp at his side. He glanced at the body and grimaced.

"Traitor!"

"I don't know, friend Railee," Tanard said heavily. "Maybe

he had it right."

Railee looked at him. "This can never be right." He pocketed the needler and sighed. "Why did he do it? We were a team!"

"They offered him something he wanted. Freedom, peace, power, who knows? He wanted more than you or I could give him."

"Well, he has it all now."

"A lesson in this for you, Mr. Railee. When you have to shoot, shoot. Don't talk."

"I shall keep that in mind, sir. I guess that after this, Manargee will not be our destination after all."

"It won't be for me," Tanard agreed.

It was over; the dreams he had, plans he made, things to do—dust in the wind. It was a matter of perspective really. The problem he had, those who ran him didn't share it.

"Oh?"

"I'm a marked man, friend Railee. That doesn't mean you need to be marked with me. You have a future that you can still shape. I have none. When you get to Manargee, contact Dame Narina. She will be a friend."

"Like Winn?"

Tanard chuckled. "I certainly hope not."

"Sir, if you think that I will desert—"

"My boy! Don't be dense!"

Railee looked like he was about to cry. Tanard walked to him and clapped his back.

"Then it's settled. What was that place you mentioned? Kerna Three?"

Railee grimaced. "It's a dump."

"Sounds good right now, but we better get out of here. We don't want to miss our flight."

"And the body?"

"We can hardly take it with us."

"But when the authorities find him—"

"They will identify him, and whoever sent him will know that I am still alive. I know. All the more reason to make myself scarce."

"They might try again."

"They might."

Tanard set the 'do not disturb' on the door and locked it. They had the room booked for two more days. With luck, it would take another day or so before someone came looking.

A communal rose off the hotel's landing ramp and climbed into a gray sky.

About the author

Stefan Vučak has written twenty-one novels, which include eight SF books in the Shadow Gods Saga. His *Cry of Eagles* won the coveted Readers' Favorite silver medal award, and his *All the Evils* was the prestigious Eric Hoffer contest finalist and Readers' Favorite silver medal winner. *Strike for Honor* won the gold medal.

Stefan leveraged a successful career in the Information Technology industry, which took him to the Middle East working on cellphone systems. Writing has been a road of discovery, helping him broaden his horizons. He also spends time as an editor and book reviewer. Stefan lives in Melbourne, Australia.

To learn more about Stefan Vučak, visit his:
Website: www.stefanvucak.com
Facebook: www.facebook.com/StefanVucakAuthor
Twitter: @stefanvucak

More Books by Stefan Vučak

https://www.stefanvucak.com/Books/

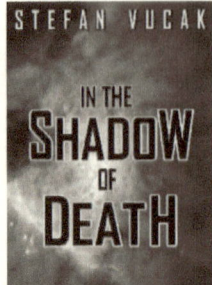
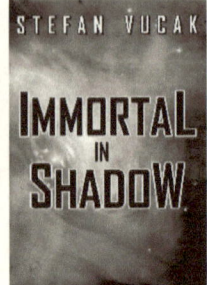
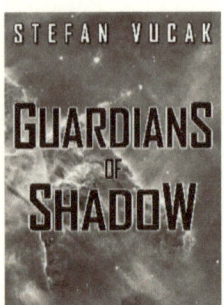

www.ingramcontent.com/pod-product-compliance
Lightning Source LLC
Chambersburg PA
CBHW020655110726
47901CB00001B/198